the AFFAIR

the AFFAIR

Colette Freedman

KENSINGTON BOOKS
www.kensingtonbooks.com

This is for Jill:
Who always listens unconditionally . . .

I'd like to thank several people for making this happen:

Audrey, Martin, and everyone at Kensington

Mel Berger at WME

The Boston contingent: David, Zachary, Dylan, Kim, and Amy

Those who listened, especially: Jill, Fred, Jade, Rebecca, Alli, Diana, and Hannah Hope

Dippy, Moses, and Miriam for their inspiration

My parents for their unconditional love and support

Barry for believing

and Michael, for absolutely everything else.

Book 1

The Wife's Story

Did I suspect?

I've asked myself that question a hundred times, and I could lie to myself and say that I did. But, no, if I'm being perfectly honest, I never suspected.

I trusted him.

I loved him.

Are they one and the same emotion? Trust and love? They are . . . or, at least, I think they are.

But once the doubt crept into my mind, then everything he did was suspect. From that moment on, I couldn't believe a word out of his mouth.

And when I finally discovered the truth, I hated him.

CHAPTER 1

Thursday, 19th December

Kathy Walker nibbled on a chocolate-glazed Dunkin' Donut as she signed the Christmas card with a flourish.

Love from Robert, Kathy, Brendan, and Theresa.

She turned the card over, pushed it into the red envelope, licked the flap with two quick movements, making a face at the taste of the gum, then picked up her pen.

And stopped.

What was the address? She looked up from the pile of envelopes and frowned; 21 something—Hammond, or was it something—Hawley Street?

Kathy stepped away from the kitchen table and pressed her hands into the small of her back, working her neck from side to side, hearing muscles pop alarmingly. She had been writing cards for nearly two hours and was exhausted. These were her "Perfunctory" cards, polite-and-expected-and-completely-meaningless cards. It was a chore she hated, one she always left until the last minute—and she was now stiff and sore and just a little irritated. She looked at the doughnut in her hand; the sugar high wasn't helping. Kathy took another bite and sighed. It was the same every year; she wrote all of the cards, and she signed for both of them, naturally putting his name first—Love from Robert, Kathy . . . Why was she conditioned to put his name first? Probably because the majority of the cards were going out to Robert's business associates.

Next year would be different, she promised grimly, hunting for her address book. Then she smiled, and for an instant looked younger—much younger than her forty-three years—remembering that she'd made the same vow last year. And probably the year before that too.

Kathy found her address book under a pile of last year's unused cards. For the last couple of years, she'd ordered Christmas cards from one of the online card shops in boxes of forty—cheesy pictures of her family dressed in Santa hats posing awkwardly around the trimmed tree—and each year she left three or four unused cards in the bottom of the box, promising to eventually send them. She never did.

Leaning over the table, she flipped open the tattered black book, hunting for the address of Robert's cousin. She'd met the dour man at their wedding eighteen years ago and doubted if she'd recognize him today if he stood in front of her. Also, Mr. Personality never sent a Christmas card. This was the last year she was sending him one, she decided. She was going to make a list of those who sent cards and cross-reference it with the list of what she sent out. Perhaps she was being petty, but life was too short. Next year she'd only send cards to those people who had sent one to them. That was fair. She smiled again. She was also sure she'd made the same promise last year. And yet, this year she seemed to be sending out twice as many cards.

Kathy looked up at the clock: just after five. The mailman usually came at five thirty. She'd have just enough time to stuff the letters in the mailbox. Robert hated when she did that; he felt it was unfair on the mailman. However, she believed it was his job and had no issues with leaving the letters in the mailbox for him to take away. It was a lot easier than driving or, God forbid, walking eight blocks in the freezing temperatures to the closest post office. Besides, it was snowing. No need for her to go out unnecessarily. Then, as a treat for doing all the cards, she was going to order in rather than cook: Indian from The Curry House for Robert and herself, Chinese from Lucky Wah for Brendan and Theresa. If she timed it right, the kids would get home right about the same time the food arrived.

Only four cards left, all of them to Robert's business colleagues. She sat down at the table again and turned the cards over in her hands. These needed a personal touch; he should really write them himself, she decided. She pushed them into their envelopes, but left the flaps open. She'd address them, so he'd have no excuse. The first was to the head of the little multimedia company he used in East Cambridge. The second to the talent agency near Copley Square that supplied extras for crowd scenes. She smiled as she scribbled the address. It didn't seem that long ago that she'd delivered these cards by hand, trudging across Boston to put them into the mailboxes because they couldn't afford the stamps.

How quickly things had changed.

Robert and Kathy's struggling independent television-production company had landed one small job, an insert for a documentary on racism. It was a small, self-contained interview segment with an African American hip-hop artist. They'd recorded it over a weekend and thought nothing more about it. Then the artist had won an award, made the cover of *Esquire,* and the documentary had won a Palme d'Or award. Robert had ridden the coattails of that success. He had new corporate brochures printed up that managed to give the impression that R&K Productions had won the award themselves. As usual, no one bothered to check, and the little lie became self-perpetuating. Kathy remembered a dinner where she was introduced as "one half of the company that won the Palme d'Or for that marvelous documentary..." She'd been so embarrassed, she hadn't had the nerve to contradict the speaker.

The company flourished and in doing so had taken its toll on them both over the years. Building a business meant that certain things—family, friendships, personal time, vacations—went by the wayside. R&K Productions still made documentaries, but nowadays principally concentrated on advertising: corporate training videos and commercials; they also shot local-color pieces—inserts—for foreign videos. She knew Robert finally accepted—and regretted—that he'd never now make huge, landmark documentaries for National Geographic, the Discovery Channel, or HBO. Kathy didn't share those regrets; the money was regular and, with two teens and a mortgage, she'd take financial security over artistic integrity any day. It had always been one of the fundamental differences between them.

She looked at the envelope in her hand. *Burst Postproduction House.* She said the words aloud, surprising herself, her voice sounding unusually loud in the silence of the kitchen. Post-Production—a new business in itself, where computers cleaned up the errors humans made.

Kathy rifled through the address book looking for Burst, though she doubted she would find it. This was one of the new companies Robert had only started working with this year. He never wrote the most recent addresses in the old address book. He preferred to store them in his iPhone.

Kathy wandered out into the hallway. Although this would be their sixth Christmas in this home, she'd never quite gotten used to the sense of space, particularly in the hallway. Their first house had had a short, dark, narrow hallway that led straight into the kitchen; this one boasted a large, circular foyer that, to be truthful, she thought just a bit wasteful. She would much rather have had bigger rooms. It was also cold; the ornate marble floor was lovely to look at, but it radiated the chill like a fridge.

"Robert!" She leaned on the blond wood railing and looked upstairs. "Robert!" Tilting her head to one side, she could faintly hear the thrum of the shower in the bedroom.

She tapped the cards in her hand against the banister; then, sighing, she started up the stairs. On the landing her feet sank into the deep pile of the impossible-to-keep-clean cream-colored carpet. Their bedroom was at one end of the house; the kids' rooms were at the other. It afforded all of them a measure of privacy. She pushed into the bedroom, blinking in surprise at the image of the petite woman with the heart-shaped face reflected in the mirrored doors of the closets. She paused for a single moment, assessing herself: She needed to lose at least four inches around her waist, and gray roots were showing through her chestnut-brown hair. She was already depressed at being on the wrong side of forty—she certainly didn't want to look fifty! Right after Christmas she was going to stop eating carbs, join Weight Watchers or Jenny Craig or both, and go back to the gym. She'd go in the afternoon when all the trim, Pilates-obsessed, young yuppie mothers who filled the morning classes were picking up their equally perfect kids from school. Real women, with real figures, worked out in the afternoons, she decided.

The shower was louder now, and she could see tendrils of steam creeping from beneath the en suite door. The water would be scalding; she didn't know how he could stand it so hot. Robert was humming something vaguely Christmassy—"Do They Know It's Christmas?" she thought, but it would be impossible to tell, because, even though she loved him dearly, she would be the first to admit that he was tone deaf.

Robert's clothes were scattered across the bed. Automatically, she stooped and lifted a crumpled purple silk tie off the floor. She'd given it to him as part of his Christmas present last year. She felt a guilty twinge: She'd gotten him another tie this year. Red paisley. He was impossible to buy for; anything he wanted, he simply bought. Shirts and ties were always a safe bet.

Kathy sat on the edge of the bed and looked around the too-white bedroom. She'd change it this year. White was too cold, too hard, and the mirrored doors bounced the light back, making her squint, deepening the lines on her forehead and around her mouth. Even the peach-colored duvet looked pale and washed-out. She'd go to Benjamin Moore and get some color charts after Christmas, adding it to the growing list of things she was going to do "after Christmas." She also knew that the list would probably not survive into the second week of the New Year.

Kathy spread out the cards on the bedspread and reached into the pocket of Robert's jacket, which was thrown across the end of the bed, and pulled out his cell. Thin and sleek, it was a combination phone and pocket computer, with a large rectangular color screen. When he had first gotten it, he'd sat up in bed beside her one night and demonstrated several applications that he had eagerly downloaded, only giving up when she finally fell asleep.

Kathy turned it on. The Apple icon lit up on the screen, then gave way to his screen saver: a picture of their dead cocker spaniel Rufus. She shuddered. It was morbid to keep the picture; why would he want to relive the loss, everyday? Her lips twisted in a wry smile. Robert always had trouble letting things go.

Kathy unlocked the screen, revealing brightly lit rows of colorful icons. She touched the little brown Contacts icon at the top of the screen, and a listing of names and addresses appeared. She started to scroll down the names to the *B*'s, looking for Burst Postproduction.

Bryant, Edward.

Burford, Kenneth.

Burroughs, Stephanie.

The name stopped her cold. Burroughs, Stephanie.

For an instant, a single moment of time, the room shifted, all the colors becoming brighter, sharper, though the sounds were muted. For the space of a single heartbeat her entire concentration was on that name glowing black on pale blue on the screen.

Burroughs, Stephanie.

Stephanie Burroughs.

There was a name she hadn't come across in a long time, a name she had never thought she'd see again.

There was a tiny red flag on the screen beside the entry.

The shower changed tempo and then died, Robert's off-key singing becoming louder.

Moving quickly now, fingers fumbling, she turned off the phone. Shoving it back into Robert's jacket pocket, she darted from the room.

"Kathy? Were you looking for me?"

Robert's voice trailed her down the stairs. But all she could hear was the thundering of her blood in her ears, thumping in time to the name echoing inside her head: Stephanie Burroughs.

CHAPTER 2

Kathy's heart was hammering so hard in her chest that she could actually feel the flesh tremble beneath her skin. She stood in the kitchen doorway, gasping for breath in the chill December air. Stray snowflakes spiraled out of the darkness and kissed her cheeks and forehead. She was blinking furiously, but she would not cry. Not yet. Not now.

Stephanie Burroughs.

With a little red flag beside her name.

The conscious part of her brain suggested that it might be nothing. Stephanie Burroughs was in advertising; Robert was sure to have the names of just about everyone in the business in his phone. But instinct and emotion kept flashing back to the little red flag icon beside the name. You only put a flag beside something important, didn't you?

It could be perfectly innocent.

But she knew it was not.

Kathy shook her head savagely. She brushed at her eyes with the palm of her right hand, pushing away the threatened tears. She could be wrong. She might be wrong. She wanted to be wrong.

But she knew she wasn't. Not this time. Not now.

Stephanie Burroughs was back.

Six years ago, around about the same time they'd moved into this house, Robert had had an affair with Stephanie Burroughs. He'd denied it, but Kathy knew—she knew—he'd had an affair. She'd always been slightly nervous about Stephanie's association with her husband, and then, when a friend—who was no longer a friend—had spotted Robert and Stephanie together at the Stones concert at Fenway Park and had gleefully told her, her suspicions had been confirmed. Three months of too many lame excuses, too many late nights at the office, too many weekend business trips. All of it had suddenly made sense. Everything had pointed to one inescapable conclusion: Her husband was having an affair.

On one terrible summer evening, with the sun low and red in the New England sky, she had turned and faced him. He'd been standing over the barbecue in the backyard, head wreathed in smoke, hamburger meat crisping on the grill. Without preamble, she had asked him flatly if he was having an affair with his researcher. In the instant when his eyes had slid from hers she'd known the truth even before he denied it. Flat-out denied it, with enough anger and outrage to rattle her convictions. She'd brought out her suspicions, and he'd managed to counter every one of them with a rational excuse. She'd never managed to prove it, and weeks of recriminations and anguish had followed. Then Stephanie had left the company and moved away, and with her departure a lot of the heat had gone out of the argument. Things drifted, then Robert and Kathy had settled back into their old routine.

Kathy had almost, but not quite, forgotten about the woman. It had been a long time since Stephanie's name had flitted across her consciousness, though she still felt that little shiver of insecurity when she saw her husband looking at a pretty woman at a party.

But now, Stephanie Burroughs's name was in his new phone, with a little red flag beside it.

"Hey, what's up—it's freezing out here!" Robert came up behind her, wrapping his strong arms across the top of her shoulders, resting his chin on the top of her head. He smelled fresh and clean, of soap and water and a hint of some cologne she didn't recognize.

Kathy pulled away and stepped back into the kitchen. "Just getting a breath of air; the kitchen was stuffy. Nice cologne."

"Yeah. It's new. I didn't know if you'd like it."

"I do," she said curtly as she closed the door and spun away from him, not looking into his eyes, fearful that he would see something in her face or that she would see something in his; after eighteen years of marriage it was difficult to keep a secret. She began to put return address labels on the last few cards. They were tacky wreath-decorated labels sent from a charity in their annual plea for money. Kathy always wondered if it was bad karma to use the preprinted labels without actually donating to the charity. "I left a couple of cards on the bed," she began.

"I saw them. . . ."

"I don't have the addresses, and besides they're personal cards— it would be better if you wrote and signed them."

"What's wrong?" he asked quickly.

Kathy glanced sidelong at him. "Nothing."

He'd been thirty-one when she married him, tall and gangly with a shock of black hair that refused to stay combed. The hair had remained more or less intact and he'd filled out some, but in truth he'd aged well. Extremely well. Unlike her, she thought bitterly. He'd matured; she had gotten old.

"Why do you ask?" she added.

Robert smiled, the corners of his lips creasing, and he tilted his head to one side, a movement she'd once found endearing, but which now irritated her. "Because you've got the tone in your voice."

"Which tone?"

"*That* tone." His smile deepened. "The tone that tells me that you're pissed off at me."

Kathy sighed.

"Oh, and the sigh is another sure sign. The sigh and the tone. You're like a great jazz band, Kathy . . . always in syncopation."

"Look, I'm tired. I've been writing cards for hours. Mostly your cards, to your friends and your colleagues," she added bitterly. "I do it every year. And every year it's last minute, and I'm always missing addresses. You don't help."

She watched the smile tighten on his lips. "Kathy, I've just come in from a ten-hour day," he said, his voice still light and reasonable. "I had a meeting in Framingham, the Pike was a parking lot, and I've got a really important presentation in the morning. Just . . . give me a minute to decompress, and I'll go through my address book. Or you can; I've got nothing to hide."

"I've done them all," Kathy said tightly, fully aware that people who claimed they had nothing to hide always had plenty to hide. "The four on the bed are all you have to do."

"We're arguing over four cards?" he asked.

"No," she snapped. "We're arguing over the one hundred and twenty I've already written. Without your help."

Robert nodded and shrugged. "I should have taken some into work with me." Then he glanced up at the clock. "I'll go and get the kids."

Before she could say another word, he turned and strode from the kitchen, across the dining room, and out into the hallway. She could see him snatching his leather jacket and scarf off the rack behind the door, and then he left, pulling the front door shut quietly behind him.

Kathy leaned on the kitchen table and listened to the car start up and gently pull away. He'd done it again. Managed to twist and turn her words until suddenly she felt she was in the wrong, that she was arguing about nothing. And then, of course, he'd walked away. He was good at that. In all the years she'd known him, he had always walked away from an argument.

A classic coward.

If that had been her, she'd have slammed the door and revved off at high speed, spattering gravel against the side of the house. He was always just too damned controlled, a true Libra, far too evenly balanced.

Kathy turned away from the table, opened the refrigerator, and grabbed a wedge of Skinny Cow cheese. There were only thirty-five calories in each piece. She ripped open the thin tinfoil packaging and popped the tiny triangle into her mouth. She hadn't managed to lose any weight for the various Christmas parties they'd been invited to—and was feeling slightly guilty because she'd avoided going to a couple of business-related events that she knew would be populated by gorgeous twenty-somethings as thin as sticks, with designer little black dresses artfully draped on their bones. Robert had gone to the parties on his own; he didn't seem to mind.

Somewhere, in the distance, there was a long shrill ring.

He'd left his phone.

Kathy stopped suddenly. He'd left his phone. He never left his phone. An oversight? Or, perhaps, the universe was conspiring with her. Tossing the empty foil into the garbage can, she darted up the stairs. As far as she could remember, he hadn't had his phone in his hand when he'd come into the kitchen. She knew he hated carrying it in his pants pocket; it was just a little too bulky, and he usually wore it clipped to his belt, like a kid wearing a toy gun, or he carried it in his inside jacket pocket like an oversized wallet.

She raced into the bedroom. His jacket was where she'd left it, and there, just visible, was the silver edge of the phone.

She was abruptly conscious that the decision she made in the next couple of seconds was going to have repercussions for the rest of her life. She could hear her mother's voice now, clear and distinct, the slightly bitter waspish tones managing to irritate her even though the woman had been dead eighteen months.

"Never ask a question unless you're prepared for an answer you don't like."

Was she prepared for an answer she didn't like? Her last accusation had almost ruined her marriage and destroyed the family. It had been based on instinct, rather than evidence.

Kathy Walker sat on the edge of the bed and cradled the phone in her hands, index finger hovering over the screen. Somewhere deep inside her, she already knew the answer. All she was looking for now was confirmation. Something tangible. Something to corroborate her suspicions. Six years ago, she had been plagued with doubt. She wasn't going to make the same mistake she had made the last time. Proof. She was looking for proof.

And once she knew the truth, she could prepare for the consequences.

Kathy Walker tapped the screen.

CHAPTER 3

Stephanie Burroughs.

All of the lines beside her name in the phone were filled in: an address, a phone number, a cell number, two e-mail addresses, a note of her birthday. And a little red flag beside her name.

Kathy's fingers felt numb, hands trembling slightly as she tapped the flag on the screen. The calendar opened, a series of little rectangles representing the days of the month. Friday last had a little flag on it; the flag on Stephanie's name was linked to it. She tapped the screen again, bringing up the day.

Friday had been a busy day for R&K Productions—or at least for the R part of it. There had been breakfast with a client at eight a.m., then a ten a.m. meeting followed by a voice-over session at the studio at eleven thirty. Artwork was scheduled in for three o'clock, then nothing.

Except for a red flag at five. No notation.

Kathy frowned, remembering. Last Friday . . . Robert had been home late last Friday; he'd been meeting a client, he said. It had been close to midnight when he'd arrived home.

Conscious that time was slipping by, she changed back to the month view and moved to the next red flag. It was for the previous Tuesday. Again, late in the afternoon, the last event of the day, with no appointments scheduled after it. The flag before that was for the previous Friday. She nodded quickly. He'd been late that Friday, but she couldn't remember anything about the Tuesday. Robert was often late getting home from work; in fact he was late more often than not. The flag before that was for the first Tuesday of the month. Leave it to her husband to develop a red flag pattern.

Now she scrolled forward in the calendar. The next red flag was for tomorrow night, Friday night. Red flag at four, with no appointments following it. Apparently, Tuesday nights and Friday nights were date night in the world of red flags, Kathy thought bitterly.

She changed back to the Contacts app and quickly scrolled down through the names. She only came across two other names with red flags, and she recognized both as longstanding clients.

Feeling unaccountably guilty, she went through the other jacket pockets, not entirely sure what she was looking for. He'd taken his wallet with him, and all she found were a couple of parking receipts, a packet of mints, and a receipt from Au Bon Pain in the CambridgeSide Galleria. Two beverages. She smoothed out the receipt on the bed, trying to decipher the date.

It looked like last Tuesday, at 5:10 p.m. What had Robert been doing in Cambridge last Tuesday? Robert hated shopping, hated shopping malls particularly. Getting out to the shopping mall in pre-Christmas traffic would have been a nightmare; getting back, even worse. When Robert wanted to pick up a quick gift, he usually just popped over to Brookline Booksmith and bought a book.

Lights suddenly flared against the bedroom window as a car pulled into the driveway. Calmly, Kathy put the parking receipts and the mints back into his jacket pocket. She stuffed the Au Bon Pain receipt into her own pocket. Then she slipped the phone into her husband's jacket pocket, and she was in the process of descending the stairs when the hall door opened and Robert, followed by Brendan and Theresa, bundled into the house in a tumult of noise and chill air.

"We got takeout," Brendan called, holding up the brown paper bags.

"More than takeout, I see," Kathy muttered. There was a smudge of chocolate on her son's upper lip, the hint of white on his cheek. They'd probably stopped for ice cream on the way home.

She looked up at Robert. He saw her looking at him and raised his eyebrows in a silent question. Kathy wondered when Robert had become the "fun" parent who took the kids out for dessert before dinner and she had become the disciplinarian who nagged them about homework and chores. She could be fun. She was fun . . . She used to be fun. Kathy smiled at Brendan. "Great. I was going to suggest takeout." She was looking at her husband, at the man she had thought she knew and realized she didn't.

Robert caught the quizzical look and tilted his head. "Everything okay?"

"Fine," she lied, "just fine."

CHAPTER 4

"I was thinking," Kathy said suddenly.

"Always dangerous..." Robert quipped.

Kathy could see him through the bathroom door, standing in those ridiculous L.L. Bean pajama bottoms designed with pictures of little duck boots that she absolutely hated. She was sitting up in bed, supported by a trio of pillows, holding a *People* magazine in front of her face. Although her head was tilted down, as if she were reading, she was watching him over the top of the page.

"You've been working so hard lately...."

The electric toothbrush began to buzz and whine. Robert was paranoid about his teeth. Two years ago, when they'd least been able to afford it, he'd spent nearly three thousand dollars having them straightened and bleached. Now he went to the dentist every three months to get them whitened. They were shockingly bright against his tanned face, and she thought they looked artificial and false. Lately, he'd been talking about having LASIK on his eyes, even though he only needed glasses for reading and close work on the computer screen. "I can still hear you," he said.

But Kathy waited until the whine of the toothbrush faded away, then she tried again. "I've been thinking, you've been working so hard lately, I've barely seen you. We should try to have a date night."

"Good idea. Great idea," he said around a mouthful of toothpaste.

Kathy heard the faucet turn on and she raised her voice. "What about tomorrow?" And how will you answer, she wondered. Will you say yes to me, and make me feel ridiculous because I've doubted you or will you . . .

"I can't." He shut off the water and came out of the bathroom, patting white toothpaste off his chin with a towel. "Not tomorrow night. I'm entertaining a client. Christmas drinks and some dinner." He stared directly into her eyes, with those huge brown innocent eyes of his, as he smiled at her.

"You never said."

"I'm sure I did." He pulled on the pajama top.

"I'd have remembered."

He shrugged and turned to toss the towel back into the bathroom. It missed the rail and slid to the floor, where she would pick it up in the morning. She caught him looking at himself in the mirrored closet doors, just a quick glance. She saw him straighten, suck in his belly, then nod.

Still keeping her head down, turning the magazine pages slowly, pretending to read, she raised her eyes and looked at her husband. Really looked at him, trying to see him anew. She'd once read in a magazine that you really only looked at someone when you first met them, and after that you never really looked at them again. The picture the brain establishes in that first glance is the one that remains. How long ago was it since she'd looked at her husband, seen him as a person, an individual, she wondered.

Was it her imagination, or was he was looking a lot more tanned and toned? He'd always been careful about his weight and was positively obsessive about his hair. Squinting slightly, she stared at his hair and noticed that some of the gray was gone. A few years ago he'd started to develop gray wings—distinguished and handsome, she'd thought—just above his ears. Now she saw that they had faded and almost vanished. Indeed, his hair was lustrous and shining, making her wonder if he had started to color it. It looked like he'd lost a little weight too; his stomach seemed flatter, and there was the hint—just a hint—of muscle. Even though it was the depths of winter, and they hadn't been on a tropical vacation, his skin was an even tan. She couldn't see a tan mark on his wrist where he habitually wore his watch, but the tan looked too perfect to have come from a bottle—there were no streaks, no darker patches. Good God—was he going to a tanning salon?

Kathy turned the page of the magazine. The words were dipping and crawling across the page and she was unable to make sense of them, but she concentrated on moving her head as if she were reading. Who was he tanning for? Not for her, certainly. Suddenly that single thought—not for her—deeply saddened her. When had he stopped trying to impress her? When had she stopped being impressed by him?

"Who are you meeting tomorrow?" she asked casually.

"Jimmy Moran," Robert said without missing a beat. "We're having dinner and drinks at Top of the Hub." He threw back the covers and slipped into the bed, sending a wave of chill air radiating through the sheets. "You didn't turn on the blanket," he said, almost accusingly.

"I didn't think it was that cold." Ever since she'd started to put together the pieces, she'd been running hot and cold. She felt almost schizophrenic. She was forty-three; maybe menopause was coming early? Both her mother and older sister had gone through the change in their early forties. Perhaps her paranoia was simply a matter of out-of-control hormones. She tossed the magazine onto the floor and slid down in the bed, pulling the covers up to her chin.

"Aren't you going to read?"

"No." She reached up and turned off the light over her side of the bed.

"Well, I'll read for a bit, if you don't mind."

She knew even if she did mind, he'd still keep the light on. He reached down to the side of the bed and lifted up the book he was reading, *The Road Less Traveled.*

She waited in silence for a moment, then she heard a page turn.

He was an infuriatingly slow reader. She could read two books a week; he'd been reading his current book for at least a month, maybe longer. Not looking at him, she asked, "When do you think we'll have a chance to get a night out?"

There was a pause. She heard another page turn. "I think we should wait until after Christmas. It's a nightmare trying to find a place to eat, and parking is impossible." He attempted a laugh. "All the restaurants in the city are full of people like me, treating clients like Jimmy to too much wine." She heard the book hit the floor, and then his light clicked off. "After Christmas, we'll find a little time. Maybe even head out to the Cape for the weekend. Or Martha's Vineyard. What do you think?"

"That would be nice," Kathy said. He had said the same thing last year. They hadn't gone away; there wasn't time.

There was never enough time.

CHAPTER 5

Friday, 20th December

"So how sure are you?" Rose King rested her elbows on the kitchen table and reached out to take her friend's hands.

Kathy Walker shook her head. "I'm not sure."

"But you're suspicious."

"I'm suspicious."

"And you've been suspicious before?"

Kathy nodded. "I have."

"Hell, I'll bet there's not a woman in the Greater Boston Metropolitan Area who hasn't been suspicious about her husband at least once."

"Have you? Been suspicious, I mean?"

Rose's smile tightened, lips thinning, lines appearing at the corners of her mouth. "I have. More than once."

"Of Tommy?" Kathy was unable to keep the squeak of surprise out of her voice.

"Yes. Tommy."

"But he's . . ." Kathy wasn't sure how one could discuss Tommy's weight in a politically correct manner.

"Big boned? Fat? Chunky? Or shall we go straight to clinically obese? It's okay; you can say it. And I know what you're thinking: Tommy shouldn't have a chance with women."

"I didn't say that."

"You were thinking it. I could hear you thinking it. My Tommy. My blubbery and bald Tommy swaying that enormous manhood of his. I'm not sure who I feel sorry for more: me, or the unfortunate woman who had to take a gander at that without being warmed up. I had years of the Thin Tommy before the fatty deposits took over."

"He's very polite," Kathy murmured.

"Oh, don't tell me you want him too?" Rose laughed. Rose King was fifteen years older than Kathy and looked five years older than that, with what looked like a frizzy burgundy perm that had gone out of fashion in the seventies, but which was her own hair. No matter what she did to it—whether she had it cut, colored, or straightened—within a matter of weeks it returned to its unruly mop. A short, stout woman, she had raised four boys and two girls, the youngest of whom had just left home. She'd recently told Kathy that this would be the first Christmas in more than twenty years that she and Tommy would be alone. She was dreading it, she added, without a trace of humor in her voice.

Rose and Kathy had formed the unlikeliest of friendships, starting twelve years ago when Brendan had been starting school. Kathy had walked past Rose's slightly disheveled front lawn twice a day. A brief hello had turned into a few words as the weeks went by, which had gradually developed into longer chats. Soon Kathy was stopping for a cup of coffee, then Rose was dropping in. On the surface they had nothing in common, besides being neighbors, but they had no secrets from one another. Even when Kathy had moved from gritty South Boston to posh Brookline, the two women had kept in touch and remained friends.

"But how could you suspect your Tommy of having an affair . . . ?" The words trailed away. Even the thought of Tommy—fat, pompous, and, when he wasn't wearing a ridiculous wig, as bald as an egg—having an affair, brought a smile to her lips.

Rose shrugged. Then she grinned and rasped, "My Tommy.

My beer-bellied Tommy. But he wasn't always fat and follically-challenged." She shook her head in wonderment. "I know for certain that he's had one relationship that lasted two years."

Kathy stared at her blankly.

"Oh, and there's definitely been two other briefer affairs. Six months each," Rose added.

Kathy was shocked, but she wasn't sure whether it was at the thought of Tommy's having an affair or by the calm, almost conversational way that Rose announced the news. More to disguise her incredulity, she got up and grabbed the poinsettia plant that her kids had given to her a week earlier. Turning to the sink, she busied herself watering it. "I never knew. . . . You never said."

"It's not the sort of thing you drop into conversation, is it?" Rose's mouth twisted in an ugly smile. "Love your new blouse. By the way, did you happen to know that Tommy's dating the twenty-two-year-old bartender at the Purple Shamrock? And I don't really mean dating either."

Pain and anger soured the older woman's voice, and Kathy turned to look at her. They had been friends for over a decade, and Kathy had never suspected the hurt Rose was hiding.

"Don't look at me like that, Kathy. The fact is, it's easier just to ignore. Make my solid contribution to the annual WASP handbook of don't ask, don't tell."

"A two-year relationship . . . two six-month relationships. That's three years of your life with him while he was with other women? Three years."

"Honey, they were the best three years of my life!"

"Rose!"

"What? I got a lot done." Rose drank her coffee and stared at Kathy.

"How long ago . . . I mean, when did you first suspect?" Kathy whirled around. "I'm sorry, I shouldn't have asked. It's none of my business."

"Ten years ago was the first time," Rose continued as if she hadn't heard Kathy. "I don't know her name; I never bothered to find out." Rose hesitated for a second. "Okay, that's a lie. Gladys Schwartz. I read the e-mails," she admitted. "What? Just because I didn't confront him about the affair, didn't mean I didn't want to know everything. I needed to know, and it sort of made it easier to manage."

"Did you ever see her?"

"No. Yes, of course I did." Her face tightened, then creased into a smile. "Gladys Schwartz was as big as a house. Made Tommy look practically anorexic."

Kathy forced a smile. Rose had looked through Tommy's e-mails. That was a complete violation of privacy. She would never consider going through Robert's e-mails. That would be a violation of trust. . . . But she'd already scrolled through his phone. Still, that was different. And if he was having an affair . . . well, hadn't he already violated that trust?

Rose interrupted Kathy's thoughts as she nattered on. "Gladys was an old flame, I think, one of his many previous girlfriends. They'd kept in touch on and off; then they started seeing one another for a drink. The drinks turned to meals; the meals turned to . . . well, I don't know what they turned to, but I suspect that they ended up in bed together." Rose delivered the statement in a flat monotone. "Must have been a big bed," she added.

Kathy shook her head. Through the kitchen window, she could see out into the grim-looking winter garden, the trees stripped of leaves, the ornamental pond, which she hated, covered in a scummy layer of brown. Reflected in the glass, she could see Rose's face, staring at her.

She turned back from the sink and sat at the kitchen table again, not sure what to do or how to respond. She had waited until Robert had gone to work and the children had raced to catch the bus before inviting her friend over. She had thought she would tell Rose her story and get some advice; she certainly hadn't expected to hear something like this.

Rose laughed shakily. "I know. It's absurd. My Tommy. But, you know, he can be so charming, so kind. So deliciously self-deprecating. That's what first attracted me to him. Trust me, he was no Brad Pitt, but by God, he made me laugh. I read somewhere that that's what women go for. Forget the good looks; most women just want to laugh. That's why liars get all the girls."

Kathy got up to pour herself more coffee. "I read that too."

"A couple of years after that," Rose continued, "I suspected he was carrying on with the blonde from number fifteen."

Kathy snorted, the sound unexpected. "The one with the big . . . ?"

Reflected in the kitchen glass, Rose nodded. "The very same. Tommy started doing the accounts for her husband's store just before his business folded. Remember, her husband ran the little appliances store just off Broadway. He had the big closing-down sale, everything must go, all items dirt cheap. Well, he made a fortune that day, then took off with the takings, the contents of their bank account, and the scrawny redhead who worked the register."

"I bought a vacuum cleaner there."

"I got a deep-fat fryer. Well, my Tommy started popping over once a week. Then it was twice. Then . . . well, I don't know. It finished when she moved out."

Kathy brought the coffee pot back to the table. "You said there were three occasions . . ." she gently prompted Rose.

"About two years ago, I suspected something was going on. It's when online dating became so popular. One day he left his computer on, and I saw instant message texts on his screen from a bunch of women. He'd joined Match.com. Set up his profile as GlassHalfFull33. Ha. More like GlassCompletelyEmpty63. Still, these women actually wrote to him . . . and he wrote back. Sexy messages. The fat bastard's profile actually said he was divorced," Rose added with a wry grin. "That's when he started getting really conscious about the hair, and got the wig."

"I remember." The wig was absolutely ridiculous. It was a confection of hair that seemed to balance precariously atop Tommy's head, and it never moved, not even in a hurricane.

"You know, he thinks no one has noticed the wig," Rose said, "because no one ever asked about it. That's another slightly difficult subject to slip into conversation. 'Nice rug, Tommy.' 'Where'd you get the wig, Tommy?' 'You better check out your head, Tommy, a porcupine is humping your scalp.' Seriously, Kathy, I know if I were to ever mention it, I'd burst out laughing in his face."

Rose started to laugh. She had a deep, masculine chuckle, and suddenly Kathy was laughing with her, the two women giggling and chuckling together, and for an instant it was just like one of hundreds of other shared mornings, when all was right with the world. Then Kathy abruptly sobered. Things had not been perfect those other mornings; Rose had been living with the belief that her husband was having an affair.

"Did you ever ask him?"

"About the wig?"

"About the affairs. About the lies. About the fake Internet dating profile."

Rose concentrated on pouring coffee, then adding a tiny touch of low-fat milk. "I thought about it," she said eventually. "I thought about it long and hard, and then I asked myself what I'd do if he copped to it."

Kathy nodded. She'd been thinking about the same thing all through the night.

Rose sipped her coffee. "What was I going to do if he admitted to the affairs? I could ask him to leave, but we still had eight years to pay on the mortgage. What happened if he left? Who would pay that?" She shrugged awkwardly. "I know it sounds like an incredibly practical, maybe even cynical thing to think about, but that's what crossed my mind. And then I wondered, what would happen if I asked him to leave and he said no? I couldn't stay with him, could I? So I'd have to go, to leave my home and go ... go where? I didn't have any job skills other than running my home, and my nearest relative—an aunt—was in Providence, and she wasn't going to take me in. Nor was I going to ask her. And then, of course, the big question: What would happen to the children? Christine was applying to colleges at the time, and little Beatrice was still in grade school. The boys were scattered in between, set in their schools, in their sports, in their lives. I had to think about them: How would this trauma affect them?"

Kathy took a deep breath. The same thoughts had been milling around in her head all night. She wondered if every woman, faced with the same situation, would have the same concerns. She reckoned they would.

"So what did you do in the end?"

Rose looked Kathy directly in the eye. "I feigned ignorance. I did nothing."

"Nothing." The word hung flat and uncompromising between them.

"Nothing. I decided he was having some sort of midlife crisis, and I let it go. I said nothing, did nothing. I stopped looking at his ridiculous profile riddled with exaggerations and untruths. I guess . . . I was just hoping he'd realize he had much more to lose if he left me. I was gambling that he would come to his senses. And he did. Eventually."

"You did nothing."

"Sometimes doing nothing is a decision too," Rose said gently.

"Are you saying I should do nothing?"

"No, I'm not saying that. I'm telling you that's what I did."

"I don't think I could do that."

"Before you make any decision, you've got to be sure of your facts. At this moment, right now, you don't know for sure."

Kathy nodded. "But I'm almost sure."

"Almost sure is not sure enough. And you were almost sure before."

"But I was right then."

"Were you?"

Kathy hesitated a bit too long before answering. "Yes. I know I was. I just . . . had no proof."

"Then you need proof before you confront him," Rose said simply. "And even then, even when you are one hundred percent sure, you've got to be prepared for the consequences."

Kathy shook her head from side to side, and suddenly there were tears in her eyes, but, for the first time since the ugly suspicion had been planted in her mind, they were tears of anger. "If I knew he was having an affair, and I didn't confront him, I couldn't live with myself."

Rose reached over and caught both of Kathy's hands in hers. "That's what I thought in the beginning. Then I realized that Tommy still came home to me every night. We had built something together that I didn't want to throw away. He was still my best friend. These other women were just a distraction, nothing more. He's a man, for God's sake. Let's face it, Kathy. Men stray. It's in their nature, whether we like it or not. It goes back to the time of cavemen. . . . Men hunted and women nurtured. Tommy was just . . . hunting. If I'd confronted him, I would have destroyed our marriage, but I knew if I was patient I would win out. And I did."

"I can't do that."

"I know you can't. Not right now. It's still too fresh. Too raw. But think about it. Have it at the back of your mind as an option."

Rose released her hands and picked up her coffee cup. Not looking at Kathy, she asked, "Are you still having sex?"

Kathy opened her mouth to make a quick response, then stopped. Things in the bedroom . . . were different. When they had first started dating, they had made love every day. The sex had been magical.

Inspired.

Adventurous.

Fun.

Then, as the months and years passed, their lovemaking had waned, to perhaps twice a week. After the children came along, it slipped into an irregular Saturday morning routine when Brendan had guitar lessons and Theresa had soccer. Then even that pattern shifted and drifted away. They made love on special occasions: birthdays, anniversaries, Valentine's Day. In recent years it had died away to almost nothing. Kathy honestly couldn't remember the last time they had made love. She was only forty-three. She still felt sexy. Despite being a bit overweight, she felt sensual . . . yet, Robert didn't look at her that way anymore. She tried to remember the last time he had told her that she was beautiful. She couldn't remember the last time he had looked at her with lust, with the passion of a man who wanted her. She started to get angry. Was Robert simply replacing her with a younger, fitter version of herself? Was he trying to recapture the lust they had felt in their first few years together when everything had been so new, when their senses had been so heightened, when the sex had been fantastic rather than . . . ordinary?

But no, a marriage wasn't just about sex, a marriage was . . .

"What?" Rose asked, seeing the expression on the younger woman's face.

"Something struck me. Something important, something I've never thought about before." Kathy licked suddenly dry lips. "What is a marriage? What makes a marriage?" Rose opened her mouth to respond, but Kathy raised her hand. "Is it living together, is it the commitment, the sex, the shared experiences, the trust, the truth? Love? What is it?"

"When I was younger," Rose said, very quietly, "I would have said all of those things. Now," she shrugged, almost defeated, "now, I think it might just be habit."

CHAPTER 6

Rose's parting words had been, "Don't make a decision until you have concrete evidence. And this time, Kathy, be sure. Be really, really sure. No marriage can survive those sorts of accusations—especially if they're untrue. And if you are sure, then be prepared for the consequences. Not just the immediate ones, but the long-term ones also."

Kathy stood at the front door and watched Rose make her way down the path. Her friend stopped at the white picket fence and raised her hand and smiled, then got into her used Volvo and headed back home. Kathy watched her drive off and raised a hand to wave good-bye. Then she turned back into the hallway, closed the door, and rested her back and head against the cool glass. It would be so easy to pretend that nothing had changed . . . and yet everything had changed.

She now saw Rose differently.

She hadn't exactly lost respect for her friend, but . . . something was different, and she knew that things would never be the same between them again, though at that precise moment, she was unsure why.

She could hear her mother's words again: Never ask a question unless you're prepared for an answer you don't like.

Isn't that how most affairs started: because one partner never asked the questions? Where have you been, why are you late, who were you with? But you couldn't do that. Even asking the questions would destroy a relationship. A relationship was built on trust; if you trusted someone, you didn't have to ask the questions.

Folding her arms across her chest, she moved silently down the overlarge chill hallway. Abruptly she knew why things would never be the same between Rose and her again. When Rose had admitted that she'd known her husband had been having an affair—affairs—and had chosen to remain ignorant, to do nothing, Kathy had lost respect for her.

You were supposed to do something.

You had to do something.

She just didn't know what you were supposed to do.

Kathy wandered around the house, moving from room to room, looking at them again, seeing them with new eyes. Somewhere at the back of her mind she was wondering what she would take with her if she chose to leave . . . or what Robert would take with him if he left. The painting they had bought together in Italy. The red leather couch they had gotten at forty percent off because it had been used in one of their commercials. The custom-made bookshelf filled with books she'd collected over the years. Kathy couldn't imagine dividing the beloved book collection into his and hers piles. Rose had a point about the convenience of staying together. Not only for the kids, but also for the practicality. If Robert was having an affair, then he'd surely come back to her when it was over. Wouldn't he? No. That wasn't even an option. If he was having an affair, she couldn't stay with him.

But would he leave?

Would she ask him to go?

And if he didn't, then would she stay? Could she?

The Walkers lived in a large, four-bedroom Colonial in Brookline, one of Boston's most prestigious suburbs. When they had first moved into South Boston, eighteen years ago, they had lived in a tiny apartment while they had grown the business. When the kids were born, there were few good public school options. Kathy had been to private school and wanted her kids to go to public school; however, she wanted them to get the best education possible. After researching school districts, Robert and Kathy set their sights on moving to Brookline, because the upmarket neighborhood was the best option. The price of their first home had pushed them to the very limit of what they could afford. There had been months when they had lived on ramen noodles just to make sure they had enough to pay the mortgage. But they had been happy times. They had laughed a lot then. More than they ever did now.

Six years ago, they had moved into this house. It was less than two miles from their first home, but it was larger and was near a park. They had bought the house for exactly half of what it was worth now. Robert had said it would be a fabulous investment; he had been right then. He was right most of the time.

She had once loved that about him, loved his absolute confidence and self-assurance. She didn't think she had ever once heard him express any doubts about what he was doing and the direction he was taking their lives. But what she once had accepted as confidence, she now recognized as arrogance.

There was nothing of his in the living room. It was rarely used, a habit she'd picked up from her mother: a room kept aside as a "good room" for visitors, where the children never ventured. Kathy smiled at the irony. What was the point of a living room that wasn't lived in? A chunky black leather suite dominated the room and made it seem smaller than it was. She'd never wanted the suite and would have preferred something lighter and brighter. But when they'd bought it, Robert was still entertaining at home, and he thought the dark leather sofa and love seat set gave the right impression, one of prosperity and success. The china cabinet against one wall had been her mother's, and was filled with a mismatched assortment of Waterford crystal and Wedgwood china. She had never gotten around to completing any of the sets and doubted if she ever would now. The cabinet also housed a collection of Hummel Dolls, also inherited from her mother, which she kept meaning to sell on eBay. She doubted she'd ever do it, but it amused her to go online and see how much they were now worth. There was no television in the room—in fact, it was probably the only room in the house, with the exception of the bathrooms, which didn't have a TV set in it.

The family room, which led directly into the kitchen, was where they spent the most time. To the left of the black marble fireplace, an enormous fifty-inch flat-screen television took up one corner, along with the Blu-ray player, Brendan's Xbox, and Theresa's Wii. Speakers connected to a surround-sound system trailed around the floor. Discs were scattered on the floor alongside the television. Robert would want some of those, though she was sure he hadn't watched any of them, and probably never would. He was always buying DVDs for "a rainy day" or for when he got a few hours of free time. Lately he'd had no free time, or if he had, he was too busy, and she realized now just what he'd been doing....

She veered away from that thought. She didn't want to go there just yet.

The couch here was older, the seats slightly bellied from years of wear, though she'd had it reupholstered recently. When it had been re-covered, it had looked brand new for about a week. She'd been promising she'd get rid of it for months now and had a vague idea about looking for a new couch in the February President's Day sales.

On top of the fireplace was the hideous 1930s clock that Robert had inherited from his grandfather. Kathy hated it, with its yellow, nicotine-stained paper face and a mechanism that whirred and clicked just before it struck the hour, reminding her of an old man grinding his teeth. Robert would want that, and if he didn't want it, he was going to take it away with him, because she wasn't going to tolerate it in her house.

Her house.

Her home.

Hers.

She was the one who spent the time in it, day in and day out. She cleaned it, cared for it, turned an empty shell of a house into a loving home for Robert and her children. She knew every nook and cranny, every squeaky floorboard, every crack in the paint; she knew where the cobwebs gathered, the taps that dripped, and which windows stuck. This was her home. She had decorated it. She had cared for it. She had nurtured it. And she wasn't going to give it up.

Hers, hers, hers!

She shivered suddenly, chill air trickling down the back of her neck; it frightened her that she was thinking like this. But as she began to examine the past and try to establish a future, she was forced to look at words like "separation" and "divorce." And that meant looking at words like "his" and "hers," words that she'd never considered before. It had always been "theirs," even during those terrible days six years earlier when she'd accused him of having an affair with Stephanie. She'd never once thought of divorce then.

Kathy took a deep breath. Rose was right. Before she even started to journey down that road, she was going to need evidence. Strong, incontrovertible evidence.

She walked into the small dining room, which was filled with a large dining table and eight chairs. One of the chairs was mismatched, from the time one of Robert's obese clients had broken the original and they'd been forced to replace it with the closest match. The family ate there on special occasions, but there had been few of those of late. It had last been used last Christmas and would be used again next Wednesday for Christmas Day dinner. Now it was covered with the remnants of Theresa's handmade Christmas cards.

Kathy wandered back into the kitchen and automatically cleared the cups from the table. She stood by the sink and ran them under the tap, rather than popping them into the dishwasher. She wanted—needed—to be doing something with her hands.

She glanced at the clock and wondered what time Robert would get home tonight. Then she remembered that he was going to be late; he was meeting a client. A *client*. Or at least that's what he had told her. She stopped, frowning. He had said he was taking . . . whom? Jimmy. He was taking Jimmy Moran to Top of the Hub.

Or was he?

*　*　*

"Information, what listing please?"

"Top of the Hub. It's a restaurant. In the Prudential building." Her voice surprised her; it sounded strong and confident, loud in the silence of the kitchen. She hadn't realized she was going to make the call until she found the phone in her hand, her fingers tapping out the number for directory assistance. Isn't this what suspicious wives around the world did, she thought bitterly: check up on their husbands?

"Please hold and I'll connect you."

Didn't his lie spill out into everyone else's lives? Friends would lie for him, colleagues would lie, and now here she was, about to add to the fabric of little white lies that surrounded his affair.

"Thank you for calling Top of the Hub. This is Elise. How may I help you?"

"Yes, hello. I'm just calling to confirm a reservation. Robert Walker for this evening, seven thirty. Party of two." It was her best professional voice, efficient, slightly bored. She'd played the part often enough in the early days when Robert was setting up the production company, pretending to be his secretary in an effort to convince clients that it was more than a one-man, one-woman operation.

"I don't have a reservation here under Walker."

Her lips went dry, and her mouth was suddenly filled with cotton. At the corner of her right eye, a muscle began to twitch uncontrollably. "Try R&K Productions." Once you discovered the first lie, she thought bitterly, the rest followed easily enough.

"I'm sorry, ma'am, nothing under that name either."

Ma'am. Even over the phone they could tell she was no longer a "miss." Kathy felt painfully old. "Well, thank you for trying. Let me get back to my boss. I'm sure there's a simple explanation."

There was no reservation at Top of the Hub. She wasn't surprised with the discovery; she hadn't expected that there would be. Of course, it could be a simple mistake on Robert's part—but Robert rarely made mistakes. Maybe it was a different restaurant.

Or he'd lied to her. And he was meeting his mistress. As he had on every other red flag day.

CHAPTER 7

Kathy Walker stood outside the door to her husband's study. She rested her hand gently on the doorknob, but hesitated, reluctant to turn the handle and step into his domain.

To cross the boundary, both figuratively and literally.

The events of the past few hours had moved so swiftly that it had left her little time for contemplation. Less than twenty-four hours ago, she'd seen the red flag against that woman's name on her husband's phone, and she'd jumped to a conclusion. Maybe she was wrong. Her head desperately tried to convince her heart that maybe it was entirely innocent.

And her heart told her it wasn't.

She had known, because she had suspected for a long time that something was amiss. And once you suspected, wasn't that the first indication that something really was wrong? If you knew—truly knew, without question, without hesitation, without doubt—that your partner loved you, you would never suspect him of having an affair. But Kathy wasn't convinced that Robert loved her anymore. Liked her probably, was used to her certainly, even tolerated her, but loved her? No, she didn't think so.

When she had seen that red flag, lots of little things, lots of half-formed questions and slightly curious incidents started to form themselves into a convincing truth. And now, for her sanity's sake, she needed proof.

But once she stepped into his room, once she crossed this line, there was no going back. Even if she found nothing inside, even if she discovered evidence that completely exonerated him, and even though he would never know that she had been searching, things could never be the same between them again. She would be betraying his trust.

He'd betrayed her once.

The thought crept, icy and bitter, into the back of her mind. Betrayed her with the same woman. Or so she believed. She'd had no proof then, no concrete evidence, just fears and suppositions.

And she needed to know the truth.

With no further hesitation, Kathy Walker pushed open the door and stepped into her husband's study.

It had originally been the second largest bedroom in the house, and at one stage they'd planned on giving it to Brendan when he got older. Robert had claimed it when they first moved into the house, set up his computer and his files, his bookshelves and his computer-editing suite, and even back then she had known Brendan would never get the room.

The room was a perfect square, with a large double window looking out over the back garden. Robert loved it because it was so quiet. A row of filing cabinets took up the left wall, while a drafting table was placed directly in front of the window. Robert preferred to first sketch out the storyboards for his scripts, whether they were for a documentary or an ad, rather than just using a computer program. He felt more creative that way. A custom-built long, blond wood table took up the entire right wall. It held all the office equipment: printers, faxes, scanners, a twenty-seven-inch iMac, and a space where the shiny MacBook Pro laptop usually sat, alongside the digital editing suite where he spliced images, dialogue, and music into the advertisements that were R&K's bread and butter. When they had first set up the business all those years ago, they had sent everything out for editing. Now, with the advances in technology and the invention of Final Cut Pro, it was possible to do most of the editing in-house on a powerful home computer.

She rarely came into this room—it was very much Robert's domain—but she was always struck by how incredibly neat it was. It was an aspect of his personality that she found contrasted sharply with the real man. In his daily life and his personal appearance, Robert was always slightly dishevelled, slightly scattered. She'd once thought it was part of his charm. He'd turned up on a date more than once wearing odd socks, and he still had the boyhood habit of incorrectly buttoning his jacket. Lately however—even before she'd become suspicious—she'd been aware that he'd started taking care of his appearance. She'd noticed some new shirts with strong vertical stripes in the closet, along with a couple of new silk ties in bright primary colors to match them. A sharply styled new suit in a dark, Italian wool-silk mix had appeared behind his row of classic Brooks Brothers suits. She remembered the brand: Forzieri. It had sounded so pretentious, and when she had looked it up online later, she discovered that it was. Since when did her husband invest in luxury Italian suits? When she had first met him, his idea of dressing up had been wearing a blazer from the Gap. Recently, he had started getting regular haircuts. It wasn't that long ago that he'd sat on the edge of the bath while she trimmed his hair with her sewing scissors.

When had these changes started? And why hadn't she given them a second thought when she first noticed them? Perhaps, because she just hadn't been paying attention. Or was it that she wasn't interested?

Kathy stood in the center of the room and looked around. She was looking for something. She just didn't know what she was looking for. She'd know it when she saw it: It would be another red flag item.

She started with the papers on his desk. A neat pile was stacked in a wire basket to the left of his computer. She knew from experience that he'd notice anything out of place, so she'd have to take care to leave everything exactly as she found it. She turned the basket upside down, emptying all the papers onto the desk, facedown. Then, she went through them, one by one, replacing them in the wire basket, right side up.

Invitation to a product launch . . . letter from a client . . . art student looking for a job . . . Visa bill . . . invoice from a secretarial agency . . . speeding ticket . . .

Kathy stopped. Robert had never said anything to her about getting a speeding ticket. It was a hundred and fifty dollar ticket issued in Jamaica Plain last October 31, at 11:12 p.m. He had been going forty-five miles an hour in a twenty-five mile an hour zone. She sighed as she put the ticket back into the basket; that was an expensive ticket. And it was going to bump up their insurance even more. She knew why he hadn't said anything to her about it. Like most men, he was incredibly vain about anything related to his driving and probably felt embarrassed.

The next sheet of paper was a complaint from Tony O'Connor. Now there was a name from the past. She remembered Tony. He'd been one of their first clients. He had a number of small carpet and tile shops scattered across Massachusetts and employed R&K to do his deliberately cheesy advertisements. Tony insisted on being the star of his own commercials, and his over-the-top, hard-sell delivery had made him a local celebrity. Despite R&K's commercials helping to nearly triple his profits, Tony always complained, even when he'd signed off and approved an ad. Some things never changed. Shaking her head, she put Tony's letter in the basket on top of the speeding ticket.

And stopped.

Something cold settled into the pit of her stomach. She picked up the ticket and looked at it again. October 31. Halloween. She remembered last Halloween because there had been some trouble in the neighborhood. A group of older boys, whom Brendan sometimes hung out with, had gotten some unbelievably powerful fireworks and had set them off into the early hours of the morning. Fireworks were illegal in Massachusetts, but were legal to purchase in New Hampshire and Connecticut. The boys had picked up the fireworks just over the border in Seabrook, New Hampshire, and had set them off in the park near the house. She clearly remembered sitting on the bed with Brendan and Theresa on either side of her, watching the colorful explosions of light. The noise was incredible—a mixture of what sounded like gunfire, crackles, and tremendous explosions. A bonfire blazed in the distance, and showers of sparks filled up the sky. Even in the bedroom behind the closed triple-glazed windows, the air had tasted of burnt rubber tires. At one stage a spent rocket had fallen on the roof, then rolled and clattered off the tiles. The three of them had jumped in unison, thinking the roof was coming in.

The three of them . . . because Robert had not been there. She'd remembered being almost grateful. He would probably have wanted to go out and argue with the boys, and God knows how that would have ended up. That night he had been in Connecticut having dinner with a prospective client; he'd stayed over and come back the following morning.

But how then could he get a ticket in Jamaica Plain at 11:12 p.m.?

Because—stupid—he had not been in Connecticut.

Because—stupid—he had been driving through Jamaica Plain.

She quickly rifled through the rest of the papers. Something else had bothered her. Yes. There was a Visa bill. Why was it here? She took care of the bills. In the early years of their marriage, Robert had looked after all the bills, and they'd ended up paying interest on more than one occasion because he'd forgotten to pay on time. Now, she paid all the bills and utilities. They had two platinum cards, one with Bank of America and one with Wells Fargo. They ran all the house expenses on the B of A card, and the business expenses on the Wells Fargo card.

Kathy turned over the Visa bill again. It was an MBNA Platinum card. She frowned; she hadn't known they had an MBNA account, and why had she never seen it before? Then she realized the bill had been sent to Charles Street, which was the office address in the city. It seemed to be entirely for Internet purchases: books, CDs, computer stuff. Kathy hadn't known Robert bought anything online except for the occasional book from Amazon, and they tended to be work-related titles. There was nothing unusual in the bill . . . until she turned the page. There were three items listed on the second page. A purchase from QVC that came to $320. A bouquet of flowers ordered online from ProFlowers that came to $95 dollars. The most recent entry was for L'Espalier, the French restaurant in the Back Bay that Kathy had been dying to go to. It was for $210 dollars, and that expense had been incurred just over two weeks ago, on Tuesday, the third of December. Last night, looking at her husband's phone, she'd noted that the Tuesdays were usually red flag days.

She looked at the few pieces of information her cursory search had revealed. He had a credit card he'd told her nothing about; he had purchased a meal at a posh French restaurant two weeks ago when he'd supposedly been working; and—most damning of all— she was able to place him in Jamaica Plain in October, when he had told her he was in Connecticut. She also knew for a fact that he was not having dinner at Top of the Hub this evening.

What more evidence did she need that he was having an affair?

She hurried through the rest of the documents. But there was nothing of any interest in them. Robert was, by nature, a cautious man, and she was more than surprised that he'd left the incriminating papers on his desk. Kathy started to get angry; he was obviously counting on her docility and stupidity, or else he had so little respect for her that he thought that even if she did come into his room, she wouldn't notice. She had a sudden temptation to rip every file out of the cabinets, shred them, then pile them up in the center of the floor and let him come home to an unholy mess. She wanted to pin the speeding ticket and the Visa bill to the bulletin board above the computer.

She wanted to pick up the phone and scream at him.

But not yet.

Not yet.

She would confront him, but in her own time and on her own terms. The last time she'd raised the subject of his relationship with Stephanie Burroughs, he had managed to convince her that she was obviously going out of her mind. She'd had no real evidence last time, only a woman's intuition that something was amiss. She would not make that mistake again.

It gave her a certain small pleasure to use the scanner—his scanner—to make copies of the speeding ticket and the Visa bill. When she did confront him this time, she would have the hard evidence in her hands.

Kathy carefully replaced the papers in the wire basket and turned to the desktop computer. Robert loved his technology. If he were conducting a relationship with anyone, she would certainly find the evidence in his computer. The only problem was, it was password protected. "In case it was ever stolen," he had told her, "or the kids get into it." She realized now that he'd never volunteered the password.

Kathy remembered the last time she'd watched Robert turn on the machine. She had been standing against a filing cabinet looking for a copy of the most recent letter they had sent out to their accountant. The IRS was claiming they had never received a tax return for the previous year. Robert had sworn he'd written to the accountant and then had sat down at his desk and booted up his computer.

Kathy now crossed the room to stand against the filing cabinet, in the same position she'd held when she'd spoken to him. She closed her eyes, remembering. Robert had been sitting directly in front of her, facing his computer screen. The log-on screen had appeared, and his fingers had rattled in the password. Except . . . except only the fingers on his right hand had moved, and they had been positioned at the right top of the keyboard.

Kathy stepped up to the computer and looked at the keyboard. The possible keys he could have used were P, O, I, U, Y, H, J, K, L, 7,8,9,0.

Pulling out his ergonomic Herman Miller Aeron chair, she sat at his desk and looked around for a combination of letters or numbers, just in case he had left the password scribbled somewhere. But there was nothing.

She closed her eyes and concentrated again, remembering. She hadn't really been looking at him . . . but she had heard eight distinct taps, hard and definite. She opened her eyes and grinned, scanning the potential letters. Robert was nothing if not predictable. Most people used combinations of letters or figures that were familiar to them. Or that had some emotional meaning. She'd lay money that Robert's password was the name of his beloved childhood beagle. A dog whose framed picture he kept alongside the family pictures on the mantle. He had been a silly little dog with an even sillier name.

Kathy brought the machine to whirring life and then waited while the screen flickered, blinked, and then cleared again.

Please Enter Password

She hesitated, wondering whether, if she were wrong, the machine would lock up and Robert would somehow know that she'd been into it. Then she discovered that she simply didn't care what he thought.

Please Enter Password

She tapped the letters in carefully, Poppykoo, then hesitated a moment before hitting Enter. Kathy nodded. She was right; she knew she was. Her little finger brushed the Enter key.

A light on the front panel of the computer flickered yellow, indicating that the hard disk was working, then the machine chimed musically and opened up to a desktop of icons.

She was in.

CHAPTER 8

Two hours later, Kathy stepped away from the computer. There was a tightness across her shoulders, and her eyes felt gritty and tired. She had been convinced—absolutely certain—that she would find evidence of Robert's affair on the machine.

She hadn't found what she'd set out to find. There had been no illicit e-mails, no secret dating accounts on Match.com, no concrete evidence. However, what she had discovered had disturbed her. Frightened her even.

She'd gone for the My Documents folder first, painstakingly and systematically going through folder after folder, reading letters and memos, all to do with business. It left her feeling depressed and a little guilty; she hadn't quite realized that Robert was working so hard. Nor had she understood just how precarious R&K's situation was. He'd said nothing to her about the state of the company, but from what she was seeing, while they were not exactly in trouble at the moment, they were certainly heading that way. There seemed to be less business out there, and the independent production companies were constantly undercutting one another simply to get the jobs. He was taking on more and more subcontracting work, most of it funneled through one of the large agencies in the city. She came across one letter to a record label that documented how Robert had been forced to cut nearly three and a half thousand dollars off the quote for a job simply to get the work. She noted that he'd sent out the e-mail at two o'clock in the morning. She discovered other e-mails sent out at two thirty, two forty-five, even three ten in the morning.

Robert worked late, both in the office and at home. She'd grown used to it over the years. He worked on into the night, claiming that he got his best work done when the house was quiet and the phones had stopped ringing.

Last night, lying in bed, with visions of that red flag still throbbing in time to the migraine headache behind her eyes, she'd imagined him conducting his affairs by e-mail and phone late at night. Her fears had drifted into fragments of dreams in which she stood outside Robert's office door, her ear pressed against the cool wood, and heard whispers of intimate conversations, the muted chatter of phone sex, the frantic tapping of his fingers across the keyboard as he sent out erotic e-mails and furtive sexts.

Yet, there was nothing; she found no evidence of a single untoward letter.

She'd gone through his Outlook program. She'd read every e-mail he had received and sent. She'd checked his deleted files and his archive folders. And she'd found absolutely no evidence of anything illicit going on. On the contrary, all the evidence pointed to a hardworking and conscientious man. If he was sending e-mails to Stephanie Burroughs, he was obviously using another e-mail account, but she had no way of checking that. She turned to look at the empty space on the table. Unless he kept that data on the laptop. Robert carried the laptop into the office with him every morning and brought it home again every night; maybe it would contain the evidence she was looking for.

But maybe, just maybe, there was no evidence, the rational side of her brain insisted. Maybe the few scraps of paper she had collected so far were all that would be available. Maybe there were even reasonable explanations for all of them. No, there were too many maybes.

She sat back down at the desk and blinked her eyes a few times before focussing her attention back on the computer screen. She moved the mouse onto the Contacts section of Outlook and quickly scrolled through the names until she came to the *B*'s and then slowed.

Stephanie Burroughs.

There was a little red flag pinned to the name. She double-clicked on the name, and Stephanie Burroughs's details opened up. Her name, address, phone number, mobile, e-mail . . . and a little photograph of the woman. Kathy stared long and hard at the picture. It had been six years since she'd last set eyes on her, and if this was a recent photograph—and she suspected that it was—then those years had been kind. A round face was dominated by huge dark eyes and framed by deep brown, almost black hair. Kathy guessed she was now in her early thirties. She imagined that she would still be slim and elegant.

But what struck her now—as it had struck her all those years ago, when Robert had first introduced them—was how much they resembled one another. They might have been sisters. She had always thought that Stephanie Burroughs was a younger, prettier version of herself. She clicked on the Details tab. It was another page of contact details, including Stephanie's birthday. The sixth of November. A Scorpio.

Kathy hit the Print button, and the little laser printer whirred to life, and almost immediately the page of Stephanie's details whirred out of the machine. She added it to the rest of her evidence.

She went to the Calendar page. It was a mirror of the calendar she had seen on his phone, and she realized that the programs on the computer and in his phone were probably synched. The same flags appeared on the same days. She scrolled back to the month of November, looking for the sixth, Stephanie's birthday. There was a little red flag pinned to the day, and a single notation: *NYC.*

New York City.

Kathy remembered the day now: Robert had taken the train down to New York to meet with a potential client. He'd been due back that night, but had called late in the evening to say that he'd had a few drinks and was going to spend the night. The following day, which was a Thursday, he'd phoned to say that he was going golfing on Long Island with the client and would not be back until Friday morning. He had finally arrived home late Friday evening.

Kathy sat back in the creaking chair and stared at the screen, remembering. There had been a lot of meetings over the years. A lot of overnights in a lot of cities. She'd never thought about it before, but she couldn't remember if any of those meetings had ever resulted in a new client's signing up with R&K Productions. In fact, considering what she'd just discovered about the state of the business, she could definitively say that none of these trips with clients had resulted in extra business.

Which meant . . .

Which meant that either Robert was a very poor salesman or perhaps this affair had been going on far longer than she had thought. The last she'd heard about Stephanie was that she'd moved away and was working somewhere in Florida. Or had she? Kathy couldn't even believe that anymore. Had Stephanie left, or had Robert just told her that to lull her into a false sense of security? Had he been seeing her all these years, sneaking off to cities and towns dotted along the East Coast to conduct his sordid affair, meeting his mistress in places where they would be least likely to be recognized? Or had he simply been heading off to—she checked the address on the sheet of paper—to an apartment in Jamaica Plain where Burroughs lived?

She had no way of knowing. Circumstantial evidence certainly, but no proof.

Kathy wrapped her arms around her body, feeling sick and chilled. She realized now that she could not believe a single word her husband had told her.

And the doubts, the questions, the confusion were tearing her apart.

CHAPTER 9

"You were always such a procrastinator."

Kathy moved the phone away from her mouth and took a deep breath. Sometimes her older sister's schoolmarmish tone set her teeth on edge. "I know, I know. Can you do it?"

"Seriously, Kathy? Brendan is seventeen, and Theresa is fifteen. I really don't think they need a babysitter. . . ." Julia Taylor began.

"—Fine," Kathy interrupted, a little more sharply than she'd intended. "I'll ask Sheila." Sheila was Julia and Kathy's younger sister, and Kathy knew that Julia was always a little envious of the amount of time Sheila spent with Kathy's kids.

"I didn't say I wouldn't do it," Julia said hurriedly. "I was just saying that I thought they were old enough to take care of themselves."

"I know they are, but at least if you're here they'll both study for their last few exams, instead of vegging out in front of the TV all night."

"I suppose Robert is out."

"He's entertaining a client," Kathy said smoothly, the words tasting bitter and flat in her mouth.

"And you're left to do the Christmas shopping, I suppose." Julia never made any secret of her dislike for Robert.

"Can you do it or not?" Kathy allowed a little of the terrible, bubbling anger that seemed to be caught in the pit of her stomach to come to the surface. "Yes or no? I don't need the lecture."

"Yes, I'll do it." There was a long pause, then Julia added, "Are you all right? You sound upset."

"I'm just tired. It's too close to Christmas, and I've barely done anything. I guess I'm just panicking a little. All the stores are open late, and if I cross a few more presents off of my list, I'll be happier."

"No problem. What time do you want me to come over?"

"Right now."

"Aw, Ma, not Aunt Julia!" Brendan was halfway through buttering what looked like an entire loaf of bread. He was making himself a quick snack. "I'm seventeen!"

Kathy gathered up the clean laundry from the dryer and dumped it into the cracked plastic basket. Brendan was a younger version of his father and looked and sounded enough like him to disconcert her on occasion.

Theresa burst into the kitchen in a billow of icy air. She too had inherited her father's looks, but not his height. "Practice got out early. I'm starving," she announced and snatched a slice of buttered bread from the pile Brendan was busily creating. Normally it would have instigated an argument.

"We've got Julia babysitting us tonight," Brendan said glumly.

"Ma!" Theresa turned the single word into an accusation.

"I know, I know," Kathy snapped.

The two children read the warning signals and kept quiet.

"It would be great to be able to go out and trust you both to get your homework done. But I can't. That's why I've got to get your Aunt Julia to watch you. Trust me, I like it even less than you do. I'm the one who had to listen to her lecture me." Hugging the basket of clothes like a shield, she hurried from the kitchen before she said anything else.

Kathy thumped up the stairs, angry with herself for getting annoyed with the children. It wasn't their fault. She'd spent the day trying to make sense of what she'd discovered in her husband's office. All the bits and pieces went around and around in her head, a hideous jigsaw of half-truths, suppositions, and lies. By the time the kids had come in from school, there was a sick headache sitting behind her eyes and a ball of acid indigestion lodged in her stomach. Even watching Brendan butter the bread was enough to nauseate her.

Balancing the laundry basket on her hip, she dumped the clothes on her bed and began to sort through them, the simple, mundane task distracting her. Theresa's socks—every one a different shade; Brendan's school tee shirts, all of them stained yellow beneath the arms; Robert's boxer shorts. She stopped and held them in her hands. The material was still warm from the dryer. When had he started wearing boxers?

It was another question. Suddenly, she had nothing but questions. She'd been married to Robert for eighteen years and had known him for three years before that. Twenty-one years. She knew a lot about him—she had thought she knew everything. But now it was becoming apparent that she knew damn little about the man she'd married. She shook her head suddenly, the savage movement setting off the pain behind her eyes. This wasn't the man she had married. The Robert she had married would not have lied to her. The Robert she had married respected her. Loved her.

She wondered when that had changed.

When they'd first married, he had worn Jockey briefs. Always the same brand, always plain white. She frowned, trying to remember when that had changed. A year, no, almost two years ago. About the time he'd started going to the gym.

He'd taken up going to the Boston Sports Club on Bulfinch, near Government Center. He had told her the three-year membership came courtesy of a client. Then one day he had come home with a packet of boxer shorts that he'd bought at the Gap in Coolidge Corner. All the guys in the gym were wearing them, he told her; he felt a bit out of place wearing briefs.

Wadding the boxer shorts into a ball, she shoved them into Robert's underwear drawer. Was it a lie? Was it the truth? Nothing made sense anymore.

Kathy then did something she rarely did: she turned the lock in the bedroom door, locking herself in. She then took off all of her clothes and looked at herself. Really looked at herself, naked, vulnerable, exposed. Standing with her back against the wall, she stared at herself in the unforgiving mirrored doors. She saw the pasty, slightly flabby body of a forty-three-year-old woman who looked at least three—maybe even five—years older. Her breasts were heavy. They were a nice shape; however, they had already lost their elasticity and were hanging lower than she would have liked. Her belly was similarly full, soft, with a circle of baby fat that had never quite disappeared. Her legs were good, Kathy thought, and she allowed herself a brief moment to admire her long legs before she glanced at her unmade face. There were lines around her eyes, etched into the corners of her mouth, tiny vertical strips on her top lip. The bags under her eyes looked bruised, and the whites of her eyes were threaded with burst veins from crying. When she looked at herself from head to toe, fully exposed, naked and raw, she saw someone who looked like her late mother.

Was that what Robert saw?

Her lips moved, shaping the next question: What do you see when you look at me? She didn't know, because he never told her. He rarely told her she was pretty. He used to compliment her all of the time. Not that she needed to be complimented . . . but occasionally, it was nice. Especially from the man you loved. She frowned. When was the last time he had told her that he loved her?

When was the last time she had told him that she loved him?

The question blindsided her. "I always tell him," she said aloud. Reflected in the mirror, she could see the lie in her eyes. She didn't always tell him, nor could she remember the last time she'd told him.

Kathy slid open the closet door and began hunting out clothing. Men were so needy. Had she not given him enough attention? Had she driven him away, into the arms and bed of another woman? It was a question she didn't want to tackle, didn't even want to examine, because she was afraid of the answer.

When was the last time he had told her that he loved her . . . and meant it? There was a time he had said it every morning before he went out to work. "I love you." Then again, last thing at night, beginning and ending every day with the simple statement. That didn't happen anymore.

In the early years of their marriage she had been a voracious reader. She'd often sit up half the night reading. When Robert got into bed he would snuggle down beside her, head almost lost beneath the duvet, arm draped across her stomach. When he heard her light click off, he would mumble, "Love you." And then he would turn, the small of his back resting against her, comforting her. His breathing would settle, and he would fall asleep almost immediately. Last thing at night and first thing in the morning. His warm touch and a simple sentence bracketing her day. It had given her extraordinary pleasure.

Kathy dressed hurriedly, pulling on a pair of black jeans and fishing out a thick turtleneck sweater. The temperature had been falling steadily, and the forecasters were suggesting that there might be a white Christmas. She found her UGGs in the back of the closet. Robert had given them to her as part of her Christmas present two years ago. They were hardly the sexiest of presents, but they were practical and comfortable. Something easily taken for granted. Just like Kathy. She pushed her left foot into a boot and tried to remember what he'd given her last year. Something very ordinary, she knew, something . . . Kathy shook her head. She couldn't remember.

Last year, amongst other things, she'd given him a state-of-the-art digital camera. When he had opened the box, his only comment had been that he hoped she'd kept the receipt so they could claim it as a business expense.

What had he given her last year? That was going to bother her for the rest of the night.

Kathy pulled her leather jacket out of the closet, then pushed the mirrored door closed and examined her reflection. Bundled up, she still looked frumpy, she decided. Frumpy and undesirable. Her self-esteem was starting to quickly spiral downward, and she left the room before she lost her nerve to do what needed to be done.

"I'll be gone a couple of hours," she announced to Brendan and Theresa. They were sitting in the kitchen, which now stank of burnt toast.

The two children nodded. They were glued to the small TV set high on the wall. Meredith Vieira was quizzing a contestant on *Who Wants to Be a Millionaire?* At least it was educational.

Kathy went through the kitchen door, which led to the garage, pulled it closed, then opened it again. "Can either of you remember what your father got me last Christmas?"

"The new Jodi Picoult novel and that perfume you don't like," Theresa said quickly, without taking her eyes off the screen.

"Right. Thanks. See you later. Please be good for Aunt Julia." She pulled the door closed and headed out to the garage. A book and perfume. She remembered now. The book had been great, but the perfume wasn't even her brand. She remembered he hadn't even taken off the price stickers. He'd picked up both at Downtown Crossing. How much thought had gone into that present?

Kathy wondered what he'd gotten his girlfriend.

CHAPTER 10

Kathy passed her sister's SUV at the bottom of the road. Julia didn't see her; she was clutching the wheel of the big vehicle with white-knuckle intensity, staring straight ahead. Kathy knew her sister hated driving the SUV because of its size, but she drove it because she thought it was a status symbol. Robert didn't like Julia; he always said that she was shallow.

At least Julia's husband wasn't having an affair.

The thought, icy as the winter weather, slid cold and bitter into her consciousness. Julia and Ben had been married for twenty-seven years, and there'd never been any doubts that they loved one another. You just had to look at them together to realize that. Kathy wasn't a big fan of her English brother-in-law. He'd met Julia three decades earlier when she'd spent a year in London and, rather improbably, the pair had fallen deeply in love. They were a strange couple, but clearly devoted to each other.

Kathy wondered what someone looking in on her relationship with Robert would think. Would a stranger or even a friend imagine that after eighteen years of marriage, everything was fine between them, that they were still in love, or would he or she be able to tell that something was desperately wrong? What were the signals when something was amiss with a relationship?

She suddenly smiled, realizing that she was holding the steering wheel in the same white-knuckled grip as her sister. The smile faded. If—and it was still only an if—it turned out that Robert was having an affair, she was not looking forward to telling either of her sisters, especially Julia. She knew that Julia would commiserate, though she suspected that secretly her sister would be thrilled. Her opinion of Robert would be vindicated; she would be able to say "I told you so," and would insist on dispensing unwanted advice. Sheila, her younger, unmarried sister, would be genuinely sympathetic. Kathy resolved to speak to her first.

Kathy flicked her headlights on to high beam. They picked up stray chips of ice and snowflakes spiraling out of the sky, making it look as if she were falling into the snow. She flicked the lights back and dropped her speed.

This was insane.

No, this was necessary.

She was heading into the heart of Boston a week before Christmas, right into rush-hour traffic with what looked like a snowstorm coming in. She thought about heading back and, for a single moment, considered it seriously. But if she went back she knew she would have lost momentum. Tomorrow was a day closer to Christmas and, for some reason, that date—that significant, family-orientated date—was assuming a huge importance. She had to know the truth before Christmas. Perhaps it was simply that she did not want to go into the New Year knowing—or not knowing—that she was living a lie, that her marriage, her relationship, her love was compromised, that her future was uncertain and her past unknown.

She turned the heat on at full blast. It made little difference to the temperature as far as she could see. At the bottom of the road she turned to the right, which bypassed one of Brookline's main streets. She could see that it was solid with cars, no doubt drawn to any one of the quaint little shops that did terrific business at this time of year. Traffic was heavy, but most of it was heading out of the city. Commuters going home for the weekend.

Kathy nervously eased the big car out onto Commonwealth Ave, trying to remember the last time she had driven herself into the city at night. Whenever they went out in the evening, Robert drove.

Deep in the folds of her coat, her cell phone chirped and buzzed. Keeping her eyes on the road, she fished into the pocket, pulled out the phone, and hit the button that turned it into a speaker-phone.

"Kathy?" Robert's voice was tinny and brittle. "Where are you?"

"In the car," she said, knowing it was an answer he hated. He knew she was in the car—he wanted to know exactly where she and the car were.

"I've just called home. The kids told me you're heading into the city to go shopping."

She could hear the incredulity in his voice.

"Yes," she said, keeping her voice carefully neutral.

"Kathy, I really don't think this is a good idea. Traffic is shit, and the weather is closing in. Forecasters are promising more snow and maybe black ice this evening."

"I need to get a few things. I thought I'd head to Newbury Street," she continued, ignoring his statement. Then she smiled bitterly. "If there's a problem with the weather, I could always drop into Top of the Hub, meet you there. We can drive home in your car, and I'll come in with you in the morning to pick up my car."

There was a long pause. She was determined not to break into it.

"Did I lose you?" came his voice at last.

"I'm still here," she said shortly. The traffic ahead of her was a wall of stationary metal. She groaned; she should have just taken the T. It would have been faster and safer. "Where are you?" she eventually asked.

"Still at the office. Jimmy's coming here around seven." There was a crackle of static. "...I really don't think it's a good idea to head into the city tonight. And if I have a few drinks with Jimmy, I might have to leave the car myself. That'll be two cars in town. I was half thinking I might even stay overnight. He says I can crash at his apartment."

There was another long pause. Robert obviously expected

Kathy to fill the silence, but she said nothing. She turned right onto Storrow Drive. She realized she was just a few miles from where Robert had gotten the speeding ticket. Traffic was almost at a complete standstill, cars bumper to bumper, windows fogged up.

"Kathy..."

"You're breaking up. I can hardly hear you," she lied.

"Can't you get what you're looking for in Brookline?"

"No," she said truthfully. "I'll see you at Top of the Hub later..."

"No, not Top of the Hub..."

Kathy kept her eyes fixed firmly on the road, refusing to glance down at the phone's lit screen. She took a breath before responding, careful to pitch her voice just right. "I thought you said last night you were going to Top of the Hub...."

"Kathy, I'm having trouble hearing you. Listen, there was a screw-up. I phoned earlier to confirm, and they couldn't find the reservation."

Kathy frowned. She knew this to be the truth. So maybe everything else was explicable also. Maybe all her suppositions had a rational explanation. She shook her head; they didn't. "So where are you going to go?"

"Don't know yet."

"Well, look, call me when you find a place, and I'll drop by. I haven't seen Jimmy for ages. How is Angela?"

"They've separated. He wants a divorce. She says no."

Kathy shifted in the driver's seat, feeling trapped by the traffic. The lights of Boston burned amber and white in the distance. "Listen, I've got to go, there's a cop nearby, and I shouldn't be on my cell," she lied again, and stabbed a finger to end the call.

If Robert wanted a divorce would she say no?

Kathy shook her head. She'd say, "Go."

If he didn't want her, if he'd chosen some slut over her, she certainly wouldn't want him hanging around. But if he was going, she would make sure she'd keep everything that was rightfully hers.

It took forty minutes to get down to Beacon Hill. The stores were open for last-minute shoppers, and street parking was at an absolute premium. She drove around the hilly side streets, looking for a place to park.

For years, Kathy and Robert had run R&K Productions out of their home. About ten years ago, when the company started making some money, they had decided that they needed a legitimate address. It had to be close enough to the city center to impress clients; a respectable address always suggested success, Robert had told her. After all, perception was everything. They'd eventually taken a single room on the first floor of a Federal-style row house on Beacon Hill, less than a mile from the State House. When a second room had become available, they'd taken that. Now R&K Productions occupied a suite of four ground-floor rooms, an outer office, a large conference room, a tiny kitchen, and a bathroom. Kathy had always thought it was an outrageously extravagant expense; Robert claimed it was good for business. And deductible, of course.

As she drove through Beacon Hill, she smiled, as she always did in this neighborhood. Why did people pay so much to live in narrow row houses that were hundreds of years old? The same reason Robert wanted to set up the company here. Location. Location. Location. And the homes were charming. When she got to Charles Street, she could see the offices; they were in total darkness. Kathy glanced at the clock on the dashboard. The amber digits said it was six forty-five. She drove around the block. There was no sign of Robert's car.

She was . . . disappointed.

What had she been expecting? To see Robert's car outside the office and then the door opening and Robert and his mistress coming out arm in arm? And if she had seen his car outside, what would she have done? Gone in, or skulked outside in the shadows, watching like some shabby detective in a cheap novel?

Kathy made one last drive around the block before heading toward the Charles River back onto Storrow Drive. There was one other destination she had to visit.

She found Stephanie Burroughs's address easily enough. It was in one of Jamaica Plain's historical Victorians that had been broken up into condominiums. Holding the printout she'd taken from Robert's computer in her hand, she peered out, trying to make sense of the numbering.

"Can I help you?" The voice was querulous, suspicious. The tiny figure of a coat-bundled old lady materialized out of the shadows. She glared into the car at Kathy.

"Yes . . . no . . . possibly." She tried her best smile.

"Well, make your mind up," the old lady growled.

"I'm supposed to deliver a Christmas present to a Miss"—she deliberately consulted the sheet of paper—"a Miss Burroughs. I think she lives here."

"Number eight." The old woman turned and pointed up to the cupola, toward a brightly lit window. A fully-lit miniature Christmas tree twinkled behind the bubbled glass. "Used to be one building, but it got broken up into four units. I'm on the ground floor in number two. Stephanie Burroughs is above me in number eight. Smallest unit but she seems to like it. Did some construction there when she first moved in, but other than that she's been a model neighbor." The old woman drew a breath, delighted to have a captive audience. "Now, there's a married couple in six who are quiet but they have a baby on the way. And don't get me started what that noise is going to be like. Thankfully, they're at the back off the building. In number four, there's a man I don't particularly care for. He's a hippie."

"Oh, so I do have the right address!" Kathy interrupted before the old woman could speak again.

"You do. But you've wasted a trip. She's just gone out."

Kathy tried her winning smile again. "I don't suppose you know where she was going?"

Now the old lady looked at her suspiciously. "Why? You make personal deliveries?"

"This is a special delivery. I'm under strict instructions to place it directly into her hands. It's supposed to be a surprise."

"A surprise? Oh, I love surprises. Bet it's from her boyfriend. She's always getting flowers delivered."

"He must be a very thoughtful man," Kathy said evenly, choking back the panic. "If you do see her, would you mind not saying anything about the surprise? I don't want to ruin her present."

"Mum's the word. I'm the soul of discretion, young woman. The soul of discretion."

"Thank you so much. Merry Christmas."

"And a Merry Christmas to you too."

CHAPTER 11

It was after nine by the time she got back, and everyone—Julia, Brendan, and Theresa—was in a foul mood. Robert hadn't come home yet.

Julia started putting on her coat the second Kathy turned her key in the lock. "I thought you'd be back an hour ago," she snapped.

"I went as fast as I could," Kathy said. She opened her mouth to say more, but closed it quickly again. She knew she had a tendency to talk too much, especially when she was nervous, and she was terrified she was going to blurt out her fears to her sister. "Were the kids all right?"

"They were fine, I suppose, though they insisted on ordering takeout. I don't believe in fast food, Kathy, you know that. You never know what you're eating."

"It's not fast food, it's—"

"It's unhealthy. Full of salts and sugars and monosodium glutamate."

"They only have it once in a blue moon as a treat."

"Really, Sis? Because they seemed pretty familiar with the menu," Julia said, voice thick with suspicion. "Brendan seemed to know it by heart. He ordered his kung pao chicken by number."

"Should I open a bottle of wine?" Kathy asked, moving past Julia, heading into the kitchen. She knew Julia would refuse.

"No, no, I should go. Ben will wonder where I am."

Kathy moved back down the hall and gave her sister a quick peck on the cheek. Julia smelled of lavender powder, the same talc their mother had worn. Kathy wondered if it was by accident or by design. As she'd got older Julia had come to physically resemble their late mother; she had her hair cut and styled in a slightly more modern version of both their mother's cut, and that of her namesake, Julia Child. Like their mother and the late chef, Julia always wore a string of pearls, blue blouses, and sensible skirts. And flat shoes. Always flat shoes. She looked old, but then, she had always looked old, even as a child.

Julia stood in the door, wrapping her coat tightly around her. "You'll be coming over on Boxing Day." Julia turned the question into a statement.

"I haven't mentioned it to Robert yet," Kathy said truthfully. "But I'm sure we'll be there."

"It means a lot to Ben. You know he loves to see the children."

"I know." Kathy wanted to pour herself a large glass of wine; however, her sister had suddenly decided to get chatty.

"Have you seen Sheila?"

"Not recently."

"Is there a new boyfriend?"

"I've no idea," Kathy said, which was not entirely true. There was a new man in their younger sister's life, someone Sheila was excited about, but was being equally secretive about at the moment. But there were always new men in Sheila's life—each one more unsuitable than the last.

"She needs to settle down," Julia said and sniffed. "She's getting a little too old for all this running around."

"She's thirty-six. That's hardly old."

"I was married with two children by that age. So were you," Julia added. "Okay, I'd better go." She turned to kiss her sister quickly on the cheek, the slightest brushing of her lips, then she rubbed her thumb under Kathy's right eye. "You look exhausted. You've got bags under your eyes. I'll bring you some under-eye cream the next time I'm over." She let herself out of the door and hurried down the path, her footsteps crunching slightly on the frost.

Kathy stood in the doorway, arms wrapped tightly around her chest, and waited while her sister slowly and carefully backed the big SUV out of the drive. Only when Julia straightened the car on the road and revved away, wheels spinning on icy patches, did she step back and shut the door. The hallway was so cold she could see her breath frosting in front of her face.

Brendan and Theresa were in the family room, sprawled in that peculiarly loose-limbed way that only young children and teens can manage, watching TV. CBS was running a *Big Brother Christmas Special.*

"Did you get your homework done?"

They both grunted.

"Any word from your father?"

"He called earlier," Brendan volunteered, "but said he'd try you on the cell."

"I spoke to him."

"I hope he gets home soon," Theresa said. "There'll be snow later."

"If it gets too bad out, he might stay in the city," Kathy said, more to reassure her daughter than to repeat the lie he'd told her.

Theresa nodded without looking up. "Good. That'd be better. Safer."

Kathy went into the kitchen and poured herself a glass of wine. Robert was a good father, she had to admit. The children wanted for nothing . . . except perhaps a father. Much of the rearing had been left to her. He had so rarely been home in the early years of their marriage; he'd often gone to work in the morning before the children awoke, and had returned late in the evening when they were in bed and asleep. They only really got to see him on weekends. And even then he was invariably working. Kathy put down her glass and began to clear up the take-out bags and foil containers. She gathered up the plates and opened the dishwasher. The children had a good relationship with him now though. . . .

She stopped and straightened. Did they? Did they have a good relationship? What constituted a good relationship? she wondered.

He bought them everything they wanted. Christmas was no longer special, because he gave them presents out of season and often came home with pieces of jewelry for Theresa and video games for Brendan. They both idolized him; how were they going to react when . . . no, not *when,* just *if.* At the moment, it was still if.

But how much time did he give them?

She began to slot the plates into the dishwasher. She couldn't remember the last time he'd spent time with them, when he'd simply taken them out with him for the sheer pleasure of their company. The last movie they'd been to see as a family had been . . . She shook her head; she couldn't remember. He'd missed Brendan's recitals and Theresa's games because he'd been working.

Or had he?

Again, the poisonous, insidious thought curled around the question. Had he been genuinely working, or had he been playing with his mistress? Every excuse he'd ever given her was now suspect.

On impulse, she picked up her phone where she had tossed it on the table and dialed his cell. His voice mail picked up immediately; he must have the cell turned off. She went back to her purse and pulled out the sheet of paper with Stephanie Burroughs's details on it. Then she picked up the phone and was just about to dial the number when she realized that her number would show up on Burroughs's screen. Sitting at the kitchen table, she spent ten minutes trawling through the phone's menu looking to switch off Send Own Number. When she'd set it, she phoned her own home to check the caller ID. *Private Number* showed on the screen. She had a few more sips of wine, and then she called Stephanie Burroughs's number. It rang and rang. She was just about to hang up when it was answered.

"Hello."

The voice was crisp, professional, brusque even. There was the tinkling of a piano in the background, the hum of conversation, a clinking of glass. A bar or a restaurant.

"Hello?"

"Hi. Is this Becky?"

"No, you have the wrong number."

"Rebecca McFeel—" Kathy began, but the phone had already gone dead. Stephanie had killed the call. "Now what exactly did that achieve?" Kathy asked aloud.

"Mom, you're talking to yourself again." Theresa padded into the kitchen. She went straight to the cupboard and pulled out a box of cornflakes.

"I thought you had food delivered."

"I did. But that was hours ago. I'm famished." Theresa filled a bowl to the brim with cornflakes, then added milk. She glanced sidelong at her mother. "Did you get everything you were looking for in town?"

"Not everything," Kathy said truthfully. "I made a start." She turned to look at her daughter. "What do you want for Christmas?"

"I gave my list to Dad."

"I haven't seen it yet."

Theresa concentrated on her cereal.

"Would that be because I might have a problem with some of the items on the list?" Kathy asked.

Theresa shrugged, a mere shifting of the shoulders.

"But you know your dad will get them for you."

"It's just one or two small things," Theresa said defensively.

"You mean one or two pages of small things. I'll talk to your father about them."

"He said he'd get them for me."

"I'll have a look first."

"Don't be mean, Mom. Dad said he'd get them; he had no problem with the list!" She gathered up her bowl and padded back into the family room, ignoring the no-food-in-the-family-room rule. Kathy was too tired, too drained to argue. She could hear Theresa speaking urgently to her brother, no doubt explaining how mean their mother was going to be over the Christmas presents.

They had this battle every year. Theresa would produce a list of just about everything she had seen on TV, on the Internet, found in a magazine, or that her friends had talked about. Kathy would then edit the list down to one or two big presents, plus some small stocking fillers. The trick was always to try and make sure both kids were opening approximately the same number of presents on Christmas morning. More recently, however, Theresa, who was her father's pet, had discovered that if she asked him directly for something, he would more often than not just get it for her. Last year there had been a major upset on Christmas Eve, when Kathy discovered that Robert had bought Theresa just about everything on her list. She'd had sixteen presents to unwrap. Brendan had had eight.

Robert had promised her that it would be different this year. Obviously he'd forgotten.

Kathy tidied up the kitchen, put her wineglass in the dishwasher, and filled the coffeemaker for the morning. Robert had started to forget lots of things: points on his license, a new credit card account . . . and the fact that she was still his wife.

"Time for bed."

"Ma."

"Aw, Mom!"

Kathy crossed the floor in two quick strides and shut the TV off. "Bed. You'll be on Christmas break soon. You can stay up late then." She picked cushions off the floor and tossed them back on the chairs. "And, Theresa, when I call you in the morning, get up. If you miss the bus I'm not driving you to school."

Theresa uncoiled from the chair and marched out of the room, leaving her cereal bowl on the floor. Kathy was going to call after her, but Brendan hopped up and grabbed the bowl and spoon. "I'll get it."

"Thanks."

"Is everything all right?"

She glanced up, struck by the note of concern in his voice. He looked so much like his father. She'd first met Robert when he was in his late twenties, and she had worked for him before they had started dating. He'd been handsome then—still was, she supposed—and Brendan had inherited his father's dark good looks. He was seventeen now and had had several on-and-off-again girlfriends. She'd discouraged them, trying to get him to concentrate on his studies. The problem was that Robert had already promised him a place in the company when he left school. Brendan had then decided that there was little point in breaking his back studying, inasmuch as he already had a job to go to. Since then, his grades had slackened off. Too many C's, a couple of D's. Before he'd talked to his father it had been mainly B's and a few A's.

"Mom?" Brendan asked again.

"I'm fine. Tired. Too much to do with Christmas coming."

Brendan nodded, though he didn't look convinced. "When's Dad getting back?"

Kathy shrugged. "Who knows? I don't." Something in her voice betrayed her. She caught the frown that appeared on her son's face and added quickly, "It's a busy time for him, wining and dining clients. So much of the business he gets comes from networking. He could be home at any time."

Brendan nodded. But she could tell that something was disturbing him. She opened her mouth to ask, then shut it again. She didn't want to run the risk of upsetting her son, and maybe have him go to Robert.

"Go to bed, honey. I'll lock up down here."

"Good night."

"Good night, and no computer games," she added. "It's late enough."

She waited until she heard Brendan's door click shut before she moved around the house, turning off lights and locking doors. She flicked on the porch light, then stood in the hall watching isolated flakes of snow drift past the cone of light.

She wondered if her husband was on the way home to her, or if he was going to spend the night with his mistress.

CHAPTER 12

It was close to two thirty in the morning when Robert finally returned home.

Kathy wasn't asleep. She'd tried reading for a little while—the
new Patricia Cornwell—but she gave it up when she discovered
that she'd read the same paragraph at least half a dozen times and
it still didn't make any sense. Dropping the book on the floor by
the side of the bed, she'd flicked off the light, then climbed out of
bed, pulled back the heavy curtains, and stood by the window, staring down the road. Watching. Waiting. Though she was not entirely sure what she was watching or waiting for.

For the first few years of their marriage, she had never gone to
bed until Robert returned home. As the clock ticked on beyond
midnight, she'd feel her tension increase as she began to imagine
the worst: a drunk driver, a car accident, a carjacking. She couldn't
remember when she had stopped waiting up for him. When he had
started staying out regularly, she supposed, when it became the
norm rather than the exception.

Finally, chilled through to the bone, she had climbed back into
bed and had lain on her back, staring at the patterns cast by the

streetlights on the ceiling. She was trying to make sense of the last two days, but she couldn't.

It kept coming back to questions, with one question dominating all others: Why?

Why would Robert have an affair?

Was it something she'd done? Something she hadn't done?

Why?

Kathy dozed off with the question buzzing in and out of her consciousness.

The dream was formless, incidents from eighteen years of marriage running together into an endless sequence. In the dream she was always alone, alone in the house, alone with the kids, shopping alone . . . alone, alone, alone.

Weekends alone, weekdays alone, vacations alone.

Alone, alone, alone.

Kathy came awake with a start, suddenly snapping from disturbing images to consciousness.

Even fully asleep she'd heard a key turn in the lock. She was out of bed and at the window before she realized what she was doing. A curious mixture of emotions—relief and disappointment— flooded through her when she saw Robert's car in the driveway. Then she slipped back into the warm bed and pulled the blankets up to her chin.

Alone.

Listening to Robert moving around downstairs, trying and failing to be silent, she realized that the abiding emotion of the dream had remained with her. And it overpowered her.

She felt lonely.

Where had the boyfriend she'd married gone? What had happened to the man with whom she'd shared everything? Where was the man she'd fallen in love with?

A flush of emotion brought tears to her eyes. She blinked furiously, then brushed her fingers roughly across her face, wiping away the moisture. And suddenly, she was able to identify that empty feeling she'd been living with for the past few years.

She was lonely. She was just so, so lonely.

She filled her time—she took classes, she volunteered—but there was always something missing. She had the children to keep her busy, friends to keep her company, her sisters to confide in and fight with . . . but it still didn't fill the emptiness.

She heard Robert start up the stairs.

And then she knew that if he walked away and left her in the morning, she'd miss him certainly, miss his presence in the house . . . but probably not much else. He'd withdrawn from her a long time ago, little by little. She was only realizing it now.

Would his departure make any real differences to her life, she asked herself? She didn't even have to think about the answer, and it burned in her stomach. If he left, it would make very little difference to their lives.

And that realization disturbed her more than any other.

"I wasn't sure if you were coming home tonight."

"I'm sorry, I didn't mean to wake you."

"You didn't wake me," Kathy said.

She watched the vague outline of him pull off his tie and fling it in the general direction of the dressing-table chair. She heard the silk hiss as it slid to the floor.

"I only had a couple of drinks, and the roads weren't too bad." He pulled off his jacket, folded it over the chair, and began to unbutton his shirt.

"I called earlier."

"I didn't get it."

"It went straight to your voice mail."

"We went to the Union Oyster House—bad place to get a signal."

Your precious girlfriend had a signal, she wanted to add, but didn't. Instead she asked carefully, "How's Jimmy?"

"Jimmy's fine. He sends his love."

"I'm surprised he remembered me."

"Of course he remembered you."

"So you didn't get into Top of the Hub?"

Robert's white shirt reflected brightly in the streetlights. He peeled it off and dropped it on top of his jacket. "I'm going to call and complain in the morning. They said there wasn't a reservation."

"That's strange. Maureen usually doesn't make mistakes like that." Maureen had manned the front desk of R&K from the very beginning, and Robert always said employing her was the best decision he had ever made. She'd started out in the City of Boston Film Bureau as a production assistant, and had spent twenty-five years there before she went freelance. She knew just about everyone in the business.

"It may have been the temp who made the booking. Maureen's out sick at the moment."

"You never told me!"

"Oh, I'm sure I did."

She allowed a snap of anger in her voice. "You did not! I most certainly would have remembered. I worked with Maureen, remember?" For a long time Maureen had been their entire staff, and the two women had worked closely together. When Kathy's mother had died suddenly and unexpectedly eighteen months earlier, leaving the three sisters distraught, Maureen had made all of the funeral arrangements. "How long has she been out sick?"

"I dunno. Three weeks . . . four," Robert mumbled.

"And you never told me!" Her voice rose, and she lowered it again with a deliberate effort. "You never told me. I would have called her, visited her."

"I've been busy. I must have forgotten."

"What's wrong with her?"

"Chest infection or something. Doctor's note says she won't be back until January. And it's the busiest time of year," he added almost petulantly.

"You make it sound as if she got sick deliberately. I can't remember the last time she was ill. Can you?" she accused.

Robert didn't answer. Naked, he stepped into the bathroom, pulled the door closed, and clicked on the light. She heard the buzz of his electric toothbrush. That was another of his tricks: When he was confronted with a question or situation where he knew he was in the wrong, he simply would fail to answer, or he'd change the subject.

"Who's the new receptionist?" Kathy asked when he came out, flooding the room with light, temporarily blinding her.

"A temp. Illona. Russian, I think. I got her from an agency. She's very good."

Kathy had used the few moments while Robert was in the bathroom to cool her temper. She had been close to losing it when she'd learned that her friend Maureen was out sick. For a moment, the conversation had threatened to drift, and she needed to keep it on track.

"Maybe Illona made the reservation?" she suggested.

Robert pulled out a fresh pair of pajamas and tugged on the bottoms. "Maybe. But it was about four weeks ago; I'm pretty sure Maureen was still around then. It's not a big deal. I'll complain to the restaurant in the morning, if I get a chance."

"Do you want me to do it for you?" she asked, expecting him to say no.

He shrugged into the top. "That'd be great. Table for two, Friday night, seven thirty, in either my name or Jimmy Moran's. I used his name too just in case he got there first."

Robert got into bed, wafting icy air under the sheets. He leaned across and kissed her politely on the cheek, and she caught a hint of alcohol on his breath. Nothing else. No perfume, no scents of soap or shampoo that would indicate that he'd recently had a shower.

"Night," she muttered and rolled over, utterly confused, second-guessing herself. Was she completely wrong? Had he really been having dinner with Jimmy Moran?

Robert's breathing quickly settled into a gentle rhythm, but Kathy couldn't sleep. Was she being nothing more than the paranoid, mistrusting, insecure wife of a handsome man?

Or was she slowly unraveling half-truths from a tissue of lies her husband had so carefully crafted?

CHAPTER 13

Saturday, 21st December

Kathy sat in the car facing the Mount Auburn Cemetery and stared through the windshield at the Bigelow Chapel outlined against an eggshell-blue sky. She was chilled through to the bone, but it had nothing to do with the icy December air; it was the cemetery. She hated the finality of the place, the huge headstones, the carved angels, the great slabs of decorated concrete placed over the graves.

Her mother and father were buried there, sharing a grave in the heart of the old cemetery. Scattered in other graves, some marked, others without a marker, were various aunts and uncles and assorted cousins. Kathy hated the place, always had. She possessed a vivid imagination, and it was easy—too easy—for her to imagine the bodies in the ground, some still clothed in flesh, others nothing more than bones. In her imagination, they always had eyes that snapped open to look at her.

When she and her sisters were kids, it was a Sunday family ritual to come and visit Mount Auburn. Every week, as they walked through the gates, her father would make the same joke, the "dead-center-of-Cambridge" joke, and every week she, and her two sisters, would groan aloud in unison. It became part of the ritual.

They would start with the graves of her grandparents and gradually work their way, Sunday after Sunday, to the graves of all their dead relatives, cleaning them up, plucking out weeds, washing down the headstones with soapy water from lemonade bottles. She knew all the names by heart, all the dates, and even though she had never met any of the people, she felt she knew them intimately. She knew that Aunty Mae had fought with Cousin Darren and that they didn't speak for nearly thirty years; she knew that Cousin Jessica—who wasn't really a cousin at all—had been left at the altar by Tim, who later went on to marry Aunt Rita, and that Uncle Fitz had a special coffin made because he was so fat. It was only later, much later, that she realized that was how her father had kept alive their family history. Even now, all these years later, she would have been able to find each and every one of those graves. She knew for a fact that her own children wouldn't be able to find their grandparents' graves. They knew precious little about her side of the family, and even less about Robert's.

But Kathy wasn't planning to go into the ground with a stone slab raised over her head. When she died, she was going to be cremated and her ashes scattered in the Boston Harbor.

The clock just inside the gate clicked onto nine, and Kathy checked her watch. She'd wait another couple of minutes.

The cemetery was busy, and the woman selling flowers outside the gates had a huge display of Christmas wreaths and poinsettias. Kathy glanced over her shoulder at the backseat. She'd brought a small bouquet of flowers, and suddenly it seemed too small, too inconsequential to mark her parents' grave. She'd get a wreath, she decided.

It had been six months since she'd last visited the grave. She could come up with any number of excuses why she'd stayed away so long, but the truth was simpler: She hadn't wanted to come. This wasn't the way she wanted to remember her parents, cold and dead in rotting wooden boxes in the ground. To her, they would both always be alive and vital. She remembered a quote she'd read somewhere: Nothing ever truly dies while it remains alive in the memory.

Except love. Love can die.

She didn't want to think about that just now. She opened up her purse and fished out the two small memoriam cards she carried tucked into the front pocket. Holding one in each hand she looked at the fuzzy, slightly out of focus photographs of her mother and father. Her father's card was cracked and faded, the paper slightly yellow; her mother's card still looked new. Margaret Childs had died only eighteen months ago. There had been no reason, no illness. She simply went to bed and never woke up. Johnny, her father, had died seventeen years ago, a year after she'd married Robert. Johnny had been a smoker all his life, and a third heart attack had finally taken him.

A tap on the window made her scream and physically jump.

Kathy rolled down the window. "Jesus Christ, you almost gave me a heart attack!"

"Well, you're in the right place for it." Smiling brightly, Sheila Childs leaned into the car to kiss Kathy's cheek, filling the car with cold air and a slightly bitter floral perfume. Then she saw the cards in her sister's hand, and the smile faded. Sheila lifted their father's card from Kathy's palm and tilted it to the light. "I was thinking about him only the other day, and I couldn't find my card." She handed the card back to Kathy.

Kathy shoved both cards into her purse, rolled up the window, and climbed out of the car. "I think about him a lot," she said. She reached into the backseat to lift out the small bouquet.

The two sisters linked arms and darted across the road. They could not have been more dissimilar. Sheila stood at least three inches taller than her older sister and was thin to the point of emaciation. The color of her hair tended to change with the seasons, but lately she'd been going back to her natural deep red, adding golden highlights to emphasize her pale, flawless complexion. Kathy was sensibly dressed in a three-quarter-length black leather coat, black trousers, and low-heeled black boots, while Sheila was elegant in a cream-colored belted Marc Jacobs raincoat and impossibly high-heeled ankle boots. She looked like she'd just stepped off of the runway.

They were through the cemetery's tall, wrought iron gates before Kathy remembered her intention to buy a wreath. Suddenly it didn't seem to matter.

This section of the cemetery was deserted, and they had the narrow pathways to themselves. The air was crystal clear, and although the winter sun was without heat, it painted the tumbled stones and ancient trees in sharp relief, making them look almost artificial. Frost and frozen snow glittered in the shadows and dusted the tops and crevices of some of the more ornate headstones.

The two women walked in silence, turning right down an avenue of evergreens, heading into the heart of the old cemetery. A robin darted into the middle of the path, cocked its head at them, then twisted away. Sheila turned her head to follow its path through the trees. "It's so peaceful here," she said. "I love it."

Kathy looked at her in surprise. "You love it?"

"Always have. Remember those Sundays when we were younger, when Mom and Dad would take us here to clean all the graves?"

"I hated those trips."

"I loved them. I loved the peace and tranquillity of this place. No matter how hot it was, it was always cooler here." She gripped her sister's arm and stopped. "Listen."

Kathy stopped. "I can't hear anything."

"Exactly," Sheila smiled. "That's what I love about this place. It's like a cocoon."

"You always were weird." Kathy squeezed her younger sister's arm to take the sting from the words.

The two women wound their way past the crypts of the cemetery's more famous historical residents like Oliver Wendell Holmes and Winslow Homer and turned left, long shadows dancing ahead of them. The graves in this section were old, most no longer tended and forgotten, but dotted amongst them, like strange blooms, were newly dug graves, a profusion of colored wreaths and cards amidst the withered grass.

"Are you going to tell me what you wanted to see me about?"

Sheila asked finally. "It's not every Saturday morning I get a call from my favorite sister."

"I'm glad you said favorite sister. Your big sister was asking after you last night."

"Your? Don't you mean *our?*"

"When she's in one of her moods, you can have her all to yourself."

"I'm afraid to ask. . . . How is she?"

"Wants to know if you have a boyfriend yet."

"Tell her if she wants to know she can pick up the phone and ask me herself," Sheila snapped. "She's not my mother." Then she smiled. "She only thinks she is."

"If it's any consolation, she's the same with me. Are you going to her place for Christmas?"

"I might. I haven't decided yet."

"You could shock her and bring your boyfriend with you."

"No way. I'm definitely not bringing Alan."

"So he has a name. Alan."

"I told you that."

"No, you haven't! You've been completely secretive about him. I was beginning to wonder what was wrong with him."

"There's nothing wrong with him. He's perfect."

"Sure. The last one was perfect. And the one before that. Even the one with the lazy eye was perfect," Kathy reminded her.

Sheila laughed, the sound loud and startling in the silence of the graveyard. "Okay, maybe he wasn't perfect. But he was extremely rich and that compensated for a lot of his other failings."

"Sheila!" Kathy was genuinely shocked.

"What? I'm just being honest. But this isn't why you asked me here this morning, is it, to talk about my taste in men? I can't remember the last time you wanted to visit Mom and Dad's grave. What's up?"

Kathy walked a dozen steps in silence. "I need to talk to you about something," she said finally. "I need some advice."

"Wow, this is a first. You've never asked me for advice before in my life."

"Well, this happens to be an area in which you're an expert."

"Which is?"

"Men."

Sheila started to smile. "I'm not sure that was meant as a compliment."

The two sisters turned left onto a narrow pathway. Their parents' grave was about halfway up on the right-hand side, a simple white headstone, with the surface of the grave covered in fine white pebbles. A single black pot stood in the center of the grave. Wilted and long withered carnations drooped from the vase.

"Julia was here," Kathy muttered.

"But not recently," Sheila added.

The two sisters moved silently around the grave. Kathy emptied the dead flowers and carried them off to the nearby trash can. When she got back, Sheila had arranged Kathy's bouquet in the bowl and was rubbing down the surface of the stone with a tissue. They then stood side-by-side and stared at the stone.

" 'A loving father. Sadly missed,' " Kathy read aloud. "We should have added a line when Mom went down. Something similar."

"It's funny—I know he's been gone longer, but I remember him more than Mom," Sheila said.

"I have better memories of him. Fonder memories," Kathy agreed.

In the last five years of her life, Margaret Childs had become increasingly bitter and disillusioned with life. She had found fault with everything, and it had reached the stage that the grandchildren—and indeed her own daughters—had found it difficult to visit with her. Family occasions were a nightmare, and she'd ruined Julia and Ben's twenty-fifth wedding anniversary celebration with her bickering and fault-finding.

"When I go, I want to be cremated," Kathy said.

Sheila shrugged. "I don't care what you do with me when I'm gone. Have a party. I'd like that."

"You're the youngest. You'll outlive all of us."

"Maybe." Sheila smiled, but it was the slightest twisting of her lips, and her eyes remained distant. Then she turned to look at her sister. "So?"

Kathy took a deep breath. "So, I think Robert is having an affair." Her breath steamed on the air, giving the words a form. "I don't know what to do about it." In the chill December air, it sounded so cold, so matter-of-fact, so unbelievable. She glanced sidelong at Sheila. "What do you think?"

Her younger sister looked shocked. She finally took a deep breath. "Are you sure?"

"Nearly positive."

"Nearly positive doesn't sound too sure," Sheila said quietly. She took her tissue and rubbed it absently over the top of the headstone, not looking at her older sister. "Tell me everything."

Kathy sat down, perching on the edge of the stone. It was cold and hard beneath her, but in a strange way she welcomed the chill. The last couple of days had been so unreal, dreamlike almost. This was real: sitting here, now, on the icy stone in the deserted cemetery. She could no longer take anything for granted. The illusion of her safe, secure world had been shattered. Maybe the last week had not been the dream; maybe the weeks and months and maybe years preceding it had been the dream. And now she'd finally woken up.

"Six years ago ..."

"Whoa, this started six years ago?" Sheila was stunned. How could she not know this? How could she be so close to Kathy, yet know so little about the important details of her life? Then again, Sheila realized, she had her own secrets she'd elected not to share with Kathy.

"Yes. Well ... in a way it did." Kathy ran her gloved hand over the pebbles on the grave. "Six years ago, I first suspected that Robert was having an affair. A woman called Stephanie Burroughs joined the company as a researcher on a project, a documentary. Young, about your age, ridiculously pretty, extremely bright. They spent a lot of time together. It was around that time he started coming home later and later at night. Her name kept cropping up in conversation. Eventually, it got too much for me; I confronted him and accused him of having an affair with her."

"With what evidence?" Sheila wondered.

Kathy lifted her head to stare into her sister's dark eyes. "Intuition."

"I wonder how many marriages intuition has ruined?" Sheila asked softly, then waved Kathy on before she could comment.

"I confronted him. He denied it. Naturally."

"But you got over it. You must have; you're still together."

"We got over it, sure, but it was hard. We'd just moved into the new house, and there was a lot going on. It was easy enough to concentrate on other things and just . . . well, just let it slide. Stephanie Burroughs moved away, and Robert stopped talking about her."

Sheila wrapped her arms around her chest and sank down on her haunches beside the headstone. "So what changed?"

"The day before yesterday I came across her name—Stephanie Burroughs's name—in his iPhone." Even as she was saying it, it sounded flat to her ears.

Sheila looked at her blankly, obviously expecting more. "And?"

"Her name was in his phone, with a little red flag alongside it."

Sheila dug in her pocket and pulled out her own phone. She ran her index finger across the screen before handing it across to her sister. "Scroll through this; I'm sure you'll find the names of the last four men I've dated. That doesn't mean I'm still seeing them. I'm also Facebook friends with most of my exes. I think you're jumping to conclusions."

"But her name is on Robert's new phone. He only got it a couple of months ago."

Sheila shoved her phone back into her pocket. "I got this less than a month ago. All that happens is that the names are stored on the SIM card in the phone. When you pop the card into a new phone, all your contact details are there."

"There was a red flag beside her name."

Sheila stared at her sister, saying nothing.

"I know, I know. It sounds completely pathetic, doesn't it?" Kathy straightened suddenly. "Look, I'm sorry for dragging you out here. Maybe I'm losing my mind."

"Honey, maybe you're just reading too much into a situation."

Kathy dusted down her coat. She faced the grave, crossed herself automatically, then turned away and headed back down the narrow path. Sheila hesitated a moment, then followed her. They walked a few yards in silence together.

"I searched his study," Kathy said suddenly. "He had a credit card account I knew nothing about. He'd bought flowers, some stuff from a shopping channel, and a meal at L'Espalier restaurant."

"I'm dying to go there."

"So am I," Kathy said pointedly.

"Oh."

"I also found a speeding ticket for a time when he was supposed to be in Connecticut." Spoken aloud, in the cold light of day, she realized again just how weak her accusations were. "He spends a lot of time away from home. He works late," she added. Now that just sounded petty, she thought.

"So what are you asking me?" Sheila said.

"Do you think he's having an affair?"

"Do you really want my advice and opinion or do you want me to support you?" Sheila asked. "Because they are not the same thing. If you want me to support you, I'll do that. But I don't think you want my advice."

"You don't believe me?"

"I didn't say that."

"You don't have to. How can you explain the evidence?"

"What evidence?"

"The credit card."

Sheila reached into her pocket and lifted out an olive Hobo wallet. She snapped it open. There were four credit cards in little plastic windows. Tucked into folds behind them were at least another half dozen plastic cards, Starbucks, Anthropologie, Banana Republic, Peet's Coffee. "At home, I get an offer of a credit card at least once a day. Gold cards, platinum cards, AmEx, Visa, MasterCard, Bank of America, First National. Maybe he simply took up the offer of a good rate."

Kathy rounded on her sister. "What about the speeding ticket? He got it in Jamaica Plain on Halloween. The same night he was supposed to be in Connecticut."

"Did he drive or take the train to Connecticut?"

Kathy opened her mouth to reply, then closed it again, suddenly feeling sick. Had Robert taken the train that time? He sometimes did. Particularly if he was going to be away overnight—he hated driving on 95. He'd been taking the train more recently. He had even gotten an Amtrak frequent traveler pass. "But how would that explain the car?"

Sheila shrugged. "Ask him. Did he lend it to someone? Was it in the garage?" She turned and caught her sister by both arms. "You've got to be so careful, so sure of your facts. You've already made one accusation you couldn't back up. Some men would have walked away at that point. Now you're about to make another accusation. Be sure. Be very sure this time."

"Whose side are you on?" Kathy asked shakily.

"Yours. Always yours." They reached the gates of the cemetery. Sheila stopped and held her sister's hands. "I've been there, but from the other side. I was once stopped in the street by a woman I'd never met. She accused me of having an affair with her husband. I knew the man, I'd worked with him on a couple of occasions, but I was most certainly not having an affair with him. Turned out he hadn't been having an affair with anyone. The couple broke up almost immediately after that. He couldn't live with the mistrust. Don't make that mistake, Kathy. Don't throw away eighteen years of marriage." Sheila hesitated before giving her parting words of warning. "Don't find an affair if there isn't one to find."

CHAPTER 14

At least he hadn't changed the locks.

Kathy Walker pushed open the door of R&K Productions and stepped into the office. A blast of warm air hit her, and she frowned. He'd left the heat on over the weekend. If Maureen had been there, she would never have allowed that to happen.

Then the alarm began to blip.

Had he changed the code? Kathy doubted it as she shoved the door closed and pulled open the little box on the wall behind it. *ENTER CODE* was flashing in bright green digital letters. She entered #328—their anniversary—and the blipping stopped. When they had first moved into the offices, she had chosen #328 because Robert had managed to forget every other combination of numbers. And, so that he'd remember their anniversary.

The office was more or less as she remembered it, though she hadn't stood in it in nearly six months. Back when she had been more involved in the business, she had been there almost every day. There were a few new framed posters on the wall, stills from print jobs and brochures that R&K had worked on. The iMac on the receptionist's desk looked new. Otherwise, it was the same: black leather and chrome furniture, looking a little tired now, and the same combination television and DVD in the corner. Just inside the door, a dispenser for Poland Spring water sat alongside the coffee pot. The ceramic mugs had been replaced by disposable cups. So much for being environmentally friendly. She was tempted for a moment to take a cup, but she didn't want to leave any evidence that she'd been in the office.

She still wasn't sure why she had come to R&K's offices. Because of the traffic, the drive across the city had taken over an hour, and parking was impossible. Luckily, she'd eventually found a space around the corner from the office behind Hill House on Mt. Vernon Street. Maybe it was her sister's parting words, "Don't find an affair if there isn't one to find," that had sent her here. Is that what she was doing—looking for an affair, looking for an excuse?

An excuse to do what? Leave Robert? Throw him out?

What was she looking for? Two days ago, when she'd first suspected that he was having an affair, she'd known instantly what she would do: She would ask him to leave. No, not ask—demand. That had seemed so clear the day before yesterday. Today, she was less certain.

But she had to know. For her own peace of mind, if nothing else, she had to know. However, on the exhausting stop and start drive, she'd come to a decision: If she found nothing concrete in the office, then she'd forget about it. She would try to push it from her mind and would make a conscious effort to pay more attention to both Robert and the business. If her fears about an affair had forced her to do nothing else, they had made her evaluate her own behavior over the past few years. And she wasn't thrilled with what she had discovered. Yes, it was all too easy to say that they had drifted apart. Easier still to blame him and the pressures of work. But what had she done? Or, more specifically, not done. As she had become more absorbed in the children and the new house, she'd certainly taken him and the work he was doing for granted. Reading his e-mails yesterday, discovering how hard he was struggling to keep the business afloat, she felt ashamed. When had she become so consumed with her own life that she had started to ignore his?

Kathy stepped around behind the receptionist's desk. It was pristine—not a paperclip out of place. The new receptionist was certainly neater than Maureen, she thought. She pulled open the drawers looking for a diary or notepad; all receptionists usually had a scratch pad where they jotted down the names from the incoming calls. Even the drawers were neatly organized; even though she'd never met the new receptionist, she wasn't sure she liked her.

Kathy finally found a pad under a well-thumbed version of the Oxford English Dictionary in the bottom drawer. It was a red and black spiral-bound notebook. Across the top of each page was a date and below it the times and names from all the phone calls into the office. Kathy carried the notepad to the window and tilted it to the light. She didn't want to risk turning on any of the interior lights and drawing attention to the premises. Most of the names and numbers were unfamiliar; a few were recognizable to her from the days she'd worked the desk. She ran her finger down the calls for the previous day.

There was no Stephanie Burroughs listed.

Kathy fished out the sheet of paper from her purse with Stephanie's details on it and checked the number against the incoming calls. Nothing.

Before she returned the notepad to the bottom drawer, Kathy looked back over the week's calls, but as far as she could see, no phone calls had come in from Burroughs on the office line.

Maybe she was using the cell, a little malicious voice argued. Maybe she wasn't calling at all, an even smaller inner voice countered.

Kathy pushed open the door and stepped into Robert's office. It was exactly as she remembered it. The only change was the scattering of Christmas cards on the liquor cabinet and a real Christmas tree in the corner, scenting the air with pine. The small tree was decorated with winking white lights that had been left on and the Waterford Crystal ornaments her parents had given them for their first Christmas together. Kathy and Robert had decided that they were too good to use at home—the children might break them—and that they would make a much better impression in the office.

She ran a fingernail down one of the handblown pieces, vaguely touched that he'd kept them for all these years and was still using them.

The room was a long rectangle. There was a circular conference table at one end of the room, while Robert's desk occupied the other. A large window took up one wall, while an oak bookcase stood against another wall. It proudly displayed the various awards the company had won in the last two decades: Tellys, CLIOs, ADDYs, Summit International Awards, and Communicator Awards. The statuettes were crammed into the three bottom shelves, while a framed picture of Robert holding the Palme d'Or stood proudly alone on the top shelf. The conference table gleamed, papers piled neatly on the center of the table. She touched a page, spinning it toward her. It was a headshot of an incredibly handsome young man. She quickly looked over the other pages. They were all related to DaBoyz, a boy band she'd never heard of. It looked as if Robert was pitching to shoot their next music video. He knew nothing about music videos, but she guessed that the band didn't know that.

She crossed the office and stood before Robert's desk. It felt strange to be here, sneaking like a thief into her own company. Because she did own half the company; fifty percent of the shares were in her name. What would happen if they broke up, she wondered. Would the company have to be sold or broken up, or would he have to buy out her share? And what happened then to his share of the house? Would she have to buy him out in turn?

Kathy deliberately drifted away from that thought.

As Sheila had reminded her, she had to be sure of her facts before she went off making wild accusations.

She moved around Robert's desk and sat in the heavy leather chair. It sighed beneath her weight. She'd bought him this chair shortly after they had moved into this office. Like his office at home, the desk was clean and bare except for a fountain-pen set that was placed at an angle off to one side, alongside a modern desk lamp. Mirroring it, on the left-hand side of the desk was a silver photo frame in three panels. Kathy reached for it, then stopped, unwilling to touch and possibly move it. She forgot her fear about drawing attention to the building and turned on the lamp, flooding the desk in warm, yellow light. The frame held three photos: Brendan in the left frame, Theresa in the right, and Robert and Kathy in the middle frame. It was an old photograph taken in New York just before they were married, with the Empire State Building in the background. She'd almost forgotten about the photo. That had been a fabulous vacation, just the two of them, madly in love, engaged to be married, with the world full of possibilities and hope.

If Robert was having an affair, he was hardly likely to keep photos of his wife and children on his desk, was he?

She tried the drawers. They were locked. So this trip had been for nothing. No, not for nothing. At least it had gone a long way toward confirming that Robert was not seeing Stephanie. She wasn't phoning him every day, and there was a family photo on the desk, which at least suggested that his mistress was not visiting him in the office.

Placing her elbows on the desktop and cradling her head in her hands, she squeezed her eyes shut. She felt sick and yet curiously elated. She'd overreacted. She was tired, exhausted, stressed out by the season. Next year they would go away for Christmas. Boycott the holiday.

Well, at least she'd had a wake-up call. The last couple of days had highlighted some problems in her marriage, but problems that could be solved. After Christmas, the pair of them would finally get away for that weekend at the Cape or the Vineyard, and talk. It had been a long time since they had talked, really talked about stuff that mattered. With the constant pressures of modern life, it was so easy to lose touch with what was really important.

Thank God, she hadn't said anything. . . .

She was leaving the office when she saw the filing cabinet behind the door. She hadn't noticed it when she first came in. It was a small, two-door, dark oak cabinet that matched the bookshelf. On impulse, she pulled at the top drawer, expecting to find it locked. It clicked and slid open easily. The files were all neatly tabbed and color-coded, and she saw the hand of the new secretary in it.

The top drawer seemed to be mainly brochures, letters to and from other production companies, pitches for projects.

Kathy knelt down and rummaged through the second drawer. It was full of invoices and bills. She hesitated, then lifted out the file marked AT&T. All of Robert's cell phone bills were neatly arranged in chronological order. She pulled out the most recent bill.

And her heart almost stopped.

Robert Walker phoned Stephanie Burroughs seven or eight times a day. The first call of the day and the last call at night from his cell phone were either to her home phone or her cell.

Kathy's heart started to pound hard enough to vibrate through her flesh. She swallowed bile.

Calls ranged in duration from a couple of minutes to an hour. And texts. Innumerable texts. Mostly to the same number. Kathy flipped to a random page and ran her finger down the list of fifty numbers. Two of the text messages had been to her own cell; the other forty-eight were all to the same number: Stephanie Burroughs's number.

Every day.

Seven days a week.

Hundreds of calls. Hundreds of texts.

Kathy barely made it to the toilet before she threw up.

CHAPTER 15

"Kathy!"

"Hi, Maureen."

Kathy stood on Maureen Ryan's doorstep, a bunch of flowers held awkwardly under one arm, a bottle of wine in a tightly wrapped brown-paper bag under the other.

"Come in, come in. I wasn't expecting you. I'd kiss you, but I don't want to give you whatever I have." Maureen stepped back and allowed Kathy to squeeze past her. "Go straight through into the kitchen."

Maureen lived in Mission Hill in a row house near the Triangle District. She'd been born in the house, and she always said she would like to die there as well.

"I should have called," Kathy said slightly breathlessly, walking down the narrow hallway and into the kitchen. She stopped, shocked. From the outside she had been expecting dark and gloomy Formica and linoleum; instead she was blinking in brilliant light, looking at the latest in Swedish kitchen design, polished blond wood and cool chrome. The rear window, kitchen door, and a section of the wall had been removed and replaced with French doors that led down into a circular conservatory that was bright and fragrant with Christmas blooms. "This is gorgeous," she said.

"Isn't it fabulous?" Maureen said, voice wheezing a little as she came up behind her. "We did a pilot for a reality makeover show a couple of years ago. It never got off the ground, but I volunteered my house for the pilot. Not only did I get a new kitchen, a patio, and a conservatory, I actually got paid for it as well."

"It's fantastic. And you've decorated it beautifully." Kathy turned to look at the older woman. She handed her the flowers and the wine. "I'm so sorry, Maureen. I only found out last night that you were sick. Robert forgot to tell me. He insisted he had, but he hadn't."

"I'm sure he's had a lot on his mind lately," Maureen said. She turned away, set the flowers and wine down on the counter, and started to fill the kettle. "Sit down. Go out into the conservatory. It's my favorite part of the house."

Maureen Ryan was twenty years older than Kathy, a tall, masculine-looking woman, with strong, sharp features, pale green eyes, and a shock of snow-white hair that she wore in a single tight braid that hung to the small of her back. When Kathy had first met her, she'd worn half-moon glasses, but she'd thrown them away in favor of contact lenses, claiming that the glasses made her look old. She had never married, but over the years had been romantically linked with several minor politicians and one equally minor movie star. Maureen liked to say that the stories were only half true; it had been a dozen minor politicians and two not so minor movie stars. Normally, she kept up with the latest fashion trends, and she was still slim and svelte enough to get away with jeans and boots. Today however, she was in a plum-colored velour tracksuit and incredibly ratty slippers.

Kathy stepped down into the conservatory. The air was perfumed with the scent of the flowers and the musky odor of a fat candle burning on an ornamental stand. Two enormous, fan-backed white wicker chairs were placed on either side of a circular glass table. A Stephen King paperback, his book *On Writing,* was open on the table. Kathy remembered that Maureen had always talked about writing a novel based upon her experiences of forty years working in and around the entertainment business.

"How are you feeling?" Kathy asked.

"I'm fine. Slowly getting better." Maureen's voice echoed down from the kitchen. "I picked up a cold, which turned into a chest infection. Pleural effusion is the official medical diagnosis. I wanted to continue working, but there was so much fluid that I had trouble breathing. So, for once in my life, I took some good advice and took some time off."

"You should have let me know. I've have visited you sooner."

"I thought Robert might have told you," Maureen said, stepping out into the conservatory. She was carrying a wicker tray, which held a hand-painted teapot and two matching cups. "Aren't these fun? I got them in Ayia Napa."

"In Cyprus? Isn't that the place where all the young people go for raves?"

"There and Mykonos, but I've already been there and done them," Maureen suggested with a mischievous glint in her eye. "And I like to think of myself as one of those young people."

"Hey, you're the youngest person I know. I hope I've still got your energy when I'm . . ." She allowed the sentence to trail off.

"When you're my age, you mean." Maureen grinned.

"Something like that." Kathy sank into the creaking wicker chair and watched Maureen pour tea. "What keeps you so young?"

Maureen lifted her head and grinned, showing perfectly white teeth. "I used to say 'regular holidays and Spanish waiters,' but lately I've been saying 'attitude . . . and Spanish waiters.' I picked an age and stuck to it."

Despite the sick headache throbbing at the back of her skull, Kathy smiled. "What age?"

"Twenty-two."

"I thought most people chose eighteen."

"I knew nothing at eighteen. I knew it all by the time I was twenty-two. By the time I turned twenty-three, I knew too much." Maureen passed the cup to Kathy, then waited while she added milk. "I don't think I'm old, therefore I'm not old. That's why I hate this chest infection; reminds me that I'm not as resilient as I once was."

The two women drank their tea in silence, looking out over the tiny rectangle of garden.

"This conservatory must make you the envy of your neighbors," Kathy said eventually.

"I started a trend. There are three similar conservatories in this block alone. It was a shame we couldn't get the makeover show off the ground. I had plans to have the whole house transformed." She sipped her tea. "I must come out and see what you've done with your place. How long have you been there now—five, six years?"

"Six, and it's still a work in progress. Somehow there never seems to be the time. I seem to have become a professional chauffeur now that the kids are both involved in sports and clubs and band and student government; they seem to be coming and going at all hours of the day. But next year, I've plans to get in and make some more changes. I definitely want to renovate the kitchen. . . ." Realizing that she was babbling, Kathy abruptly shut up.

"How's Robert?" Maureen asked.

Kathy blinked at her in surprise.

"What? I haven't seen him in nearly six weeks," Maureen added.

Kathy shook her head in disgust. "He said you'd been gone for three or four weeks."

"I went out sick early in November. Other than a couple of e-mails, I really haven't spoken to him."

"He hasn't called?" Kathy asked, getting angry now. R&K owed much of its growth and success to this woman. But more than that, she was a friend.

"Oh, sure, he called for the first few days, usually when he wanted something, or had lost something, or couldn't find a file. I wasn't really expecting him to keep in touch. This is a busy time of year for him. He's probably run off his feet."

"I haven't really seen a lot of him," Kathy admitted. "Let me apologize for him—"

"Don't," Maureen said quickly, raising a hand. "I've worked with him for a long time. I know what he's like."

"And he hasn't . . . hasn't done anything stupid, has he, like stopping your salary, or anything like that?"

Maureen laughed and then wheezed a rasping cough. "Are you kidding? He's terrified he'd lose me to one of his rivals. He knows both Hill Holliday and Digitas have been chasing me."

"Good. Good." Unsure what to say next, Kathy concentrated on her tea.

Maureen sat back into the wicker chair, then lifted up both legs and tucked them beneath her. "I get the impression that this may be more than a social call," she said gently.

Kathy stared miserably into the dregs of her tea. She nodded. "I really did only find out you were sick last night. It's a long story, but Robert was out with Jimmy Moran . . . or at least, he said he was out with Jimmy Moran," she added softly.

"That's an odd thing to say," Maureen said, putting down her cup. "You sound as if you don't believe him."

Kathy put down her own cup and looked Maureen in the eye. "I don't." She breathed deeply. "I believe Robert's having an affair with Stephanie Burroughs. What do you think?"

And she knew, even before Maureen answered, what the answer was going to be. It suddenly seemed colder in the conservatory.

The older woman nodded. "I have suspected that for a long time."

It took Kathy a moment to catch her breath and when she spoke, her voice was little more than a whisper. "When did you know for certain?"

"About a year ago. I was suspicious for a little while before that."

"A year! A year and you didn't bother to tell me!" Kathy bit back the wave of anger that surged through her body.

"I thought about it often enough. I wanted to tell you . . . but it never seemed to be the right time."

"You should have told me!" Kathy's voice rose as she surged to her feet. "I had a right to know!"

"I'm not the one you should be angry with." Maureen said quietly.

Kathy sank back into the chair and put her head in her hands.

"If the roles were reversed, would you have told me?"

Kathy opened her mouth to snap a "yes" but closed it again without replying. Would she, could she, put another woman through the agony, the self-doubt, the self-loathing, the fear, the anger she'd experienced over the past two days? She wasn't sure. She wasn't sure of anything anymore.

"I've just come from the office. I went looking for something—something to tell me that he was having an affair, hoping to find nothing. I'd almost walked out the door when I discovered his cell phone bills."

The older woman smiled bitterly. "That's how I found out too. I was doing an analysis of the bills, looking to see where we could cut costs, when I saw that he kept phoning the same number. I initially thought it was your cell, then I realized he was calling it late at night when he would have been home with you."

"Tell me what you know," Kathy said fiercely. "Tell me everything. I have a right to know," she added desperately.

Maureen stood. Wrapping her arms tightly across her chest, she turned her back on Kathy and stared out at the empty December garden. "I think they've been having an affair for about eighteen months. Maybe a little longer, I'm not sure."

"A year and a half," Kathy said numbly. "He knew her a long time before that. I suspected them of having an affair six years ago when she worked for us as a researcher."

Maureen frowned. "I don't think they were. I know they worked closely together, but I don't think they were having a relationship then."

"Are you sure?"

"No. But if they'd been having a relationship six years ago, I would have found out," Maureen said confidently. "I know something is going on now."

"But you've known for a year and a half. Why didn't you tell me?"

"It's complicated."

"Complicated," Kathy whispered. "What does that mean? I've just discovered my husband of eighteen years has been having an affair for the last year and a half, maybe longer, and you couldn't tell me because it's complicated! What's so complicated about that?"

"Stephanie Burroughs sends a lot of business our way." Maureen turned to look at Kathy, her face hard and expressionless, but her big eyes were brimming with tears. "Stephanie is the account manager with one of the largest advertising agencies in the city— she got us a lot of work. Without her, we would probably have gone under this past year."

Kathy stood and backed away from the older woman. "You let my husband continue his affair because you didn't want to lose your job?"

"His affair was none of my business," Maureen said, biting the inside of her cheek to keep her calm. "His affair is between you and him. No one else. That's why I didn't tell you. I'm not one of those women who go running to their friends with news that they've seen their husbands with other women. Don't you blame me for this, Kathy. This has nothing to do with losing my job. If R&K goes under, sure, I'll lose my job, but I'll get another. But you'll lose your house, and in this economy a man pushing fifty isn't going to be getting another job any time soon. People like him are a dime a dozen, and the kids coming out of school will work twice as long for half the salary. If I'd told you, you would have confronted him and then what? We'd all have lost, you and Robert most of all."

Kathy licked dry lips. Her tongue felt swollen in her mouth. "You're saying he slept with her to save the business."

"I'm saying nothing of the sort."

"But that's what you're implying."

"I'm not implying anything. I'm simply telling you the truth."

"Then what exactly are you saying, Maureen?"

"Kathy . . ."

"Tell me," Kathy demanded, voice rising to a scream. "Why is he sleeping with her?"

Maureen sighed. "I've seen them together. I think they're in love."

CHAPTER 16

Sunday, 22nd December

The remainder of Saturday passed in a blur, and Kathy had no memory of driving back from Maureen's house. She'd kept out of Robert's way, busying herself around the house with the Christmas preparations. Robert had gone out in the morning with the kids to buy the Christmas tree, so by the time she got back the house smelled of pine and echoed with Theresa's squeals as she decorated the tree. A trail of pine needles led from the back door, through the kitchen, and into the dining room.

Maureen's words had frightened her, confused her. She could almost accept that Robert was having an affair with another woman, but that was sex, wasn't it, nothing more? Maureen had said she thought they were in love with one another, which implied . . .

She wasn't sure what it implied.

Kathy had gone to bed early, claiming a headache, which was true, and had lain in the darkness, listening to the sounds of the TV from the room below and the noise of the regular weekend argument coming from next door. The young, good-looking couple next door did everything together—golf, hikes, tennis, movie nights.

They had great barbecues and were excellent hosts. Only Kathy knew that they had screaming matches in the backyard, usually about this time every Friday or Saturday night when one or the other—or both—had a little too much tequila. In the six years she'd lived in this house, she'd learned all the details of their unhappy lives. But when they stepped out on the streets, neighbors only saw a perfect couple....

When people looked at her and Robert, what did they see? A happily married couple, with the standard two children, nice house, and two cars? Or could they see the cracks ... the distance that had crept in between them? She suddenly wondered how many other people knew about Robert's affair. She felt her heart beat too quickly and a panicked tightness squeeze across her chest at the idea. The entertainment business in Boston was a tight-knit community; someone must have seen Robert and his mistress together. If they had, would they have made the connection and assumed the couple were sleeping together? Or would they think Robert and Stephanie were just colleagues? Friends even. Kathy hated the thought that people knew and were pointing fingers as she drove past or walked down the street, whispering behind her back. No, if that were true, someone would have told her. The reality was, most likely no one suspected.

She hadn't.

Kathy fell into a fitful sleep, only snapping awake again when Robert crept into the bedroom. He undressed in the dark and slid in beside her, sighing with contentment as his head hit the pillow. She had not intended to speak to him, afraid that she might blurt out something, or rage or scream at him, but she needed to say something. The rhythm of his breathing was changing, slowing, as he drifted toward sleep.

"I went to see Maureen today."

There was a long pause and, for a moment, she thought Robert had fallen asleep. There was movement in the bed as he turned to look at her. In the reflected streetlights, she could see the sparkling whites of his eyes.

"How is she?"

"Getting better. But she won't be back till the New Year."

"Didn't think so," he mumbled.

"She's not as young as she pretends to be."

"I know." He shifted again, rolling onto his back. "The new girl, the Russian . . ."

"Illona?"

"Yes, Illona. She's very good. Does what she's told, doesn't have an attitude, is in on time, and takes exactly an hour for lunch. Maureen does it her way, treats me like a boy, and has no concept of a one-hour lunch."

"You're not thinking about firing her, are you?"

"It's crossed my mind," he admitted.

"It's not going to happen," Kathy snapped. "I forbid it."

"Forbid it?" There was something in his voice she didn't like: sarcasm or contempt. "You forbid it?"

"I still own half the company, remember? Maybe it's time I started to take a more active interest in it." She sat up in bed and turned on the light.

Robert groaned and shielded his eyes. "It's almost one, for Christ's sake. Can we talk about this in the morning?"

Kathy ignored him. "Now that the kids are older, I'm thinking in the New Year I might start coming in with you three or four times a week. Even when Maureen comes back, she's not going to be able to work full-time. I can go back to doing what I used to do: helping you run the company. Put the K back into R&K Productions."

"Where are you going to find the time?"

"I'll make the time. I'll concentrate on getting new business; you concentrate on making the material. Remember? The way we used to."

"Yeah, that would be great," he said, sounding less than enthusiastic. "Let's talk about it in the morning."

"Maureen said the company was in the red."

Robert shuffled up in the bed. "Maureen should have kept her mouth shut. Can we talk about it in the morning?"

"We rarely get a chance to talk anymore, Robert. We're running in opposite directions."

"C'mon, Kathy, it's only temporarily, and it's Christmas. That always brings its own drama."

"No, it's not only temporarily, and it's not just Christmas. We've been doing it for months, maybe longer. I barely see you anymore. You're home late four nights out of five, you go in to the office on the weekends, and when you are home, you're locked in your office, working."

Robert shrugged. "It's been crazy busy."

"Put my mind at ease; tell me the business is going well."

Robert sighed deeply. "Look, we've gone through a rough patch, but I've landed a few new accounts. Next year will be good."

And Kathy knew where those new accounts had come from.

"Does that mean you'll end up working eighty hours a week next year too?"

"While the work is there, yes. Kathy, I don't have an option. It's one of the joys of being self-employed; you know that."

"Then I'm even more determined to help you. Starting in the New Year, you've got a new colleague: me. You can give your Russian girl notice."

Robert made a face and shook his head.

"What's wrong?"

"Nothing's wrong. But here's what's going to happen. You'll come work with me for a week, maybe two, then you'll have to take time off to be home for some reason: Theresa's sick; you have to get to Brendan's concert on time; you have to be home for the refrigerator repairman."

"Really? That's your worry, my needing to be home for the repairman?" Kathy was getting angry.

She noticed that Robert was completely ignoring her. He kept trying to justify himself. "Then you'll take more and more time off, and soon enough, we'll be back to the way we are now. Except I'll have to go looking for a secretary again."

"So, you're using the fact that I'm prioritizing my kids . . ."

"Our kids, and I'm not saying that, Kathy."

"You sound as if you don't want me to work with you."

"I didn't say that."

Kathy took a deep breath. The conversation was not going the way she had hoped it would. "Look, Robert, I want to be more involved. I feel . . . I feel like we're drifting apart."

Robert reached out to take her hand, but Kathy slid her fingers away. "We're not drifting apart; we're just busy. And it's Christmas. That's all. I'd love you to be more interested in the business." He lifted the clock off of the nightstand and held it up. "Jesus, can we please continue this tomorrow? I have to get an early start in the morning."

"Okay," she agreed, turning off her light and sliding down beneath the covers. "But we will continue it," she promised.

"Fine," he said.

"Fine," she parroted.

Lying in the dark, listening to her husband's breathing deepen beside her, Kathy realized that there was no way he could allow her to be around the business—not if he was using it as the base for his affair.

Kathy awoke Sunday morning with a blinding migraine.

She made the kids brunch and then the three of them decorated the tree. Robert was of no help: he spent the entire day in his study. Kathy went to bed and fell asleep watching an old Hitchcock film.

The entire day had passed and she and Robert had never continued the previous evening's conversation.

CHAPTER 17

Monday, 23rd December

"Are you free tonight?" Kathy tucked the phone under her ear as she picked through the clothes in the closet. "I hate to ask. . . ."

"I can be free. What do you need?" Sheila's voice was breathless, and Kathy could hear music and a cheery voice in the background.

"I'm sorry, I didn't realize you had company."

"Two-dimensional company. It's a workout video. The Bar Method. Really lifts the butt." Each sentence came in short bursts.

"Like your butt needs any more lifting," Kathy said, unable to keep the touch of envy out of her voice. "I was wondering if you could stay with the kids. I asked Julia the other night, and I don't want to ask her again."

"Sure. Where are you off to?" There was a silence, and Kathy heard the television click off. "This is something to do with Robert, isn't it?"

"Yes."

"What are you going to do?"

Kathy pulled out a black polo turtleneck and tossed it onto the bed.

"I went to see Maureen Ryan on Saturday. You remember Maureen, the office manager at R&K?"

"Of course, she's great."

"She knew about the affair, Sheila; she knew about it, and she didn't tell me."

"I'm not that surprised," Sheila said softly.

Kathy blinked in surprise. "Would you, if you had known? Would you have told me?"

"Honestly?"

"Of course."

"If I had known for certain, I would have talked to Robert first before I spoke to you. What did Maureen say?"

"She says it's been going on for over a year. They meet every Monday night at the Boston Sports Club on Bulfinch, and then usually go out for dinner afterward."

Sheila's voice was deadly serious. "What are you going to do?"

"I want to see them together. That's all. Nothing else. I promise."

"I'm coming with you," Sheila said immediately.

"But the children . . ."

"Are not children anymore, and they're big enough to look after themselves for a couple of hours. They're teenagers, for Christ's sake. Brendan will be eighteen in a few months. He's practically a man."

"I really want to do this on my own. . . ."

"And what happens if Robert sees your car? What happens if you have a crash on the way home because you're upset at something you see? I'm coming with you. I'm your sister."

"Do I have a choice?" Kathy's voice was shaky, but she was secretly relieved. She'd been dreading doing this on her own.

"Of course you do. You could ask Julia to go with you."

Kathy laughed, a short barking sound that was completely without humor.

"We'll use my car. He won't recognize it," Sheila said. "I'll be there in an hour."

"You really don't have to do this," Kathy said.

"I want to," Sheila answered.

*   *   *

The two sisters were sitting in Sheila's car on the street below
the Boston Sports Club. Sheila had run into Starbucks, which was
just across the plaza, and they were nursing cappuccinos as they
observed the brick building. The entire second level of the building
had floor-to-ceiling windows. Through the tall glass they could see
people working out on the gleaming gym equipment.

The sisters had cruised around the block twice before they finally spotted Robert's Audi tucked away close to the hedge in a
puddle of shadow. There was a silver BMW parked alongside it,
but plenty of empty spaces in front of and behind the two cars.
Kathy had leaned forward, squinting through the windshield at the
BMW. Was that Stephanie's car?

"This is a good spot." Sheila had tucked her Honda into a darkened corner of the street that afforded a good view of the front entrance to the building to the left and Robert's car to the right. "This
is very exciting. We're like private eyes." The moment she turned
off the engine, the heater shut off, and chilly air began to invade the
car. "I wonder how long they'll be in there?" she said.

"Maureen told me that they usually leave about eight."

Sheila leaned forward to look at the gym. "No matter how fa-
natical I was about my fitness, I'm not sure I'd be spending the
night before Christmas Eve working out. Talk about neurotic."

"No, instead you're sitting in a car with your hysterical sister
spying on her philandering husband. That's not neurotic at all."
Kathy smiled. "Trust me, I'm sure you could have found better
ways to spend your twenty-third of December. Didn't you have
something planned with Alan?"

Sheila didn't answer immediately. She hit a switch and the windshield wipers swished across the windshield, wiping away stray
flakes of snow. "Nothing that couldn't be canceled." She smiled, a
flash of white teeth. "Doesn't do any harm to keep them off balance; keeps them on their toes."

"Is that where I went wrong, do you think?" Kathy wondered
aloud. "He stopped guessing about me; I became too predictable,
too ordinary."

"You've done nothing wrong. You've raised two wonderful children and kept the house going; you gave Robert the freedom that allowed him to grow the business. That's called a partnership."

Sitting in the darkness, staring out at the lights, Kathy gave voice to the questions that had been troubling her from the moment she had first seen Stephanie Burroughs's name and known—absolutely known—that Robert was involved with her. "I keep asking myself what I could have done differently, how I could have kept him."

"Do you want to keep him?"

Kathy sucked in a deep, ragged breath. "I don't know. Everything's just come at me so quickly. When I try to think logically about it, I get lost in issues like the house and the business and the children. . . ."

"Forget all that for a minute. Focus on yourself. What do you want?"

"I . . . I don't know," Kathy whispered. "I'm not sure. When Maureen told me she thought they were in love . . . I hated him . . . and I immediately wanted him back. I wanted to take him away from her. The woman who had stolen him from me." She shook her head. "What's wrong with me?"

"You're saying it was easier when you thought it was just sex?"

"Of course. Having sex with someone is one thing. But loving her . . . giving yourself emotionally to her. That's the deeper betrayal."

The windshield wipers worked again, squeaking slightly on the glass. Sheila took a long sip of her coffee before turning to her sister. "Alan is married," she said softly.

It took a long moment for the sentence to sink in.

"Your boyfriend Alan is married?"

"Married for twenty years with three children." Sheila's voice was a monotone.

"Sheila! What were you thinking?" Kathy turned, pushing back against the door, twisting in the seat to look at her sister in horror.

Sheila didn't look at Kathy. Reflected Christmas lights ran red and white down her face. "I didn't know he was married when I first met him, and he tried to hide it from me for a while, but it's easy enough to find out. The married ones never have that endless free time the single ones do. Weekends were out of bounds; holidays were impossible. It's easy to spot. But . . . he was fun. I enjoyed his company. And he made me laugh. I've dated a lot of immature guys, Kathy, and I wanted a man, not a boy. I wanted someone mature, someone who would look after me, respect me."

"But a married man!"

"I know. But I never wanted him as a husband; I never wanted to take him away from his wife. I enjoy my freedom too much. I was absolutely fine just being the mistress. We have good times, great meals, fantastic sex. It was like being twenty again . . . except this time we had the money and the credit cards to enjoy it."

"Does his wife know?"

"I'm not sure . . . maybe."

"Jesus, Sheila, if you knew what I've been through, you would never put another woman through it."

"It was all going fine," Sheila continued as if she hadn't heard her sister, "until he fell in love with me. Now he's talking about leaving his wife and kids. He's talking about getting a divorce. He wants to marry me." Her voice was suddenly shaky. "Can you imagine it: me, married?"

"You don't love him?"

"No," Sheila said emphatically. "Like him, yes, love him, no. I was going to see him tonight, talk to him, try and break it off with him, before he does something idiotic like tell his wife. Recently, he has started talking about how much fun it would be to go on a honeymoon with me. I may not be the brightest bulb in the box, but that's when the alarm bells starting ringing for me."

Kathy was shivering, and not with the cold. She couldn't believe what she was hearing. Her sister, Sheila, her baby sister, was a married man's mistress. But her sister wasn't a bad person, not an evil person. She hadn't deliberately set out to trap a married man; in fact it looked as if she was doing everything in her power to ensure that he remained with his wife.

"You're going to tell me that I should never have taken up with him in the first place. But I'm a big girl; I went into this with my eyes open. And when I discovered that he was married, I didn't walk away, did I?"

"Why . . . why did you stay with him?"

Sheila shrugged. "Who knows? We always want what we can't have."

"You've no regrets about his wife?"

"No. If she'd been looking after him, been interested in him, he would have never wandered in my direction."

Kathy looked away. Is that what had happened? Had Robert drifted away because she was no longer interested in him?

"There they are," Sheila said, pointing.

This was the man you married.

This was the man who proposed to you, the man with whom you exchanged wedding vows, the man who carried you over the threshold, who had made love to you, gotten you pregnant, stood in the hospital and held your hand while you gave birth.

This was a man with whom you bought a home, started a business, raised a family.

This was the man whose flesh you knew, whose clothes you washed, whose hand you held, whose lips you kissed.

This was the man you loved and trusted.

This was your husband.

And he was holding the hand of another woman.

Kathy Walker watched Robert stride out from the main entrance of the gym. There was a woman by his side, pretty, slim, bright-eyed, smiling. Stephanie Burroughs.

Neither was wearing gloves, and their hands were wrapped together, fingers interlinked. They moved easily alongside one another, confidently, their steps in rhythm. Glance at them quickly, and you'd see just another happy couple.

They were both laughing.

Kathy didn't remember the last time she and Robert had laughed together, didn't remember the last time they had held hands so easily, so intimately.

The couple strolled over to the two cars. Both sets of lights flashed in unison as they hit their remotes simultaneously, and they laughed again, the sound high and brittle on the chill December air.

Robert opened the door of Stephanie's silver BMW. The interior light popped on. The woman threw her gym bag onto the passenger seat and turned to Robert. She wrapped her arms around his neck, pressed the palm of her right hand against the back of his skull to bring his head down to a level with hers. Then she kissed him. Robert responded by dropping his gym bag to the ground and pulling her close.

The kiss went on for a long time. Kathy forced herself to continue watching, refusing to look away as this stranger passionately kissed her husband . . . and her husband returned the kiss with equal passion.

Finally the couple broke apart, and Stephanie climbed into her car. She waved once and drove away. Robert picked up his bag and moved around the front of his car.

Kathy pulled out her cell and hit a speed dial.

"What are you doing?" Sheila hissed, snatching for the phone.

It was too late. The call connected.

"Hi, it's me," Kathy's voice was level, remarkably controlled.

Up the street, less than a hundred yards away, Robert stood with his phone pressed against his ear.

"I'm just wondering what time you'll be home?"

Kathy and Sheila saw Robert lift his left arm to look at his watch. "I'm just leaving the office. I should be there in about forty minutes."

Kathy's hands were trembling so hard that Sheila had to take the phone out of her hand and switch it off.

"Now what?" Sheila asked when Robert's car pulled out of its spot.

"I'm going to see Stephanie Burroughs tomorrow," Kathy said, her voice growing firm and cold with resolution. "I have to talk to her."

"Is that a good idea?"

"I don't know whether it's a good idea or not. I don't care. I have to talk to her."

"It will bring everything to a head," Sheila said.

"It'll bring everything to a conclusion," Kathy said firmly. But even as she was saying the words, she didn't believe them.

Book 2

The Husband's Story

At first, I didn't know what I was doing.

That's not an excuse. Simply a statement of fact. But I swear I didn't set out to have an affair. It just happened.

And then things got out of control. They got complicated.

By the time I knew what I was doing, it was too late. I was in too deep.

I was already in love with her.

CHAPTER 18

Thursday, 19th December

Robert Walker sighed as the hot spray hit his body. There was an iron bar of tension stretched across his shoulders and what felt like a red-hot coal in the base of his spine from sitting in traffic.

He hated Christmas.

Hated everything that it stood for: its falseness, artificiality, pressure to spend, the cloying Christmas songs, and the traffic—he especially hated the traffic. One year, just one year, he would love to take off in early December and return around the middle of January and give the entire Christmas and New Year's nonsense a miss. Play hooky from the holidays.

Robert touched the dial, inching up the hot water. He dipped his head and turned, allowing the water to dance across his neck.

Also, this year R&K Productions had shot a Christmas advertisement in June—when finding a Christmas tree had been next to impossible—and early in December had shot a segment for a docudrama that was set in the middle of August. Inasmuch as finding sunshine in Boston in the middle of winter was nearly impossible, and the budget wouldn't stretch to moving cast and crew to a sunny locale, they had ended up using a few incredibly expensive

HMIs to light the sets in such a way as to suggest brilliant weather. It meant that his entire year was topsy-turvy.

But it was the traffic he really hated. Inner city Boston traffic multiplied to the power of ten because it was Christmas. Add lousy weather, and the seemingly never-ending construction, and the city was practically at a standstill. The politicians had claimed that traffic would get better after the Big Dig. But the Big Dig had become the Big Dug and, as far as he could see, there was no difference. The never-ending construction was suffocating.

Robert tilted his face to the water. He ran his long fingers through his hair, pulling it back off his forehead. Then he grimaced and opened his eyes; a few strands had come away in his hands, entangled in his fingers. He was losing his hair. There had been a time when it wouldn't have bothered him—he didn't like to think of himself as vain—but things had changed.

Not so long ago, it had been experience that counted in his business, and no one really cared what you looked like. But with the impossibility of getting real work—or what he called real work, artistic television documentaries—he had been forced to make more commercials. And he quickly discovered that in this end of the business, looks were everything. He was in the running to shoot a pop video for a boy band at the moment, trying to convince them that he was the right person to create something dark and cutting-edge to match their song. There was no way they were going to give the gig to someone who looked like their father. He would have to get some more Botox in his forehead, and perhaps Restylane injections in his mouth creases. He had to make himself look younger.

He squeezed some shampoo into his hands and began to hum as he rubbed it gently into his scalp. Maybe it was also time to look at some of the treatments that were supposed to restore hair. He had started taking Propecia, but he wasn't sure if it was working. He needed something faster, something that would have more immediate results. Robert saw ads in the papers all the time, special shampoos, electric caps, brushes that massaged the scalp . . . maybe there was a documentary in it. He grinned; he could try out all the treatments and charge it to the company as research. Although, with the way his luck was running, he'd probably go bald. Tilting his head back, he allowed the shower to rinse away the soap, then turned off the tap and stood for a moment, dripping, before pushing open the shower stall door and stepping out onto the bath rug.

When the new power shower had been installed, he'd used the opportunity to redo the en suite bathroom. It was clean and white—he knew Kathy thought it was too cool and clinical—and one wall was completely covered in mirrored tiles. He felt that it gave the otherwise small room a great sense of space, but she had told him she hated the reflections, which allowed her to see all of her imperfections at the same time.

He looked at his reflection in the glass. He was forty-nine years old and looked a couple of years younger. The age showed in the set of his jaw, the lines on his face and around his neck. But he was still in relatively good shape for a man pushing fifty, and although his waist had thickened a little, there was still no hint of a paunch. He worked out regularly and paid particular attention to his stomach and chest. He'd had a couple of sessions on a tanning bed—the new turbo kind, which you stood up in—and he was really pleased with the results. Now, if only he could save his hair.

Robert stepped up to the mirror and patted his hair dry with a towel. He'd done a piece for a hair company a couple of years ago, and he remembered they advised that patting and gently rubbing were better than briskly scrubbing the hair with a towel. That damaged the delicate follicles. He tilted his head to one side. Earlier in the year, he'd noted the first real and dramatic signs of gray appearing. However, he'd gotten hair-coloring foam that blended it away before anyone noticed.

Well, Kathy hadn't noticed.

Stephanie had.

She'd spotted it immediately. She preferred his silver wings; she thought they made him look distinguished. He thought they aged him and blended them away despite her objections.

Wrapping a towel around his waist, Robert reached for the aftershave. He thought he heard a sound in the bedroom outside and popped his head around the door. "Kathy?"

There was nothing there but a depression on the bedcovers that was gradually filling in. There were a few red Christmas envelopes on the bedcovers alongside the clothes he'd stripped off before climbing into the shower.

"Kathy?" He stepped out of the bathroom and pulled open the bedroom door. He was in time to hear the kitchen door click. He picked up one of the Christmas cards, leaving damp fingerprints on the envelope, and glanced at it. Then he tossed the card back on the bed again; he knew what this was all about. Every year, Kathy would fight with him about Christmas-card addresses. She never seemed to have them, even though she'd sent out cards to the same addresses every year. He simply didn't have the time to write dozens of cards. She did. What did she do all day anyway? His iPhone was sticking out of the pocket of his jacket, and he picked it up and turned it on, checking the screen for any missed calls. There were none.

He splashed on some of the new cologne that Stephanie had bought him, wrinkling his nose at the musky smell. He hadn't been sure about it at first, but it had slowly grown on him. He also liked the fact that it would mask the heavy musky perfume that she sometimes wore when they went out at night.

He dressed quickly in jeans and a cashmere sweater and hurried down the stairs. The house was still and silent . . . and cold, very cold. There was a chill to the air. He trailed fingertips along the tops of the radiators, but they were scalding hot.

When he pushed open the kitchen door, he discovered the cause of the chill: The back door was wide open, and Kathy was standing on the step.

"Hey, what's up—it's freezing out here." He came up behind his wife, wrapped his large arms around her waist, and rested his chin on the top of her head. He felt her stiffen and knew immediately that she was going to draw away from him.

Kathy stepped back into the kitchen, forcing him to release her. "Just getting a breath of air; the kitchen was stuffy. Nice cologne."

He couldn't tell if she was mocking him or not. "Yeah. It's new. I didn't know if you'd like it." He spoke evenly and watched her pull the door closed and move to the table to clean up the cards.

"I do. I left a couple of cards on the bed," she began.

"I saw them. . . ."

"I don't have addresses, and besides they're personal cards—it would be better if you wrote and signed them."

After eighteen years of marriage, he'd come to know when something was amiss. He could tell from the set of her shoulders, by the way she refused to meet his gaze. "What's wrong?" he asked quickly.

"Nothing. Why do you ask?"

"Because you've got the tone in your voice."

"Which tone?"

"That tone." He smiled, covering his growing irritation. "The tone that tells me that you're pissed off at me."

Kathy sighed.

"Oh, and the sigh is another sure sign. The sigh and the tone. You're like a great jazz band, Kathy . . . always in syncopation."

"Look, I'm tired," she snapped. "I've been writing cards for hours. Mostly your cards, to your friends and your colleagues. I do it every year. And every year it's last minute, and I'm always missing addresses. You don't help."

Robert bit back a response. He was going to say, you've had weeks to do it, but you always leave it to the last minute, and you always blame me. You could have been doing these a few at a time instead of sitting on your ass watching *The View* and *Judge Judy*. But the last thing he wanted was an argument. Instead, he said calmly, "Kathy, I've just come in from a ten-hour day. I had a meeting in Framingham, the Pike was a parking lot, and I've got a really important presentation in the morning. Just . . . give me a minute to decompress, and I'll go through my address book. Or you can; I've got nothing to hide."

"I've done them all," Kathy said tightly. "The four on the bed are all you have to do."

"We're arguing over four cards?"

"No," she growled. "We're arguing over the one hundred and twenty I've already written. Without your help."

Robert nodded and shrugged. "I should have taken some into work with me," he said. Then he glanced up at the clock. "I'll go and get the kids." He turned and hurried from the kitchen before he said something he regretted. It was the same argument every year. They probably even used the same words. He snatched his leather coat off the rack behind the door and left, resisting the temptation to slam the front door.

He pressed the remote, and the Audi clicked open. Sliding into the driver's seat, he grabbed the steering wheel and took a deep breath, calming himself. He counted to ten before slowly exhaling the air from his lungs, trying to push out the frustration as well. Today was Thursday. This would be the third argument this week. An argument over nothing. Or over something so small that it counted for nothing. Easing the car out of the driveway, he turned left onto the quiet street. Ice crackled under his tires; it would freeze hard later on.

They had been married for eighteen years, and he recognized that an argument never really came from nowhere, and it was never— *never*—about the subject under discussion. Everything had subtext. Today, Kathy was arguing about Christmas cards. Yesterday she'd fought with him because he had forgotten to bring home milk; earlier in the week she'd had a go at him because he had failed to get home in time to go to a parent-teacher conference.

He had explained to her—more than once—that this was his busiest time of year. He simply didn't have the time; but she found it difficult to accept that. Plus it was particularly awkward now with Maureen out of the picture. The new receptionist was good, very good indeed, and she came without all the awkward baggage that know-it-all Maureen brought to the job, but he found he had to check and double-check everything, and that just increased his workload and his stress level.

Kathy liked to think that she knew about the business, but in the years since she'd stepped back from being involved in the day-to-day running of R&K, things had changed. And not only his business; Kathy had been home for too long and had become isolated from the realities of doing business in the real world. And the real world now included traffic. Incredible traffic. Standstill traffic. She simply didn't understand that it made no sense to leave the office at five thirty and sit in traffic for an hour, when he could just as easily leave at six thirty and sit in moving traffic for twenty-five minutes.

Plus, of course, it allowed time for him to see Stephanie.

Robert smiled as he pulled up outside the kids' high school. Both Brendan and Theresa were home late on Thursdays; Brendan had extra classes, and Theresa had basketball practice. Brendan was slipping behind in just about every subject, whereas Theresa was ranked second in her class this year. She took after her mother, he thought proudly.

Robert turned off the engine and dropped the window a fraction. Icy wind curled in around the stuffy interior of the car. He pushed the CD button and a Christmas compilation that had been given away free with the *Boston Herald* came on. He found himself humming along with the Bing Crosby–David Bowie version of "The Little Drummer Boy," and he felt a little of the tension ease away.

Maybe after Christmas they would find time to get away together. Have a talk, mend some fences; he could tell her exactly what was going on with the business. And Stephanie? Would he talk about Stephanie Burroughs? Would he tell her about his mistress, and why he needed to keep her sweet?

"Dad!" Brendan wrenched open the door, with all the force and enthusiasm of a seventeen-year-old, jolting him from his thoughts. "I wasn't expecting to see you here."

"Thought I'd surprise you." Robert reached over and squeezed his son's shoulder. "How was school? And don't say boring," he added quickly.

"Almost boring," Brendan grinned. "Math sucks, Dad. . . ."

"I know. I know. But you heard what your mother said. Junior year's your most important year for grades on your college application. She wants you to get into a good school. And so do I," he added, turning the key in the ignition and easing the car down the street.

"But you said I could join you in the company."

"And you will. After college. The business is changing. It's hard to get hired without an education, even if your old man owns the company. Technology is evolving. The latest digital video technology is moving ahead in leaps and bounds. Wasn't so long ago video cameras recorded on tape. Next it was CDs and then Blu-rays, and now it's all digital recorder." Robert turned down the narrow side road that led to the gymnasium where the Brookline Warriors practiced. "I can't keep up with all the new technology—but you can. That's why I really want you to go to college, come out with a degree, and take R&K to a new level." He squeezed his son's shoulder again. "You know it makes sense."

"I know," Brendan said unhappily. "But Mom's really on my case about this. I even have to study over Christmas for my SATs. Seriously, Dad, it's so unfair."

"I'll talk to her."

"Does this mean I can't work at the company on weekends?"

"Of course you can. I'm talking to a boy band about shooting their new pop video. I could use you on that."

"That'd be awesome. I could be a second-unit director."

"Hey—this is R&K Productions, not 20th Century Fox. We don't have second units. We have one unit—and that's me with a Steadicam. You can be an associate producer, maybe."

"Okay," Brendan said slowly. "So . . . what does that mean exactly?"

"Means you make the coffee."

"Tight," Brendan said glumly. He suddenly leaned forward and pointed. "There's Theresa."

"Yeah, J.P. Licks!" Brendan shouted and high-fived his sister.

"Wait until I park . . . ," Robert began, but Brendan pulled open the door and bounded out of the car toward the ice cream shop. "Dad, you're the best."

Robert pulled up alongside Zaftigs Deli and parallel-parked between two oversized SUVs, maneuvering the Audi into the tight space. Satisfied, he pulled up the brake and turned off the engine.

Theresa waited for her father while he put money into the Pay Station. She was very maternal, just like her mother. He reached down, and she slipped her hand into his. "So tell me," he said, "how was school?"

"The usual. How was work?"

"The usual," he said. "Although I've got some really cool stuff coming up."

"You can't say cool, Dad," Theresa said quickly. "Not at your age. It's not . . . cool."

"When I was young, we used to say cool all the time."

She squeezed his hand, a quick tightening of the fingers. "Well, you're not young now."

"Gee, thanks."

"Gee, you're welcome."

Theresa would probably be the one taking care of him in his old age. Brendan would want to put him into a home, but Theresa would insist that her father live with her and her family. Robert swallowed hard, pushing away the sudden image of his little girl all grown up with a family of her own. It seemed like only yesterday when he'd cradled his babies in his arms . . . and now they were teens. Soon they would make their own way out into the world, and he'd lose them to husbands, wives, and lovers . . . but they would always be his children, and he would always strive to make them happy. To give them what they wanted, no matter what the cost. They would have everything he never had. Including ice cream before dinner.

Theresa had been "starving" after basketball practice and she "couldn't wait" for dinner. And even though it was below freezing outside, the air cold enough to make blinking painful, she wanted ice cream. Coconut almond chip ice cream.

"Dad, please, Dad, please."

When Theresa asked Robert for something, it was hard for him to say no. For years, they had had a father-daughter tradition that on the first day of every month, he'd buy two large Hershey chocolate bars with almonds at CVS, and they'd wolf them down in the car. Kathy had never found out.

Kathy didn't approve of kids eating sugar, but Robert was of the opinion that a little chocolate never hurt anyone, especially when it afforded him a little bonding time with his daughter.

Because he had been working so hard for so many years, Robert cherished any time he could get with his kids. For far too many years, by the time he got home at night they were either in bed or, more recently, watching TV or doing homework. By that time he was too mentally exhausted to engage with them, and often a whole week would go by with less than a couple of words spoken between them. On the rare occasion he got home early enough from work to pick them up from school and spend time with them, well, he tried to make it last. So, when Theresa begged for ice cream before dinner, Robert simply couldn't refuse.

Robert wrapped his daughter's small hand in his as they walked down Harvard Street. Robert smiled; he wondered if his daughter would ever be "too old" to hold her dad's hand. He blinked at the sudden image of him leading his daughter down the aisle of a flower-filled church.

"You're like a million miles away," Theresa said as they entered the ice cream store. Brendan was already at the counter, pointing to the vat of chocolate M&M ice cream.

"I was just thinking that you're growing up so fast. You'll be getting married soon."

"Dad!" Theresa squealed. She had just gotten her braces off, and Robert knew it was only going to be a matter of time before he was going to be subjected to the stress of a dating daughter. "That is seriously not happening any time soon." Then her smile faded as she searched his worried face. "What's wrong?"

"Nothing, pumpkin. Just don't grow up too quickly, promise me that."

"Sure, Dad. Hey, can I add hot fudge and marshmallow sauce?" She pulled him up to the long counter.

"You're going to ruin your appetite, and you know how your mother feels about dessert before dinner."

Theresa chuckled. "Trust me, I won't. I'm totally starving." She squeezed her father's hand again. "Besides, what Mom doesn't know won't hurt her."

"Don't underestimate your mother," Robert said, reaching for his wallet. "She's a lot smarter than you think."

Robert drove back to the house with the two children chatting happily together in the back of the car, which now smelled like a combination of Indian and Chinese take-out food. There were only two and a half years between Brendan and Theresa, and they got along really well. Robert was particularly happy about that. He didn't really have a relationship with his three brothers, all of whom were older than he was. His parents had divorced when he was fourteen, and although he'd stayed with his mother, his regular weekends with his father and older brothers had been uncomfortable outings. He'd stopped going when he was sixteen. By then all but one of his brothers had moved out of the country—and a year later, his eldest brother, Stephen, had gone to New Mexico. There were still occasional letters, the odd Christmas card, congratulatory e-mails when the Red Sox won the World Series, but the last time he'd actually seen all of them had been at his father's funeral fifteen years ago. Only Stephen had come home for their mother's funeral nine months later.

"Dad," Theresa chimed up around a mouthful of fries. She was dipping them in curry sauce, and Robert felt his stomach grumble. He'd missed lunch—again—and all he'd had to eat since breakfast was a packet of peanut M&M's and rum raisin ice cream. So much for taking care of himself. He had promised Stephanie that he would start eating more healthily, and today's diet had consisted of sugar, sugar, and more sugar. "Dad, hello, are we going to have to go to Aunt Julia's the day after Christmas?"

"Well, you have a choice," he said carefully. "Either we go over to your Aunt Julia . . . or she'll come to us. Now, if we visit her," he continued slowly over the groans, "we can leave. If she comes to us, we'll never get rid of her."

"But we go there every year!" Brendan protested.

"It's a tradition. It's called Boxing Day."

"A British tradition. We're American."

"I know, but the tradition is important to Ben, who's British . . . and Julia who pretends she is." Robert said patiently.

"Well, I think it's time to break the tradition," Brendan grumbled. "We're missing some of the best television."

"That's why we have TiVo," Robert sighed. He too hated going over to Kathy's sister's house in Wellesley for her annual Boxing Day party, but he knew how important it was to his wife. "Let's do it this year, and we'll see if we can do something about changing it for next year. Deal?"

"Deal," the kids echoed.

"And we should probably not bring this up with Mom," Theresa guessed. "Like the ice cream."

"Probably not." Robert grinned. He pulled into the driveway and turned off the engine. The bedroom light was on upstairs. As they climbed out of the car, it clicked off. He put his key in the lock and pushed the hall door open, allowing Theresa and Brendan to shove their way into the hallway.

Kathy appeared at the top of the stairs, hand lightly trailing along the banister.

"We got takeout," Brendan called, holding up the brown paper bags.

Kathy smiled. "More than takeout, I see."

There was an expression on her face that Robert could not identify, and he wondered if she was coming down with something. "Everything okay?"

"Fine, just fine," she said tightly, then swept past him into the kitchen.

Robert wandered into the family room and sank into a chair. He hit the remote to turn on the television, absently flicking from channel to channel. Sitcom, sitcom, bad sitcom, really bad sitcom, marine documentary, cooking program. All the sitcoms had a Christmas theme, the marine documentary was set in someplace snowy, and *Iron Chef* was doing a mince pie cook off. It had probably been recorded in June, he thought glumly.

"Are you having yours in here?" Kathy asked, standing in the doorway.

"No, no, I'll eat in the kitchen." He eased himself out of the chair and went into the kitchen. Theresa and Brendan were sorting through the food, doling it out onto plates, squabbling over the number of fries each had. They put their plates onto trays and carried them into the family room to watch TV.

"I got you some lamb curry. It's mild," Robert said.

"I'm not really hungry."

"Well, have a few mouthfuls anyway."

"I said I'm not hungry."

Robert concentrated on emptying his own food—plain old chicken curry—from the foil containers onto his plate.

"That'll stink up the kitchen," Kathy said, pushing open the windows, "and you'll reek of garlic for the rest of the night."

"Keep the vampires away," he said lightly. He sat and ate, chewing slowly and methodically, determined not to get a stomachache. He turned on the small TV set high on the wall and found the *Iron Chef* program. From the corner of his eye, he watched Kathy open the plastic medicine box and pull out two aspirin. She swallowed them quickly. "Are you all right?" he asked again.

"Just a touch of a headache. I'm going to bed," she said, and hurried from the room, leaving him alone in the kitchen with his curry and the TV for comfort.

Robert watched several chefs competing against each other with the sound muted. The two children were a room away and Kathy was upstairs, and he was alone in the kitchen, eating his dinner: just another night in the Walker household. He felt desperately lonely. He couldn't remember the last time the family had sat down to a meal together, nor could he remember the last time Kathy had asked him about work, how things were going, whether it had been a good day or not.

In fact, he couldn't remember the last time she had shown any interest in anything about him: emotionally or physically.

CHAPTER 19

"Hi."

The phone popped and crackled, then Stephanie's voice, intimate and clear, whispered down the line. "I was going to call you later. I'm really missing you tonight."

Robert crossed the floor of the room he used as a home office and checked to make sure the door was locked. "I know. I miss you too," he said quietly. "I was working on the DaBoyz pitch. Then I decided to get away before traffic got too awful."

"How's it coming?"

"Good, I think."

"You can do it. I know you can."

Robert sank back into his office chair and nodded. "I hope so."

"Of course you can." Her voice was enthusiastic, cheerful. "It'll be a new direction for the company. Do one good pop video, and you'll be the next big thing. All the bands will flock to your door."

"You're right. I know you're right." And in that instant he knew he could do it; Stephanie had absolute confidence in him and his abilities. "Thanks again for getting me the pitch meeting."

"What's wrong?" Stephanie asked suddenly, surprising him.

"Nothing."

"Yes, there is. I know there is."

"How can you tell?" Robert wondered, genuinely curious now.

"Short sentences. When you're tired or bothered, you reply to me in short, staccato sentences."

"You and your Ivy League education," Robert grinned.

"Nothing to do with Princeton. 'The Interpretation of One's Lover's Moods' was never covered in Contemporary Literary Theory."

Robert could hear the laughter in her voice and found himself smiling in turn.

"So what's bothering you?"

"Oh, the usual. I'm just tired. It's been a long day."

"And Kathy?" Stephanie suggested lightly.

Robert shrugged, uncomfortable discussing his wife with his mistress. "She's not great," he admitted. "I saw her taking some pills; I think she may be coming down with something."

There was a silence on the other end of the line.

"You think I'm making excuses for her, don't you?" Robert said, filling the silence and immediately regretting it. The last thing he needed was to have an argument with Stephanie. One cold shoulder he could manage; two cold shoulders would leave him none left to cry on. "I'm sorry. I shouldn't have said that. I'm tired. Yes," he admitted, "there were a few words this evening. But only to do with Christmas. It's the pressure of the season."

As soon as the words were out of his mouth, Robert squeezed his eyes shut and shook his head from side to side. Christ, he must be tired. He'd been avoiding bringing up the subject of Christmas with Stephanie.

"Am I going to get to see you over Christmas?" Stephanie asked. He had come to recognize that when she was being serious, her Midwest accent became more pronounced. Stephanie Burroughs had grown up in Madison, Wisconsin.

"Of course you will," he said quickly.

"Any idea when?"

"Well, I'll see you on Christmas Eve. Give you your present," he added. "And then probably the day after Christmas."

"So I won't see you Christmas Day?" Stephanie asked sharply.

"No, not on Wednesday, Christmas Day. But the day after. Actually, no, shit, not the day after, scratch that."

"What's wrong with Thursday?"

"We always have dinner with Kathy's sister Julia on Boxing Day. Her husband's British. It's a tradition."

"Oh. A tradition."

There was a long pause, before Stephanie added, "I remember you did that last year. And, I'm pretty sure you said then it was going to be the last one you went to."

"I think I say that every year."

"Do you enjoy it?"

"No," he said simply.

"So, given the choice, dinner with your sister-in-law or spending time with me, what would it be?"

"No contest. Spending time with you," he said immediately.

"Then do it."

"It's not that easy."

"It is if you want it to be."

"You know I want it to be."

Stephanie sighed. "I know you do. I'm sorry. I shouldn't pressure you. I guess I'm tired too. I'm seeing you tomorrow though?"

"Actually, that's what I wanted to talk to you about. I double booked. I've got Jimmy Moran lined up for dinner tomorrow night. I'm really sorry. Blame it on the situation in the office. I thought Maureen had canceled him, and Illona never thought to check. I'm sorry."

"It's no problem. These things happen. Any sign of Maureen coming back?"

"January. Maybe." He sighed. "I sent her a few e-mails but she cannot—or will not—give me a straight answer."

"You need to start thinking with your head rather than your heart on this one," Stephanie suggested. "And if you do manage to get the pop video gig, do you want someone who looks like a glamorous granny at the front desk or do you want a gorgeous young European?

"Well, since you put it that way..."

"This business is all about first impressions," Stephanie interrupted. "Come on, Robert. Who do you want to be the face of your company, Maureen or Illona?"

"You're right. I know you're right." He sighed. "But I don't feel good letting Maureen go before Christmas."

"You're too soft," Stephanie murmured. "Though I usually change that," she added quickly, her voice soft and husky, catching him off guard.

"You're bold!"

"Sometimes. So I won't see you tomorrow at all?"

"I've got the pitch in the morning, then dinner in the evening."

"Wanna have a sleepover after dinner?" she purred.

"Maybe," he said coyly.

"Maybe." She laughed, the sound high and light. "Just maybe?"

"Would it be worth my while?" he asked.

"Absolutely," she promised.

"I'll see what I can do."

"You do that," she said, and hung up.

CHAPTER 20

"I was thinking," Kathy said suddenly.

"Always dangerous . . ." he quipped. He hit the switch on the electric toothbrush as his wife began to speak.

"You've been working so hard lately. . . ."

She stopped talking, and he caught the flash of annoyance on her face in the mirror.

"I can still hear you," he said through a mouthful of toothpaste, but she went back to her magazine. He'd spoken to her a dozen times about the amount of money she spent on magazine subscriptions. Eventually, he'd simply stopped talking about it, because the argument went nowhere and she retaliated by throwing every expense she could think of in his face. When he'd had his teeth done, she'd given him hell about it for weeks. He turned off the toothbrush, and Kathy started immediately.

"I've been thinking, you've been working so hard lately, I've barely seen you. We should try to have a date night."

"Good idea. Great idea," he said automatically. And it was. With Maureen gone and the temp not knowing her way around the office, plus the scramble for new work, combined with the craziness of Christmas, he had been working longer and later recently. He hadn't seen a whole lot of his wife, and their encounters lately tended to be brief and chilly. He remembered when they had first started dating, how they would save their money to go skating on Frog Pond on Boston Common. They would skate until their faces were bright red from the cold, and then they'd have hot chocolate and talk for hours. There always seemed to be time then. Lately, time had started to gain a chokehold on him and he couldn't breathe, let alone find the time for frivolities. Perhaps, after Christmas, when things had settled down, he'd take her out for a nice meal, maybe even talk to her about the situation with the business, try and convince her to cut down a little on her spending. He turned on the faucet and splashed some water on his face. Just as he was reaching for a towel, she started again.

"What about tomorrow?"

He walked toward Kathy, toweling off his wet face. "I can't. Not tomorrow night. I'm entertaining a client. Christmas drinks and some dinner."

"You never said."

"I'm sure I did." He frowned. He had told her, hadn't he? But he'd had so much on his mind recently. Had he told her? The biggest problem with having an affair was juggling the lies. He thought he had done a good job, but he had been so tired lately that one little lie was bound to slip through a crack.

"I'd have remembered."

Robert shrugged and turned to toss the towel back into the bathroom. It missed the rail and slid to the floor.

"Who are you meeting tomorrow?"

"Jimmy Moran," Robert said. "We're having dinner and drinks at Top of the Hub." He threw back the covers and slipped into the bed, then jumped with the chill of the sheets. "You didn't turn on the blanket," he said, almost accusingly. He loved sliding under his electric blanket at night and liked it on the highest setting. He was annoyed, though not entirely surprised that Kathy hadn't made the effort to turn it on. It was one of those small, seemingly insignificant thoughtful gestures that she had stopped doing for him. They used to be second nature to her, and he'd only noticed them when they'd stopped.

"I didn't think it was that cold." She tossed the magazine onto the floor and slid down in the bed, pulling the covers up to her chin.

Robert turned on the blanket and glanced sidelong at her. "Aren't you going to read?"

"No." She reached up and turned off the light over her side of the bed.

"Well, I'll read for a bit, if you don't mind." He reached down to the side of the bed and lifted up the book he'd been reading on and off for the past two months, *The Road Less Traveled* by M. Scott Peck. Despite Stephanie's recommendation, he simply couldn't get into it and managed less than a page a night. She was always reading self-help and self-improvement books. He'd enjoyed her last recommendation, the *Chicken Soup for the Soul* series. He had loved the little stories that revealed the essential goodness of man. He had bought one for Kathy—*Chicken Soup for the Woman's Soul*—thinking she'd enjoy it. It was on the floor, close to the bottom of the pile of paperbacks, still unread.

"When do you think we'll have a chance to get a night out?" Kathy's voice was muffled, coming from beneath the covers.

Next week was Christmas week; the whole idea was too ridiculous for words, but it just went to show how out of touch she was. Robert bit his tongue, taking a moment to work out how to phrase his response properly, determined to fall asleep without a major argument. "I think we should wait until after Christmas," he suggested. "It's a nightmare trying to find a place to eat, and parking is impossible." He attempted a laugh. "All the restaurants in the city are full of people like me, treating clients like Jimmy to too much wine." Robert dropped *The Road Less Traveled*—The Book Never Read in his case—to the floor, and turned the light off. "After Christmas, we'll find a little time. Maybe even head out to the Cape for the weekend. Or Martha's Vineyard. What do you think?"

"That would be nice," Kathy mumbled, but she didn't sound too enthusiastic about it.

Robert lay in the darkness, listening to the house settle and creak around them. A house alarm was wailing in the far distance, the sound like an animal cry, while closer to home, a drunken voice was butchering "White Christmas."

Kathy's breathing shifted, and when he was sure she was fully asleep, he moved closer to her, resting the side of his face against her back. Sometimes, he thought that was the only thing keeping them together: the comfort of her touch in the darkness. The warm feeling of flesh touching flesh, connecting in a silent union, reminding him of how things had once been with his wife.

Of how things had become with his mistress.

Robert couldn't help but compare Kathy's attitude with Stephanie's. Stephanie was encouraging and interested; Kathy was the complete opposite. Kathy simply didn't understand his world and, as far as he could see, had no interest in even trying to understand. Her world had shrunk to the kids, the home, her friends, and her sisters. Because he was running so fast now, running just to stand still, it was a world he had little time for and, except for his children, even less interest in.

And when he came home to a night like tonight, when there was an argument over nothing, then he really appreciated having someone understanding and loving to talk to, someone like Stephanie.

His job required him to be able to compartmentalize and prioritize. The production business was essentially one of time and people management, and although he could be disorganized in his personal habits, he had always been able to manage his business.

Kathy lived in one compartment; Stephanie in the other. He sometimes liked to imagine the three of them as three circles. His personal Venn diagram. He remembered, when he was Theresa's age, using a protractor to make the three circles, classifying set groups and objects in intersecting geometric circles. His circle intersected with Kathy and Stephanie; their circles intersected with his. But, in his diagram, the women's circles could never intersect. That would complicate his life tremendously, though he knew he didn't have to worry. Kathy was disinterested in him and the business; Stephanie was interested in every aspect of the business—and every aspect of him too. He smiled into the darkness.

Stephanie had a healthy appetite toward lovemaking, whereas over the years he and Kathy had drifted apart in that department too. He was as much to blame as she was; he was often exhausted after too many hours in the office and fell asleep the moment his head hit the pillow. He'd also be the first to admit that they'd become just a little bored with one another sexually. With Stephanie, every time was new and exciting.

Stephanie spoke to him every day, and, more important, listened to him. Kathy told him practically nothing. When he asked how her day had gone, Kathy would say "Fine," and that would be the sum total of information.

Of the two, Stephanie was more demanding. She wanted to spend time with him. And he adored spending time with her. She made him feel young; she made him feel special again.

Kathy made him feel like an inconvenience.

And yet, and yet, and yet . . . he loved Kathy. Not passionately, not sexually, not extravagantly; he just loved her. She was his—God, he hated the phrase—his rock. She had been with him right from the beginning, had worked side-by-side with him to build the business, even when she was pregnant. She had supported him when he wanted to set up his own company, even though it meant giving up a regular paycheck and a pension. The bond they'd forged together ran deep, and if their relationship had changed . . . well, after eighteen years, that was hardly surprising.

What was surprising was that he'd fallen in love with Stephanie too.

That was the problem. He'd never believed it was possible to love two people equally; he'd always imagined that love was some sort of exclusive emotion. And he had discovered that it wasn't. He had discovered that it was possible to love two people simultaneously.

Robert turned over in the bed and looked at the glowing red digits on the clock: 12:55. He needed to get to sleep; he needed to be refreshed and alert tomorrow morning for the presentation. Yet his mind would not quiet.

He loved Stephanie.

Or did he?

The emotion had crept upon him over the past couple of months, surprising and frightening him in equal measure. He'd never really thought about the words, "I love you." Three little words, over-used, bandied about with little thought to their real meaning. In the television and advertising business especially, it was a phrase that everyone used. It was a phrase he used with Kathy every day . . . although he had recently drifted out of the habit of saying it to her. It was a phrase he had tucked the children into bed with every night, until they had grown too big and he got too busy to be home when they needed tucking in.

And then, about six months ago, he had first used the phrase to Stephanie and meant it.

It had shocked them both.

And it had frightened him.

Robert had first met Stephanie Burroughs almost seven years earlier. R&K had been struggling, and the position was made all the more difficult because Kathy had stepped back from the business to look after the children. Her mother, Margaret, had been helping out up till then, but she had started to become increasing bitter and gloomy, and both Robert and Kathy became genuinely concerned for the children's welfare around her. Also, Brendan and Theresa simply didn't want to spend any more time with Granny Childs.

Stephanie had joined the company as a researcher. She'd been a freelancer, a couple of years out of graduate school, and had im-pressed Robert in her job interview with her intelligence and port-folio. Her Ivy League pedigree didn't hurt either.

R&K had landed a small, but lucrative project: *One Hundred Years Ago on This Day*—little two-minute inserts that told, in news-report form, the events of one hundred years previously. The pieces required intensive research and sharp writing. Stephanie had ended up doing all the work on the pieces: researching, writ-ing, finding the pictures and archive footage where needed, and also the locations, costumes, and jewelry for the dramatic recon-structions.

Robert and Stephanie had worked very closely together on the *One Hundred Years* project, which had, by necessity, taken them up and down the East Coast, keeping them away from home for days at a time. He had to admit that he'd found himself attracted to her. But that's all it had been, an attraction, and he'd never done anything about it, never tried to take it any further. Stephanie was a bright, vivacious, lively, fun-loving young woman. Neither he nor Stephanie had said or done anything to move it onto another level. It was only later, much later, that he had realized that all he had been waiting for was a hint from Stephanie that she was interested. Then things might have been different. . . .

Close to the end of the *One Hundred Years* project, when everything had been shot and they were in the final stages of editing, Kathy had accused him of having an affair with Stephanie. It had been a lazy Sunday afternoon, and he'd been standing at the barbecue in the back garden at peace with the world, content and unsuspecting when she'd made the accusation out of the blue. The hamburgers had burnt to carbon as he listened to Kathy's wild allegations, and it was months before he'd been able to stand the odor of meat again without feeling sick to his stomach. He'd denied his wife's accusations of course, because they weren't true, but deep in his heart he felt guilty, because he knew how close he'd come.

He'd never told Stephanie, but he'd immediately terminated her contract with a little cash bonus as a thank-you. They'd kept in touch intermittently, and then she'd gotten a lucrative job down in Miami as an accounts manager for Saatchi & Saatchi. In the first few weeks after her departure, while Kathy had persisted in her suspicions, he'd thought of Stephanie often, and then, when everything calmed down at home, she had rarely crossed his mind again.

Two years ago, Robert had bumped into Stephanie at an awards dinner. She had returned to the Northeast as the accounts manager for Ogilvy & Mather, one of the biggest ad agencies on the East Coast. Within weeks, they had rekindled their earlier friendship, and this time it was different.

Stephanie had grown, matured. And his relationship with his wife had changed and altered over the years. Previously, he could not have had an affair. But now . . .

* * *

Kathy turned over in bed, breathing in short, sighing breaths. Robert turned to look at her. In sleep her features changed; the lines on her forehead and around her mouth disappeared altogether, and her mouth drooped open, elongating her face, turning it ugly.

In sleep, Stephanie's face remained unchanged, keeping her beautiful.

The comparison came unbidden, and he turned away from his wife, glancing at the clock again: 1:20.

He remembered the first time he'd slept with Stephanie. They had been circling the event for weeks. Casual lunches had turned into regular events, their occasional dinners were becoming habit, and their conversations were becoming more and more suggestive.

Then Stephanie had gotten R&K a lucrative little contract to shoot an ad for bottled water. She had given Robert a list of locations and told him to scout the best one. He'd recommended Tiverton, Rhode Island, just on the water, and she had suggested they both visit it, check out the light in the evening and again in the morning. They had both known it was completely unnecessary, and they had both known where the evening was leading.

There had been absolutely no doubt in his mind as they drove out to the coast in his car that they were going to end up in bed together. But that was it; he hadn't been thinking beyond that. They would have an enjoyable meal, and then . . . well, then the old adage beloved of television and film crews everywhere would apply: What happens on the road, stays on the road.

He could recall every detail of that night.

All his senses had been heightened. He remembered the meal, the intense flavors of the meat, the sharp bitterness of the wine, the hint of Stephanie's perfume, the peaty odor from the fire. She had worn a white silk blouse over skinny jeans, a thin gold chain around her neck, gold hoops in her ears, no rings. Her nails were short and blunt and coated with an iridescent, clear lacquer, and she'd allowed her hair to tumble onto her shoulders.

They'd taken adjoining rooms in the little hotel.

When the meal was finished, they'd retired upstairs. They had stopped outside Stephanie's room, and Robert had dipped his head to kiss her good night. She turned her head at the last moment and instead of brushing her cheek, he'd kissed her lips. And she had returned the kiss.

They had made love for hours that first night. Robert had been shocked by Stephanie's enthusiasm, inventiveness, and obvious enjoyment of the act. He always had the impression that Kathy treated lovemaking as a duty, something to get finished as quickly as possible. Stephanie relished it.

And later, much later, as the first rays of wan morning sun were touching the window and he was lying naked in bed, with Stephanie wrapped into his body, he had realized that he felt alive. For the first time in years, he had felt energized, creative, and excited. He had felt young again.

It crossed his mind that he had betrayed his wife and their wedding vows. But he hadn't felt the slightest bit guilty.

CHAPTER 21

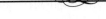

Friday, 20th December

Eyes gritty, head pounding, Robert Walker pushed open the door of R&K Productions with his foot. He was carrying a triple latte in one hand and was juggling his laptop, briefcase, and keys in the other. The alarm started to blip warningly. He placed the coffee on Illona's desk and returned to the box behind the door to punch in the alarm code #328. He kept promising to change it. Maybe if he really did pluck up the courage and let Maureen go, that would give him the impetus to change the code and locks.

There were two calls flashing on the answering machine. Robert hit the Play button and left the door to his office open so that he could listen to them as he carried his coffee and briefcase inside.

The mechanical female voice announced: "You have two new messages. New message left Thursday, December 19, at 6:59 p.m."

"Hello, mate, it's Jimmy. It's about seven o'clock, Thursday evening. I'm phoning to confirm that dinner is still on tomorrow night. Really looking forward to it. If it gets too late, or there's a little too much of the red stuff consumed, you can always stay over at my place. You know I've still got that apartment in the North End.

My God, but it was the best investment I ever made. Talk to you tomorrow."

"New message left today, Friday, December 20, at 7:55 a.m."

"Good morning, Robert, Eddie Carson, DaBoyz Management here. I understand from Stephanie that you start early. Will you give me a call as soon as you get in? I need to reschedule our appointment."

"End of new messages."

Robert glanced at the clock. Ten past eight. The message had come in fifteen minutes ago. Most of the DaBoyz presentation was spread out on the conference table, and he had the latest updates on his laptop. The band and their manager were due to come in at ten, but it would only take him half an hour to get his act together, so he could see them at nine if they needed to pull the appointment forward.

Before he phoned DaBoyz however, he had one other call to make. It had become a habit: the first call of the day and the last call at night. He hit the speed dial on his cell. "Good morning, gorgeous."

"My God, what time is it?" Stephanie's voice was muffled and woolly with sleep.

"Ten past eight. Wake up, sleepyhead. I thought you'd be on the way into the office."

"I'm going in later. I had a late call with Beijing; the thirteen-hour time difference is a killer."

Robert moved around the office, opening the blinds. "Speaking of calls, there was a message from Carson on my answering machine this morning; he wants to rearrange the appointment. Shouldn't be a problem."

There was a rustle of bedclothes, and when Stephanie spoke again, her voice conveyed that she was awake and more alert. "Tell me what he said, exactly what he said."

"Well, he just said . . . Actually, hang on a second and I'll play you the message." He carried his cell to the outer office and hit the Play button.

"You have no new messages. You have two old messages."

Robert fast-forwarded through the first message, then he hit Play again and held his phone to the speaker.

When the message finished, he put the phone to his ear again. "That's it," he said brightly. "It's not a problem. Obviously, I'll clear my calendar to see them, you know that."

"It is a problem," Stephanie snapped. "This is just bullshit. I told Carson we were lucky to get you. Call him back and do not— do you hear me—do not allow him to rearrange the appointment. You've got to show this little bastard who's boss; otherwise he'll walk all over you."

"It really isn't a problem—" Robert began.

"Just do as I say. Be tough with him. Tell him you can meet this morning or not at all, then shut up and say nothing. Wait for his response."

"Okay," Robert said dubiously.

"Trust me on this," Stephanie said in a slightly gentler tone. "Do it now, and then phone me back."

"Yes, ma'am!" Robert mimed a salute as he hung up. He went over to the conference table and rooted through the pages until he found Carson's business card. Left to his own devices Robert would call Carson and arrange to see the band at their convenience. But he had to accept that Stephanie was very good at what she did, and she handled some of the biggest accounts in the showbusiness world.

"Eddie Carson." The call was answered on the first ring.

"Morning, Eddie, Robert Walker, R&K Productions. I just missed you."

"Yeah, Bob, thanks for calling back. Listen, I need to rearrange DaBoyz's meeting for tomorrow or maybe Sunday. What's good for you?"

Robert opened his briefcase and took out his laptop, settling it onto his desk. "None of those work for me, Eddie. Today works for me. I made time for you today."

There was a long pause. Robert could hear traffic whizzing by and guessed that Eddie was still on the freeway. He fired up the laptop and rattled in his password. The screen cleared and opened to an almost empty desktop, with just a few icons lining the left-hand side of the screen. He clicked into My Documents, then My Pictures. He highlighted one picture and hit Enter. It opened immediately. He had taken the picture last Christmas. It showed Stephanie wearing only tinsel and Christmas balls, kneeling provocatively beside a tiny Christmas tree in her apartment. The tip of the tree was in line with her large pink areola. There was a sign on the carpet by her feet: *Robert's Christmas Present. Can be opened anytime.* He zoomed in on her face. She was smiling impishly. She was always in control, always knew just what to do. He just hoped that she knew what she was doing now.

"That's really not possible. DaBoyz are in great demand—"

"So am I, Mr. Carson," Robert said coldly. "It's this morning or not at all."

There was a long pause. Robert opened his mouth several times to break the silence, but, mindful of Stephanie's advice, closed it again.

"I might be able to fit you in later today," Carson said smoothly, and in that moment, Robert knew he had won.

"I have you down for ten o'clock. Will you be here or not?"

There was another silence. "I'll juggle some stuff. We'll be there." Then Carson hung up.

Robert's fingers were trembling as he hit the speed dial. The call was picked up on the first ring. "You were right. What would I do without you?"

"Let's hope you never have to find out."

CHAPTER 22

"I told you." Stephanie strode around the office. She was dressed in a pinstriped power suit whose severe lines were only softened by the cream silk blouse she wore beneath the jacket. She wore her hair pulled back off her face, looped and held in a sleek, tight ponytail with an ornate butterfly comb, which Robert had given her last Christmas.

Robert was sitting behind his desk, staring intently at his monitor. He was putting the finishing touches to the latest version of the DaBoyz presentation, which incorporated the changes he had agreed to with Carson and the band members earlier that morning. "Your advice was absolutely spot on," he said without looking up from the screen. "They turned up at ten on the dot. The boys were as good as gold, a little overawed by everything and very much under Carson's thumb. He made all the creative decisions."

Stephanie stopped at the conference table and spread out the drawings of the band at the Haleakalā Crater in Maui. "These look very good, very exciting. Different. Dark and just a little exotic. Just what the band needs at the moment—it'll take them in a new direction."

"Carson was complimentary. Apparently everyone else was suggesting something light and bright and fluffy with tween appeal. He wants to take the band up into an older age range." Robert came out from behind the desk and joined Stephanie by the table. He arranged the images into a sequence, laying out the pop video. "You'd think I'd been doing this all my life," he muttered. "Carson wanted a few changes."

"Of course he did. It's a power thing with him, like trying to change the time of the appointment this morning. I've seen him do that so often. He thinks he's managing U2, not just another cookie-cutter boy band."

Robert was abruptly conscious of Stephanie's perfume, something sharp and citrus, and the heat from her body as she bent over the table alongside him. A stray curl of hair brushed his face; it felt like an electric shock.

"And if you hadn't called him on it, then he would have given you the runaround for the next couple of weeks. Even if you had gotten the gig, he would have interfered every step of the way. Hawaii was a good location choice. Everyone loves Hawaii. . . ." Stephanie's voice trailed away to a husky whisper. She turned to look at Robert. Her face was inches away from his. He could smell the coffee on her breath. As he watched, her pupils dilated, and she brushed the tip of her tongue across her lips. She smiled and raised her eyebrows a fraction, then glanced toward the open door.

Robert took a deep breath to settle his fluttering heartbeat and stepped away from Stephanie. He could feel himself straining against his jeans. He never wore jeans to pitches; he was an old-school suits kind of guy. However, Stephanie had instructed him on his wardrobe. They had even gone shopping together for it: Rock & Republic skinny jeans, an Ed Hardy tee shirt, and a gray wool Theory blazer. The outfit made him look young and hip. And now he was desperate to get out of it. Glancing at the clock, he strode out into the outer office to where Illona was systematically working her way through an office-supplies catalog. "Are you busy, Illona?"

The slim Eastern European girl looked up, eyes huge and dark in her pale face. She spoke English with a British clip that was now showing traces of a Boston accent, which Robert found incredibly disconcerting. "Not especially. The phones are quiet."

"Look, it's just after four. Why don't you head out? Maybe get some shopping done, or beat the Friday evening traffic."

"Well, if you are sure you do not need me . . . ?"

"Stephanie and I still have to go through the DaBoyz contract. We'll be a while, and there are no other appointments this afternoon, are there?"

"None."

"Okay. Switch the phones over to the answering machine, but leave your computer on; I'll shut down the system before I leave."

Illona gathered up her coat and bag and headed for the door. She stopped and glanced back over her shoulder, looking past Robert to where Stephanie was standing at the conference table, seemingly absorbed in the designs. She raised her voice slightly. "Good night, Miss Burroughs."

"Good night," Stephanie called, without looking up.

The receptionist looked back at Robert. "Try not to work too late."

Robert just nodded. Was there something in Illona's expression, something knowing, a smirk almost? Did she suspect? He knew for certain that Maureen suspected—she had revealed her dislike of Stephanie in a score of ways. It was one of the reasons he was seriously thinking about letting her go. But even that was no longer a clean decision; if he let Maureen go, then she might take her suspicions to Kathy.

Who would have thought that a simple affair would have such complications? There wasn't a single aspect of his life left untouched and unaltered by the relationship.

He'd tried very carefully to keep his affair with Stephanie a closely guarded secret. When he'd finally become aware that what had started out as a fling was turning into something more serious, he'd consciously tried to ensure that they never ate in the same restaurant more than once and, when they stayed away overnight, it was always outside of Boston where they stood less of a chance of being recognized. It was really no one's business but his and

Stephanie's, but Boston was a city filled with prying eyes and big mouths, and the last thing he wanted was for the news to get back to Kathy. If anyone was going to tell her, he would.

When the time was right.

And the time was most certainly not right, not now.

Robert followed Illona to the door and held it open for her. "See you on Monday."

"Good night, Robert." Illona wrapped her coat tighter around her shoulders and disappeared into the fading light.

Robert waited until she had rounded the corner, then closed the door and locked it. "I think she suspects . . . ," he began, walking back into the office.

"Who cares?" Stephanie had already undressed down to her lace bra and panties. "She's a receptionist." Then she caught Robert by his lapels and pulled him toward her, tilting her head and pressing her lips against his.

Her passion took him by surprise. His own response—immediate and hungry—shocked him. Every time with Stephanie was like the first time: exhilarating and exhausting. He backed her up against the conference table and pushed her back onto it, scattering pages in every direction. His fingers fumbled at the hooks on her bra.

Before he had met Stephanie, the only place Robert had ever made love was in bed. In the early years of their marriage, he and Kathy had been more spontaneous with their lovemaking. They often made love during the week, but as the years went by, that changed too, and they'd fallen into the routine of many married couples who had children: Saturday or Sunday morning, when the house was still quiet and the kids were either in bed or downstairs watching TV.

Stephanie sat up on the table and pushed him away from her. She undid her bra strap with one hand, exposing her gorgeous breasts. Robert tugged off his blazer, hearing a button pop and dance across the room.

More often than not, Stephanie was the one who instigated their lovemaking. Robert could never remember Kathy initiating sex; he always had to make the first move. Before he had made love to Stephanie that first time, he hadn't had sex with Kathy for over four months. Since he had begun his relationship with Stephanie, he had not made love to his wife once. Nor had he tried; it didn't seem right somehow. Like he would be cheating on his mistress. But he made love to Stephanie almost every day.

Suddenly, Stephanie was completely naked on the conference table and he was eagerly pulling off his jeans, saluting his mistress with a flag raised to full mast. Stephanie looked at his eagerness approvingly. "Nice to see you're still interested in me."

"I thought we were discussing a contract . . . ," he murmured, approaching the table.

"We will. But first things first. Priorities are important." Stephanie's voice was husky with lust. "And you are my priority. Now, where were we?" She lay back, opening her arms, spreading her legs, and inviting him, welcoming him, into her body.

Stephanie stepped out of the tiny shower and accepted the towel Robert wrapped around her. The shower cubicle in R&K was too small to hold two people, so they had to wash in turn. This was not the first time they had made love in the offices. There was always something especially exciting about it, Robert thought. Only earlier that day, as he'd sat at the table with the boy band, he'd had a sudden flash of a naked Stephanie spread-eagle on the table. It had been very difficult to hold a sensible conversation after that.

He stepped into the shower and adjusted the heat, pushing it up to its highest level. Even at full power, the water pressure was little more than a trickle. Through the frosted glass, he could see Stephanie drying herself un-self-consciously. He watched the sway of her hips as she stepped out of the bathroom and began to gather her clothes off the chairs where she had tossed them. His clothing was strewn around the room. The neat drawings and printouts he had prepared for the DaBoyz presentation were scattered across the floor, many of them crumpled and crushed. He didn't care. When he made love to Stephanie, nothing else mattered. He gave himself fully and wholeheartedly to the act. So did she. Whenever Kathy made love to him, he was always aware that she was distracted, distant even, almost as if she was going through the motions. After eighteen years, he wondered, was that so unusual?

Robert turned off the shower and stepped out into the bathroom. Stephanie's towel was still damp, but he used it, unwilling to use a second towel. If Illona was suspicious, then he didn't want to leave her clues that anything was going on.

"Will I see you later?" Stephanie stood seductively in the doorway, only wearing her light pink lace-trimmed bra and a tiny matching thong.

"I'm not sure. Do me a favor," he added. "Get dressed, please."

"Why?" she said archly.

"Because if you don't I'll just have to have you again."

"Promises, promises." She smiled, but she stepped away from the door and started to dress. "What about tonight?" she asked again.

"Tonight's all screwed up." He tossed the towel on the rail and padded naked out into the office and started to dress. "You know Jimmy and I were supposed to have dinner in the Prudential building at Top of the Hub? Well, I got Illona to phone to confirm the reservation. And it turns out there was none. And you know that place is impossible to get into, especially this time of year."

"What happened?" Stephanie tugged on her trousers, but her blouse was still undone, and Robert reached out and stroked the swell of her breast with the back of his hand. The movement was unconscious, tender. Stephanie caught his hand and pressed it against her hard nipple. Then she brought his fingertips to her lips and kissed them.

And it was these movements, the small, tender, intimate movements, that meant so much to Robert. These were what he missed with Kathy: the tiny intimacies, the touches, the casualness, the comfortableness with one another. For a long time, he'd felt like a stranger with his own wife.

"I'm not sure whose error it was, Illona's or Maureen's. Maureen's, I think. But that's not the point. I've got an old friend meeting me here in just over an hour, and I've no place to take him to dinner."

"It'll be difficult finding a posh place to eat this close to Christmas."

"I know. And Jimmy won't want to go far; he was talking about spending the night in his apartment in the North End."

Stephanie finished dressing. She grabbed her tiny clutch and went back into the bathroom to repair her makeup.

"Be upfront with him," Stephanie advised. "You never know, maybe all he wants is to have drinks. If you get out relatively early, you might check out the Union Oyster House. They serve food at the bar, and they have the best oysters in town."

"Great idea."

"But that doesn't answer the question I asked earlier: Are you going to spend the night with me? Should I wait up?"

Robert grinned. "If I do spend the night, I'll be sleeping. You exhaust me."

"If you can get to me before one o'clock, then come over. But if you're going to be any later, then forget it. Text me when you've got an idea what's happening."

"Good plan."

Stephanie appeared out of the bathroom, looking immaculate and composed.

"There is no way to tell that less than half an hour ago you were lying on this table making passionate love."

Stephanie blinked at him in surprise. "I have absolutely no idea what you're talking about, Mr. Walker. I was closing a very important business deal." She leaned over and kissed him, a gossamer brushing of her lips against his. "And I do like the way you close a deal," she added.

CHAPTER 23

When Stephanie left, Robert tried to put some order back in the office. It looked as if a bomb had gone off in it. Papers were scattered all over the floor, some of them clearly bearing the imprint of damp bare feet, others crushed beyond all recognition. He made a note to reprint them. Making love with Stephanie could not be done in halves. At the point of orgasm she cried aloud, a sound between a grunt and a shout of pain. It wasn't so bad in the office, but he was sure that the neighbors in the condos adjoining hers could clearly hear what was going on. In the beginning it had embarrassed him; now he had no such reservations. It was another of Stephanie's gifts: She had taught him to let go, to be free.

Clearing up the papers, he turned his attention to the table. It was covered with sweaty palm prints, and there was the clear imprint of a bottom on the polished wood. He found some paper towels and furniture polish under the sink in the tiny kitchen and set to work on it.

It was just after six when he finished. He sprayed some citrus air freshener around the room to disguise the scent of sex, then stood back to examine his handiwork. The office looked pristine, the table gleaming, papers piled neatly, pens arranged alongside. Hard to image that two naked people had recently cavorted there.

Robert hit the speed dial on his desk phone to call home.

"Hello?"

For an instant he thought he had phoned the wrong number. It sounded like Kathy's voice, but altered somewhat.

"Hello?"

Then he recognized his sister-in-law Julia's waspish tone. He forced a pleasant tone into his voice. "Julia, it's Robert."

"I thought it was."

"I take it if you're there, then Kathy isn't."

"She had a few things to do; I said I'd keep an eye on the children, though, to be perfectly honest," she added quickly, "they're old enough to look after themselves."

"I agree, but at least if you're there, they'll study rather than just watch TV," he said, unconsciously mirroring the same words his wife had used a little earlier that day. "Can I speak to Brendan—is he nearby?"

Robert had no time for Julia. There was simply too much bad blood between them, going back over too many years; she considered him beneath her sister, and he thought Julia was a stuck-up cow. He often sympathized with Ben, a shy Brit who was her long-suffering husband.

"Dad?"

"Bren. Where's your mom?"

"Gone into town."

"Why?"

"I dunno, but she's left Aunt Julia in charge of us," Brendan added, lowering his voice to a whisper. "Seriously, Dad. I'm seventeen; I don't need a babysitter."

"I know. How long has your mother been gone?"

"Twenty minutes, maybe half an hour. Can we order takeout tonight?"

"Didn't you order in last night?"

"We did. But there's nothing in the fridge."

Robert frowned. That was unlike Kathy. She usually kept a packed refrigerator and shopped at Trader Joe's once a week, filling both the freezer and the fridge with a huge variety of foodstuffs. She was a wonderful mother, and the children wanted for nothing. "Any idea where she's gone?"

"No idea. She just kinda announced it out of the blue."

"That's all she said? Nothing else?"

"Oh, yeah. She wondered what you'd given her for Christmas last year. Maybe she's gone into town looking for your present."

"Maybe." He experienced a twinge of guilt. He still hadn't gotten Kathy her present, and he had sworn, after last year's debacle, when he'd ended up grabbing a few things at Macy's, that he'd get her something nice this year. "I'll call her on the cell. Be good for Julia. I'll be home late tonight."

"Later, Dad." Brendan hung up.

Robert sat at his desk and tried to make sense out of what he had just heard. Kathy did and didn't do many things, but she never did anything without a good reason. Why was she coming into the city, for Christ's sake? Especially when she hated to drive. He hit another speed dial and transferred the call to the speaker. It rang six times before it connected.

"Kathy, where are you?"

"In the car."

Robert took a deep breath. He knew she was in the car; he was calling her on her cell. Telling him that she was in the car was telling him nothing. If anything, it proved that she was still pissed off at him. He wasn't quite sure what it was about this time, but lately there didn't need to be a reason. He tried a different tack. "I've just called home. The kids told me you're heading into the city to go shopping." Even as he was saying it, he was aware of just how ludicrous it sounded.

"Yes," Kathy said, her voice neutral and flat.

Robert put his elbows on his desk and cradled his head in his hands. "Kathy, I really don't think this is a good idea. Traffic is shit, and the weather is closing in. Forecasters are promising more snow and maybe black ice this evening."

"I need to get a few things. I thought I'd head to Newbury Street," she pressed on, ignoring him. "If there's a problem with the weather, I could always drop into Top of the Hub, meet you there. We can drive home in your car, and I'll come in with you in the morning to pick up my car."

Somewhere at the back of his mind a warning bell—a tiny, bitter sound—went off. Something was amiss. Why was she coming into town in the first place, and why was she talking about popping into Top of the Hub? It was almost as if she was checking up on him. "Did I lose you?" he asked when he realized that there had been a long moment of silence.

"I'm still here," she said shortly. "Where are you?"

"Still at the office. Jimmy's coming here around seven." There was a crackle of static. "I really don't think it's a good idea to head into the city tonight. And if I have a few drinks with Jimmy, I might have to leave the car myself. That'll be two cars in town. I was half thinking I might even stay overnight. He says I can crash at his apartment."

There was another long pause.

"Kathy . . . ?" he asked eventually.

"You're breaking up. I can hardly hear you." He could barely make out her static-laden gibberish as the phone kept cutting out. Why did she want to meet him? It was completely out of character for his wife to behave like this. And there had definitely been a note of suspicion in her voice. He'd lived with her long enough to recognize it. He'd heard it before, on that terrible occasion when she'd accused him of having an affair. But she didn't know . . . she couldn't know about Stephanie. Could she? No, he'd been too careful.

"Can't you get what you're looking for in Brookline?"

"No." Suddenly her voice was crystal clear again. "I'll see you at Top of the Hub later."

"No, not Top of the Hub."

"I thought you said last night you were going to Top of the Hub. . . ."

"Kathy, I'm having trouble hearing you. Listen, there was a screw-up. I phoned earlier to confirm, and they couldn't find the reservation."

There was a slight pause before Kathy answered. "So where are you going to go?"

"Don't know yet."

"Well, look, call me when you find a place, and I'll drop by."

Robert nodded. That was the third time in the same conversation she'd made a definite reference to dropping by and seeing him. He couldn't remember the last time—certainly not in the last year, maybe even the last two years—that she'd made such a suggestion. She was definitely suspicious. He frowned. Had he said or done something to alert her? Had someone said something? Had she discovered something?

"I haven't seen Jimmy for ages. How is Angela?"

"They've separated. He wants a divorce. She says no."

"Listen, I've got to go. There's a cop nearby, and I shouldn't be on my cell."

The phone immediately went dead, and the office descended into silence. Maybe she really was just doing some last-minute Christmas shopping. Why was he suddenly acting so paranoid?

He'd never set out to have an affair with Stephanie, but once it had happened, it was the most exciting thing in his life. But he was also determined that he would do nothing in the world to upset Kathy. He'd spent eighteen years of his married life protecting and looking after her; he would continue to do that. He wasn't one of those men who went to bed with a woman and was then forced by a guilty conscience to confess everything. But there would come a time when Kathy would find out. And the longer it went on, the greater the likelihood became. How much longer could he keep it from his wife? And what would happen when she found out?

He had never imagined that the affair with Stephanie would continue on for this length of time. At first he had thought they'd drift apart after a couple of weeks or even months; instead, the affair had deepened; it had intensified.

And then it became complicated.

He had actually been on the verge of breaking up with Stephanie almost eleven months earlier. He'd gone through an intensely busy patch looking for work, and they hadn't seen each other for the best part of a month. In that time, he had made the decision to break it off; he was becoming fearful of the feelings he was having for the woman. This was no longer about sex or affection or some combination of the two: This was love.

He had decided he would speak to her on a Friday night. He would invite her around to the office and break the news gently over an expensive bottle of wine. They would remain friends, but he could no longer be her lover. That was the plan. But on that Wednesday she'd come to him with a proposal. She knew R&K was in trouble, and she suddenly found herself in a position to send a little business his way, good business, lucrative business. Was he interested?

R&K wasn't just in trouble; the company was on the verge of going under. Of course he was interested. Stephanie only had one condition: No one in her office must know that they were involved. She could lose her job if people knew she was directing contracts toward her lover's company. There was nothing illegal about what she was doing, but there was certainly a conflict of interest. As long as she pushed him for the lowest possible price, people wouldn't suspect her favoritism.

That single connection kept the company afloat.

Suddenly he couldn't let her go; he couldn't afford to. The jobs, large and small, that she sent his way had saved R&K from going bankrupt.

But if they got the DaBoyz contract, things would be different. He wouldn't need to rely so heavily on Stephanie for work. Also, because of some of the other work she had gotten him, small jobs had started to trickle his way again. Referrals. It was mainly advertising work, shooting infomercials, which he hated, but which paid the bills. He also knew R&K was in the running to shoot the new Zipcar ad, and he'd pitched what he thought was a very good idea for the forthcoming Sam Adams campaign.

After Christmas, he would break up with her. She'd understand; he was sure she would. She'd see the sense in it. They were having fun, but the instant gratification of sex and companionship wasn't worth the emotional stress he was starting to feel. He was starting to get an ulcer. He couldn't carry on this way, splitting himself in two.

Christmas really highlighted the problems of trying to juggle a wife and a mistress. The lies became even more complicated.

He desperately wanted to spend time with Stephanie—it was always fun and sexy; they would laugh and eat and make love. Kathy, on the other hand, might condescend to speak to him and, then again, she might not. There was usually an argument over something—these days there almost always was. So really there was no argument about whom he wanted to spend Christmas with . . . except . . . there were the children to consider. He couldn't very well spend Christmas away from his children. . . . It was out of the question.

Robert got up and began to move around the office, shutting off lights and locking up for the night. He glanced at his watch; where was Jimmy?

Robert was extremely proud of Brendan and Theresa. He could truthfully say that they had brought nothing but joy into his life. And he would never hurt them. He loved the way they looked up to him, the way they came to him for advice, the way they shared their triumphs and disasters with him. He was devoted to his children. He loved them and they loved him, of that he had absolutely no doubts.

And he couldn't afford to lose that love.

That would destroy him.

His own father, Robert Senior, had been a cold, distant, aloof man. Not once did Robert remember his father being proud of him or saying, "I love you." His own kids would not be able to say that; he constantly told them how proud he was of them and made sure to tell them that he loved them every day. If it ever came to a toss-up between the children and Stephanie, then Stephanie would lose.

It was a cliché to say that he was staying with Kathy for the sake of the children, but it was very close to the truth. There were so many great things in his life—including Kathy, when she was in a good mood—and he knew that his affair with Stephanie was casting a shadow over all of them. One slip, one stupid mistake, and he stood to lose everything. The few friends he and Kathy had were joint friends—he'd probably find himself ostracized by them. At least he'd be able to hang on to the business. . . . Except, he realized with a sinking feeling, Kathy owned half of it. What would happen if they split up? He veered away from that thought; it was not going to happen.

A sudden tapping on the glass made him jump. He could see Jimmy's round face peering in.

The smartest thing Robert could do would be to end the affair. But whenever Stephanie touched him, pressed herself against him, breathed in his ear, he felt young again. He felt alive. And he could feel his resolve failing.

Jimmy tapped on the glass again.

Robert shook his head fiercely. He wasn't going to lose anything. He was too careful. Much too careful.

CHAPTER 24

"I'm really sorry about Top of the Hub," Robert said again as they looked up at the Prudential Center in the distance.

"There's no problem," Jimmy said again. "Really. None at all." He reached out and patted Robert's shoulder. "Forget about it. Besides, that food's too rich for my blood anyway." He patted his stomach. "I'd spend the next two days paying for it."

In his youth, Jimmy Moran had been one of the handsomest men in his hometown of Dublin, Ireland. Tall, elegant, and fine-featured, the director and producer had been a regular in the social pages and had been involved in bringing some huge movie productions to his homeland in the eighties and early nineties. It had been confidently expected that he was going to be Ireland's answer to Francis Ford Coppola. But he had never lived up to those expectations; two hugely expensive productions had foundered with enormous debts and had tainted him with the whiff of scandal when it was discovered that he'd made sure to pay himself before anyone else, including the internationally famous stars. Time moved on, and a lifetime of excess had blurred his fine features, bloating his nose and dappling his cheeks with broken veins. Jimmy was fifty-two—he looked sixty—though his hair was still jet-black and he swore he didn't dye it.

Jimmy had left Ireland twenty years earlier, and he'd deliberately kept his Irish brogue. Initially, he'd hoped to continue his directing work in Los Angeles; however, he had quickly discovered it was a town of young people with young ideas. He had moved to Boston where the film community was smaller, more manageable, and less ageist. He'd managed to get a small, no-frills quiz show off the ground, which paid the bills, and then he soon started finding success in front of the camera rather than behind it. Jimmy had gotten regular bit work as a heavy in many of the Boston-based films, including *The Departed, Mystic River,* and all of the Ben Affleck films. There had been a time when he might have been able to translate that success into something bigger, but his fondness for the drink put paid to that.

Jimmy had originally met Robert when he had auditioned for and gotten a part in a beer campaign Robert was directing. The beer spokesperson gig had a long successful run and had kept Jimmy flush for several years. With little in common, the men became unlikely friends. "So, where are we going?" Jimmy asked again.

"Wherever we can get in," Robert grinned. "I'll buy you a drink or two, even if we can't have dinner. Let's walk by Faneuil Hall, grab a couple of beers, and figure out a plan."

There was an Enchanted Village in City Hall Plaza, where children stood in line to meet Santa. Nearby, carol singers gathered around the huge Christmas tree. Wearing white coats with tinsel-trimmed Christmas hats, they were singing "Silent Night" with more enthusiasm than skill. A girl whose cheeks matched the color of her red hair shook a plastic bucket under Robert's and Jimmy's noses. "Help the homeless!"

Jimmy laughed as he dropped a handful of coins into the bucket. "That's me," he said brightly.

"What?" Robert asked, unsure if Jimmy was joking or not.

"Technically, I'm homeless at the moment," Jimmy said ruefully.

"Angela is going to take the house from me." They continued across Congress toward the water, walking into the boisterous crowd milling outside Faneuil Hall, and suddenly further speech was impossible. "Fill you in later," Jimmy shouted. The noise in the outdoor marketplace was incredible. A brass band was playing something vaguely Christmassy, while the enormous crowd of chattering, laughing, and singing tourists stretched the length of the pedestrian-only cobblestone street, waiting to get into Cheers. Even though the show had been off the air since 1993, reruns ensured the bar never went out of fashion. Farther down the street, a fire-eater was juggling tinsel-wrapped flaming torches to roars of applause. The two men pushed their way back through the crowd and turned to the left, toward the North End.

"Even we're too old for this noise," Robert grinned.

"Speak for yourself, old man."

"Okay, crazy idea." Robert pointed to a quaint building up the street. "What about the Union Oyster House? Best oysters in town and six different Sam Adams varieties on tap," he added.

"That's me in then," Jimmy smiled as the men crossed North Street.

"Too bad there's no good Chinese nearby. Remember the place we used to always go in Chinatown?"

"Peach Farm, best dumplings I've ever had," mused Jimmy as he patted his stomach again. "Can't do that anymore. It's bad for my stomach."

"I thought you said it was an ulcer."

"It was. Until I had the docs look at it." Jimmy glanced sidelong at his friend. "Don't look so alarmed. It's nothing major. Okay, I admit it. . . . I'm getting old. There are certain foods I can no longer eat, and I'm afraid anything with MSG in it is out for me."

"That's too bad." Robert shook his head. He had a lot of happy memories of the pair of them on location for the beer shoots, always looking for the Chinese or the Indian with the hottest curry on the menu. A little place on an Arlington back street still held the record.

"I'm finally paying for my lifetime of sins," Jimmy said, then added, "but they were great sins, and I enjoyed every one of them."

"Didn't Oscar Wilde say something about sins? . . ."

"Ah, Oscar said something about everything. And most of it was utter shite."

They walked up Union Street and turned into the Union Oyster House, going directly to the only empty seats at the bar. "Two Sam Adams Winter Lagers and two dozen oysters." Robert gave the bartender his gold AmEx card to start the tab.

The bartender quickly brought two tall tumblers filled with the deep ruby-colored beer.

Jimmy raised his glass, and Robert raised his.

"You look good, Jimmy."

"Aye, Robert. If bullshit was music, you'd be a brass band."

Robert smiled as their glasses pinged together. "What'll we drink to? That next year is better?"

Jimmy grinned ruefully. "Bollocks. That might be too much to ask for and is probably tempting fate. Let's stick with the classic: to health and happiness. May they never clunk into each other and feck things up."

"Health and happiness," Robert agreed. He sipped the beer. It was bitter and sharp and as he swallowed, he realized he could still taste Stephanie's flesh on his tongue. "You don't sound too sure about next year?"

"I'm not." Jimmy glanced sidelong at him. "This year has been a pisser. An absolute pisser. I'll be glad to see the back of it."

In the dim light of the bar, Robert saw that Jimmy looked old—more than old, he looked weary, beaten. There were bags under his eyes, and his normally spotless suit was shabby, with the evidence of an old stain on the lapel. The collar was dappled with dandruff.

"Again, I'm really sorry about Top of the Hub, I wanted to take you out in style," Robert offered.

"Forget about it."

"But I wanted . . ."

"Jayzus, relax. The rest of the world's forgotten about Jimmy Moran, but you keep remembering me every Christmas. That's plenty."

"What are you talking about? You're my lucky clover, Jimmy. If you hadn't starred in our first Harpoon commercial, R&K would have never gotten off the ground.

"Jayzus, those were the days, weren't they?" Jimmy mimicked hurling a harpoon into the water and thickened his brogue. "If you don't have the luck of the Irish in getting women, have a Harpoon, and it just won't matter." He laughed. "Who wrote that bloody shite?"

"I did. And it was enough bloody shite for their revenue to go up. I could use that kind of inspiration again."

"You get me all hot when you talk about advertising, Bobby. I could do with a gig."

Robert smiled. "My brilliant copy and your scruffy mug sold a lot of beer."

"That it did. I wonder why?"

"The accent helped."

"Oh, everyone loves an Irish accent, especially in this town."

"And you used to be good-looking," Robert teased.

"That I was." Jimmy's face suddenly soured, the weight of the world bearing quickly down upon him. He took a long pull on the glass and swallowed hard. "Angela's taking the house from me."

"Shit. Do you want to talk about it?"

"Not unless you can get Angela *not* to take the house from me."

"I'm really sorry," Robert said gently.

"What's to be sorry about?" Jimmy sighed. "It's my fault. I cheated for years and got away with it too. I was on borrowed time, and I was finally caught. Ye can't blame Angela. I've been a feckin' eeijet." He downed his beer and signaled to the bartender for another one. "Remember I told you that Angela wouldn't give me a divorce? Well, she's changed her mind, or rather her very expensive lawyer has changed her mind for her. But she wants the house as part of the deal."

"But the house is fabulous!"

Jimmy and Angela owned a stunning house in Quincy, right on the water. It was a colonial with twelve thousand square feet of private beach. Over the years, they had restored it with an extraordinary amount of love and too much money.

"Well, to be honest, I don't get down there much anymore, so I'm resigned to letting it go."

"You spent years fixing it up."

"I know. But if that's the cost of getting out of a loveless marriage, then that's the price I'm prepared to pay."

"That's what you meant when you said you were homeless earlier?"

Jimmy nodded.

"But you have the place around the corner, in the North End?"

"For the moment, yes. Angela wants a bite of that too. I may end up paying her half its value."

"But it must be worth what? Half a million?"

Jimmy smiled, showing startlingly white teeth. "Almost double that. Angela's lawyers had it valued recently; two real estate agents estimated it at nine hundred thousand. Even with the recession. So, I'll either have to pay Angela almost half a mill—which I can't afford—or put it on the market and give her half of whatever I get."

"Jesus, Jimmy, what a mess."

Jimmy Moran finished the last of the drink in one quick swallow, then grimaced as it hit his stomach. "Of my own making, remember. I've always told you: Everything has a cost; you just have to be prepared to pay the price. Angela just got fed up with me screwing around and drinking. You can't blame her."

Robert couldn't. Angela had put up with a lot. Events had come to a head three years ago when Jimmy's long-running relationship with Frances, an up-and-coming actress many years his junior, had hit the headlines. The girl had been desperate for a part in a big-budget movie and had sold the story to one of the tabloids, hoping that the resultant publicity would help her get the job. It hadn't, and Frances hadn't really worked since. Surprisingly, Jimmy had continued the relationship with the actress, and she'd quickly become pregnant. Remarkably, the press had not yet got wind of the fact that Frances had borne Jimmy a son. Following her disastrous publicity stunt, she had disappeared completely from the public eye. Robert was one of the few people who knew that Jimmy had set her up in a quiet job at The Thoreau Institute at the Walden Woods Library.

"How is Frances?" he asked.

"Someone told Angela about the baby," Jimmy continued, ignoring the question. "And Angela contacted me through her lawyer, said that if she'd known I had fathered a child she would have given me the divorce I wanted ages ago. No child deserved to be without a father, she said." He shook his head at what was obviously a painful memory. "She's bitter, very bitter indeed. She'll take me for everything she can."

"What are you going to do?" Robert asked.

Before Jimmy could answer, their oysters arrived, heaping plates of freshly opened oysters garnished with horseradish and lemons.

Jimmy shrugged. "I'll divorce Angela—it'll probably bankrupt me—and I'll marry Frances, which will probably kill me. I'm fifty-two, far too old to be a first-time father. I'd be a lousy da."

"Jesus, Jimmy, I'm not sure if I'm supposed to say sorry, or congratulations."

"Both, I s'ppose."

The two men nibbled at the food without speaking. The noise level at the restaurant had increased appreciably.

"How are things with you?" Jimmy asked, arranging the empty shells in a neat circle on the bar.

"They're okay. I'm struggling a bit. There's not a lot of work out there. But I've been lucky recently."

"And Kathy, how is she?"

"Good. She's good. She's busy with the Christmas preparations. I was talking to her earlier; she said she might drop in to see us at Top of the Hub." He fished out his cell. "In fact, I really should let her know where we are. She might stop by if she's close." Also, it actually suited him to have her stop by now; at least then she'd get to see that he was genuinely out with a client. His screen said *No Network*. "I don't have a signal. What about you?"

Jimmy pulled out a flip phone that was at least five years out of date. He tilted it to the light and squinted at the small, green screen. "No. No signal. Must be the thickness of the walls."

"You need to upgrade that," Robert smiled. "Noah probably used that model to talk to God about the Flood."

"I think it's retro chic. Besides, I'm not a conformist." Jimmy reached out for Robert's phone. "Very fancy. I presume it does everything except butter your toast."

"I think it might even do that."

Jimmy handed Robert back his phone and asked abruptly, "Is it true y'er fucking around with Stephanie Burroughs?"

"What?" For a single instant, Robert wasn't sure if he had heard right. He felt his stomach cramp. "Who said that?"

"Me. Just now." Jimmy smiled sympathetically. "This is a small city, Robert. Small minds and big mouths. People talk and make assumptions. Some uppity prick saw ye together and made the connection."

"People should mind their own fucking business!" Robert barked, surprising himself with his vehemence.

"So it's true then?"

Robert opened his mouth to bark a response and deny it, but then he abruptly nodded. "It's true." Even as he was saying the words, he felt an extraordinary rush of emotion; it took him a moment to recognize it as relief. Jimmy was the first person—the only person—to whom he would confess his affair with Stephanie. It was as if the balloon of tension he had been carrying in the back of his neck for the last several months had quickly deflated, allowing the stress and guilt to hiss out with it. "Stephanie and I are . . . together."

Jimmy leaned across and caught both of Robert's hands in his. "Is she worth it?"

Startled, Robert drew back. "What?" This was not the reaction he'd expected. Jimmy's affairs and one-night stands were legendary.

The bartender came to clear their plates, and the two men drew apart. Robert needed some time to gather his thoughts. Jimmy knew about his affair. Other people knew about the relationship. The question was: Who else knew, and for how long? Even though the Oyster House was now hot and noisy, he felt surrounded by a bubble of chilly silence.

"Is she worth it?" Jimmy asked again.

"Yes. Yes. I think so. Who told you?"

"I was at an audition recently. A callback for some Celtics

promo. I was in a group, and I overheard someone from the production company talking about Stephanie's company. He mentioned that they'd given you three major contracts over the past year and wondered how that had come about when you didn't exactly have a track record in shooting advertisements. Simon Farmer . . ."

"Little prick," Robert interjected immediately.

"Little prick," Jimmy agreed. "He said it was because you were shagging their accounts manager. He said it like it was common knowledge." Jimmy signalled to the bartender for another drink.

The beer and oysters curdled and soured in Robert's stomach, and he felt as if he was about to throw up. His fingers were trembling slightly as he lifted his glass and drained it in one long swallow. It seared its way down his throat. He should have been feeling a little buzz from the beer on an empty stomach, but right now he was stone-cold sober, and he imagined that no matter how much he drank tonight, he would not be able to get drunk.

Jimmy sipped his beer, then pulled Robert's glass over and emptied half of his into it. "It took me a moment to figure out that it was Stephanie he was talking about."

"Shit. And is it . . . common knowledge, I mean?"

"I'd not heard it before," Jimmy admitted. "I've suspected about the pair of you for a while however. I will confess whenever I saw the two of you together, there was a comfortableness between you that made me uneasy."

"Uneasy? How?"

"Because I saw myself and Frances in the way the two of you stood, the way you casually looked at one another, the innocent and apparently accidental touching of hands. The casual chat that was anything but."

"And you never said anything to me about it?"

"None of my business, was it? Besides, with my reputation, I'm not the one to be telling you how to live your life."

"I need to talk to Stephanie. I need to let her know. She might lose her job over this."

"I doubt it. She wouldn't be the first colleen to do favors for her lover, and besides, I'm sure the work you did for her company was top-notch. As long as you weren't overpaid and didn't under-deliver, you'll be fine."

"She said she might lose her job if anyone found out."

Jimmy shrugged. "If she worked for me, I'd be asking hard questions," he admitted, "but if she's done nothing illegal, I would have no cause to sack her. She's a tough cookie; she'll have protected herself somehow."

Robert put his elbows on the bar and cupped his head in his hands. "I didn't think anyone knew. I've been so careful."

"Bob, I'm tellin' ye what I heard. Hearsay. Repeated by a bitter little wanker, pissed off because he didn't get the accounts. And because he wasn't shagging Stephanie Burroughs himself, probably. Look, even if there was nothing going on, people would be talking. If a man and a woman are out together, people suspect. Didn't you ever watch *When Harry Met Sally*?

"You've been in this position before," Robert said desperately. "What should I do?"

"You're really asking me two questions: What should you do, and what should you do if anyone asks?"

Robert thought about it for a moment and then nodded in agreement. There were two questions. He opted for the easier one. "What do I say if anyone asks?"

"You have two choices: deny or accept. If you accept it, you have to be prepared for the consequences, which will affect home, the children, friends, and work. My advice is to lie. Deny it and stick to your guns. Make sure Stephanie denies it. But make sure that Kathy knows about the rumors before anyone tells her. Tell her you've heard that this story is going around and you're bringing it to her attention first. You have to make her believe it's not true. If Kathy believes that nothing is going on, then you're okay; however, if she has any suspicions, then you will only be confirming them."

Robert opened his mouth to say something, but Jimmy held up a hand.

"And don't tell me you don't want to lie to her. You've already done that. This is just an extension of the lie. That's the thing with lying. It's a gift that just keeps on giving."

Robert slumped on his barstool and motioned to the bartender.

"Can I have the bill, please?" He looked at Jimmy. "I'm really sorry. I need to get out, get a breath of air, clear my head."

"I understand."

Robert laughed, a short bark. "You know what's so ironic here? I had decided just a couple of hours ago that I'd suggest to Stephanie that we really should consider stepping back from one another in the New Year."

Jimmy's face remained a blank mask.

"Maybe this will precipitate that," Robert continued.

"Bob, are you just screwing around with Stephanie, or do ye really love her?"

There was a long pause, and then Robert's lips formed the words, unheard over the noise in the bar. "I really love her." He licked dry lips and repeated it aloud. "I really love her."

"Shite. And Kathy? Do ye still love her?"

"Yes."

Jimmy squirmed uncomfortably. "Then you're banjaxed. It's always so much easier if it's just sex."

"I know that."

"Let me give you some advice. Never tell a woman that you're dumping her—no matter how nicely you phrase it. That road leads to disaster."

"I should never have gotten into this situation. But at the time . . ."

"I know. It was easy. Easier to get into than to get out of. Remember what I said about everything having a price. Well, payment is a bitch."

CHAPTER 25

"I never did ask you what I should do."

The two men shivered as they came out of the Oyster House. The temperature had plummeted, though that seemed to have had no effect on the line of people waiting to get in, or the milling crowd of smokers gathered on the street.

"That's not a question you should be asking me," the older man said.

Robert offered to walk Jimmy back to his apartment, but in light of the new information, refused his offer of staying over. They headed down busy Hanover Street, passing the brightly lit window of Mike's Pastry. The air smelled of baking and sugar.

Robert dug his hands into the pockets of his long black overcoat. "I just don't know what to do. I've never been in this situation before and—"

"I have." Jimmy smiled, but there was nothing humorous in the twisting of his lips. "Believe me, I have. But you know something? All of the affairs I had—and I'll not deny that there were many—none of them tempted me to leave Angela. Except Frances. And,

I'll admit this to you and to no one else, if she hadn't gotten pregnant, I'd not be in the mess I'm in now. Angela and I never had children. We tried; we wanted them. We got medical advice, but there was nothing wrong; we just never conceived. We talked about adopting, but my life was too erratic; I was all over the place; the money was too irregular. Even if we had managed to adopt, it would have meant Angela would have been left to raise the child herself. We kept putting it off, and suddenly that option was closed off to us. But when Angela learned that Frances had given birth, that was the last straw in our relationship. She had forgiven me so much over the years, but I think she saw that as the ultimate betrayal."

"You're saying I shouldn't leave Kathy."

"I didn't say that."

"I love them both!" Robert said loudly, shocked by the sound of desperation in his own voice. His voice carried on the chill air, and tourists, taking pictures of Paul Revere's statue, glanced over at him.

Jimmy gripped his arm and hurried him across the road, weaving through traffic, which was at a standstill. "So what? Love is not some exclusive emotion that you give to one person. We love lots of people, our parents, wives, children. We love them unconditionally. I'm not talking about love. I'm talking about commitment. Which one of the women are you committed to?"

They turned right past Nico Ristorante heading down Hanover Avenue. The narrow avenue was jammed with smokers spilling out from the restaurant, some sitting on the icy curb. A bachelorette party in matching Santa outfits that ended high on their thighs was click-clacking its way across the street. Their bare flesh looked blue and alabaster with the cold.

Jimmy paused at an entranceway. "Here's where I leave you. Are you sure you won't come up for a nightcap?"

"I'd better not; I'm driving."

"Think about what I've said. This is no longer about love—since you love them both—this is about commitment. Commitment in the past, commitment now, and commitment in the future.

You wouldn't be where you are today if Kathy hadn't been there to support you."

"I know that. But the business wouldn't have survived without Stephanie."

"Yes, it would, Robert. It would just have survived differently." Jimmy suddenly reached forward and embraced Robert, hugging him closely. When Jimmy spoke, his words were warm and moist against the younger man's ear. "Which is more important to you: your marriage and your family, or your mistress and your business? This time next year, where do you want to be? Who do you want to be with?" He broke away and took half a dozen steps, before glancing over his shoulder. "Oh, and Merry Christmas." Then he turned, buzzed in his code, and was swallowed up by the dark hallway.

Robert waited until he was out of the noisy North End before reaching for his phone. He was about to call Stephanie, then he stopped. What was he going to say? His head was spinning. Events were slipping out of control; there was just too much to deal with at the moment.

He darted across the road, car horns blaring, an angry shout fading behind him, and walked toward Beacon Hill. Couples walked toward him, arm in arm, happy, laughing, smiling, and he found himself wondering how many of them were having affairs, how many of them were in genuine relationships. But was that to suggest that an affair was not a genuine relationship? It was. He found himself nodding. His relationship with Stephanie was genuine.

But was it fair?

The answer was stark and simple. It wasn't fair to anyone. He fished his phone out of his pocket and hit the speed dial for Stephanie. The call was answered almost immediately.

"I was just about to call you," she began.

"Where are you?"

"Heading home. I met Izzie for a drink at Clink. Is everything all right?"

"I'm not sure. I'll meet you at home. I'm just heading out of the

North End; I left the car outside the office. It'll take me forty-five minutes."

"Robert . . ." Stephanie began, but he hung up the phone. He didn't want to talk to her just now; he needed a little time to think.

This was not how he had planned to end his day, walking cold and heartsick through the colorfully lit streets of Boston. This should have been a good day: it looked as if he had tied up the DaBoyz contract; he had made love to a beautiful woman and then had dinner with an old friend.

Until Jimmy had told him about the rumors. And then everything had changed. Was he overreacting? Jimmy had said that Simon Farmer had told the group that Robert was having an affair with Stephanie. He knew Farmer, an obnoxious little no-talent shit, but one who was incredibly well connected. Farmer's company managed, year after year after year, to get some plum contracts. Farmer himself was a loud-mouthed drunk, and he and Robert had bumped heads on a couple of occasions. They had sat on a couple of awards committees together some years ago and had simply not gotten along. Thinking back to those committee days, Robert remembered that one of the things he had particularly disliked about the man was that he was a gossip, delighting in telling tales and spreading bad news. How many people had he told?

Robert walked up Causeway past North Station. For a second, he contemplated just taking the T to Stephanie. The Orange Line would let him off at Green Street, just a few long blocks from Stephanie's condo; however, he didn't want to feel vulnerable without a car in case things didn't go well. He turned up Staniford and made a right onto Cambridge. He had to accept that if Farmer knew about his relationship with Stephanie and had noticed that she was directing business toward Robert's company, then Farmer would complain. His stomach lurched; maybe he already had.

Robert pulled out his iPhone and stepped into a nearby Starbucks, where he ordered a double espresso. He scrolled down through the names in his contacts list until he eventually found Jimmy's. The call was answered on the first ring.

"Jimmy Moran."

"It's Robert."

"Changed your mind? Come on over." Robert distinctly heard a pop and then a clink as Jimmy opened a bottle and poured liquid into a glass.

"I can't. I'm going to see Stephanie. She and I need to talk."

"Good idea."

"Jimmy, how long ago were you talking to Farmer? How recent was that audition?"

"It was the last weekend in November. I can get you the exact date if you like."

"No, that's great. I just was trying to work out how long Farmer has known."

"Robert," Jimmy said seriously, "when he announced the news, no one reacted like it was a big surprise. I think you have to accept that people know and have known for a while. . . . And you know something—most people don't give a shite, which is as it should be. Now go and talk to Stephanie. And you know you can call me anytime. Anytime," he emphasized.

"I know. Thank you, Jimmy, you're a good friend." Robert hung up, pushed his phone back into his pocket, and downed his drink. He left Starbucks and hurried up the street. He needed to get back to the car, needed to get to Stephanie, needed to talk to her.

But if people knew, then why had no one said anything to him? He'd been at a CLIOs meet-and-greet in New York City six months earlier. One of his old colleagues from Leo Burnett was being honored, and pretty much anyone who was anyone in creative marketing was at the Skylight Soho. No one had said anything to him about Stephanie. Not even Farmer. They'd exchanged a few civil words. He frowned, trying to rerun the event in his head. Was there something he had missed, some subtle hints, some knowing looks? Had people been looking at him, whispering behind his back, talking about him?

He laughed, a sudden barking sound that made the young couple walking toward him veer away suddenly. He was being paranoid. Paranoid and stupid. Of course no one was talking about him; Jimmy was right. No one cared.

But this was certainly no way to live his life, wondering if people were talking about him, concerned about what they thought of him, terrified in case his wife caught a hint of the rumors. Or had a taste of the truth. He had to sort this out.

Tonight.

CHAPTER 26

Robert pulled the Audi into the empty space in front of number 8, alongside Stephanie's silver BMW. He sat in the car for a few moments, listening to the engine tick, looking at the apartment. The house was in almost total darkness, just a few of the windows lit up, including the cupola, which sported the miniature Christmas tree they had bought together a few weeks earlier. He guessed that everyone was either out or gone home for the holidays.

He didn't want to do this, he realized. He didn't know what to say, and he was afraid that if he even brought up the subject, it would somehow change the nature of their relationship. Shaking his head ruefully, he climbed out of the car and pressed the door closed. He wanted her. . . . He wanted to finish with her. The truth was he didn't know what he wanted . . . or maybe he just wanted it all. A wife at home and a mistress nearby.

Although he had a key to Stephanie's apartment, he rarely used it, and he hit the bell, two short, distinct rings.

A moment later, light flared, and there was movement behind the bubbled glass. Stephanie pulled open the door and stepped to one side. She was wearing a peach-colored silk dressing gown, her hair wrapped in a towel. Her body, still damp from the recent shower, was clearly outlined against the thin fabric, nipples hard and pointed against the cloth. She smiled archly. "I really wasn't expecting you."

"There was a change of plans." He kissed her quickly and brushed past her, through the door to the left, up the stairs, into her apartment.

Stephanie's apartment offered a stark contrast to his home. He always felt slightly claustrophobic in the small rooms. Stephanie preferred comfort over form, and the combination living room/ dining room was cluttered with patterned furniture from Pottery Barn and a hideous dark-wood display cabinet filled with scores of pictures from her past: her family, her days at Princeton, and a few men whom Robert suspected were past lovers although he never asked. Dozens of paintings in just about every medium crowded each wall. There was little empty space, as if Stephanie had made it her mission to cover every inch of the quirky condo. Tall bookcases filled with everything from classics to comic books dominated either side of the fireplace. A flat panel TV hung on the far wall and below it, a micro-CD player was running, filling the air with the ambient New Age music that Robert hated and Stephanie adored.

"You look like you need a drink." Without waiting for a response, she turned away into the small kitchen, which was just off the dining area.

"Coffee, no alcohol," Robert called after her. He shrugged off his coat and tossed it onto a chair, then followed her to the kitchen and leaned against the doorway. The kitchen was tiny and pristine, and it was obvious that she rarely cooked. The gas oven looked unused, but the worktop was strewn with kitchen devices: kettle, toaster, microwave, water filter, and a state-of-the-art black and silver Keurig coffeemaker.

She bent over to open the fridge. "Are you sure? I've got a nice Pinot chilling. . . ."

"I'd better not. I'm driving."

Stephanie straightened, and a frown flickered across her face. "You're not staying?"

"No, not tonight. I can't."

"That wasn't the initial plan." She smiled.

"The plan changed."

Stephanie started to make coffee. Robert watched her in silence while she plucked an individual coffee packet from the cupboard and put it in the machine. What was it about this woman that he loved? How had she completely captivated him? She was pretty, but not spectacular. In fact, he suddenly realized, with what felt like a growing sense of panic, she looked a little—no, she looked a *lot*—like Kathy, a slimmer, younger Kathy. Robert stared intently at the woman, shocked, horrified, and fascinated by what he had just discovered. How had he never seen it before? Perhaps because he'd never asked himself what had attracted him to her in the first place.

He watched her move, aware—all too aware—that she was naked beneath the silk robe. She poured water into the coffeemaker, and her robe gaped open, allowing him a glimpse of her breast. She flicked him a quick sidelong glance, and he knew he'd been caught. She reached to pull the robe closed.

"Don't," he whispered.

"You've seen them before."

"The day I get tired of looking at them is the day I'm dead."

But there were differences, huge differences between the two women. Kathy would never make coffee in the kitchen wearing nothing more than a flimsy robe. Kathy didn't make him laugh anymore, didn't arouse him anymore either. Stephanie did all of that, and more.

But somewhere at the back of his mind, he knew that he wasn't being entirely fair to Kathy; he worked hard with Stephanie, worked to make her laugh, to make her happy, bringing her little presents, small treats, occasional bunches of flowers. He couldn't remember the last time he'd brought Kathy a small present or a bunch of flowers.

"Tell me what happened?" she said. "I presume it's something to do with Jimmy, since you were fine—more than fine—when I left you a couple of hours ago. Is he okay?"

"He's far from okay. His life's a mess."

"His life has always been a mess," Stephanie remarked. "Honestly, I think he thrives on the drama. He's an actor, remember?"

"He's not getting any younger. And this time the mess is bigger than usual. His wife's finally giving him the divorce he's wanted."

"Well, that's good news. . . ."

"And taking half of everything he owns."

Stephanie looked at him sharply. "Good for her. That's her right."

"You heard that Frances, the girlfriend, had a baby?"

"I heard something about it."

"Well, he's going to marry the girlfriend and raise the child with her."

"So he should."

Robert shrugged noncommittally. He found he was vaguely uncomfortable with Stephanie's reaction; she wasn't exactly sympathetic toward Jimmy's plight.

"You don't look so sure," Stephanie observed, watching him closely.

"Frances sold her story to the press. She used him to get free publicity, hoping she'd get that movie part."

The coffee started to percolate, and the rich aroma of Kenyan filled the small kitchen.

"That was really the beginning of the end for him and Angela." Robert sighed.

"But he's still with Frances," Stephanie said, pulling open cupboard doors and taking out two packets of Stevia. "He went back to her, got her pregnant."

"You haven't got sugar, have you?"

Stephanie didn't look at him as she poured the Stevia into the coffee cup. "Sugar is bad for you."

Robert shrugged. "Frances ruined Jimmy's reputation in return for fifteen minutes of fame."

Stephanie laughed, the sound high and bright. "She did not. He had no reputation to ruin. So he was a big deal back in Dublin. So what? Here, he's just another actor. And not even a good one, and actors are a dime a dozen. And he has a reputation as an alcoholic womanizer." She handed Robert the coffee. "Everyone knows about him."

Robert accepted the mug from her hand. He sipped it, grimacing and yet relishing the harsh, bitter taste. "People know about us, Stephanie," he said quietly. "Jimmy told me tonight."

Stephanie's eyes met his for a long moment before she sighed. Then she poured herself a large glass of white wine and walked past Robert into the living room. In one deft movement, she curled up on the sofa, tucking her bare legs beneath her.

Robert followed her into the room. "Did you hear what I said?" He sat down in the easy chair facing Stephanie. "People know about us."

The room was still, silent save for the sound of ghostly wind chimes coming from the CD player. Something about Stephanie's stony demeanor and her reaction finally clicked: She hadn't been surprised. He had been stunned when Jimmy had told him; her reaction should have been similar, unless . . .

"You knew." He was shocked and felt curiously betrayed. "You knew and you never told me."

"Yes, I knew."

Robert licked dry lips and drank deeply from the coffee. "How long . . . I mean, why didn't you . . . what about your office?"

"There have been rumors floating around about us for the last couple of months," she said simply. "I ignored them. This business of ours thrives on innuendo and gossip. And when two people are regularly seen together, tongues wag, even if there isn't truth to the rumors."

Robert groaned. His world was collapsing in on him, much faster than he had expected.

"And your boss? Does he know?"

"About a month ago, Charles Flintoff himself asked me outright if you and I were an item."

"You said no," Robert said immediately.

"I said yes."

Robert looked at her blankly, mouth opening and closing wordlessly.

"Having a relationship with you is one thing—he doesn't give a damn about that. Putting business your way is another. But as long as everything was aboveboard, well, that's still marginally okay. However, lying to my boss was out of the question. The very fact that he was asking me the question suggested that he already knew the answer. I told him the truth."

Robert was speechless. There were questions he wanted, needed to ask, but he could not formulate the words.

"And it was the right thing to do. He had the contracts for the jobs I'd given you, plus the estimates. He'd done some comparisons with the other bidders and had gotten an independent assessment of the final result." She shrugged. "He could find no fault with it."

Robert finally managed to find his voice. "So how many people know?"

Stephanie frowned. "Jesus, Robert, I could have lost my job over this." She looked at him hard. "Why? What's the problem?"

"Because if people know, then it's only a matter of time before Kathy finds out."

Stephanie's face became an expressionless mask. She concentrated on her wineglass.

"I wanted to be in a position to tell her myself. When the time was right."

"And when would the time be right, Robert?"

"When it's right," he muttered.

"And when would that be?"

Robert concentrated on his coffee. This was not going the way he had planned. On the drive over, he had rehearsed versions of the conversation he intended to have with Stephanie. He needed to explain to her that people in the business suspected that they were having a relationship and that, for the sake of her job, it might be best if they were to cool it for a while. They'd let things cool down, maybe not see one another for a few weeks or a couple of months, and then pretty soon people would forget. Stephanie's revelation—that her boss knew and that she had admitted to him that the stories were true—changed all that.

"We've been lovers now for eighteen months, Robert. Where do we go from here? What's the future?"

He had asked himself the same questions.

"You've told me how unhappy you are at home. You suggested to me—no, more than suggested, you *told* me that you would leave Kathy. . . ."

"I never said that!" he said immediately, a touch of panic clearly audible.

"Maybe not in those words, but that was my clear understanding. I would never have gotten involved with you otherwise. You told me you would leave her when the time was right."

He heard the bitterness, the anger in her voice.

He nodded briefly. He had said that. He remembered saying it. They'd spent the day in bed. He had been exhausted, a little drunk. He'd said a lot of things.

"Well, when is the right time? This month? No, it can't be this month because it's Christmas, and you don't want to ruin Kathy's Christmas. Of course you have no trouble ruining my Christmas, but that's another story. So, when? Next month? No, that's the New Year, not an ideal way to kick off the New Year. What about February? No, that's Theresa's birthday, and that's not the sort of gift you want to give your daughter. Do you want me to go through the whole year? Do you?!"

He shook his head.

"There is never a right time, Robert." Stephanie suddenly stopped ranting. Then she sighed. "Look, I'm tired and feeling incredibly bitchy, and my period's overdue. I don't want to be having this conversation with you right now."

Robert nodded. He didn't want to have it either. He had been shocked by the intensity in her voice.

"I had a drink with Izzie earlier. . . ."

"Does she know?"

"Of course she knows! Do you think I could handle this alone? Without a girlfriend to confide in, to get advice from? Izzie's been my rock; she knew from the very beginning. She was the first to know."

Robert squeezed his eyes shut. Who didn't know?

"And she warned me, right from the start, not to get involved with a married man. She explained to me exactly what would happen, and you know what? So far, she's been right. Just spot-on."

"Stephanie," Robert began. He was alarmed to see tears in her eyes. "Maybe this isn't a good time. We're both tired. Let's get some sleep."

"I think that's a really good idea." She stood up smoothly, picked up Robert's coat, and handed it to him.

"I'll see you tomorrow. We'll talk."

She nodded as she walked him to the door, then she laid a hand on his arm. "I don't want to think that you've been making a fool of me. I don't want to think that you've been using me. Maybe I just want to think that we have a future together." Then she leaned up and kissed him gently, brushing her lips against his. "Tomorrow. Tell me the truth."

"We'll talk tomorrow," Robert said, tasting her lipstick on his lips, surprised by how husky his voice sounded.

"Tomorrow," she said, pushing him out the door.

He headed down the stairs, out of the building, and walked over to his car. Robert hit the remote, opened the door, and climbed in without looking back. Sitting in the driver's seat, he was facing the front door of the Victorian. Stephanie hadn't even walked him down the stairs. Usually, she waited in the doorway until he drove off but tonight was different. The bedroom light in the cupola came on, warm and yellow against the drapes, and he saw her shadow move behind them. He knew what that bedroom looked like, knew what the bed felt like beneath his naked flesh. He waited a moment, wondering if she would look out. She didn't, and the light flicked off, leaving only the twinkling Christmas lights to silently mock him. Robert stared at them until his eyes filled with tears and the lights fractured. "What a mess," he breathed, the words white on the air before him.

Brushing his fingers over his eyes, he turned the key in the ignition, and backed out and drove home.

CHAPTER 27

"I wasn't sure if you were coming home tonight." The voice whispered out of the darkness, startling him.

"I'm sorry, I didn't mean to wake you."

"You didn't wake me."

Kathy was awake. It was the perfect opportunity. Now or never. He could sit on the edge of the bed and tell her the truth, whispering his secrets into the darkness.

And tell her what?

Once he started to tell this story, he had to go right through to the conclusion. And he wasn't sure what the conclusion was. Which version of the truth did he want to tell? It was the question that had gnawed at him on the drive home.

Did he want to stay with Kathy, or did he want to go with Stephanie?

He tugged at the knot in his tie, pulled it open, the raw silk hissing like a zipper, and threw it onto the chair by the nightstand. It slipped onto the floor.

Of course, it wasn't quite that simple. If he told Kathy that he'd been having an affair, would she still want him? He remembered how she had reacted when she had confronted him six years ago. Maybe if he admitted it to her now, she'd tell him to get out, and the decision would be made for him. Is that what he'd wanted all along? For Kathy to find out, for Kathy to make the decision? Robert squeezed his eyes shut, suddenly disgusted with his own cowardice.

"I only had a couple of drinks, and the roads weren't too bad." He pulled off his suit jacket, folded it over the chair, and began to unbutton his shirt.

"I called earlier." Her voice was crisp and clear; she sounded wide awake.

"I didn't get it," he said.

"It went straight to your voice mail."

"We went to the Union Oyster House—bad place to get a signal."

Driving home, he'd thought about telling Kathy. But, Stephanie was right; it was too close to Christmas.

Merry Christmas. Guess what, sweetheart? I'm having an affair.

That was the emotional response. Then the rational part of his mind kicked in, asking him why he should tell Kathy anything. Simple. He wanted to get to her before anyone else did, so he could tell her the story in his way, give her his version. He was a spinmaster, someone who lied for a living: making toothpaste look whiter and apples look fresher; making marginally talented boy bands look and sound like Radiohead. Robert knew how to twist something to his advantage.

Guess what? People are saying I'm having a relationship with Stephanie Burroughs. Remember her? She's back, and she's sent a lot of business our way. Business we really need . . .

No. As soon as Kathy heard Stephanie's name, she would guess the truth.

And before he spoke to Kathy, he needed to talk to Stephanie again. He hadn't liked the way the conversation had drifted this evening. Previously, their relationship had been lighthearted and fun. Sure, he'd always been vaguely aware that she expected more, but that was going to happen at some future date, some indefinable time when *things would be different.*

Whatever that meant.

Whenever that was.

"How's Jimmy?"

"Jimmy's fine. He sends his love."

"I'm surprised he remembered me."

"Of course he remembered you."

"So you didn't get into Top of the Hub?"

And there it was again, the probing suspicion. This was not paranoia brought on by the events of the day; this was something more, something definite. "I'm going to call and complain in the morning. They said there wasn't a reservation." This was probably the longest conversation they'd had in a long time.

"That's strange. Maureen usually doesn't make mistakes like that."

"It may have been the temp who made the booking. Maureen's out sick at the moment."

"You never told me!"

He could hear the accusation in her voice. "Oh, I'm sure I did."

"You did not!" she snapped. "I most certainly would have remembered. I worked with Maureen, remember? How long has she been out sick?"

"I dunno, three weeks ... four," Robert mumbled. Shit, shit, shit. Why had he opened his mouth and mentioned Maureen's name? Now there was every possibility that Kathy would want to talk to her. And that was the last thing he wanted at this moment. He'd decided on the way home that he really needed to get to see Maureen before Christmas, bring her a little present, tell her about the new business that Stephanie had brought the company. And yes, buy her loyalty.

"And you never told me. . . ." Her voice rose, and she lowered it again. "You never told me. I would have called her, visited her."

Christ, couldn't she understand that he had a lot on his mind at the moment? Maybe if she'd shown more interest in the company, she'd have known about Maureen. Maybe if she'd shown more interest in him, he would not have had an affair. Maybe this was really Kathy's fault. "I've been busy. I must have forgotten."

"What's wrong with her?"

"Chest infection or something. Doctor's note says she won't be back until January. And it's the busiest time of the year."

"You make it sound as if she got sick deliberately. I can't remember the last time she was ill. Can you?"

Robert didn't answer. He stepped into the bathroom, pulled the door closed, clicked on the light, and picked up his electric toothbrush. So what if she wanted to visit Maureen? He suspected that Maureen knew about his affair; shit, it sounded as if the entire industry knew about it. Even if Kathy got to her before him, Maureen was no fool. She knew the state the company was in, knew too that it was only the business Stephanie had sent their way so far that had kept them afloat and paid her salary. She'd keep her mouth shut. Still, it would be better if he could get to her quickly. Maybe tomorrow. No, Sunday maybe, or Monday. Maybe he'd call her. It wouldn't do any harm to remind her—subtly—who paid her salary; at her age she wasn't going to get another job as cushy as this. Maureen liked to think that her contacts in the business were second to none. But time was passing her by, and slowly, one by one, her contacts were becoming useless as her old friends were replaced by new people. Younger people.

He'd call her in the morning because women, in Robert's limited experience, stuck together. Like Stephanie's meddling friend Izzie warning her off him in the first place; why didn't she just mind her own business? If Kathy went to Maureen voicing some vague suspicion, God only knows what Maureen would say. Actually, it might be better if he popped by her place in the morning, maybe bring a bunch of flowers and a Christmas bonus. He nodded into the mirror. That's what he'd do; it would keep her sweet.

"Who's the new receptionist?" Kathy asked when he came out of the en suite bathroom. White light flooded the bedroom, and he watched her raise her hand to shield her eyes. He quickly shut off the light.

"A temp. Illona. Russian, I think. I got her from an agency. She's very good."

"Maybe Illona made the reservation?" she suggested.

Robert pulled out a fresh pair of pajamas and tugged on the top. "Maybe. But it was about four weeks ago; I'm pretty sure Maureen was still around then. It's not a big deal. I'll complain to the restaurant in the morning, if I get a chance."

"Do you want me to do it for you?"

Something in her voice, some eagerness, some expectation alerted him. He'd heard that tone before, and he knew then, knew for a certainty that Kathy was suspicious. Only this time there was a reason. He was aware that his heart was racing. It was beating so hard and so fast, he could actually feel the skin vibrate. Christ, that's all he needed right now was a heart attack. He took a deep breath and forced his voice to remain calm, and then he smiled in the darkness. "That'd be great. Table for two, Friday night, seven thirty, in either my name or Jimmy Moran's. I used his name too just in case he got there first." Let her check up; she'd find nothing, and it might allay some of her suspicions.

Robert got into bed. The sheets were icy, but maybe that was because he felt as if he were burning up. He leaned across and kissed his wife quickly on the cheek.

"Night." She muttered the single word as she rolled over, turning away from him. He found himself getting angry. Why did he put up with this? Was this his future? Was he destined to spend years going though this loveless routine, gradually becoming more and more distant from Kathy, until there was nothing left between them but bitterness?

But there was an alternative.

There was Stephanie.

She loved him, and he loved her. She loved being with him. There was an opportunity for a future for both of them. A happy future. But she wouldn't wait forever.

But the children. What about the children?

When he eventually fell asleep, he tossed and turned in dreams where he chased Brendan and Theresa through endless corridors. They were always just out of reach, and Kathy and Stephanie appeared around every corner, watching, waiting, accusing.

He awoke around four and didn't sleep for the rest of the night.

CHAPTER 28

Saturday, 21st December

"I told you we should have gotten the smaller tree."

"Dad! You know we always get the biggest tree we can find," Theresa said.

"And then we always spend ages cutting the end off," Brendan reminded his sister.

"Who's this we?" Robert asked. "Looks like I'm the only one sawing at the moment."

"Hey, we're holding it steady," Brendan reminded him.

Robert, along with Brendan and Theresa, had gone thirty miles outside of Boston to buy a Christmas tree at Doe Orchards in Harvard. It had become a tradition over the years to buy their tree as close to Christmas as possible, a tradition that was becoming increasingly difficult to keep as trees began appearing in neighbors' windows earlier and earlier in December and surviving long into January. The other part of the tradition of course was that Kathy would complain about the tree—it was too big, too bushy, too thin, too lopsided, and, Robert's favorite, too environmentally incorrect to cut down a live tree.

But at least they had been spared Kathy's complaining this

morning, and, for that small mercy, Robert was grateful. Although Kathy had been in bed when the trio had set out to buy the tree, she'd left the house by the time they had returned a few hours later. A scribbled note on the kitchen table said: *Gone Shopping.*

It suited Robert perfectly. Once he got the tree into the house, and dug the decorations out of the garage, he needed to see Stephanie. He glanced at his watch; he wanted to be gone before Kathy came back.

But the tree was too tall; it wouldn't fit into the house.

He spent a frustrating half hour sawing off the base of the tree, getting covered in sticky sap and pricked by scores of needles. And every moment he expected to see Kathy's car turn down the road. Finally, he managed to chop and saw eighteen inches off the end of the tree, and, with Theresa holding the top, Brendan the middle, and him taking up the rear, they backed the tree through the kitchen door and into the house.

"We could set it up in the hall," Robert said, voice muffled behind branches, which kept swatting him across the face.

"Dad!" Theresa squealed in disgust. He made the same suggestion every year, and every year they placed the tree in the family room.

With the tree finally set up in its usual corner, standing in a bucket filled with stones, and more or less straight, Robert turned to Brendan.

"I know, I know," the young man said. "Vacuum up the needles. I'll get on it."

"Right. I'll get out the decorations, then I need to wash up and head into the office for an hour or so."

"Dad! Do you have to?"

"This is to do with DaBoyz!" He leaned over and patted Theresa's cheek. "Just think, if I get this gig, you can come on set when I shoot their video."

Theresa looked distinctly unimpressed, with that look that only teenage girls perfect. "Yeah, I don't think so!"

"I thought they were good," he said, surprised. "Up and coming. They were on *Ryan Seacrest*."

"And they were crap," she said. "Their last single didn't even chart. And Gideon, the lead singer—"

"Which one is he?"

"Shaved head, little pointy beard."

Robert nodded, vaguely remembering the young man. He'd thought all five band members looked alike.

"Gideon's gay. He's dating Vic, the drummer," she said seriously.

"How do you know?" Robert knew the answer just as the words were coming out of his mouth. With media access and social networking, teenagers often knew about breaking news long before adults did.

"There were like a hundred tweets about it last week," she answered. "Everyone is expecting the band to break up." She saw the look on her father's face and grinned. "Are you sure you want to shoot their video?"

Robert licked dry lips, tasting pine and bile in equal measure. "I don't know."

"Might be a mistake, Dad," Brendan said, coming back into the room, lugging the upright Oreck. "If they're about to go bust, these bands usually blame everyone but themselves. Blaming the video is high on their list."

"Wish I'd spoken to you two sooner," he muttered, leaving the room.

"Anytime, Dad," Brendan called after him. "Say, do we get a consultant fee for this?"

Robert stepped into his home office, shut the door, then, as an afterthought, turned the key in the lock. Folding his arms across his chest, he stared out across the bare winter garden, not quite sure what to think. The big gig, the great opportunity, might just turn out to be not so big, not so great as he had imagined. He'd talk to Stephanie about it; she'd know what to do.

He sat in his chair and reached for his cell. He never called Stephanie on the home phone; he didn't want the itemized bill displaying numerous calls to a single number. He hit the speed dial and, while he waited for the call to connect, he rifled through the correspondence in his basket. He'd been so busy at work that he hadn't had a chance to attend to it. He'd stuffed all the correspondence in his briefcase on Monday last, intending to deal with it during the week, but so far, he hadn't even had a chance to glance through it.

The call connected.

"How . . . how are you feeling?" he asked immediately.

"I'm tired, Robert."

"Do you want to see me?"

"I always want to see you." He could almost hear the smile in her voice.

"I was going to come over."

"I'm about to head into the city; there's an open-air carol service in the Common."

"What time?"

"Starts about two."

"Great. Why don't I meet you there? We can listen to some carols, then go and get something to eat."

"Okay," she said after a brief silence. "Give me a call when you're in the city." The phone went dead.

Robert sat looking at the handset for a long moment. That had been very short and not so very sweet. He put the phone down and quickly sorted through the basket.

And for a moment thought he was indeed having a heart attack.

His MBNA Visa bill was in the pile. What was that doing here? He must have bundled it up with the mail he'd brought home from the office. He'd taken up the offer of the credit card shortly after he had started his relationship with Stephanie, thinking that it might be a useful way of allowing him to spend money unbeknownst to Kathy. Kathy did the household accounts and paid all the bills, and the last thing he needed was for her to start questioning some of his expenditures. He still put his legitimate business expenses on the Wells Fargo card, but expenses that were specifically to do with Stephanie went on the new card. Statements were sent to the office, and he wrote them a check every month. He filled in the check stub with fictitious business meetings.

Robert turned the statement over and over in his fingers. Had Kathy seen this? Unlikely. She rarely came into his office, and she would have no reason to go rooting through his mail.

Unless she was suspicious.

The thought crept slowly and insidiously into his consciousness. And he knew she was.

He looked through the bill. It wasn't as bad as he thought; most of the items on it he could claim as legitimate business expenses, even the books and CDs, which he'd given as gifts to Stephanie, he could claim as research material for a documentary. Documentary research covered a multitude of sins. He turned the page. "Shit!" There were three items on the second page that might be more difficult to explain. He had satellite TV piped into the office and often watched QVC, the shopping channel, when he was working, particularly when they were selling movie memorabilia, which he collected. However, he'd bought a bracelet for Stephanie—part of her birthday present—on the credit card, and he'd also ordered a bouquet of flowers online to be sent to her. He'd taken Stephanie to L'Espalier in the Back Bay, and he'd used the card to pay for that.

Okay. What was the worst-case scenario? Kathy had seen this page. If she had, then she was bound to raise the issue of the card. He could explain that away. The books, the CDs, he could explain away also. These three items however . . .

Well, the statement only showed the amount; it did not show the item.

The QVC bill could have been something for his computer. He had a couple of items in the office—wireless mouse, an external hard drive—that he could show her if necessary; she'd never know how much they cost.

The flowers. A birthday present, a thank-you gift. Maybe a get-well bouquet for Maureen. He must remember to really send her a bouquet, just in case Kathy asked about the flowers.

The dinner. Well, that could have been just any business dinner. A meeting at a hip restaurant to impress a new client.

A lie justified.

He sat back in the creaking chair, and then stopped. What was he was doing? He was creating a worst-case scenario—just in case

Kathy confronted him. But only last night he'd been on the verge of confessing to her. So just what did he want to do? To stay with Kathy or go with Stephanie?

Both, the little perverse thought at the back of his head whispered. Both. He wanted to have his cake and eat it too.

CHAPTER 29

"Shit. Shit. Shit. She didn't waste any time."

Robert slowed as he turned off Columbus Avenue. Kathy's car was parked outside Maureen's house. He remembered the row house well; when R&K had pitched a reality makeover show to FOX, they'd used Maureen's home for the pilot. She'd gotten a very nice conservatory out of it. He hoped that she and Kathy were now sitting out in that conservatory at the back of the house, rather than in the living room watching him drive by. He glanced at the bouquet of flowers on the seat beside him. He had planned to drop in on Maureen unannounced, just to "see how she was" and give her a Christmas bonus, a check for one thousand dollars. He had planned to be very careful to explain that one of the reasons he could pay the bonus was because of the work that Stephanie had brought them. Well, Maureen wouldn't be getting the money or the flowers today. He accelerated past the house, desperately resisting the temptation to glance over and look in.

It took him another half an hour to get from Mission Hill into the city, and he eventually parked the car in the Boston Common garage where, after fifteen minutes of circling, he finally found an empty space on the bottom level.

Pulling on his heavy tweed jacket and wrapping a wool scarf around his neck, he hurried through the park. The temperature was hovering around zero, but Boston looked glorious in the crisp December light. It was one of those rare winter days when the sky was cloudless and the low sunlight painted the streets in gold and shadow. All across the city, bells were tolling as the bell ringers put in some practice for Christmas Eve, and, with his breath pluming in the air before him, he felt the first touch of Christmas spirit.

This had never been his favorite time of year. There were too many bitter memories from his youth; his parents' constant arguing and his mother's drinking—exacerbated by his father's icy temper—made holidays, or indeed any time they were forced to spend together as a family unit, difficult and uncomfortable. When his parents had finally divorced, he ended up spending Christmas Day with his mother, listening to her bitch about his father, and then New Year's Eve with his father, listening to him rant about his mother.

He didn't want that to happen to his children, forcing them to choose between parents. He didn't want to place them in that position . . . and yet, his actions had certainly made that a very real possibility. When he'd first slept with Stephanie, he'd never imagined the potential consequences. It was just a bit of fun, two adults doing what adults did, not harming anyone. . . .

Except that it had. Even if Kathy and the kids never found out about his affair, it had damaged his marriage. He shook his head quickly; no, the affair hadn't damaged his marriage. He had.

The drive into the city, however, had allowed him to come to one conclusion. He was determined to get through Christmas without having to make a decision. If he boxed cleverly, danced around questions, parried issues, deflected attacks, he thought he might just be able to do that. He just needed a little more time to think things through. A couple of days, a week, maybe a month or two to make a decision.

Coward, something that might have been his conscience heckled. And he had to agree.

He cut through the Common. It was packed, and he battled his way through hordes of shoppers: teenagers wrapped around one another, mothers pushing carriages, fathers carrying children in their arms or dragging older children along behind them. Who in their right mind brought children into the city a couple of days before Christmas? But when he looked closely at the children and parents, none of them seemed to be upset. They were smiling, happy, and he remembered that when Brendan and Theresa were young, he and Kathy had taken them into the city to see the lights strung across the streets, window shop, and enjoy the festive atmosphere. They had been happy then, just the four of them; they'd laughed a lot, as a couple and as a family. He tried to remember when they'd stopped doing that. There was no one moment. It had just happened; things had changed. The children had grown up, he'd started working harder and harder to support a particular lifestyle, and he and Kathy had just drifted apart.

He ducked into the entrance of the AMC Theatre on Tremont, pulled out his phone, and hit the speed dial for Stephanie. The call went for ten rings before it was finally answered.

"Where are you?" she asked without preamble.

"In the lobby of the movie theater."

"Stay there. Don't move. I'll find you. It's chaos here."

Robert ended the call and stood nervously in the foyer. He was feeling exposed; this was probably one of the most visible spots in Boston, with crowds of people milling around. He'd already caught glimpses of a couple of neighbors.

He turned away from the crowds and focused on a poster for a WWII film he thought he'd like to see, but knew he'd end up watching it on TV. He peered at the director's name on poster, and a hole opened up in the pit of his stomach. Robert had gone to film school with him. The kid was talented, but it had been Robert who had won all of the awards, who had shown the greatest promise. Now, this guy was directing a holiday blockbuster and Robert was . . . Who was he anymore?

And then suddenly Stephanie was standing beside him. She was bundled against the chill air in a bright red ski jacket, black jeans tucked into woolly-topped boots, wearing a bright red woolen ski cap on her head. With the bulky clothing disguising her lithe body and only a tiny section of her face visible—eyes, nose, and mouth— the similarity to his wife was startling.

He leaned forward to kiss her, a quick peck on the cheek, and then caught her arm, easing her away from the doorway. "Where did you leave your toboggan?"

"Parked it upstairs alongside the sleigh."

Robert hurried her across the road, back toward the center of the Common. From within the park came the sound of "Away in a Manger," clearly audible above the noise of the traffic, the rattling of the T, and the drone of the massed people. "So, Christmas carols?"

She shook her head. "The choir is loud but not good, and the park is jammed. Let's walk around and look at the art."

A huge, open-air art exhibition was taking place near Frog Pond. Dozens of artists were exhibiting their works, the younger artists standing nervously alongside their paintings, talking to everyone who stopped to look, the older, more experienced exhibitors sitting on chairs, allowing their art to speak for them.

"Left or right?" Stephanie asked brightly.

"Right," Robert said, leading her to the right, away from the crowds.

"I'm sorry about last night," he began.

"So am I," she said immediately. "I should have told you that our relationship had been discovered. But I knew you were under so much pressure; I simply didn't want to add to it."

"It might have been better if you had. When Jimmy dropped it on me last night, I started to have a panic attack."

Stephanie glanced at him curiously before stopping to look at a spectacular abstract oil, vivid in green and gold, slashed across with daubs of red and violet. She leaned forward, toward the painting. "Tell me," she murmured, so softly that Robert had to lean close to hear her. "Do you love me?"

His instinct was to snap a quick "yes," but something about the apparent casualness of the question stopped him.

When he didn't answer immediately, she turned her head to look at him. "That's a mighty long pause."

"What? No. I suppose I was just surprised that you had to ask me."

"I want to know, Robert." She moved away from the painting, and he followed her. "I want to know how much."

"I've told you often enough."

"I know that. But have you shown me?"

"I've given you presents. . . ."

A flash of annoyance in her dark eyes shut him up. "What is love, Robert?"

"Love is . . ." he floundered, ". . . well, love."

"You're such a typical man!" she snapped. "Think about it, Robert: What is love? You tell me you love me. What does that mean?"

"It means . . . it means I want to be with you. That I love being with you."

"So, you're saying that love is commitment?"

He suddenly saw where the conversation was going, but had no way to change it. "Yes. Commitment," he agreed.

Stephanie stopped to peer at another painting, a tiny, delicate watercolor of a single daffodil. "And are you committed to me?" she continued.

"Yes."

Stephanie straightened. "Okay. So, how do you show that commitment?"

Robert was about to answer, but the overeager artist, a young woman with huge glasses and a streak of cobalt blue in her hair, came forward. "We're not interested," Robert said, before she could utter a word. He caught Stephanie by the arm and led her out of the park. "If we're going to talk, then let's talk and leave the art for another day. What do you want from me, Stephanie?"

"The truth," Stephanie said. "I told you that last night. Just tell me the truth."

"I've told you I love you. That's the truth."

"And I believe you."

Her response stopped him in his tracks. She walked on a couple of paces, before turning to look back at him. The path was busy, and for a moment he lost her in the crowd, and there was the temptation simply to turn his back and walk away. When the path cleared, she was standing in the same position, waiting for him.

"If you have something to ask me, then ask me straight out," he said.

Stephanie dug her hands into the pockets of her jacket. Her eyes were glittering and her cheeks were red, but he wasn't sure if it was from the cold or emotion.

"You tell me you love me. You tell me you want to be with me. You seem to enjoy my company. You certainly enjoy my body." She stopped and took a deep breath. "I need to know if there is more. If there is going to be more."

"More?"

"More of us. Together. Not snatched half-hour lunches or one-hour dinners, not fumbles in your office or dirty weekends away. I need to know if we're going to be together. As a couple. Openly." She looked away from him, across the park, which was bright with people. "That's all."

The answer he gave now was going to determine the rest of his life. All the thoughts of the previous night, his rambling notions had revealed nothing, had not prepared him for this moment. He could try and be cold and calculating, try and choose between the two women, choose the security that Kathy represented, or the uncertain future that Stephanie promised. He could refuse to make the decision and lose Stephanie, but in doing so, might force her to go to Kathy, and then he would lose her too. Jimmy Moran was right: Everything had a price.

"I've had plenty of relationships before, Robert; you know that. I've never felt about anyone the way I feel about you. I love you. I need to know if you love me. I need to know if you love me enough to do something about it."

They walked out of the Common together. An Old Town Trolley tour drove by, passengers snapping pictures and shouting Christmas greetings; neither Robert nor Stephanie turned to look at them.

Robert was watching Stephanie out of the corner of his eye. When they had first been falling in love, but before they had made love for the first time, they had walked. They had spent weekends together, walking through the streets of the city, along the Charles, around Jamaica Pond, through the Arboretum, walking side by side, not touching, not holding hands. She was fitter than he was; there were times when he struggled to keep up. Later, he understood what had been happening. They had both been so full of energy—nervous energy, sexual energy; this was how they had channeled it. Once they started making love regularly, they had stopped walking. Now they were walking again, but with a different energy, a different motive. Their steps were slow, grudging.

"You want me to commit to you."

"I don't want to be your mistress anymore. That was fine for a while, because I wasn't sure if you were the one."

"The one?"

"The one I loved. And I allowed myself to fall in love with you—even though you were a married man—because I believed that there might be a chance for us. A future." Stephanie took a deep breath, and Robert realized that his heart was hammering. "My girlfriends have gone away for Christmas to be with their families, but I'm going to be spending Christmas alone, because I wanted to be close to my lover. But my lover is spending time with his family. It was that way last year too; I don't want it to be that way next year. I feel so foolish, Robert. So incredibly foolish."

"Stephanie, I—" he said quickly.

She held up a hand, silencing him. "If there is no future for us, then just say so. I can handle it. It will hurt, but I'll get over it. I'll survive. And I'm not going to be stupid about it. I'm a big girl. I won't make a scene. I won't tell Kathy, if that's what you're worried about."

So there it was.

Robert took a deep breath. In a single sentence, Stephanie had removed his biggest fear. And she had given him the get-out-of-jail-free card. He could now, guilt-free, tell Stephanie that there was no future for them, at least not for a few years, until the children had grown up. He could go back to Kathy, be more attentive, more loving, more considerate, and she would never know anything about his affair. Stephanie would drift away. And things would continue on with Kathy until . . . well, until they drifted completely apart.

The children would have their own lives, their own families. He would be left with nothing.

Except now he had an opportunity.

For the first time in his life, he had a unique opportunity to make a selfish decision, to do something for himself. From the moment he had married, he'd ended up in a trap, running faster and faster to stand still, scrambling for work to keep everyone satisfied, to keep a roof over their heads. He'd sacrificed friendships and holidays, weekends and late nights in the desperate search for work in a business that was, ultimately, worthless. What had happened to his dreams of being a great director, of producing documentaries of worth, of making people think, of making a difference? His life was one of missed opportunities: his chance to be on that film poster, his chance to make a difference with his work, his chance to be happy.

Was he too old to start again?

Was this an opportunity to start again with a woman who loved him, and whom he would work with to make sure they stayed in love?

His head was spinning, and he physically swayed. Stephanie reached out and caught his arm. Even through the layers of cloth, her touch was electric.

The decision, when it came, was almost a shock to him. He felt as if pieces were sliding and slipping into place. He moved around to stand in front of Stephanie, catching both of her shoulders, looking down into her dark eyes, magnified now by unshed tears. His breath was coming in quick gasps as if he had been running.

"I love you. I want to be with you. To marry you. Will you marry me?"

And then the tears came. Stephanie wrapped her arms around his shoulders and pulled his face down and kissed him. He could feel her tears running down his collar and was sure there were tears on his own face.

"Yes, I will, yes, yes, yes."

CHAPTER 30

Sunday, 22nd December

The remainder of Saturday passed in a blur. Robert stayed up late watching television, but he couldn't concentrate. He flipped through the channels, but all he could think about was his new life.

His future. With Stephanie.

Since proposing to Stephanie, Robert felt as if a huge weight had been lifted off his shoulders. Bizarrely, he wanted to phone people and tell them his good news, his great news: He was in love with a woman who loved him.

No decisions had been made; Stephanie had been satisfied that he'd made the commitment. She'd been laughing, crying, and when they'd reached her condo, she'd invited him in, but he had resisted the temptation; once they were inside, he knew they would end up in bed together, and for some indefinable reason, he felt that would be unfair to her. Standing in front of the Victorian, she kissed him, lovingly, passionately, and thanked him.

"For what?" he asked.

"For making me so happy."

It was half past midnight when he finally headed up to bed. The house was silent. Kathy had gone to sleep early, claiming another one of her interminable migraines. The kids had drifted off to bed much later. Robert moved around the house, checking the doors, turning off lights. Who would do this when he was gone? He was startled to find himself thinking in the past tense, as if he had already left. Truthfully, he had left emotionally a long time ago. He climbed the stairs and turned off the hall light, then stepped into the bedroom, closing the door gently behind him. Undressing in the dark, he tossed his clothes onto the back of the chair and slid into bed, sighing as his head hit the pillow. This was a day he was not going to forget.

"I went to see Maureen today."

Kathy's voice startled him; he had thought she'd been asleep for hours.

He was too wired with thoughts and emotions to sleep, but the last thing he wanted to do was start chatting about Maureen. Besides, once the news broke, Maureen would have no hold—real or imagined—over him. He could let her go without a second thought. It would be a chance to make a clean sweep and start afresh in the office too. Maybe Stephanie could join him as a business partner; that was an exciting thought. He turned in the bed to look at Kathy. He could see her wide-open eyes sparking in the dim, reflected streetlight. "How is she?"

"Getting better. But she won't be back till the New Year."

"Didn't think so," he mumbled.

"She's not as young as she pretends to be."

"I know." Maureen sometimes thought—and dressed—as if she were in her twenties. He shifted again, rolling onto his back. "The new girl, the Russian . . ."

"Illona?"

"Yes, Illona." He was somewhat surprised that Kathy remembered the girl's name. "She's very good. Does what she's told, doesn't have an attitude, is in on time, and takes exactly an hour for lunch. Maureen does it her way, treats me like a boy, and has no concept of a one-hour lunch." Robert remembered one day last year when Maureen had actually taken a three-hour lunch. She simply did not respect him the way a secretary should respect her boss.

"You're not thinking about firing her, are you?"

"It's crossed my mind," he admitted.

"It's not going to happen," Kathy said. "I forbid it."

"Forbid it?" He was genuinely shocked. He bit back the crack of anger in his voice. "You forbid it?"

"I still own half the company, remember? Maybe it's time I started to take a more active interest in it." She sat up in bed and snapped on the light.

Robert groaned and shielded his eyes. "It's almost one, for Christ's sake! Can we talk about this in the morning?"

Although the company was in both their names, he ran it, he did all the work; he'd always thought of it as his business. Kathy had a perfect right—a legal right—to query or veto any decisions. But it was his company. Shit . . . Exactly what had happened to Jimmy was going to happen to him. Kathy would want half. Maybe he could do a deal with the house. . . .

"Now that the kids are older," said Kathy, "I'm thinking in the New Year I might start coming in with you three or four times a week. Even when Maureen comes back, she's not going to be able to work full-time. I can go back to doing what I used to do: helping you run the company. Put the K back into R&K Productions."

This was getting worse. He rubbed dry lips with an equally dry tongue. "Where are you going to find the time?"

"I'll make the time. I'll concentrate on getting new business; you concentrate on making the material. Remember? The way we used to."

"Yeah, that would be great. Let's talk about it in the morning." He didn't want this conversation to proceed. He needed time to think through the ramifications of what he was hearing.

"Maureen said the company was in the red."

Robert shuffled up in the bed. "Maureen should have kept her mouth shut. Can we talk about it in the morning?"

"We rarely get a chance to talk anymore, Robert. We're running in opposite directions."

"C'mon, Kathy, it's only temporarily, and it's Christmas," he said. "That always brings its own drama." He closed his eyes, trying to end the conversation, but Kathy pressed on.

"No, it's not only temporarily, and it's not just Christmas. We've been doing it for months, maybe longer. I barely see you anymore. You're home late four nights out of five, you go in to the office on the weekends, and when you are home, you're locked in your office, working."

So she had noticed. Where was this coming from? What had suddenly triggered it? He shrugged. "It's been crazy busy."

"Put my mind at ease; tell me the business is going well."

This had to have something to do with Maureen. What had that bitch told her? "Look, we've gone through a rough patch, but I've landed a few new accounts. Next year will be good."

"Does that mean you'll end up working eighty hours a week next year too?"

Next year would definitely be different, he promised himself, but not in ways she would expect. "While the work is there, yes. Kathy, I don't have an option. It's one of the joys of being self-employed; you know that."

"Then I'm even more determined to help you. Starting in the New Year, you've got a new colleague: me. You can give your Russian girl notice."

Robert bit the inside of his cheek to keep his face straight, but not before he had started to shake his head. She'd been out of the business this long; she could now stay out of it.

"What's wrong?" she asked.

"Nothing's wrong." He was getting annoyed with this nonsense. "But here's what's going to happen. You'll come work with me for a week, maybe two, then you'll have to take time off to be home for some reason: Theresa's sick; you have to get to Brendan's concert on time: you have to be home for the refrigerator repairman."

"Really? That's your worry, my needing to be home for the repairman?"

Robert ignored her and kept justifying himself. "Then you'll take more and more time off, and soon enough, we'll be back to the way we are now. Except I'll have to go looking for a secretary again."

"So, you're using the fact that I'm prioritizing my kids . . ."

"Our kids, and I'm not saying that, Kathy."

"You sound as if you don't want me to work with you."

"I didn't say that."

"Look, Robert, I want to be more involved. I feel . . . I feel like we're drifting apart."

Robert reached out to take her hand, but Kathy slid her fingers away. He took a deep breath. "We're not drifting apart; we're just busy. And it's Christmas. That's all. I'd love you to be more interested in the business," he lied. Her offer was coming at least two years or three years or even five years too late. He lifted the clock off the nightstand. "Jesus, can we please continue this tomorrow? I have to get an early start in the morning."

"Okay," she agreed, turning off her light and sliding down beneath the covers. "But we will continue it."

He heard what sounded like a threat in her voice.

"Fine," he said.

"Fine." The ice in her voice was unmistakable, and it seemed to give a chill to the room.

That settled it: another night without sleep. The rational part of his mind knew that he shouldn't be getting upset with Kathy because she was offering to help him. On any other day of the year, he might have been thrilled that she'd finally decided to become his partner again and help shoulder the burden of the business. Obviously something Maureen had told her had twinged her conscience; maybe she had revealed just how rocky things were, just how hard he worked to keep the business afloat. But right now he was more concerned with Kathy's reminders that she was half of R&K. He was going to need legal advice. He didn't want to end up in a stupid and expensive litigious process; he was hoping they would be able to decide things amicably.

That same voice, the little whisper of conscience deep in his skull, started to laugh hysterically. He was about to separate from his wife of eighteen years and he hoped they would do it amicably? She'd take him for everything he had.

And he couldn't really blame her.

Robert spent most of Sunday hidden away in his study, editing a corporate video for a new green energy company. He heard the laughter coming from downstairs as Theresa, Brendan, and Kathy decorated the tree. Although Robert wanted to participate in his family's tradition, he felt somehow it would be unfair to Stephanie, that it would be disloyal, so he worked through the day and into the night.

He just needed to focus on work, keeping Stephanie happy, and getting through Christmas. Then he would be home free.

Or would he?

CHAPTER 31

Monday, 23rd December

Robert had been on the treadmill for fifteen minutes and had already worked up a respectable sweat when Stephanie came out of the women's locker room and hopped on the machine next to his. She gripped the handles and hit the button to turn the machine on. The narrow pad beneath her feet started to move, and she fell into an easy pace on it.

"Sorry I'm late. The office is closing today, and there were drinks in the boardroom."

"No problem. I got your message. Any issues in work about . . . ?"

"About us? Nothing. No mentions. And I did hear through the grapevine that it looks as if you got the DaBoyz gig."

"That's great! I mean, I think that's great. Theresa said two of the guys are gay."

Stephanie shook her head. "So? Is that a problem?"

"No. Not at all. But she also said there were lots of tweets that they're thinking about breaking up."

"They were. That's why this single is so important. There's been a lot of investment in this group, and the investors are unwilling to cut loose their potential cash cow without one last shot. That's you, by the way. Do the video right, and you will have saved a lot of people a lot of money. Screw it up, however, and you'll never work in this town again." She laughed.

"I'm not sure whether you're joking or serious."

"A bit of both, I think. You'll do a great job. Remember, I've staked my career on it."

"So, no pressure there then," he murmured.

"And I'm sorry about yesterday. I really wanted to see you, but I'd already agreed to go shopping with Izzie before . . ."

Robert glanced sidelong at her and smiled. "Before?"

"Before us." She was wearing a simple black sports bra and black, skin-tight yoga pants. He loved the way they showed off every curve of her body.

Kathy hid her curves behind oversized sweaters; Stephanie showed hers off.

"It was probably just as well. It gave me a chance to get a lot done in the office. If you and I had gotten together, we would have . . ."

Now it was her turn to look sidelong. "What would we have done?"

"Talked. Planned."

"I know. You've made me so happy. Even Izzie is pleased."

Robert bit the inside of his cheek to prevent a comment he knew would only cause an argument. "One of these days I'd like to meet this mysterious Izzie."

"She's looking forward to meeting you too. I've told her a lot about you."

Robert had never met Stephanie's best friend and confidante, Isabel Wilson, an old college sorority sister who was an orthopaedic surgeon at Mass General. All he knew was that Izzie didn't approve of him and had done her best to separate them. "I suppose she was surprised by the news."

"More like stunned. I said we'd get together after Christmas and celebrate. She's paying."

"Good." Robert pressed the controls on the side of his treadmill, increasing the speed. "Why is she paying?"

"Because she once bet me the best meal money could buy that you would never leave your wife for me."

"Well, let's make sure that's an expensive bet. I'll book Top of the Hub myself for this one."

"Have you given any further thought to Christmas?" Stephanie asked.

Robert frowned, wondering where this was leading. "I've thought about nothing else," he said truthfully.

"Will you spend Christmas Day with me?"

Robert increased the speed of the machine again. The humming whine would make conversation difficult. "No." He caught the flicker of disappointment on her face. "Be reasonable." Realizing that some of the other patrons of the gym were looking in their direction, he discovered that he'd raised his voice. He leaned across to Stephanie. "Be reasonable. I can hardly go to Kathy and the kids tonight or tomorrow and say, 'Guess what, I'm leaving. Merry Christmas.' Can I?"

Stephanie nodded. "No, of course not."

"But I'll see you tomorrow," he added, though he was not exactly sure what excuse he'd use to get out of the house. Maybe say the office alarm had gone off, something like that.

Stephanie patted her forehead with the towel draped around her neck. "And when do you intend to tell her?"

"I was thinking the twenty-seventh, which is Friday."

"Why not Thursday?"

"Well, we're committed to going over to her sister's for dinner. It's a family tradition. All the arrangements have been made."

"So what am I supposed to do for Christmas Day? Hang around until you appear?"

Robert ignored the question. "Look, I'll tell her on Friday, and I'll spend New Year's Eve with you. We'll bring in the New Year together. Come on—meet me halfway on this. This is a big decision, a huge move for me to make. You've only got yourself to think of; I've got Kathy and the kids to consider."

Stephanie nodded. "You're right, of course. Absolutely right. Another couple of days won't make that much difference to us. And Christmas Day is really just another Wednesday."

They moved off the treadmills and onto the bikes. Stephanie set a high gear and began to pedal, the muscles in her legs pushing hard as the covered wheel whirred around. Robert pedaled at an easier pace.

"So, I have a proposition."

Stephanie looked at him and smiled. "Another one?"

"It's about the company. R&K Productions. You know the K stands for Kathy and that she has a fifty percent share in it."

"I know that."

"I was wondering if you'd like to join me in the company, take over Kathy's share. We could call it R&S Productions. That is, if I can buy Kathy out, of course."

He thought Stephanie was looking at him in surprise, and she took a long moment before she replied. "I'm not sure I'd want to give up my present position. I would think going to work in your company might be seen as a retrograde step, career-wise."

For a moment, Robert thought she was joking. He even started to laugh, until he realized that she was deadly serious.

"The other thing we'll have to bear in mind is that, obviously, I won't be able to send any more business your way. It wouldn't look good for me to be seen to be pushing business to my partner's company."

He was shocked. "No more business . . ."

"Not from me. But I'll keep my ear to the ground. I'll keep you well up to speed with what's happening in the industry."

Robert felt his head spin. Yesterday, sitting in the cold office, trying to reach Stephanie and only getting her machine, he'd doodled new R&S logos on the computer, interlocking *R*'s and *S*'s, symbolically entwined. And with the relationship between himself and Stephanie out in the open, he imagined there would be no problem with her sending him clients. Which was a good thing, because he reckoned he was going to need the extra money to pay off Kathy.

"Anyway," Stephanie continued, "I was thinking you might close R&K."

"What?"

"Maybe get a job with one of the big advertising agencies or production companies. You'd be a huge asset, Robert. You have a great deal of experience."

Robert concentrated on pedaling. He'd spent most of his adult life building up R&K, and now she was suggesting closing it down!

"It would be easier on you mentally and physically," she continued. "There would be a steady paycheck, and you could walk out at six and not have to think about it again until the following morning. Your weekends would be yours again. Ours," she added significantly.

"I'd be working for someone. I've been my own boss for a long time."

"At the moment you're working for Kathy and the children and the bank. They're your boss. This way you end up with more free time, time to spend with me. Time to spend with your children," she added.

And Robert admitted it was a persuasive argument. Ironically, he'd even broached something similar with Kathy a year earlier. Then, it had been her reminding him of the huge investment in time and money he'd put into the firm over the years. He started laughing, a dry rasp, which turned into a cough.

Stephanie climbed off the bike and thumped his back. "Are you all right?"

"I'm fine. I was just thinking . . ."

"Thinking what?"

"That you're some sort of catalyst. Change happens around you."

Stephanie leaned into him, pushing her pert breasts against his chest. "We make our own changes, but sometimes you just need someone or something to do a little nudging. I'm going to take a shower."

Robert watched her move across the floor, hips swaying. One or two of the other men in the huge gym also turned to follow her progress. He was surprised to discover that he didn't feel jealous of their interest in her. They knew she was with him, which meant that they were jealous of him.

"So, what are your thoughts about babies?" Stephanie asked, lacing her fingers through Robert's.

"I hadn't thought about it. I mean, I have two teenagers already," Robert said as they walked across the foyer toward the door that led out onto the street. "But I'm not opposed to the idea. What do you think?"

"Honestly, I'm not sure. I mean, I think I'd like children," she said as they came through the door of the gym and out into the bitter night air.

"If you did want children, when would you like to have them?" he wondered. Would he, could he, go through the process again? Diapers, sleepless nights, childcare, school plays, soccer games, recitals. He'd spent the last seventeen years being a father. He'd experienced the highs of teaching his kids to ride bikes, throw balls, and make home movies, but he had also lived through the lows: the terrible, heartbreaking feelings of guilt when he missed a game or arrived too late to a concert. Did he really want to start over again? He had a good relationship with his kids, but it was one that he was always trying to improve. Robert worked hard to be a good father to Brendan and Theresa, and he didn't want a new baby to interfere with his love for his grown children. If—no, *when* he separated from Kathy, it was going to break their hearts. A new baby was going to confuse them even further. Unconsciously, he shook his head. The precious little spare time he had, he wanted to devote to his teenage children. They were going to need all the support he could give them.

"Not immediately of course." She reached for his hand. "Well, it's a bit of a Catch-22. I'm thirty-three now. My biological clock is definitely ticking. I can't wait too long, and yet, I need another two years at least before I'm promoted. Then we could start trying for the year after that."

Two years.

Brendan would be in college and Theresa a senior in high school. How would they react to a stepbrother or sister?

How would they react to a stepmother?

They'd understand. They'd be adults. He'd be able to explain it to them . . . wouldn't he?

A sudden, terrifying thought left him breathless: If he left Kathy, would he also lose the children? He looked quickly at Stephanie. Was she worth it? he wondered.

Their cars were parked alongside one another in the darkened corner of the street. They hit their electronic car door openers together, and both sets of lights blinked simultaneously.

Robert opened the door of Stephanie's silver BMW for her. The roof light popped on, flooding the interior in soft, pearl light, washing over the leather seats. Stephanie threw her gym bag onto the passenger seat, then turned to Robert. She wrapped her arms around his neck, pressed the palm of her right hand against the back of his skull to bring his head down to a level with hers.

"Think of all the fun we'll have practicing to conceive children," she whispered. Then she kissed him. Robert responded by dropping his gym bag to the ground and pulling her close. He loved the feel of this woman in his arms, the heat of her, the strength of her. He adored the pressure of his lips on hers. He loved her passion.

Finally they broke apart, and Stephanie climbed into the car. She waved once and drove away. Robert picked up his bag and moved around the front of the car. His phone rang. He fished it out of his jacket pocket and answered without looking at the screen.

"Hi, it's me." Kathy's voice crackled across a surprisingly clear connection. He thought she sounded like she was in a good mood for a change. "I'm just wondering what time you'll be home?"

Robert checked his watch. "I'm just leaving the office. I should be there in about forty minutes."

When he hung up, he suddenly found himself wondering why he had told the white lie. She knew he went to the gym; it was no secret. But he just supposed he'd gotten into the habit of lying to Kathy. It was time to start telling the truth.

But not tonight.

Book 3

The Mistress's Story

Of course I knew he was married.

I knew he was lying to his wife, and I knew, in my heart, that he was also lying to me.

But I loved him.

Or at least I thought I loved him.

CHAPTER 32

Thursday, 19th December

Stephanie Burroughs ran the back of her hand down the length of the raw silk tie. It felt cool and soft against her skin. She glanced up at the young woman standing behind the counter. The girl was staring at her blankly, a professional smile fixed on her lips, but with that empty, expressionless face of someone who is overworked and underpaid.

"Long day?" Stephanie asked sympathetically, folding the tie back into its box.

"Long week," the girl murmured, glancing around quickly to make sure her supervisor wasn't around. "With no end in sight."

Stephanie put two boxes side by side on the counter and compared the ties—one a deep, powerful crimson, the other a rich gold—and tried to choose between them.

"You're not off for the weekend?"

"I wish!" the girl said, obviously grateful for someone to talk to. Once she started to talk, she didn't stop. "But with Christmas not falling until Wednesday, we're working right through until Christmas Eve, and then we're open again on Friday. But I've got the following Monday off," the girl added with a smile, "and Wednesday,

New Year's Day, of course. Then we're back to normal. December is seriously the longest month. I'm sorry, I'm babbling, which tie are you interested in?"

"I'll take them both," Stephanie said. She suddenly felt sorry for the salesgirl forced to spend long hours on a shop floor for minimum wage. She'd never really thought about working in a retail environment where you started at nine and finished at five thirty or six, with a late night on Thursday and open on the weekend. She thought it must be like prison. After she'd graduated from business school, she'd been seduced into the world of television research, which had more or less allowed her to set her own pace. Now, as senior accounts manager for one of the largest advertising agencies in the world, she was moving steadily along a career path that often demanded long hours, but equally allowed a lot of free time. And it paid well. Very well. And December, for her, was turning out to be a remarkably short month. There were only a few small projects to complete, then the office closed on Tuesday and wouldn't reopen until the second of January.

"Cash or charge?"

"Charge." Stephanie handed over her platinum AmEx card.

The salesgirl rang up the purchase and slipped the two long, rectangular tie boxes into a black bag. "A Christmas present?" she asked.

Stephanie nodded. "For someone special." She smiled. "Merry Christmas."

"I'm sure he'll love them. Merry Christmas."

Stephanie Burroughs wandered into Copley Place and allowed herself to be carried along by the crowd. She had a few small presents left to get and wanted to pop into Neiman Marcus. She knew Robert would like the ties; she'd seen him wearing the ones she'd bought him over the past few months. They matched the Forzieri suit he'd initially been so skeptical about. She still hadn't picked up his "big" present and, as time went by, she was finding him more and more difficult to buy for. He had the unfortunate habit of buying himself whatever he wanted. She'd had her eye on the new iPad and had wanted to get it for him before he bought it for himself.

He had the latest in cameras—he'd gotten a new one last Christmas. She was also thinking about the new iPod. The only problem was, he rarely listened to music. She found that inconceivable. For her, music was one of the great joys of life. It went everywhere with her; it played through every room in her home, even in the bathroom, on her computer, her laptop, in the car, in the office. She owned hundreds of CDs; she thought he might own two dozen. For an otherwise remarkable and creative man, she found it a curious lack in his character.

Stephanie pushed her way into Neiman Marcus. She loved the familiarity of her favorite shop, and despite its often extravagant prices, she felt comfortable there. She headed toward the men's department.

The other problem was that she loved to buy him presents. She didn't need an excuse or an event, and over the course of their eighteen-month relationship, she hadn't let a month go by without surprising him with something.

And he had done the same for her.

But this would be their second Christmas together, and she was determined to outdo herself. So far she'd gotten him some shirts in a nice Oxford weave, and now she had these ties to match. She'd picked up a stunning book of aerial photographs of the world, which she thought he'd like, and *The Godfather* trilogy on Blu-ray that she knew he'd love, but she needed just one more present, something personal. . . .

Of course, she could always do as she'd done last year: wrap herself up in tinsel and bows and present herself as his Christmas present. They'd both enjoyed unwrapping that gift.

She touched the Hermès Birkin bag he'd given her. It was incredibly impractical and way too expensive, but she carried it proudly. She was both impressed and surprised that he had been able to procure such a coveted fashion accessory, and she adored the envious looks of the other girls in the office, or women walking down the street who recognized it for what it was.

Stephanie dipped into her bag and pulled out her BlackBerry. Robert was the first number on her list. She tried his direct line in the office, bypassing Illona on the reception desk, but the phone kept ringing. She glanced at the clock: three thirty. A little early to have closed the office. She hung up and tried his cell.

It rang for six rings, and she hung up before it transferred to his voice mail. She'd catch him later.

Stephanie wandered through the men's department. What exactly did you get the man who had everything and wanted for nothing? Clothes certainly, but they weren't exactly the most exciting of presents, and he didn't play tennis or golf. He had no real hobbies as far as she could determine; his entire life revolved around his work.

Finding nothing in Neiman's, she left the shop and maneuvered her way through the mall toward Landau, the jeweler. Maybe a watch. A watch wasn't really jewelry. Watches tended to fall into two types, very thin or very chunky, and she wondered which one he would prefer. Maybe something in silver, with lots of dials and buttons—he was just like a big kid that way. She nodded, seeing her reflection in the shop window mirror the movement. A watch, a diver's watch, with three dials and a rotating bezel, silver with a black face . . .

Then came the little practical thought, the one that now accompanied, touched, and tainted everything she bought him: Would he be able to wear it without his wife noticing and asking questions about where he got it?

She sighed, her breath misting the glass before her face. Who would have thought that buying a present would be so complicated, and would have so many conditions attached?

Robert said that his wife had no interest in him—and Stephanie believed him. She saw absolutely no signs that Kathy showed any curiosity in his work or whereabouts, but that didn't mean that the woman wouldn't notice if he turned up wearing a nice chunky watch. Stephanie supposed he could always say it was a gift from a client. But she didn't want that; she wanted him to be able to wear it and say: "My girlfriend gave me this."

Girlfriend sounded better than mistress.

Maybe not a watch then. She pushed away from Landau's window, exited the stuffy and overcrowded mall, and considered whether to go into Raven Used Books or Barnes & Noble. She wrapped her scarf tighter around her neck and hurried down Newbury Street. While she loved the used book store, it would be faster for her to find a present in the large chain. Barnes & Noble was absolutely jammed with people. She thought it was such a shame he read so little that books were a limited option. He claimed he simply had no time. She'd bought him some books on CD for the car stereo for his birthday a few months earlier, but she'd noted the last time she sat in his car that they were still in their plastic wrappers, unopened.

Maybe a print, or an original painting? But, although they shared an interest in so many things, they were diametrically opposed in others, especially art. She preferred modern art, bright primary daubs of colors, loving the energy and emotion they conveyed. He preferred—if he had any real preference—photo-realism.

Besides, if she got him a picture or a print, where would he hang it? It came back to the same question, one she was beginning to tire of asking: What would his wife say? He could hardly bring it home and hang it on the bedroom wall. That would be awkward.

She turned to the right as she came out of the bookstore and headed farther up Newbury Street, glancing cursorily in the windows of the posh shops as she hurried past. An overcoat was an option—something in mohair perhaps—or a Burberry scarf, maybe a nice briefcase, a wallet, pens . . .

She stopped and grinned. She was getting desperate and stupid. She could hardly give her lover a fancy pen, could she? Besides, last year he had given her a magnificent antique gold pendant inset with a chip of opal as big as her thumbnail. And for her birthday recently, he'd given her a fabulous modern silver bracelet. He had designed it himself. He took time to look for interesting and unique presents for her. The final option would be a gift certificate, but she hated giving small, colorful plastic cards with money values for presents because they were completely impersonal.

Kathy had given Robert a gift certificate last year. And a tie. And a state-of-the-art digital camera.

Stephanie felt her cheery mood slip a little. Some days she felt as if she were living with Kathy Walker. Glancing up and down the street, she noticed a Salvation Army band was gathered around the huge Christmas tree, and the rich sounds of trumpets and cymbals were just audible over the noise of the traffic.

Lately, she'd discovered that Robert's wife was never too far from her thoughts. Mostly, when she couldn't sleep at night. Then, she would toss and turn, imagining the two of them in bed: not having sex—but the smalls of their backs touching. Sharing an unspoken intimacy that she believed was meant for her. Stephanie tried, unsuccessfully, to expel Kathy Walker from her thoughts. And at times like these, when she was buying Robert a present, she'd find herself wondering what Kathy was going to get him for Christmas, or what she'd gotten him for his birthday. Sometimes she even found herself wondering what Robert was giving his wife.

When she'd first begun her relationship with Robert, it hadn't been a problem. She had known he was married; but she also knew that he was emotionally separated from a woman who seemed to have stopped caring for him. He was attracted to Stephanie and she to him, and they were two adults, and so long as they weren't hurting anyone . . .

Stephanie turned off the busy street. Even though she was outside in the crisp air, she suddenly felt incredibly claustrophobic.

When she'd started the relationship, she had never expected it to last. She had given it three months, six at most. She'd never thought about his wife or kids, of that other life he had with them, a life apart from her. As time went by, and she had slowly, inexorably, almost unconsciously fallen in love with him. And, subsequently, she wanted to know everything about him. His likes and dislikes, his dreams, his plans, his past . . . and that's where it became complicated, because Robert's past was still very much with him, wrapped around a wife and two children and a job that he obsessed about.

Why did she have to go and fall in love with him?

Because she was an idiot.

You don't fall in love with a married man.

She'd given the same answer to girlfriends who had ended up in similar situations, and she'd always sworn she wasn't going to make the same mistake. Yet, when she fell in love with him, she had starting asking questions about his other life: the life that didn't include her. A part of her brain even pretended that the more she knew about it, the more she could demystify it, and the more she could justify her actions. Because if Robert's wife didn't love him, Stephanie could defend her own behavior.

You don't fall in love with a married man.

But she had.

The fading notes of the Salvation Army trumpets sounded like mocking laughter following her down the street.

CHAPTER 33

The condo was still and silent as she pushed open the door, then picked up her shopping bag off the step and carried it into the hall. Old Mrs. Moore, Stephanie's downstairs neighbor, watched her enter the building from her bedroom window, and for a single instant Stephanie had been tempted to wave at her, but she didn't feel like having a conversation with her. Mrs. Moore liked to chat and involve herself in people's business. She was better than a burglar alarm; she phoned the police at the slightest intimation of something amiss. Three weeks ago, when she saw two young men skulking along the alley, she'd called the police and a roaming patrol car had stopped the two men for questioning. They had been carrying gloves, screwdrivers, and masking tape in their bag. They claimed they were apprentice carpenters. They found it slightly more difficult to explain the dozen twists of silver paper containing heroin and an assortment of credit cards in different names in the same bag. A local police officer had called to personally thank Mrs. Moore for her assistance. Since then Mrs. Moore had assumed the role of security guard for the building. Stephanie made a note to get her a nice Christmas present. She should probably get presents for everyone in the building: the young couple who were expecting a baby, and the old man in number four who always reeked of marijuana.

Stephanie opened the left door to number 8 and climbed the stairs to her apartment. She immediately hit the button on the answering machine and listened to the messages as she unpacked the few groceries she'd picked up on her way home. Robert always teased her because she had a classic bachelor's fridge: beer, wine, yogurt, and salsa. But she rarely ate there—snacked, breakfasted, lunched certainly, but she'd never cooked a full meal in the oven. That's why God had invented the microwave.

"Stef . . . this is your mother. Are you there? Why aren't you there?"

Stephanie pulled open the fridge and added the half gallon of soy milk to the empty tray in the door, alongside the half-empty carton of pure orange juice and an unopened bottle of Pinot Grigio. She hated when people called her Stef.

"You're probably out enjoying yourself. . . ."

Stephanie shook her head in resignation. She knew where the lecture was going. Her mother, if anything, was consistent in her nagging.

"I was just checking to make sure that you were not going to come home for Christmas. . . ."

Stephanie added a container of Greek yogurt to the fridge. She had told her mother at least a dozen times that she'd be staying in Boston for Christmas. One year—just one—she had made the mistake of returning to the family home in Wisconsin for the holiday, and every year thereafter her mother had phoned and put pressure—subtle and not too subtle—on her to come again.

"All your brothers and sisters will be here. Your cousins too."

Stephanie Burroughs had grown up in Madison, Wisconsin, the daughter of a college professor and a high school teacher. The family was staunchly Catholic, and the seven children, four boys and three girls, had grown up in a four-bedroom house, in a Catholic neighborhood, living a quiet, respectable version of the American dream. There was only a twelve-year age difference between the oldest, Bill, and the youngest, Joan. Stephanie fell more or less in the middle of the group and had somehow managed to avoid the cliques, pairings, and groups that form in any large family. That had left her feeling slightly distant from the rest of her extended family, who seemed to spend an inordinate amount of time living in one another's pockets. She had always felt like the outsider, which had actually made it easier to leave home and move away, first to New Jersey, then up and down the East Coast. She was also the first member of the family to own a passport and was now, at the ripe old age of thirty-three, the last one left unmarried. Billy was on his third wife, much to their mother's disgust.

"Your father went online last night and discovered some last-minute flight bargains. If there's a problem with money, you know he will send it on to you...."

Stephanie poured herself a glass of water from the Brita pitcher and shook her head. Including salary, bonuses, and expense account, she earned about two hundred thousand dollars a year. She—and the bank—had just purchased this condo; she owned her own car, had weekly massages, ate out regularly, had a premium gym membership, and went to the theater and movies whenever she wanted. She flew business class and was probably the most successful and financially secure of all of the Burroughs children, and yet somehow Toni still thought of her daughter as a secretary or a lowly researcher earning a pittance. Also, because she was not married with at least one child, Stephanie knew her mother was seriously worried about her. Being the only unmarried Burroughs was one notch lower on the totem pole than her gay brother Jack, who had caused uproar in the family when he had come out three years earlier. But even Jack had a partner and a newly adopted kid from Haiti. And as soon as she had met her newest granddaughter, Toni Burroughs had "forgiven" her son for being gay. But she still hadn't forgiven Stephanie for being single. Or given up on finding her a potential mate. The last time Stephanie had been home—Thanksgiving—Toni had arranged for a string of young and eligible and not-so-young and even less eligible men to troop through the house in a somewhat macabre parade. To appease her mother, Stephanie had gone on one date with a computer programmer, and even half a bottle of chardonnay hadn't saved her from one of the dullest evenings of her life.

"It would be lovely to see you. Maybe if you ask nicely, your bosses would give you a little extra time off. Tell them you'll make it up to them in the New Year."

Stephanie still had ten vacation days left to take out of this year's allocation. She was going to try and carry them forward into the New Year. If she could persuade Robert to take a few days off, she might take him back to the Midwest, and they could travel out to Madison to meet her parents. She stopped, suddenly struck by the thought. Meeting the parents: That was a very formal thing to do. She knew they would both adore him—a successful businessman. They might have an issue with the sixteen-year age difference, but she was a big girl and she knew what she was doing. Didn't she? But you only introduced a partner to your parents if you were serious about him. And then she smiled, and her face lit up. She was serious about him—then the smiled faded slightly—and becoming increasingly serious as time went by.

"Well, call me if you get a chance, but I guess you're too busy. You might call on Christmas Eve. All the family will be here, your brothers and sisters and their spouses and all of the grandchildren. We'll have a full house here. . . ."

Here it comes, Stephanie thought, and mouthed the words along with her mother.

"*. . . All except you, of course.*"

Stephanie lay back in the thick-foaming bubble bath and pressed her cell to her ear as she repeated the conversation to her best friend. "So then she said, 'We'll have a full house here, all except you of course.' Talk about emotional blackmail!"

Izzie laughed. "My mother is exactly the same. Mothers the world over are the same. I'm sure they go to Mommy School and take lessons."

Stephanie lifted her leg out of the water and allowed the bubbles to run down her smooth skin. Putting the claw-foot tub into the condo had been outrageously expensive, but money very well spent. After a long day on her feet, even the best shower couldn't compete with a hot bath. "But you know what, I was actually tempted. It would be fun to go home, be with all the family again. See all of my nieces and nephews. Plus, I'm really conscious that both Mom and Dad are getting older."

"Well, why don't you?" Izzie asked, seriously. There was a sharp intake of breath, and Stephanie clearly heard the crackle of cigarette paper burning. She could just visualize Izzie standing outside a bar somewhere, drink in one hand, cigarette in the other. Even though Izzie was a successful surgeon, she still had all of the bad habits of their undergraduate days at Princeton.

"Why don't I what?"

"Get on a plane Christmas Eve and surprise everyone? Don't tell anyone you're coming. Just turn up."

"I couldn't!"

"What's stopping you?" Izzie asked sharply. "I bet your mother would be thrilled to see you."

"I'm sure she would."

"And you said yourself, one of these Christmases will be their last."

"I know. I don't like to think about it, but it's true."

"But . . . ?" Izzie prompted.

"But what about Robert?" Stephanie squeezed her eyes shut as soon as she mentioned her lover's name. She knew what was coming.

"Oh, yes, Robert," Izzie said coldly, and Stephanie could just see her sucking hard on that cigarette. "Let's see. Hmmm, I wonder where Robert will be? Gosh, let me think about it for a millisecond. Oh, I know: Robert will be at home with his wife and children. Like he was last year and the year before that, like he will be next year and the year after that."

Stephanie sat up and reached for the glass of Pinot Grigio perched on the edge of the tub. "You really don't like him, do you?" she said brightly, trying to avoid another argument with Izzie over Robert.

"Not much. No."

"He really is a nice man. You just have to give him a chance. One of these days I'm going to get you two together."

"Oh, I'm sure he's a wonderful man, pats dogs, kisses babies, helps old people cross the street, recycles, donates blood, pays his taxes, gives money to charity, and makes his wife breakfast in bed . . . while he's lying to her, of course."

Stephanie sighed.

"I'm sorry," Izzie said immediately. "Look, I don't want to have a fight with you. I just don't want to see you sitting home on Christmas Eve hoping for an hour with Robert, and then waiting in all day Christmas Day for a visit that will never happen. That's all."

"I know." Stephanie sighed. And she did know. She remembered last Christmas; she had never felt so lonely, so lost, so alone in all her life. She had ordered in Chinese food and watched a James Bond movie marathon, clasping the phone in her hand for most of the day, willing it to ring . . . which it never did. "I know you're right. God, I feel so pathetic. I do need to talk to him. I can't go through that again this year."

"Better do it soon, sweetie—less than a week to go to the big day," Izzie advised.

"Tomorrow night. We're having dinner. I'll talk about it with him over dinner."

"Okay then. What are your plans for tonight?"

"Absolutely none. I took a half day, then walked my feet off looking for a present for Robert, and I still haven't really found him anything. What are you getting Dave?"

"A leather jacket, impossible to get tickets for the Celtics against the Lakers, and the *Star Wars* DVD boxed set on Blu-ray. He'll probably want to watch them all in one day. He's nothing but a big kid. I also got him the hardback Stieg Larsson books in a boxed set."

"You're lucky; at least Dave reads. Robert isn't interested."

"Your Robert is a peculiar fish," Izzie agreed. "I have to admit, I don't really trust people who don't read. I'm always uncomfortable if I go to a house that doesn't have books. People who don't read . . ." Stephanie braced herself for another diatribe, but then Izzie suddenly said, "Gotta go, Dave's here. Talk to you tomorrow."

She hung up, and Stephanie clicked off her own phone. She was sure there had been a distinct tone of sarcasm in Izzie's voice when she used the phrase "your Robert." Because of course, he was not "her" Robert; he was someone else's Robert.

Izzie and Robert still hadn't met; Stephanie was deliberately keeping them apart. Izzie made no secret of her dislike for Robert; he was a married man who was playing around. She'd been tough on Stephanie too, reminding her how stupid she was for getting involved with someone like him. The two women had fought, and Stephanie's relationship with Robert had almost cost them their friendship. Finally, she came to her senses and realized that Izzie was just looking out for her, trying to save her friend from what she saw as inevitable pain and heartache.

And Stephanie had been stupid; she knew that. She'd broken one of her own long-standing rules: Don't get between another woman and her man. There were plenty more men out there. But not like Robert; Robert was different.

Stephanie leaned forward to add more hot water to the bath. She tossed in bath salts she'd just gotten from her Secret Santa at the office party, and the slightly spicy odor of green tea permeated the damp air. She stretched out in the bath, resting her head back on the foam pillow. Over her right shoulder a short fat candle guttered out. In its original layout the condo had come with a power shower but no bath. Before she'd moved in, Stephanie had brought in a team of interior designers to reconfigure part of the second bedroom and incorporate it into the bathroom, effectively taking a corner off the unused bedroom and creating a larger bathroom. She'd gone for a country estate look for the room: An antique-style freestanding bathtub, treated to look like copper, stood in the center of the terracotta floor, and while hand-painted tiles covered three of the walls, the fourth was covered with a trompe l'oeil mural that gave the impression of a door opening out onto a Tuscan landscape. She had even had a skylight installed directly over the bath, so she could look up at the stars on clear evenings. When she'd had a particularly stressful day, she'd fill the bath almost to the brim with the hottest water she could tolerate, add bubble bath or Dead Sea salts, light some candles, and just lie back and stare at the sky. Within moments, she could feel the tensions and anxieties of the day floating away.

The irony was, of course, when she'd first met Robert six years earlier, she hadn't really liked him. He wasn't especially handsome, he was incredibly arrogant and brusque to the point of rudeness, and he seemed very much under the thumb of his wife and Maureen, the old dragon of a secretary who ran the company.

She'd been aware even then that relations had been strained between Robert and his wife. He had been very careful not to say anything directly about it, but she had picked up enough by what he said, and how he said it. She learned more by simply listening to Kathy and Maureen talk about him; it was obvious that neither woman respected him and, as time went by, she started to feel sorry for him.

Stephanie had been brought in to do the research for what seemed like a simple premise for a TV show, *One Hundred Years Ago on This Day*—events from the last century presented as if they were contemporary news pieces, but with a strong Americana flavor. It should have been a straightforward gig, but the pieces had to be intensively researched, and every fact had to be spot-on because R&K Productions was hoping to sell the series, and there was talk of a DVD and a companion book. The problem was the number of programs: They had secured a twelve-week run on the Discovery Channel, five days a week, which came to sixty programs. The more she researched, the more difficult she found it to find interesting news for every day one hundred years ago. The past could be boring too, and some days nothing really happened. The other problem was that Robert couldn't afford to get another researcher, so she was absolutely swamped. That was when they had first started working together, traveling all across the country, trying to guerrilla shoot the segments on site. She had really gotten to know him on those trips and was surprised to discover that beneath the bluster and the arrogance was a clever and sensitive man who had traded dreams of directing important and worthy documentaries in return for putting bread on the table and setting up college funds for his children.

Eventually, she ended up practically producing the series herself: researching and writing the scripts, then finding the pictures and archive footage to match the words. Robert was so impressed with her work that he gave her on-screen credit as writer and producer and took the executive producer role for himself. The screen credit had, in so many ways, kicked off her own career and, for that, she would be forever grateful.

He had been her first real mentor.

She hadn't had the slightest romantic or sexual interest in Robert then. She'd just been coming out of a relationship with a minor league baseball player who was as poor as a church mouse when he was with her and had allowed her to pay for everything, but as soon as he left, had signed a multimillion-dollar contract with the Colorado Rockies. Nowadays she saw him on the back and front pages of the tabloids practically every other week having committed another gaffe either on or off the field, and considered that she'd had a very lucky escape.

The gig with R&K had ended suddenly too; she remembered that. With still three weeks left on her contract, Robert had called her into the office on a Monday morning . . . no, Tuesday; it was just after a long weekend. He had given her three weeks' salary, plus a bonus of an extra two weeks' pay, and had told her she was to finish up that day. He had never given any explanation, and it wasn't until years later, when she and Robert had become an item, that she discovered Kathy had accused her husband of having an affair with her.

Talk about the shape of things to come.

With the two weeks' unexpected bonus, she'd gone on a trekking tour through Spain, where she had met a young woman who worked as a researcher on breakfast-time TV in Britain. They had exchanged addresses, and six weeks later Stephanie had moved to London and was working on *BBC Breakfast,* first as a researcher, then, when it was discovered that she had credits for *One Hundred Years,* as associate producer. She stuck at that for a year before joining one of the largest advertising agencies in the world. Again, it was through a fortuitous meeting: Charles Flintoff, the head of the agency, was a guest of *BBC Breakfast,* and had been impressed by her professionalism. He had offered her a job on the spot and she had accepted. She had returned to the States and rented a beach-front apartment in Miami just blocks from her new job and spent a couple of years honing her skills at the agency.

Life was full of small instances, little moments when a simple decision had extraordinary consequences years down the road. If she had not taken the job as researcher with R&K, she would not have gone to Spain, would not have gotten the job on breakfast-time television, would not have met Charles and gotten her position in Miami that eventually returned her to Boston, and back into Robert's world.

She'd been in the city less than a week when she bumped into Robert. They'd chatted about old times, then gone for a drink, in the Penalty Box of all places: not exactly the most romantic pub in Boston. But that drink had led to dinner a few nights later. She often wondered if that was when the affair really began, with that single drink in the Penalty Box.

The irony of the bar's name did not escape her.

CHAPTER 34

Stephanie stood in the kitchen, wrapped in her flannel robe, waiting for the microwave to ping. A low-calorie, low-sodium, low-taste excuse for a meal spun slowly behind the glass. "Instant Meal," it said on the package; that meant it took eight minutes to cook, including standing time, which she now knew really translated as the time you spent standing in front of the microwave. Her freezer was filled with a variety of frozen healthy meals; the only thing they had in common was the tagline "Dinner for one."

Advertised loneliness in a box.

Her cell rang, and she automatically opened the microwave door before she realized what she was doing. She'd left her phone on top of the counter. Grinning, she snatched it up and glanced at the screen, seeing the three *X*'s she used instead of Robert's name, and felt her insides physically shift.

"Hi."

She put her dinner in the microwave, shut the door, and set the timer. There was a crackle of static, and she moved away from the microwave. "I was going to call you later. I'm really missing you tonight."

She heard movement on the other end of the line, the signal dipping in and out. She wondered where he was now, what he was doing, what he was wearing.

"I know. I miss you too," Robert said quietly.

She could tell immediately by the tone of his voice that he was at home. He always spoke to her in softer tones there, as if he was afraid of being overhead.

"I was working on the DaBoyz pitch. Then I decided to get away before traffic got too awful."

"How's it coming?" The DaBoyz contract was the biggest job she had so far managed to send his way and the one she had the most doubts about. He'd never shot a pop video before, and although she was sure he could, she was beginning to regret having recommended him. She left the kitchen and wandered into the living room, curling up on the sofa.

"Good, I think."

"You can do it. I know you can."

"I hope so."

She heard it then, the self-doubt in his voice. "Of course you can. It'll be a new direction for the company." She wondered who she was trying to convince. This was DaBoyz' last chance. They were on the verge of splitting up, and their manager, Eddie Carson, looked as if he was going to take one of the boys under his wing and manage him as a solo artist and dump the rest. It was a classic move in the music industry. Create a band like *NSYNC, find the breakout star like Justin Timberlake, and then navigate him on his own trajectory to stardom while the remaining band members are lucky to find a slot in the sixth or seventh season of a bad reality TV show. "Do one good pop video, and you'll be the next big thing. All the bands will flock to your door."

"You're right. I know you're right. Thanks again for getting me the pitch meeting."

He sounded flat, beaten. She'd come to recognize the signs; he'd fought with Kathy. There was a time when she had thought he was simply a coward, unwilling or unable to stand up to his wife. More recently, she'd understood that he didn't fight with her because he hated upsetting her. It had been a shocking revelation, because it begged the question: Did he still have feelings for Kathy? He said he didn't, but . . .

"What's wrong?" she asked gently.

"Nothing."

"Yes, there is. I know there is."

"How can you tell?"

She forced herself to keep her tone light and bantering. She needed him positive and focused on the meeting in the morning. "Short sentences. When you're tired or bothered, you reply to me in short, staccato sentences."

"You and your Ivy League education," Robert joked.

"Nothing to do with Princeton. 'The Interpretation of One's Lover's Moods' was never covered in Contemporary Literary Theory. So what's bothering you?"

"Oh, the usual. I'm just tired. It's been a long day."

"And Kathy?" she pressed.

There was a long moment of silence, then he said, "She's not great. I saw her taking some pills; I think she may be coming down with something."

Stephanie opened her mouth to respond, but closed it tightly without saying a word. He knew there was a problem in his marriage, but he refused to face it, and, more important, deal with it. He always made excuses for her: Kathy fought with him because she was tired, because she was ill, because she was upset. When was he going to realize that maybe she fought with him because it was the only form of communication open to her?

"You think I'm making excuses for her, don't you?" he snapped, his quick touch of temper surprising her. "I'm sorry. I shouldn't have said that," he added immediately in a much more conciliatory tone. "I'm tired. Yes, there were a few words this evening. But only to do with Christmas. It's the pressure of the season."

It was the opening she was looking for. "Am I going to get to see you over Christmas?" she asked. If he said no, then she might very well book that flight back home and surprise the family. It might be nice to have a family Christmas, especially when considering the lonely alternative. And at least if she went back to Wisconsin, it would be neither lonely nor quiet. It would be loud and joyous, with lots of shouting, crying, arguments, and food. Lots and lots of food. She'd go sledding with her nieces and nephews; her mother would bring out the photo albums; her father would set up the old slide projector, and the entire family would gather around to laugh and cry at the old photographs. She found herself nodding; suddenly home was beginning to look very attractive.

"Of course you will," he said quickly.

"Any idea when?"

"Well, I'll see you on Christmas Eve. Give you your present. And then probably the day after Christmas."

"So I won't see you Christmas Day?"

"No, not on Wednesday, Christmas Day. But the day after. Actually, no, shit, not the day after, scratch that."

"What's wrong with Thursday?" So, she wouldn't see him Wednesday or Thursday; maybe if she went online now she'd be able to book a ticket. Logan to General Mitchell Airport direct would be good, and she could rent a car and drive to Madison. There were bound to be seats left, even if they were middle seats in coach—her idea of hell. The microwave pinged, and she uncurled from the sofa to return to the kitchen.

"We always have dinner with Kathy's sister Julia on Boxing Day. Her husband's British. It's a tradition."

"Oh. A tradition." Spending Christmas with loved ones was also a tradition, she thought, but resisted the temptation to say it aloud. "I remember you did that last year. And, I'm pretty sure you said then it was going to be the last one you went to." She juggled the hot container out onto a plate and peeled back the melting plastic top with a fork to allow steam to escape. The faint aroma of Indian spices filled the kitchen.

"I think I say that every year."

"Do you enjoy it?"

"No."

"So, given the choice, dinner with your sister-in-law or spending time with me, what would it be?"

"No contest. Spending time with you," he said immediately.

"Then do it." But even as she was saying it, she knew that he was going to find a problem with the suggestion.

"It's not that easy."

"It is if you want it to be."

"You know I want it to be."

And suddenly she was tired of the sparring. She had to accept that she was not going to see him on those two days; this was part of the price of dating a married man.

"I know you do. I'm sorry. I shouldn't pressure you. I guess I'm tired too. I'm seeing you tomorrow though?"

"Actually, that's what I wanted to talk to you about. I double booked. I've got Jimmy Moran lined up for dinner tomorrow night. I'm really sorry. Blame it on the situation in the office. I thought Maureen had canceled him, and Illona never thought to check. I'm sorry."

"It's no problem." She was pleased she managed to keep her voice even and disguise her disappointment. "These things happen. Any sign of Maureen coming back?"

"January. Maybe. I sent her a few e-mails but she cannot—or will not—give me a straight answer."

"You need to start thinking with your head rather than your heart on this one," Stephanie suggested. "And if you do manage to get the pop video gig, do you want someone who looks like a glamorous granny at the front desk or do you want a gorgeous young European?"

"Well, since you put it that way . . ."

"This business is all about first impressions. Come on, Robert. Who do you want to be the face of your company, Maureen or Illona?"

"You're right. I know you're right." He sighed. "But I don't feel good letting Maureen go before Christmas."

"You're too soft," Stephanie murmured. "Though I usually change that," she added quickly, her voice raw and husky, catching him off guard.

"You're bold!"

"Sometimes. So I won't see you tomorrow at all?"

"I've got the pitch in the morning, then dinner in the evening."

"Wanna have a sleepover after dinner?"

"Maybe," he said coyly.

"Maybe." She laughed, the sound high and light. "Just maybe?"

"Would it be worth my while?" he asked.

"Absolutely," she promised.

"I'll see what I can do."

"You do that," she said, and hung up. She carried her *mattar paneer* dinner back into the living room. She hit the remote control on the arm of the chair, and the CD clicked on. Medwyn Goodall's appropriately named *Timeless* filled the air. She loved the simple, ethereal music. She concentrated on the gently lilting guitars and mechanically ate the dinner for one, trying unsuccessfully not to rerun the conversation she'd just had.

Izzie was right. Izzie was always right when it came to men. Her friend had one rule: no married men. Although Izzie was close to getting engaged to her current boyfriend, she had had scores of boyfriends in the fifteen years Stephanie had known her, but none of them had been a married man. Izzie even tried to keep her casual friendships with married or attached men to an absolute minimum. When Stephanie teased that platonic relationships were possible, Izzie laughed at her, claiming that sooner or later platonic eventually drifted into sexual, and once sex entered a friendship, then everything changed.

It had certainly changed for Stephanie when she and Robert went to bed together. The sexual tension had been building for a while. She had recognized what was happening a long time before he did. In those early days together, they would visit sites across New England, "scouting locations" they called it, and walk and talk together. She'd learned a lot about him on those walks, about the young man he'd been, full of dreams and plans and hopes for the future, and she'd learned even more about the man he'd become, with no real plan and a lot of broken dreams, trapped in a loveless marriage, and with a job that was slowly spiraling into the ground.

The first time they had made love had been . . . extraordinary. He had been passionate and gentle, fearful of hurting her, terrified of letting go, and afterward he had wept. She had never been entirely sure why; he had told her it was because he was happy and hadn't, until that moment, known he'd been unhappy beforehand. But she wasn't entirely sure if she believed him.

She had never believed she was taking him away from a loving wife. He was always incredibly loyal to Kathy, and never said anything against her, but from the scraps of information she had picked up on their walks and talks, she'd come to understand that a great gulf had opened between them. If there had been no children, they might have split up and gone their separate ways, but their relationship was wrapped around house and home, the kids and the business. It was complicated.

When he was with Stephanie, he acted like a single man and Stephanie treated him like one.

They made love because they wanted to; she didn't feel guilty, and neither did he. He was an old-fashioned and unimaginative lover, but he was considerate, and she enjoyed the physical aspect of their relationship. She especially loved waking in his arms, feeling the warmth and comfort of them around her.

Stephanie pushed away the plate; she hadn't tasted a single mouthful. She climbed slowly to her feet and carried the plate out to the kitchen where she dropped it into the sink. She knew she should wash it now, but a growing, numbing exhaustion crept over her, and all she wanted to do was to climb into bed and sleep. The CD had finished, and the condo was still and silent. She moved through the rooms, checking that the doors were locked and the lights were off. She recognized what was happening. It had taken her a long time to put a name to the emotion she was now feeling, and when she had, it had both surprised and frightened her. She felt lonely. So incredibly lonely.

It was an emotion she had not experienced in a long time. She had always been resilient, confident, and self-sufficient. She was always in control, needing no one, wanting no one in her life.

And then she had met Robert, and everything changed.

With him, she learned the meaning of loneliness.

These moments, she called them blue notes, happened occasionally when she wanted to have Robert around and, for various reasons, he couldn't be there. She was experiencing the blue notes much more frequently lately. The problem was she'd gotten used to having Robert around, to having him in her life. It had been easier, so much easier, when she'd been alone.

Then, she hadn't known what she was missing from her life. And she wasn't just talking about a man—she despised that nonsense that a woman needed a man to make her complete. She was talking about a partner, a lover, a friend. In the beginning it had been nothing but sex. It had just been a game. But the game had turned serious when she fell in love with him.

If only she could be sure that he loved her. He said he did.

But did she believe him?

CHAPTER 35

Friday, 20th December

The loud ringing of the phone woke her out of a deep and dreamless sleep. She scrambled blindly for it, almost knocking it off the table.

"Hello?"

"Good morning, gorgeous."

Recognizing Robert's voice, she pushed herself into an upright position and discovered that the bedclothes were in a knotted heap on the floor. When she slept alone she tossed and turned, but when Robert was in bed with her, she remained still and unmoving throughout the night. She squinted at the clock, trying to make sense of the digits. "My God, what time is it?"

"Ten past eight. Wake up, sleepyhead! I thought you'd be on the way into the office."

"I'm going in later. I had a late call with Beijing last night; the thirteen-hour time difference is a killer."

The call had come in around midnight, shocking her from a deep sleep. It was her newest client, a rising techno company that was a needy, albeit lucrative account. Stephanie was available to them 24-7. After the call, she had not been able to get back to sleep until the early hours of the morning, and all the time she'd been wishing, desperately, that Robert were there with her, not to make love, just to hold her.

She was aware that Robert was speaking to her, and abruptly his half-heard words leapt out at her. "Speaking of calls, there was a message from Carson on my answering machine this morning; he wants to rearrange the appointment. Shouldn't be a problem."

She shook her head and rubbed the heels of her hands into her eyes. Her intuition and business acumen were telling her that something was wrong. "Tell me what he said, exactly what he said."

"Well, he just said . . . Actually, hang on a second and I'll play you the message." She heard him walking across the room, then a click as he hit the Play button on his answering machine.

"You have no new messages. You have two old messages."

She heard the high-pitched squeal of a voice as Robert fast-forwarded through another message, then suddenly Eddie Carson's smug voice came clearly down the line.

"Good morning, Robert, Eddie Carson, DaBoyz Management, here. I understand from Stephanie that you start early. Will you give me a call as soon as you get in? I'll need to rearrange our appointment."

Stephanie shook her head in astonishment. Eddie tried the same trick with just about everyone he worked with.

"That's it," Robert said cheerfully. "It's not a problem. Obviously, I'll clear my calendar to see them, you know that."

"It is a problem," she snapped. "This is just bullshit. I told Carson we were lucky to get you. Call him back and do not—do you hear me—do not allow him to rearrange the appointment. You've got to show this little bastard who's boss; otherwise he'll walk all over you."

"It really isn't a problem—" Robert began.

"Just do as I say," she ordered. "Be tough with him. Tell him you can meet this morning or not at all, then shut up and say nothing. Wait for his response." She hopped out of bed and went to stand by the window, looking down over the courtyard. Mrs.

Moore was out sweeping dead leaves away from the front of the Victorian. Stephanie was getting sick and tired of Eddie Carson and his second-rate band.

"Okay," Robert said, but she could hear the doubt and indecision in his voice. Why couldn't he trust her? Because she was a woman and he was a man, and men always knew what they were doing in business? Bullshit. Stephanie had her finger on the pulse of the industry, and while she loved Robert, he was considered a dinosaur in a field in which rapidly evolving technology was dramatically changing the business. She had proved, time and time again, that she was right.

"Trust me on this. Do it now, and then phone me back."

"Yes, ma'am!"

She hung up. Carrying the phone in her hand, she headed into the bathroom and turned on the shower. It would be interesting now to see how Robert handled this; if he gave in to Carson, then the video would be a disaster, because Carson would effectively take charge. If Robert kept control of the DaBoyz manager, then there was still some hope for him.

But Stephanie also knew that Robert was so desperate for business that he might very well give in to Carson. He'd be even more desperate if he discovered that this was the last job he was getting from her agency. She was already compromised. She just wasn't sure how badly.

The recent Skype conversation she'd had with her boss, Charles Flintoff, had been very strained. This was the man who'd found her on breakfast-time TV and had offered her a job on the basis of a half-hour meeting. He'd mentored her, and she'd proven to be an excellent student. She got the feeling that he regarded her almost like a daughter—he had three of his own, none of whom were following him into the business—and she, in turn, was incredibly fond of him. He had heard a whisper in the trade about her involvement with Robert, and had Skyped her immediately to ask her straight out for an answer. For a single instant, she'd been tempted to lie to him and deny the rumor, but instead had opted for the truth. She respected Charles, and the truth had probably saved her job. Charles had once told her that he only ever asked questions he knew the answer to.

The other thing in her favor was that the few small jobs she'd sent Robert's way had been competitively priced, and he'd delivered the goods. Charles had made no comment about the fact that Robert was married, but he had advised Stephanie that she had compromised the agency by becoming involved with a subcontractor. She admitted that when she was giving Robert the work, she'd never thought about that. "Love can be blind," Charles said, "but infatuation can be stupid." If she wanted to remain with the company, she had a choice: She could either break up with Robert or refrain from giving him any more business. She had to do one or the other, and although he didn't say it, she got the distinct impression that Charles would prefer if she did both. She gave Charles Flintoff an assurance that she would not allow R&K to pitch for any further business and that if they did pitch, she would not consider them. "Then, we can consider the matter closed," Flintoff said in his avuncular, cut-glass British accent. "There's no need to revisit it." Stephanie knew he would never mention it again, but even on the computer screen, she could see the disappointment in his face and knew also that her credibility with the man had been damaged. She was going to have to work hard to restore it.

Stephanie wondered how Robert was going to react when he discovered that he was not going to get any more business out of her agency. She knew he was counting on her putting more business his way in the coming year. He'd even, rather arrogantly she thought, created a budget based upon that premise. She decided she would break the news to him sometime in January. Let him enjoy his Christmas.

Stephanie stared at herself in the mirror. Her hair was wild and her eyes were bloodshot after her disturbed night. The flesh on her face was sagging and creased with pillow-marks. She stepped back and looked at herself critically: Her body was in relatively good condition, her breasts were still more or less firm, stomach reasonably flat, but she was losing the battle with cellulite on her thighs. What exactly did Robert see in her, she wondered? What had attracted him to her? . . . Could it be for the business she brought his company? The thought was nasty and spiteful, but it was not the first time it had occurred to her.

Her phone rang.

"You were right." She could hear him smiling on the other end of the phone. "What would I do without you?"

"Let's hope you never have to find out."

CHAPTER 36

"I like him," Eddie Carson said, voice crackling and distorted as it came through her hands-free phone system in the BMW.

Stephanie was looking for a place to park and was tracking a pedestrian walking down Charles Street with car keys jangling in his hand. Was he walking to his car or away from it? "I knew you'd like him, Eddie," she said brightly. "Plus he's a new face, with new ideas, so you can be sure you'll get something different, a new look, for the band."

"Yeah, yeah, he had some good stuff, some nice ideas." Carson sounded bored.

"You didn't try to change the time of the appointment this morning, Eddie, did you?"

"Would I do that, Miss Burroughs?" Eddie Carson asked innocently.

"Absolutely."

The pedestrian stopped beside a blue Prius and climbed in. Stephanie pulled right up beside the car, signal light ticking. The trick now was to make sure that no one stole her space.

"It's a game, Stef; you just got to play the game. But this new boy, this Roger . . ."

"Robert," she corrected him.

"Robert. Yeah, he seems to know the rules. I understand you know him . . . personally." The leer in his voice was clearly audible.

The Prius showed no sign of moving. Stephanie ground her teeth. "What are the chances of DaBoyz breaking up?" she asked, not answering his question, keeping him off-balance. If he wanted to play games, she could play just as well—better—than he ever could.

"None. I'm drip-feeding the press the story myself. The single isn't going to make number one for Christmas, which is a shame, but if Roger . . ."

"Robert."

"If Robert can shoot a good vid, we'll have a reasonable chance at the charts with the next single in the early spring."

Stephanie knew he was lying through his teeth. The new video would be released probably a week before the band announced they were going their separate ways for "creative reasons." The creative reasons being that only one of them could sing. The sympathy vote from the dwindling numbers of fans might push the single into the top five.

The Prius finally pulled out, and Stephanie nipped the BMW into the space. "Sounds good. You have a great Christmas, Eddie. I'll talk to you in the New Year."

"Same to you, Stef."

"And Eddie . . . don't let me read in the papers that the band's broken up. Let's get the video out first."

"Keen to show off your boyfriend's handiwork, eh?" Carson said and hung up before she could respond.

Stephanie nodded. He'd won that round.

"I told you." Stephanie strode around the office, having related an edited version of the conversation she'd just had with Eddie.

Robert was sitting behind his desk, staring intently at his monitor. "Your advice was absolutely spot-on," he said without looking up. "They turned up at ten on the dot. The boys were as good as gold, a little overawed by everything, and very much under Carson's thumb. He made all the creative decisions."

Stephanie fanned out the storyboards across the conference table. This was the first time she'd seen the finished presentation, and it looked great. Robert wanted to shoot the band's new single, "Heart of Stone," in the middle of the Haleakalā Crater in Maui. He was going to shoot in color, but treat the image, making it look black and white, giving the video a stark, minimalist look. She was reminded, looking at the neatly precise and original drawings he'd made of each frame, just how creative he was when he was given the opportunity. "These look very good, very exciting. Different. Dark and just a little exotic. Just what the band needs at the moment—it'll take them in a new direction."

"Carson was complimentary. Apparently everyone else was suggesting something light and bright and fluffy with tween appeal. He wants to take the band up into an older age range." Robert came to stand beside her and started shuffling the pages into order. "You'd think I'd been doing this all my life," he said. "Carson wanted a few changes."

"Of course he did. It's a power thing with him, like trying to change the time of the appointment this morning. I've seen him do that so often. He thinks he's managing U2, not just another cookie-cutter boy band. And if you hadn't called him on it, then he would have given you the runaround for the next couple of weeks. Even if you had gotten the gig, he would have interfered every step of the way." She smiled. "Hawaii was a good location choice. Everyone loves Hawaii."

Her voice trailed away. She was abruptly, erotically conscious that Robert was standing close—much too close—to her. She could feel the heat radiating from his body, and in that instant she wanted him, with a hungry, animal passion. She had to have him, in her arms, in her body. Watching his eyes, she saw the lust bloom in them and knew that he wanted her too. She wished that she were on the crater in Hawaii with him, making love as the sun came up over the beautiful landscape.

She smiled and raised her eyebrows a fraction, then glanced toward the open door to where the secretary was pretending to be busy with a catalogue, but was obviously listening in. Robert nodded imperceptibly and stepped into the outer office.

Stephanie fanned out the images again, vaguely aware that he was sending the Russian girl home. There was a great power and energy to the images, and if Robert managed to capture it on screen, it would make a stunning video. Undoubtedly, the best pop video the band had ever had. And it was going to be released a week before they broke up. With any luck someone would see it and commission Robert to do another one for another band. She was relieved too; Charles Flintoff could not help but be impressed.

"Good night, Miss Burroughs." The Russian girl's voice disturbed her thoughts.

"Good night," Stephanie called, without looking up. She didn't particularly like the Russian girl, didn't like the way she looked knowingly at her every time she came in. And there was also the doubt, just the tiniest insidious doubt that what had happened between her and Robert could just as easily happen between the Russian and Robert. It wasn't the first time the thought had struck her. Since Robert had betrayed his wife, Stephanie had lived with the awareness that he could just as easily betray her too, which really begged the question: Did she trust him?

And it bothered her—bothered her tremendously—that she could not answer yes to that question.

"I think she suspects . . . ," Robert began, walking back into the office.

"Who cares?" Stephanie said. "She's a receptionist." Then she caught Robert by his lapels and pulled him toward her, tilting her head and pressing her lips against his. The need for him was a physical hunger, shocking and surprising in its intensity.

She pulled him back against the conference table, kissing him deeply as his fingers fumbled at the buttons of her blouse. She lifted herself up onto the table and pushed him away from her, giving her time to shrug out of her jacket and toss it on a chair. She undid the buttons on her blouse as Robert pulled urgently at his shirt. His button broke away, pinged off the table, and skipped across the room.

She was the one who usually initiated their lovemaking. The

first time they had made love, she had been forced to make the first move, letting him know that she was available. She remembered feeling a sick queasiness in the pit of her stomach that first time she had stood naked before him, waiting for him to take her or reject her, wondering why he hadn't come on to her sooner.

Later, much later in their relationship, she'd come to realize that he'd simply fallen out of the habit of initiating lovemaking. Later still he'd admitted to her that he and Kathy hadn't made love for a very long time. In the last few years when he had tried to initiate lovemaking with his wife, she was always too tired, and he felt she was rejecting him. He had simply gotten into the habit of not trying, because the rejection hurt.

Stephanie had promised that she'd never reject him. She told him that if she did not want to make love, she would tell him openly, without pretending to be asleep or to have a headache or a stomachache. And she would always hold him. That, she discovered very quickly, was what he really wanted: to be held gently and quietly.

She spread herself naked on the table and watched in amusement as he hopped around on one leg, pulling off his socks. "Nice to see you're still interested in me."

"I thought we were discussing a contract," he murmured, approaching the table.

"We will. But first things first. Priorities are important." Her voice was husky with lust as she watched him undress. When he was completely naked, she opened her arms and lifted her legs. "And you are my priority. Now, where were we?" she whispered.

She turned around in the tiny shower and allowed the trickle of tepid water to roll off her body. He really should get the plumbing fixed in this building. It was the only drawback to making love in his offices. But at least she wasn't heading back to her office. The last time they'd made love here, she'd had to go back for a meeting that had lasted for the rest of the afternoon. She could smell him on her body for the rest of the day and imagined that the rest of the attendees could also.

She dried herself while Robert stepped into the shower. She was pleased to see that he'd started to take care of himself. When they'd first become an item, he'd been heading toward flab, with the beginnings of a paunch and with skin the color of old marble. She'd encouraged him to exercise, and he'd even joined her gym, and now they worked out together. She'd booked him in for a session in a tanning salon and had sent him to her dermatologist for a consultation about getting Botox injected in the deep worry lines in his forehead.

The shower died down, and Robert pushed the door open and stepped out.

Stephanie walked back into the tiny bathroom and stood provocatively in the doorway. "Will I see you later?" she asked. She was only wearing her light pink lace-trimmed bra and thong.

"I'm not sure. Do me a favor," he added, reaching for a towel. "Get dressed, please."

"Why?" she said innocently.

"Because if you don't I'll just have to have you again."

"Promises, promises." She stepped away from the door and started to dress. If she gave him any encouragement, he would make love to her again, and she loved that passion, that need he had for her. "What about tonight?" she asked again.

"Tonight's all screwed up. You know Jimmy and I were supposed to have dinner in the Prudential building at Top of the Hub? Well, I got Illona to phone to confirm the reservation. And it turns out there was none. And you know that place is impossible to get into, especially this time of year."

"What happened?"

Robert was standing beside her. He suddenly reached out and pinched her nipple. The touch sent an electric ripple straight through to the center of her groin. She caught his hand and pressed it against her skin; his flesh felt hot against her cool breasts. Then she lifted his fingertips to her lips and kissed them. She loved this man. Loved him.

And that thrilled her and terrified her in equal measure.

"I'm not sure whose error it was, Illona's or Maureen's." For a moment, she had no idea what he was talking about; then she realized he was continuing the conversation. It took a deliberate effort of will to come back on track. "Maureen's, I think. But that's not the point. I've got an old friend meeting me here in just over an hour, and I've no place to take him to dinner."

"It'll be difficult finding a posh place to eat this close to Christmas." She was still aroused, and there was a perceptible tremble in her voice, but she didn't think he noticed.

"I know. And Jimmy won't want to go far; he was talking about spending the night in his apartment in the North End."

Stephanie returned to the bathroom to repair her makeup. "Be upfront with him," she advised. It was the advice she tried to live her life by: Be truthful and honest with people.

And was her current situation with Robert truthful or honest? she was forced to ask herself. It was, she decided fiercely, because she loved him.

"You never know, maybe all he wants is to have drinks. If you get out relatively early, you might check out the Union Oyster House. They serve food at the bar, and they have the best oysters in town."

"Great idea."

"But that doesn't answer the question I asked earlier: Are you going to spend the night with me? Should I wait up?"

Robert popped his head around the door and grinned. "If I do spend the night, I'll be sleeping. You exhaust me."

Staring intently at the fogged-up mirror, she reapplied her lipstick. "If you can get to me before one o'clock, then come over, but if you're going to be any later, then forget it. Text me when you've got an idea what's happening."

"Good plan."

Robert stood back to examine her as she stepped out of the bathroom. "There is no way to tell that less than half an hour ago you were lying on this table making passionate love."

"I have absolutely no idea what you're talking about, Mr. Walker. I was closing a very important business deal." She leaned over and kissed him, brushing her lips against his, leaving the tiniest thread of Viva Glam red lipstick on his upper lip. "And I do like the way you close a deal," she added.

* * *

She checked her phone when she returned to the car. She had one missed call on her phone; it was from Izzie.

"Here's the plan," Izzie's chirpy voice said without preamble, voice dipping and crackling. "I got your message and understand that you are now unexpectedly free tonight. So am I. We can get dressed up and go out for drinks in a noisy bar filled with loud people we just want to smack, or I can come to your place with food. The menu for tonight is pizza with extra chillies, Chinese with extra chillies, or sizzling prawns in a hot and spicy sauce . . . and extra chillies. The luxurious repast is my treat, but the wine is up to you. And I promise not to smoke, either inside or outside the house."

Stephanie hit the second speed dial, which connected her with her friend. "Where are you?"

"I'm still at the hospital. I just finished rounds."

Stephanie could hear the sound of an ambulance and wasn't sure if it was coming through the phone or was in the neighborhood. She was one street away from Mass General. "I'm literally around the corner. I'll leave the car here and meet you at the Liberty Hotel, in Clink. We'll get a quick drink, then pick up the pizza. How does that plan grab you?"

"Sounds like a better plan."

CHAPTER 37

The moment she stepped into Clink restaurant at the Liberty Hotel, Stephanie knew it was a mistake. The bar was a mass of bodies, and she recognized half a dozen faces immediately. Naturally, most of the men in the bar had turned when she'd entered, so she now had no chance of slipping out unnoticed. She quickly lifted her phone to her face in an effort to discourage them from coming over to join her. She hit the speed dial.

"Where are you?" she asked in a singsong voice.

"Right beside you," came the immediate reply, and Stephanie jumped as Izzie Wilson materialized out of the crowd.

Stephanie leaned down to kiss her friend's cheek. Izzie Wilson was a year younger than her friend and at least six inches shorter. She was blond, her features all angles and planes. The two women were the exact opposites in just about every way possible, and they were closer than sisters.

"This might have been a mistake," Stephanie suggested.

"It might," Izzie agreed lightly, "but probably not the worst mistake we've ever made. We'll stay an hour, then head back to your place, and pick up some food on the way back."

Stephanie knew that the chances of escaping within the hour were slim, and while the last thing she wanted to do was to spend an evening in a noisy pre-Christmas bar, already the boisterous, happy atmosphere was starting to lift her spirits. Although she loved being with Robert, sometimes—particularly of late, when he'd been so panicked and under so much pressure—she came away from him feeling depressed and worn down, as if she had absorbed his negative mood.

"What are you having?"

"Glass of white wine would be perfect." She positioned herself beside the door and watched in admiration as Izzie battled her way, with a combination of charm, smiles, excuse-me's, and elbows, to the bar. A throng of men was standing at the bar with their money in their hands, desperately attempting to catch the bartender's eye, but Izzie was served immediately. Stephanie thought it might have something to do with the remarkably low-cut little black dress she was wearing. Izzie returned within minutes and handed Stephanie her glass. The two women silently toasted one another.

"I wasn't expecting you to be around with—with R&K after the conversation you had with Charles."

Stephanie shrugged uncomfortably. "Well, I suggested Robert for the pop video gig, so I've got to see that to its conclusion. But it will be the last job they get from us."

Izzie sipped her wine, leaving a bright pink lipstick mark on the rim of the glass. "Does he know?"

"Not yet. I was going to tell him this afternoon, but I decided not to ruin his Christmas. Besides," she added with a cheeky grin, "we got distracted."

"Distracted?"

"Distracted."

"Oh." Izzie stared at her friend. "You didn't . . . you haven't?" she asked in a horrified, yet fascinated, whisper.

Stephanie nodded happily. "In his office. This afternoon. On the boardroom table. It was fabulous. Always is."

"Always? You mean you've done it more than once in the office? You never told me."

"We've done it a couple of times. Besides, I don't ask you how often you make out with Dave."

"Not often enough is the answer. Wow; no wonder you're ditzy this evening. And I'm supposed to be the blonde, remember?" She sipped a little of her wine. "I've always wanted to do that with Dave in my office, but the only place is the on-call room, and that would feel too much like a bad television show."

"I thought you were going out with Dave tonight."

"He's working. He got a call this afternoon—one of the guys came down with this flu bug that's going around. He was grateful for the overtime." Dave was an EMT in the same hospital, a huge, hulking bear of a man who stood six three to Izzie's five three. He earned extra money on weekends by working the doors of some of Boston's toughest clubs. He took no shit from anyone except Izzie, who bullied him mercilessly.

Izzie waved at an unusually tall, spike-haired young man at the bar, who smiled and nodded back. "I fixed his anterior cruciate," she explained to Stephanie's raised eyebrow. "He just got picked up by the Celtics." Then, not looking at Stephanie, scanning the crowd, she added casually, "You know, I think he's going to propose this Christmas."

"The Celtics player?" Stephanie asked, deliberately misunderstanding.

"Dave!"

Izzie and Dave had been an item for three years now and had lived together for the past nine months. Stephanie toasted her. "Congratulations!"

Izzie turned away from the crowd and lifted her glass. "Oh, you know Dave. He's a big old ox. Likes to think he's being very subtle and casual. He kept taking off one of my rings a couple of weeks ago and trying it on his little finger. Thought I wouldn't notice or cop to what he was doing. And he's being very secretive lately, and if he's asked me once, he's asked me a dozen times what time I'll be home on Christmas Eve."

"And what'll you do if he asks you?"

"Say yes, I suppose."

"You suppose. I thought you loved him."

"I do love him. But is he the one?" Then Izzie shrugged. "How can you be sure if any of them are the one? I'll say 'yes' of course. I could do a lot worse."

"That sounds very enthusiastic," Stephanie said sarcastically. This was rich—coming from the woman who gave her relationship advice!

"I'm happy," Izzie admitted. "He's a good man and will make a great husband and a terrific father. Sure, he's still a kid himself. His mother will be thrilled; mine will be pleased; we'll have a fabulous wedding. What more can you expect these days?"

Stephanie shook her head. There should be more, shouldn't there?

A group of young women were gathering up their bags at one of the plush couches. One glanced at Stephanie and nodded toward the seat she was vacating, with a raised eyebrow. Stephanie raised her glass in reply, then caught Izzie's arm and began to maneuver her through the crowd toward the couch. "Thanks," she said as they swapped places with the girls, who swayed out into the night, trailing five distinct perfumes in their wake.

"Now you see, men would never do that," Izzie said. "That's one of major differences between the sexes; women look out for one another."

Stephanie wasn't so sure, but she didn't want to argue with her friend. "When do you think Dave will propose?" she asked.

"My money's on Christmas Eve, at midnight."

"Very romantic," Stephanie murmured, and it was very romantic. She wondered if she would ever be proposed to in such a romantic fashion.

"If he does propose—I'd like you to be my maid of honor."

Suddenly Stephanie's eyes were full of tears. The two women had always promised that they would be each other's maids of honor. She nodded; then, blinking furiously, she attempted a smile. "That means you'll have to be my matron of honor. If I ever get married," she added, surprised at the note of bitterness in her voice.

Izzie's face remained an expressionless mask, and she concentrated on her drink.

"You don't believe that he'll ever marry me, do you?"

"I could lie to you and say yes. But I won't do that. No, I don't believe he will. I think if you even push him for some sort of commitment, he's going to run a mile. They all do."

The crowd surged and swirled around them. In one corner someone attempted to sing "Jingle Bell Rock," but was quickly drowned out by the groans of the other drinkers.

"Why do you hate him?"

"Because he's going to hurt you. Because I've been hurt by men just like him, and I know what it's like."

"Robert is different from other men."

"Robert is a man. And all men are after one thing."

"He's not like that."

But Izzie was nodding. "He is. Look, we both know the real problem here is that you've fallen for him. That means you're not thinking straight."

"He loves me too," Stephanie said quickly.

"And how does he show that?"

"Oh, please don't start that again," Stephanie pleaded.

"Start what?" Izzie demanded. "I'm your oldest friend. Your closest friend. The first friend you made freshman year when you wore that ridiculous hat," she reminded her. "No one else would tell you how silly the hat looked."

"You did."

"That's because friends look out for one another. I'm merely telling you what I see. I see an older man sleeping with a younger woman, who happens to be able to bring in some extra business to his ailing company. I'm not saying that's the only reason he's with you, but I'm sure it's certainly an added bonus as far as he's concerned."

Stephanie bit the inside of her cheek to stop herself from snapping out a response that would bring the evening crashing into an argument. She also knew that Izzie was right; her friend was only saying what she'd been thinking herself.

"I don't see this ending well. I know you didn't set out to trap him or to lure him away from his family. I know you love him, and it's all wonderful and magical and you think you're rescuing him from an uncaring, unthinking, cruel wife . . . but you know something? Consider the source. Remember, everything you know about Kathy, you've learned from him."

"Well, some I picked up from the time I worked there," Stephanie said quickly, almost defensively.

"You saw one tiny aspect of their relationship for a very brief period of time six years ago. You cannot base your entire understanding of their marriage on that. No one truly knows what goes on in a marriage, except the couple themselves."

This was part of the ongoing argument the two women had over one another's boyfriends. Stephanie had very nearly persuaded Izzie to drop Dave, and now here he was, about to propose to her.

"What do you think I should do?" Stephanie asked miserably, because deep in her heart, she knew that her friend was right.

"You've been together for eighteen months; it's time for him to put up or shut up. Force him to make a decision. Make him choose. You or the wife. And you know something? You're really asking him to be fair to both of you, because right now, he's being neither fair nor truthful with either one of you. You're looking for commitment now, not vague promises for the future. And the best commitment he can give you now is to be with you on Christmas Day." Izzie paused and put down her drink. Then she took both of Stephanie's hands in hers and stared deep into her troubled eyes. "Is that unreasonable? No, it's not. Is it unfair? Sure, he may tell you it is, but you know something—it's not. What's unfair is leaving you dangling. What's unfair is lying to you."

Deep in her handbag, Stephanie's phone started to ring. She was almost grateful for the opportunity to break away from Izzie's savage intensity. It took her a few moments to locate the phone and snap it open.

"Hello?"

"Hi. Is this Becky?"

"No, you have the wrong number." She hung up, then sat for a moment looking around the bar, watching the various couples laughing, enjoying themselves, touching one another, holding hands, being close and intimate with one another, unafraid who was watching, not caring who saw them.

She wasn't able to do that with Robert. Not in Boston anyway. He was afraid that people would see. Afraid that they would tell Kathy, and then . . .

And then what?

What would happen if Kathy knew? What would she do?

"What are you thinking?" Izzie asked quietly.

Stephanie shook her head, and her smile was touched with pain. "I know you're right. All you've done is put in words what I've been trying to articulate." She leaned forward and kissed Izzie's cheek. "Thank you. I think I'm going to head home. Talk to Robert."

"What are you going to do?"

"Ask a question and demand an answer."

"And if you don't get one you like?"

"Then we're done."

CHAPTER 38

The phone buzzed as she turned onto Green Street. She glanced at the screen and was surprised to see the three *X*'s across it. "I was just about to call you," she began.

"Where are you?" Wind whipped away some of Robert's words.

"Heading home. I met Izzie for a drink at Clink. Is everything all right?"

"I'm not sure. I'll meet you at home. I'm just heading out of the North End; I left the car outside the office. It'll take me forty-five minutes."

"Robert...," Stephanie began, but the call ended, and she wasn't sure if it she'd lost the call or he'd deliberately ended it. He sounded—strange. Not drunk; Robert drank very little and, although she'd seen him tipsy, she'd never known him to be falling-down drunk.

Stephanie pulled the car in front of the house and climbed out. She didn't need to be a genius to guess that something must have happened during dinner with Jimmy.

"There you are, dear."

Stephanie jumped with fright as Mrs. Moore materialized out of the shadows. "You almost gave me a heart attack."

"That's no joking matter," Mrs. Moore said sternly. "A heart attack took my Frank."

"I wasn't joking," Stephanie said seriously.

Mrs. Moore looked over the bags in Stephanie's hands, then glanced into the car.

"Can I help you, Mrs. Moore?"

"Did the lady not catch up with you then?"

"What lady?"

"The lady with the Christmas present. She said she had to deliver it to you personally."

"And she had this address?"

"Yes. She had it on a sheet of paper."

That was odd; very few people had her home address. She directed just about everything to the office address. Possibly something from Robert . . . No, he'd give it to her himself. Then, it could only be something from home. Maybe that was it: a care package from her mother.

"I didn't get it. I'm sure it'll come tomorrow. Good night, Mrs. Moore," she said, moving past the older woman to put her key in the lock and push open the door.

She took a quick shower before Robert arrived. If the evening went anything like the other nights they'd spent together, he'd want a quick shower before they made love—and she had no doubts, despite his earlier reservations and protestations, that they would make love. They simply couldn't help it when they were together. Then they'd probably share a bath before falling asleep in one another's arms, and then wake early in the morning and do it all again. She grinned.

Before he went home to his wife.

The smile faded.

She had just climbed out of the shower and wrapped a towel around her head when she heard the doorbell. He had a key; why didn't he use it? She grabbed the first item out of the closet, her peach-colored silk robe, and pulled it on. The flimsy material immediately stuck to her damp body—but she didn't think that Robert would mind. She hurried downstairs to open the door.

"I really wasn't expecting you." And she hadn't been; she had thought he'd end up spending the night with Jimmy.

"There was a change of plans." He kissed her quickly, casually, and brushed past her into the apartment, and she knew then that something was definitely amiss. She could almost feel the tension and something else—anger?—vibrating off him.

"You look like you need a drink." She headed into the small kitchen, wondering if she had any whiskey in the apartment.

"Coffee, no alcohol." He came and stood in the door of the kitchen, arms folded across his chest, one foot in front of the other, ankles crossed. One didn't need to be an expert in body language to know that he was wound up as tight as a spring.

She pulled open the fridge. "Are you sure? I've got a nice Pinot chilling. . . ."

"I'd better not. I'm driving."

"You're not staying?" That shocked her; Robert usually took any excuse offered to spend the night with her.

"No, not tonight. I can't."

"That wasn't the initial plan." She smiled, trying to tease out what was wrong.

"The plan changed."

She turned back to the sink and poured water into the coffee-maker. Out of the corner of her eye, she saw him lean forward, and she realized that the front of her robe had gaped open, exposing her breasts. She started to close the robe.

"Don't," he pleaded.

She smiled, knowing then that everything was going to be all right. "You've seen them before."

"The day I get tired of looking at them is the day I'm dead."

"Tell me what happened?" she said softly, allowing the robe to remain open. "I presume it's something to do with Jimmy, since you were fine—more than fine—when I left you a couple of hours ago. Is he okay?"

"He's far from okay. His life's a mess."

"Honestly, I think he thrives on the drama," Stephanie remarked. "He's an actor, remember?" She despised the misogynistic Jimmy Moran and everything he represented, with his extraordinary arrogance built on far too little talent.

"He's not getting any younger. And this time the mess is bigger than usual. His wife's finally giving him the divorce he's wanted."

"Well, that's good news. . . ."

"And taking half of everything he owns."

Stephanie looked at him sharply, surprised by the disapproving tone in his voice. "Good for her. That's her right," she reminded him.

"You heard that Frances, the girlfriend, had a baby?"

"I heard something about it."

"Well, he's going to marry the girlfriend and raise the child with her."

"So he should." Again she was surprised, and just a little disappointed, with his reaction. Surely he accepted that Jimmy had treated his wife abominably and had a duty to his girlfriend and her child. "You don't look so sure," she added, watching him closely.

"Frances sold her story to the press. She used him to get free publicity, hoping she'd get that movie part."

Coffee started to percolate, and the rich aroma of Kenyan filled the small kitchen.

"That was really the beginning of the end for him and Angela."

"But he's still with Frances," Stephanie said, pulling open cupboard doors and plucking two Stevia packets from the box. "He went back to her, got her pregnant."

"You haven't got sugar, have you?"

Without saying a word, Stephanie turned away and tore open the packets and poured them in the mug. It was her mission to make this man healthy, whether he liked it or not. "Sugar is bad for you."

Robert shrugged. "Frances ruined Jimmy's reputation in return for fifteen minutes of fame."

Stephanie laughed, shocked by the bitter tone in Robert's voice. He seemed to be blaming Frances for Jimmy's problems. But wasn't that what men did: blame the woman? "She did not. He had no reputation to ruin. So he was a big deal back in Dublin. So what?

Here, he's just another actor. And not even a good one, and actors are a dime a dozen. And he has a reputation as an alcoholic womanizer." She handed Robert the coffee. "Everyone knows about him," she added.

Robert accepted the mug from her hand and sipped it, making a face at the bitter taste. "People know about us, Stephanie," he said quietly. "Jimmy told me tonight."

So he knew. That's what was behind his attitude. She poured herself a large glass of wine and carried her glass past him into the living room and curled up on the sofa, tucking her bare legs beneath her, pulling her dressing gown tightly across her body.

Robert followed her into the room and sat down facing her. "Did you hear what I said?" he said almost accusingly. "People know about us."

What was that she was hearing in his voice? Anger . . . or fear?

Ghostly wind chimes coming from the disc in the CD player filled the silence between them.

"You knew." He looked as if he had been struck. "You knew and you never told me."

"Yes, I knew."

"How long . . . I mean, why didn't you . . . what about your office . . . ?"

"There have been rumors floating around about us for the last couple of months," she said simply. "I ignored them. This business of ours thrives on innuendo and gossip. And when two people are regularly seen together, tongues wag, even if there isn't truth to the rumors."

"And your boss? Does he know?"

She took a long sip and said simply, "About a month ago, Charles Flintoff himself asked me outright if you and I were an item."

"You said no," Robert said immediately.

"I said yes."

Robert looked at her blankly.

"Having a relationship with you is one thing—he doesn't give a damn about that. Putting business your way is another. But as long as everything was aboveboard, well, that's still marginally okay. However, lying to my boss was out of the question. The very fact that he was asking me the question suggested that he already knew the answer. I told him the truth."

Robert's mouth was opening and closing, but no sound was coming out.

"And it was the right thing to do. He had the contracts for the jobs I'd given you, plus the estimates. He'd done some comparisons with the other bidders and had gotten an independent assessment of the final result." She shrugged. "He could find no fault with it."

"So how many people know?"

Stephanie frowned. "Jesus, Robert. I could have lost my job over this." She was shocked at how selfish he was being. He was obsessed with trying to prevent people from finding out about them. Or was he obsessed with trying to prevent his wife from finding out about them? "Why? What's the problem?" she demanded.

"Because if people know, then it's only a matter of time before Kathy finds out."

She had her answer.

Stephanie let the silence hang over the room. There was so much she wanted to say; however, she was determined to make him speak first. She swirled her wine, watching the light dance off the spinning liquid.

"I wanted to be in a position to tell her myself," he finally said. Was there a tinge of embarrassment in his voice? She remained silent until he finally added, "When the time was right."

"And when would the time be right, Robert?" Stephanie finally snapped.

"When it's right," he muttered.

"And when would that be?"

Robert concentrated on his coffee and would not look her in the eye.

"We've been lovers now for eighteen months, Robert. Where do we go from here? What's the future?"

He wrapped his hands around the mug and stared into it.

"You've told me how unhappy you are at home. You suggested to me—no, more than suggested, you *told* me that you would leave Kathy. . . ."

"I never said that."

"Maybe not in those words, but that was my clear understanding. I would never have gotten involved with you otherwise. You told me you would leave her when the time was right." She remembered the moment clearly. They'd been lying upstairs in her bed, exhausted after a bout of strenuous lovemaking. He'd made the announcement out of the blue, with no prompting from her. "I'll be with you," he had said. "I'll sort things out and come to you when the time is right." The words were etched on her consciousness. He might have forgotten; she hadn't.

"Well, when is the right time? This month? No, it can't be this month because it's Christmas, and you don't want to ruin Kathy's Christmas. Of course you have no trouble ruining my Christmas, but that's another story." She was unable and unwilling now to disguise the bitterness in her voice. "So, when? Next month? No, that's the New Year, not an ideal way to kick off the New Year. What about February? No, that's Theresa's birthday, and that's not the sort of gift you want to give your daughter. Do you want me to go through the whole year? Do you? There is never a right time, Robert."

Stephanie stopped abruptly. Exhaustion, leaden, bone-numbing exhaustion washed over her, and suddenly she did not want to speak to him anymore. "Look, I'm tired and feeling incredibly bitchy, and my period's overdue. I don't want to be having this conversation with you now."

Robert nodded. It was obvious that he didn't want to have it either.

"I had a drink with Izzie earlier. . . ."

"Does she know?"

Stephanie wanted to hit him. "Of course she knows! Do you think I could handle this alone? Without a girlfriend to confide in, to get advice from? Izzie's been my rock; she knew from the very beginning; she was the first to know. And she warned me, right from the start, not to get involved with a married man. She explained to me exactly what would happen, and you know what? So far, she's been right. Just spot-on." The room fractured into a rainbow of crystals as tears filled her eyes. She was angry with herself; she always felt that tears were the cheap option, and she was not going to give in to tears.

"Stephanie," Robert began, "maybe this isn't a good time. We're both tired. Let's get some sleep."

"I think that's a really good idea." She stood up smoothly and picked up his coat. She wanted him out of the house. Right now.

"I'll see you tomorrow. We'll talk."

She laid a hand on his arm. "I don't want to think that you've been making a fool of me. I don't want to think that you've been using me. Maybe I just want to think we have a future together." Then she leaned up and brushed her lips against his. "Tomorrow. Tell me the truth."

She closed the door behind him and listened to him shuffle down the stairs. Normally, she would have walked him out, but she didn't want him to see the tears now rolling down her cheeks. Automatically, she turned out the lights and headed upstairs to bed. Without even brushing her teeth, and still wrapped in the robe, she crawled under the thick covers. A moment later, she heard a car engine start in the courtyard outside and wondered if it was Robert's. And then she realized that she didn't care.

He had one last chance; Izzie would say that it was one too many. Tomorrow night—she'd know for sure by tomorrow night.

The car drove away, a lonely fading sound.

CHAPTER 39

Saturday, 21st December

She slept remarkably well. Considering.

When she'd crawled into bed, she'd felt as if she'd been beaten and almost physically bruised. Sitting across from Robert, watching him act and react, she'd gradually realized that he was a coward, that he was never going to leave his wife, and that she'd been naïve to even dream of it.

He wanted her to keep their secret, to not even confide in her best friend. Didn't he realize the emotional toll the affair was taking on her as well? If she didn't have Izzie to talk to, she'd be going crazy by now. Robert's selfishness, his fear, made him weak. The alarm bells had gone off when she'd seen how he'd sympathized with Jimmy Moran—philandering, lying, cheating Jimmy Moran. She'd seen how he'd reacted to the news that Jimmy's wife was looking for her share of Jimmy's money, and he'd been upset that Frances expected Jimmy to pay child support. If he couldn't accept or understand the women's side of the story, then how could he ever comprehend what she was going through?

She felt him slipping from her, and there was nothing she could do about it. Had she been mistaken about him? Was he, as Izzie suggested, no different from any other married man with a younger mistress? Had he been using her?

But she didn't—couldn't, wouldn't—allow herself to think that. Not just yet.

He had to commit to her; she'd already committed to him. She didn't feel guilty asking him to choose her over his wife; according to him, he'd already done that. She wasn't asking him to do anything he hadn't already agreed to do.

But the man who had sat across from her the previous night, the man who had said little, had almost been like a stranger to her.

She'd not expected to sleep, but as soon as her head had hit the pillow, she'd fallen into a deep and dreamless sleep and had awoken surprisingly refreshed just after eight. She'd lain in bed for an hour, deliberately not thinking about the situation, not allowing him to enter her thoughts at all. There were a few things she needed to do today—including looking at the availability of tickets to Wisconsin—and there was an open-air carol service on the Common that she thought she might check out. She'd leave her car. She could walk to the T. She needed the exercise.

She was just swinging her legs out of bed when the call came in. Caller ID identified Robert's cell, and she actually hesitated for a moment before picking up. Six rings, seven, eight . . . She snatched it up.

"Robert." No hello, no good morning, just an acknowledgment of his name. She wasn't sure how she felt about him this morning. But if he was distancing himself from her, then maybe she ought to be doing the same.

"How . . . how are you feeling?"

"I'm tired, Robert." Not physically tired; emotionally exhausted.

"Do you want to see me?"

"I always want to see you." And it was true. She did.

"I was going to come over."

But she didn't want him in the house today. She wanted to meet him on neutral ground. "I'm about to head into the city; there's an open-air carol service in the Common."

"What time?"

"Starts about two."

"Great. Why don't I meet you there? We can listen to some carols, then go and get something to eat."

"Okay," she said shortly, feeling something shift and move inside her. "Give me a call when you're in the city." She hung up. And then she realized that she was smiling. She loved this man.

She leapt out of bed. Okay, so maybe she had misjudged him. When she'd seen his name on the phone, she'd half expected to hear an excuse why he couldn't see her today, and if he had refused to see her, then that would have been that. But he had surprised her.

Robert was full of surprises. It was one of the things that had first attracted her to him.

Stephanie was moving away from the carol singers, pushing her way through the crowded park when she felt the phone vibrate in her pocket. She scrambled to pull her gloves off with her teeth and finally got to the phone just before the call went to her voice mail. "Where are you?" she asked without preamble.

"In the lobby of the movie theater."

"Stay there. Don't move. I'll find you. It's chaos here."

This was the last Saturday before Christmas, traditionally the busiest shopping day of the year. People always thought Christmas Eve held that particular honor, but by Christmas Eve a lot of the shopping was complete, and people either didn't come into the city or started heading out of town early. The carol service by the baseball fields in the heart of the Common had attracted thousands of onlookers, and the park was jammed with bodies pushing in to hear the singers.

Stephanie hurried through the park and toward the big red neon letters marking the multiplex. There was an art exhibition taking place near Frog Pond, and that had brought in even more crowds.

As she crossed Tremont and approached the entrance, she couldn't see Robert. The foyer was jammed with bodies waiting for the early afternoon screening.

There he was.

He was standing a little to one side, scrutinizing a movie poster, frowning, hands pushed deep into his pockets, collar turned up, head ducked. All he needed was a hat and a cigarette, and he'd look like a forties detective. She managed to get right up in front of him before he noticed she was there. He blinked in surprise, then leaned forward to kiss her, a quick chaste peck on the cheek, before catching her arm and moving her away from the doorway. "Where did you leave your toboggan?" he asked, mocking her practical, though not entirely unflattering, winter clothing.

She smiled. "Parked it upstairs alongside the sleigh."

They crossed the road, heading back toward the park. He nodded toward the park. "So, Christmas carols?"

She shook her head. "The choir is loud but not good, and the park is jammed. Let's walk around and look at the art." She pointed with both hands. "Left or right?" she asked brightly, guessing that he would want to take her to the right, away from the crowds. She knew he hated being seen in the city with her, especially on a day like this, when they might be spotted and not be able to make a work-related excuse.

"Right," Robert said, linking her arm and leading her away toward the art show.

She was disappointed that she'd been proven right. He was just so predictable, she thought bitterly.

"I'm sorry about last night," he began.

"So am I," she said immediately. "I should have told you that our relationship had been discovered. But I knew you were under so much pressure; I simply didn't want to add to it." It was more or less the truth. She had seriously thought about telling him about her conversation with Flintoff, but Robert was no fool; he would have put two and two together and guessed that she would no longer be able to send work his way. She couldn't afford to have him panicking and going out scrambling for more work; she had wanted to keep him focused on the DaBoyz project.

"It might have been better if you had. When Jimmy dropped it on me last night, I started to have a panic attack."

Stephanie glanced at him curiously; was he such a coward? She stopped to look at a spectacular abstract oil, vivid in green and gold, slashed across with daubs of red and violet. She loved the raw emotion and energy in the painting. This was a work of passion.

Where was the man she had fallen in love with, the passionate man? What had happened to him? The early days of their relation- ship—even before they had started to make love—had been pas- sionate days, full of light and life and energy. But as time had gone by, the passion had slowly seeped away. They no longer went places; they did less and less together, and he no longer had as much time for her. He was driven by work, obsessed with the need to make money to keep the business going. If this was how he be- haved with Kathy, she was beginning to understand why the couple had drifted apart.

Leaning forward into the painting, inhaling the rich aroma of oil and linseed, she said, without looking at him, "Tell me . . ."—she waited until he had bent his head to hers—"do you love me?"

When he didn't answer immediately, she glanced sidelong at him. "That's a mighty long pause."

"What? No. I suppose I was just surprised that you had to ask me."

"I want to know, Robert." She walked away, and he fell into step beside her. "I want to know how much."

"I've told you often enough."

"I know that. But have you shown me?"

"I've given you presents. . . ."

She bit back a savage response and instead asked, "What is love, Robert?"

"Love is . . . ," he floundered, ". . . well, love."

"You're such a typical man!" She was becoming frustrated by what she saw as deliberate vagueness. "Think about it, Robert: What is love? You tell me you love me. What does that mean?"

"It means . . . it means I want to be with you. That I love being with you."

Was he just saying the words automatically, a rote response, or did he really mean them? Was he just telling her what he thought she wanted to hear? "So you're saying love is commitment?"

"Yes. Commitment," he agreed.

A tiny, delicate watercolor of a single daffodil attracted her at- tention, and she stopped to admire it. Constructed of individual sweeping brushstrokes, it had an Asian feel to it. It looked delicate, ephemeral, fragile, which was exactly how she would describe her relationship with Robert at that precise moment. It was either about to bloom or wither away. "And are you committed to me?" she asked.

"Yes."

Stephanie straightened. "Okay. So how do you show that commitment?"

Robert opened his mouth to answer, but the young female artist moved in to try and make a sale. "We're not interested," Robert said. He caught Stephanie by the arm and led her out of the park. She could feel the tension vibrating through his hand, and he was squeezing hard enough to leave bruises. "If we're going to talk, then let's talk and leave the art for another day. What do you want from me, Stephanie?"

"The truth," she said simply. "I told you that last night. Just tell me the truth."

"I've told you I love you. That's the truth."

"And I believe you."

He stopped, surprised, stunned or just shocked by her statement.

She walked away from him, then stopped and turned back. She believed him, truly believed that he loved her in his own way, on his own terms. But did he love her enough . . . enough to walk away from everything he had and start again, start afresh?

"If you have something to ask me, then ask me straight out," he said.

Love and commitment, well, they were two separate things. But they should be one. Stephanie dug her hands into the pockets of her down jacket and turned to face him. She was aware that if she blinked then the tears pooling in her eyes would roll down her cheeks, and she wasn't going to give him that satisfaction. "You tell me you love me. You tell me you want to be with me. You seem to enjoy my company. You certainly enjoy my body." She stopped and drew in a deep breath. "I need to know if there is more. If there is going to be more."

"More?"

"More of us. Together. Not snatched half-hour lunches or one-hour dinners, not fumbles in your office or dirty weekends away. I need to know if we're going to be together. As a couple. Openly." She quickly looked away and brushed the tears from her cheeks before he could see them. "That's all."

Because in the end that's what it came down to.

Not what had happened in the past, not what was taking place in the present and all that it represented, but the future: That's all that mattered now. She needed a future, either with or without him.

She looked out across the Common. The brilliant weather had brought people to the park, bringing it alive with stark color against the leafless trees. When she'd first fallen in love with him, it had been as if everything were brilliantly colored, but in the past few weeks and months of their relationship, it seemed as if the colors were leaching away.

"I've had plenty of relationships before, Robert; you know that. I've never felt about anyone the way I feel about you. I love you. I need to know if you love me. I need to know if you love me enough to do something about it."

She turned and walked away. He hesitated, and for a moment she thought he was going to walk in the opposite direction, but then he fell into step beside her. She was not going to say any more. She'd said more than she'd intended to. If he couldn't share his life with her, be open about their relationship, commit to her . . . well, then she was done. She headed toward Beacon Street. She would walk to Downtown Crossing and catch the Orange Line. She was going home.

"You want me to commit to you."

She wasn't sure if he was asking her a question or making a statement. She was numb and tired. "I don't want to be your mistress anymore. That was fine for a while, because I wasn't sure if you were the one."

"The one?"

"The one I loved. And I allowed myself to fall in love with you—even though you were a married man—because I believed that there might be a chance for us. A future." Stephanie took a deep breath. "My girlfriends have gone away for Christmas to be with their families, but I'm going to be spending Christmas alone, because I wanted to be close to my lover. But my lover is spending time with his family. It was that way last year too; I don't want it to be that way next year. I feel so foolish, Robert. So incredibly foolish."

"Stephanie, I—" he said quickly.

She held up her hand. She needed to finish this. "If there is no future for us, then just say so. I can handle it. It will hurt, but I'll get over it. I'll survive. And I'm not going to be stupid about it. I'm a big girl. I won't make a scene; I won't tell Kathy, if that's what you're worried about," she added bitterly.

They walked another ten yards up Beacon in silence, each step taking her closer to the T stop, each step moving them further apart.

Then, abruptly, Robert moved around to stand in front of her, stopping her in the middle of the sidewalk, catching hold of her shoulders, looking down into her eyes. She was suddenly conscious that his eyes were huge, magnified now by unshed tears, and his breath was labored, as if he had been running. She saw his tongue flick out to lick dry lips.

"I love you. I want to be with you. To marry you. Will you marry me?"

The city went away. The noise of the traffic and the crowds faded and dulled, and there was only Robert and his words echoing around in her head.

I love you.

I want to be with you.

To marry you.

Will you marry me?

She wrapped her arms around his shoulders and pulled his face down and kissed him, and she was crying and trying to speak, but her heart was thumping so hard she was sure it was going to burst.

I love you.

I want to be with you.

To marry you.

Will you marry me?

The world shifted and settled, and the doubts and fears were wiped away in those four simple sentences. Three statements and a question.

She loved him.

She wanted to be with him.

She wanted to marry him.

And yes was the answer.

"Yes, I will, yes, yes, yes."

CHAPTER 40

Sunday, 22nd December

"He proposed! So, what do you think of that!" Stephanie demanded triumphantly.

Izzie barely made it through the door of the James's Gate pub before Stephanie blurted out the news. "He told me he loved me, wanted to be with me, wanted to marry me." Even as she said the words, Stephanie could feel the combination of excitement and maybe even fear churning inside her stomach. And relief. Stephanie felt as if an enormous emotional weight had been lifted from her.

Izzie's eyes and mouth were wide with shock. "He proposed to you? Proposed! Okay, slow down, what's happened? Tell me."

"He asked me to marry him. Proposed. Right there in the street."

Will you marry me?

That was the phrase that had shocked her, surprised her, undone her. She was thirty-three years old; she was a strong, independent, established businesswoman. She'd never felt the need for a man on her arm or by her side to validate her. Never really needed a man before. Enjoyed them certainly, loved some of them, but not since she was a teen had she thought about marriage. Marriage was a young girl's dream, and she'd stopped being a young girl a long time ago.

And yet . . .

With those four words, he'd made her a young girl again, with all those dreams and futures made possible again.

Izzie was speaking to her, and she had to concentrate on the words. "What did you do to bring out this dramatic change?" she demanded. "I want details."

Stephanie downed her Guinness, grabbed her coat off the back of a chair, and grabbed her purse. "I really do listen to you. Maybe I just needed you to make me think about the questions I should be asking. . . . Maybe I was just too close to the situation, making excuses for him all the time. I guess I finally just got tired of waiting."

She left a three-dollar tip for the five-dollar beer, then linked her arm through her friend's. They strode out of the bar, up South Street, and made a left at the Civil War monument. They were going to walk around Jamaica Pond and then go into town, to shop for one another's presents—a tradition that had grown up over the many years of their friendship.

"I asked myself what I wanted—not for now, but for next year. Then I asked him if he loved me."

"And of course he said yes," Izzie answered. "Men always say yes, but that's because they don't really know the meaning of the word. 'Yes' is just a filler in a conversation, something to mark the place while they're really thinking about something else."

"Stop being cynical. He did it, Izzie. He did it. Told me he would marry me. I wasn't expecting that. Hell, I would have been happy with his just committing to moving in with me."

They passed a group of geese that were sunning themselves by the side of the road and crossed the Jamaicaway to stroll along the pond. With the sun fracturing on the water, it looked like a summer's day. They walked a dozen steps, then Izzie wondered aloud: "And did he say when he was going to break the good news to his wife?"

Stephanie felt her euphoric mood slip. That same thought had crossed her mind, but she'd dismissed it. "Well, no . . . we didn't get around to discussing that. We were going to meet today, but I wasn't going to cancel you for anything."

"Thanks."

"Besides, I haven't had a chance to get Robert his big present. I needed some time to do that today."

They walked another dozen steps.

"And when do you think he'll be moving in with you?"

"Oh, soon," Stephanie said confidently. "By the New Year, I should imagine. We'll have a New Year's celebration dinner—and remember, you're paying."

"Oh, trust me. If he moves in with you and commits to you—I'll absolutely pay."

Stephanie wasn't sure if Izzie was being sarcastic or not.

Izzie squeezed Stephanie's hand. "Come on; two loops around the pond then let's go buy overpriced trinkets on Centre Street, have drinks at Costello's, and have dinner at Bukhara. And we'll make a promise now not to think or talk about men for the rest of the day!"

"Is that possible?" Stephanie laughed.

"After what you've told me today, anything's possible." Izzie grinned at her friend before her voice took on a more serious tone. "I am really happy for you, Stephanie. I am. I just don't want to see you get hurt."

"I won't."

CHAPTER 41

Monday, 23rd December

Robert was wheezing like an old man when Stephanie took up her position on the treadmill alongside him. He grunted a greeting but didn't let up the pace. When she'd convinced him to join the gym, she hadn't really imagined that he would stick with it, but he'd surprised her by keeping his twice-weekly appointments. Once he had gotten over the initial shock to his system, he almost seemed to enjoy it. She'd seen some slight improvements to his body, especially around his stomach, but his pecs still needed a lot of work. After his first session, she'd convinced him to go for a tan, and that went a long way toward disguising some of his flabby sins. She had noted the last time they made love that he'd continued to top up the tan.

She started up the treadmill. "Sorry I'm late. The office is closing today, and there were drinks in the boardroom."

"No problem," he panted. "I got your message. Any issues in work about . . . ?"

"About us? Nothing. No mentions. And I did hear through the grapevine that it looks as if you got the DaBoyz gig."

"That's great! I mean, I think that's great. Theresa said two of the guys are gay."

Stephanie shook her head. "So? Is that a problem?"

"No. Not at all. But she also said there were lots of tweets that they're thinking about breaking up."

Stephanie bit back a flicker of irritation. Robert hadn't even known what Twitter was before she had taught him the importance and relevance of social networking. She helped him set up his company's Twitter, Facebook, and Pinterest accounts—all in the name of better branding R&K. Keeping them competitive. It should be of no interest to him if the band were straight, gay, or on the verge of breaking up. All he had to do was concentrate on the video. "They were. That's why this single is so important. There's been a lot of investment in this group, and the investors are unwilling to cut loose their potential cash cow without one last shot. That's you, by the way. Do the video right, and you will have saved a lot of people a lot of money. Screw it up, however, and you'll never work in this town again." She laughed to take the sting from her words.

"I'm not sure whether you're joking or serious."

"A bit of both, I think. You'll do a great job. Remember, I've staked my career on it."

"So, no pressure there then," he murmured.

"And I'm sorry about yesterday. I really wanted to see you, but I'd already agreed to go shopping with Izzie before . . . ."

Robert glanced sidelong at her and smiled. "Before?"

"Before us."

"It was probably just as well. It gave me a chance to get a lot done in the office. If you and I had gotten together, we would have . . ."

She looked at him seductively. "What would we have done?"

"Talked. Planned."

"I know. You've made me so happy. Even Izzie is pleased."

"One of these days I'd like to meet this mysterious Izzie."

"She's looking forward to meeting you too. I've told her a lot about you."

"I suppose she was surprised by the news."

"More like stunned. I said we'd get together after Christmas and celebrate. She's paying."

"Good." Robert began to run faster. "Why is she paying?"

"Because she once bet me the best meal money could buy that you would never leave your wife for me."

"Well, let's make sure that's an expensive bet. I'll book Top of the Hub myself for this one."

They ran in silence for a while, then Stephanie asked the question that had been troubling her ever since Izzie had raised it the previous day. "Have you given any further thought to Christmas?"

"I've thought about nothing else," he said quickly.

"Will you spend Christmas Day with me?"

Before he answered he reached down to increase the speed of the machine, and she had an inkling of the answer. He was now running hard, breath coming in great, heaving gasps. "No," he said eventually.

His answer chilled her, and something must have shown on her face, because Robert said immediately, "Be reasonable." Realizing that he was shouting above the noise of the machine, he leaned closer to her.

"Be reasonable. I can hardly go to Kathy and the kids tonight or tomorrow and say, 'Guess what, I'm leaving. Merry Christmas.' Can I?"

Well, when he put it like that, it sounded perfectly reasonable. But of course, all his excuses sounded reasonable. "No, of course not." She nodded, not sure what she was hearing. Was he backtracking on what he had said on Saturday, or was this perfectly genuine? She needed a few moments to think. But her initial reaction was that the bastard was backing down.

If he walked away from her now, having proposed to her, having gotten her hopes up, having made her incredibly, unreasonably happy, then she would go to his wife and tell her. If he hurt her like that, then she would hurt him back! She didn't like the person Robert was making her into. A jealous, bitter girlfriend. His actions were not backing up his words, and it was making her crazy.

"But I'll see you tomorrow."

"And when do you intend to tell her?" she asked. His answer

had helped a little, but she needed more, she needed something definite, something she could hold onto, something she could count on.

"I was thinking the twenty-seventh, which is Friday."

"Why not Thursday?"

"Well, we're committed to going over to her sister's for dinner. It's a family tradition. All the arrangements have been made."

Something like panic was beginning to creep in around her now. Panic and a terrible anger. When Robert had told her on Saturday that he wanted to be with her, she'd somehow imagined that meant Christmas Day, but when she had rerun the conversation again, she had realized that he'd never actually committed to any timeframe. "So what am I supposed to do for Christmas Day? Hang around until you appear?" Stephanie was angry. What did Robert expect? Knowing what he had promised, was she supposed to treat Christmas like an ordinary weekday? Do her laundry? Watch television? Was it going to be another Merry-lonely-Christmas?

"Look, I'll tell her on Friday, and I'll spend New Year's Eve with you," he said, trying to placate her, although not exactly answering her question. "We'll bring in the New Year together. Come on; meet me halfway on this. This is a big decision, a huge move for me to make. You've got yourself to think of; I've got Kathy and the kids to consider."

"You're right, of course. Absolutely right." Now that she had her definitive dates, she'd swap Christmas for New Year's. It was more symbolic anyway: new starts, fresh beginnings, ushering in the New Year together. "Another couple of days won't make that much difference to us. And Christmas Day is really just another Wednesday."

They switched from the treadmills onto the bikes. She started pedaling. Robert tried to keep up with her for a few minutes but couldn't and slowed back down to a moderate pace. "So, I have a proposition," he said when he'd gotten his breath back.

Stephanie continued cycling as she looked at him. She was still breathing evenly. "Another one?"

"It's about the company. R&K Productions. You know the K stands for Kathy and that she has a fifty percent share in it?"

"I know that," Stephanie said cautiously. What was he talking about? Maybe he was thinking of selling the company.

"I was wondering if you'd like to join me in the company, take over Kathy's share. We could call it R&S Productions. That is, if I can buy Kathy out, of course."

She looked at him in blank surprise. Whatever she had been expecting him to ask her, it hadn't been this. She eased up on the bike, allowed the wheel to spin to a stop. There was no easy way to say this, but it had to be said, and better he hear it from her. She took a moment to try and phrase the response as diplomatically as possible.

"I'm not sure I'd want to give up my present position. I'm rising fairly rapidly in the agency, and I would think going to work in your company might be seen as a retrograde step, career-wise."

Robert started to laugh, then she watched the laughter die on his lips as he realized she was serious.

And, since he had raised the issue of the business, she thought she might as well tell him the rest. If he was being totally honest with her—and she thought he was—then she owed it to him.

"The other thing we'll have to bear in mind is that, obviously, I won't be able to send any more business your way. It wouldn't look good for me to be seen to be pushing business to my partner's company."

He looked as if he had been struck. "No more business . . ."

"Not from me. But I'll keep my ear to the ground. I'll keep you well up to speed with what's happening in the industry. Anyway," she continued, "I was thinking you might close R&K."

"What?" Beneath his tan she could see that he'd actually paled. Had he been counting that much on the work she could get him?

"Maybe get a job with one of the big advertising agencies or production companies." She pandered to his ego. "You'd be a huge asset, Robert. You have a great deal of experience."

He wouldn't look at her now, merely stared straight ahead with what looked like a defiant—or sullen—expression on his face.

"It would be easier on you mentally and physically," she pressed on. "There would be a steady paycheck, and you could walk out at six and not have to think about the job again until the following morning. Your weekends would be yours again. Ours."

"But I'd be working for someone. I've been my own boss for a long time."

"At the moment you're working for Kathy and the children and the bank. They're your boss. This way you end up with more free time, time to spend with me. Time to spend with your children," she added.

He started laughing, a dry rasp, which turned into a cough.

Stephanie climbed off the bike and thumped his back. "Are you all right?"

"I'm fine. I was just thinking . . ."

"Thinking what?"

"That you're some sort of catalyst. Change happens around you."

She leaned into him, deliberately pushing her breasts against his chest. "We make our own changes, but sometimes you just need someone or something to do a little nudging." Izzie had nudged her; she had nudged Robert. "I'm going to take a shower." She spun away, aware that he—and some of the other men in the gym—were watching, and enjoying their attention.

Next year was going to be so different, so very, very different.

"So, what are your thoughts about babies?" Stephanie asked. She had stepped out of the dressing room to find Robert leaning against the wall, checking his messages. He put the phone away and kissed her quickly, and she laced her fingers through his. The sudden thought had come out of the blue while she was showering, and she figured she might as well put all of the cards on the table.

"I hadn't thought about it. I mean, I have two teenagers already," Robert said as they walked across the foyer toward the entrance. She realized he must have sensed her vulnerability when he added quickly, "But I'm not opposed to the idea. What do you think?"

"Honestly, I'm not sure. I mean, I think I'd like children," she said as they came out into the bitter night air. She'd never thought about having kids before he'd proposed on Saturday. And now she couldn't stop thinking about them. And if she wanted them or not. Many of her friends had babies and toddlers, and she recognized the extraordinary amount of work that went into rearing a child. She had nothing but admiration for women who managed to juggle a career and family, but the very nature of her job, which involved travel and odd hours, made having a child simply out of the question. Well, out of the question if she was alone. But if she had a partner . . . that might be different. Maybe this was what she had first seen in Robert: the possibilities. She had looked at the lonely, slightly desperate, trapped man and recognized the potential surrounding him. When they were together, and when the time was right, she would love to have a child. Boy or girl, it didn't matter; it would be theirs.

"If you did want children, when would you like to have them?" he wondered.

"Not immediately of course," she said, just in case he had any ideas about an instant family. She squeezed his fingers, relishing the warmth and strength of them. "Well, it's a bit of a Catch-22. I'm thirty-three now. My biological clock is definitely ticking. I can't wait too long, and yet, I need another two years at least before I'm promoted. Then we could start trying for the year after that."

But was thirty-five too old to be thinking about conceiving a first child? Did she want to have to deal with in vitro and all of the new technologies that made having a kid later in life possible? It was expensive and time-consuming. Her mother had had her and her siblings the old-fashioned way when she was in her early twenties. And Stephanie's mother had managed just fine. If Stephanie was going to have a baby, now was definitely the most logical time. Maybe she'd think about a career break, have the baby then go back to work, possibly in a part-time capacity. She wasn't necessarily the most maternal person, but she could manage a kid. Couldn't she? Besides, Robert would help her. She knew he would. He adored his own children and, from what she understood, they loved him. He would be a wonderful father to a child. To *their* child.

Stephanie smiled as she walked toward her car. Her entire

world was changing. She was looking at possibilities that simply hadn't existed forty-eight hours ago.

The cars were parked alongside one another in the darkened corner of the street. Stephanie and Robert hit their electronic car door openers together, and both sets of lights blinked simultaneously.

Robert opened her car door, and she threw her gym bag onto the passenger seat, then turned to him. She loved this man. And she would love to have his child. She reached up, pressed the palm of her right hand against the back of his skull to bring his head down to a level with hers. "Think of all the fun we'll have practicing to conceive children," she whispered. Then she kissed him, passionately and deeply. Finally they broke apart, panting slightly. Without saying another word, Stephanie climbed into the car, waved once, and drove away. She was thinking about baby names as she glanced in the rearview mirror and saw him still standing by his car, talking on the phone.

And would she keep her own name or take his?

She quite liked Walker. She tried it out, saying it aloud. "Stephanie Burroughs-Walker." No, just Stephanie Walker. That's what she would become.

Mrs. Walker.

CHAPTER 42

Christmas Eve
Tuesday, 24th December

When Stephanie Burroughs opened the hall door, she instantly recognized the woman standing on the doorstep. A dozen emotions flickered through her—shock, fear, anger . . . and, surprisingly, relief.

"Hello, Stephanie."

"Hello, Mrs. Walker. Kathy."

On the drive over, Kathy Walker had rehearsed her conversation with Stephanie Burroughs a hundred different ways. She'd gone through every emotion: from anger to resignation, from disgust to horror, and what was left was . . . nothing. An emptiness. A hollow feeling inside.

She knew, right up to the moment she pressed the doorbell, what she was going to say to her husband's mistress, but when Stephanie Burroughs opened the door and looked at her with instant recognition in her eyes, all of Kathy's carefully laid plans, her nicely ordered words and phrases deserted her. Instead, she stepped forward and cracked Stephanie across the face with the flat of her hand.

The two women blinked at one another, each surprised, shocked, horrified by what had just taken place. Kathy felt herself start to shake; she'd never raised a hand to another person in her life.

Stephanie pressed her hand against her stinging cheek. She had absolutely no intention of striking back. She bore the woman no animosity; Kathy had done nothing wrong. Almost from the very first moments of her relationship with Robert, Stephanie had been dreading—and expecting—an encounter with Robert's wife. She knew once Robert told Kathy that he was leaving, she could expect a visit. And if she ever ended up calling at the home of her husband's mistress, she'd belt her one too.

"I'm sorry!" Kathy began, abruptly breathless. "I promised myself I wasn't going to do that. I'm sorry."

Stephanie hadn't been expecting a visit this soon; she hadn't thought Robert was going to tell his wife until after Christmas.

Kathy gathered herself. "We can . . . ," she began, but her voice was trembling with emotion. She swallowed hard and tried again. "We can have this conversation here on your doorstep, or you can let me in."

Stephanie looked at the woman. She didn't want to speak to her . . . but somewhere deep inside her, she felt a twinge of sympathy. Kathy deserved an answer. Mrs. Moore's curtains twitched, making the decision for Stephanie. She moved aside. "Yes, absolutely, you should come up."

The older woman hesitated a moment, then nodded and stepped into the foyer. Stephanie directed her through the door on the left to number 8, up the stairs to Stephanie's apartment, where she found herself standing in a large room with skylights that was a combination living room and dining room.

Stephanie took her time closing the door, composed herself. There were tears in her eyes, more from the fright than the slap across the face. She glanced at herself in the hall mirror: The imprint of Kathy's fingers was clear on her pale cheek.

Stephanie hung back in the doorway, a hand pressed to her cheek, and watched Robert's wife. The woman was not entirely as she remembered her: older certainly, the skin on the face sagging a little, black bags under bloodshot eyes. She was simply dressed in a cream blouse over black pants, with plain jewelry, a gold necklace, a gold bracelet, and gold wedding and engagement rings. Stephanie got the impression that Kathy Walker had taken some time dressing for this encounter.

Stephanie couldn't help but wonder how she would look if her lover had just said he was walking out. How would she feel? How was Kathy feeling right now? In that moment, Stephanie felt an extraordinary rush of pity for the other woman. She folded her arms across her chest; she couldn't afford to feel pity for Kathy. This was the woman who had effectively driven her husband away with her uncaring indifference.

Kathy looked at the quaint room and found that she liked it; it wasn't her taste, it was just a little too fussy, but it was homey and comfortable, not at all what she'd imagined it was going to be. She'd somehow imagined that Robert's mistress would be a slave to fashion and have an apartment straight out of *In Style* magazine. It was spotlessly neat of course, but it was easy to keep a house clean if you didn't have two teens running about.

Kathy turned a full circle. "It's very nice," she said eventually. She was relieved to find no pictures of Robert and Stephanie on the walls, no signs that he was already living there. "I suppose you know why I'm here."

Stephanie looked at her closely, spotting the remarkable resemblance between them, and realized with a frisson of horror that she was seeing herself as she would be in ten years' time. Or at least as she would be if her husband had just left her for a younger woman. "So he's told you about us?" she asked coldly.

Kathy shook her head. "No. Robert didn't tell me."

Stephanie nodded slowly. Trying to prevent her voice from trembling, she said coolly, "So, you found out."

"I found out," Kathy said, her voice as icy as Stephanie's. "I found out about you and him." Anger began to edge her words.

"I thought he'd told you. He said he was going to."

"Robert says he's going to do lots of things. Then he forgets," Kathy added bitterly. "I just want some answers. That's all. I can't ask him—I can't ask him anything—because he'll lie. He'll lie to me. I've discovered that he's been doing that a lot lately. And since I can't ask him, I thought I'd ask you instead."

And although Stephanie did not want to speak to this woman, she felt that she owed her that much. She nodded. "I was going to make some tea. Would you like some?"

"Yes. Please." Kathy pulled off her coat and folded it over the back of a chair while Stephanie disappeared into the kitchen. Kathy hesitated a moment, then followed her, unconsciously taking up the same position and the same pose that Robert had adopted on Friday night.

"On the way over here I knew down to the last word everything I was going to say to you. Now that I'm here, I can't think of anything worthwhile to say. But I never intended to hit you," she added, embarrassed by the action. "That was ... unnecessary."

"I'd have done the same thing. If you want to shout at me, scream at me, I'd understand that too."

Kathy shook her head. "What's the point?"

Stephanie nodded.

"Why?" Kathy asked simply. "Why did you take my husband from me? Why would you do that?"

Stephanie concentrated on the kettle. "It just ... happened," she said, surprisingly softly. "It just happened."

"Things don't just happen," Kathy said. "People make things happen. You made this happen."

"And Robert too," Stephanie added.

Kathy nodded, forced to agree. "Yes, he did."

"And you." Stephanie rounded on Kathy. "You had a part in this too."

Kathy was taken aback by the fervor in the other woman's voice. "I did nothing ... ," she began.

"Exactly," Stephanie snapped. She was getting angry, terribly angry. She wasn't going to shoulder the entire blame for this. Kathy was responsible, Robert was responsible, and she was responsible too. "I want you to know that I never set out to have an affair with him. I've never had a relationship with a married man before. I got together with Robert ... I allowed myself to get close to Robert because I understood that you and he had parted. Emotionally, I mean."

Kathy opened her mouth to snap a denial, but then she closed it again. Was it true? Could it be true? She watched the younger woman make tea in the rather sterile-looking kitchen. She'd recalled Stephanie as being much more glamorous than she was, slimmer, prettier. Maybe that was just her memory playing tricks; the Stephanie she was looking at now was rather ordinary looking in a well-kept sort of way. Was this the woman Robert was thinking of leaving her for?

Kathy accepted the tea from Stephanie's hand, noting the slightest tremble on the surface of the tea. But maybe it was her own hands shaking.

Together the two women went back into the living room, Stephanie taking up her usual place, Kathy settling into the chair usually occupied by her husband. They drank their tea in silence, not quite looking at one another.

"I saw you last night," Kathy said, breaking the long silence. "Coming out of the gym. I was so angry then, but only for a moment. Just a single instant. Then I felt . . . nothing."

Stephanie nodded, not entirely sure what to say. She was trying to remember what they had said and done last night. They'd been talking about children, and she'd kissed him. Had Kathy seen that? Probably. Stephanie found herself wondering how she would feel if she saw Robert kissing another woman.

"What do you want to know?" she asked eventually.

"I'm not sure," Kathy said truthfully. "When I set out to come here, I was going to fight for him. I was going to plead with you to let him go, ask you not to take him away from me, from his children. But I'm not sure I want to do that anymore."

"Why not?" Stephanie whispered.

"I want my husband back . . . but I don't want him to come back to something he doesn't want to commit to."

Stephanie nodded. She could understand that all too clearly.

"Tell me something . . . ," Kathy continued.

Watching this woman, Stephanie tried to analyze her own emotions; unexpected feelings that were churning through her at this moment. Stephanie had never really thought too much about Kathy. Izzie had been right: Everything she knew about this woman had been filtered through Robert, and he, no doubt, had edited the story to make it his version of the truth. It worried her now that she was beginning to feel the first stirrings of sympathy for Kathy.

"Six years ago, when you first joined the company, did you have an affair with Robert?"

"No," Stephanie said simply, "I didn't. I was an employee, nothing more. I swear to you that there was absolutely nothing between us."

And Kathy believed her. She took a moment to absorb the answer, looking at the woman sitting across from her. They were strangers, with nothing in common—except the one man. Her man. The man who Stephanie Burroughs had tried to take from her. But that feeling was changing; her perspective was altering. Stephanie was right. She was not entirely to blame. Stephanie might have made herself available to Robert, but he, in turn, had responded and made himself available to the younger woman. And suddenly Kathy was forced to ask herself what she had done. She had distanced herself enough from him to allow him to act—and think—like that.

"Do you believe me?" Stephanie asked.

Kathy nodded. Her eyes filled with tears. "I was wrong then. I was wrong."

"Wrong?"

"I made a mistake back then—about you and him."

"Yes, you did. I didn't realize until very recently that you'd made the accusation. Have you accused him again?"

"Not yet. This time I wanted to be sure. I wanted to speak to you first."

"Maybe you should have done that before," Stephanie snapped.

"Maybe I should have," Kathy agreed.

"When did you find out about us?"

"Thursday evening. By accident. I needed an address for a Christmas card, and I discovered your name in Robert's phone. There was a little red flag beside it. I jumped to a conclusion: the same conclusion I jumped to six years ago. Then I was wrong; this time, I was right. When I went looking for proof I discovered that it wasn't that hard to find. Sometimes I think he wanted me to find out and save him the trouble of having to face me and tell me himself."

"As far as I can see, he's done everything in his power to keep this a secret from you. He didn't want to hurt you." Stephanie was unable to keep the trace of bitterness from her voice.

"I've been trying to analyze over the past few days when exactly the rot began in our marriage. I think I can pinpoint it back to that moment, six years ago, when I accused him of having an affair with you. I made a mistake then; am I paying for it now?"

"I've told you: We weren't involved then."

"I believe you," Kathy said.

"Why did you accuse him in the first place?" Stephanie had the sudden urge to reach out and touch Kathy's hand.

"He was always with you, always talking about you, spending time away with you. You were so young, pretty, idealistic. I was jealous, I suppose. I thought it was inevitable that he'd sleep with you."

"But it wasn't. He never even hit on me. Remember, we were working all hours of the day on that huge project. He couldn't afford to hire a second researcher, and you'd backed away from the business to raise your kids. That's how we were thrown together."

"But I made the accusation. He denied it of course. I called him a liar, doubted him, and you know something, once you doubt someone, then there's no way to come back from that. It taints everything."

Stephanie nodded. She'd spent weeks doubting Robert's intention to commit to her. And even now, even with the words said, she still had the vaguest of niggling reservations.

They drank their tea in silence.

"I've been thinking about this a lot over the past few days," Kathy continued, "and there were times when I hated you. Absolutely despised you. I wanted to know if you were seducing him just because you could, like it was some sort of game, or . . ."

"It wasn't like that," Stephanie said urgently.

"Then what was it like? What gave you the right?"

"You did. You gave me the right," Stephanie snapped.

Kathy looked at her blankly.

"When you pushed him away, pushed him out of your life. Then I allowed myself to be interested in him."

Kathy opened her mouth to respond, but Stephanie held up a hand.

"And then I fell in love with him." Stephanie took a deep, shuddering breath. "And that changed everything."

Kathy felt her stomach churn. It was hard to sit there and listen to this woman talk about loving her—*her*—husband. "Maureen said she'd seen you together. She told me that she thought you were in love with him."

Stephanie shrugged. "It just happened. I didn't plan it."

Kathy pressed on as if she hadn't heard Stephanie. "And I remembered why I had fallen in love with him. He was very charming."

Stephanie nodded.

"And he was gentle and hapless, and he made me laugh. And he was passionate. So passionate about his work. He had such dreams."

"He still has," Stephanie whispered.

"He doesn't tell me anymore."

"Why not?" Stephanie asked, and she was genuinely curious now.

"I don't know. When I left R&K to raise the children, I guess he assumed that I'd no further interest in the business. He no longer saw me as a business partner, only as a wife and mother. He stopped telling me what he was doing, stopped asking my advice. I was bringing up two young children. He had no idea how exhausting that was—still is. He was leaving early in the morning, coming home later and later at night. I had the sole responsibility for raising the kids twenty-four hours a day. By the time he got home, all I wanted to do was sleep."

Stephanie stood up and took Kathy's empty cup and her own. She returned to the kitchen to fill them. Was it only last night she'd been thinking about having a child with Robert? How would that affect their relationship? How would he regard her once the child was born?

Robert had never really talked to Stephanie about his relationship with his kids. He'd simply spoken about them in a general way, but she'd never realized just how much of the parenting responsibilities had fallen to Kathy. When she was together with Robert, their relationship was entirely a selfish one: They concentrated on one another. She'd never really thought about his children. . . . What would happen to them when he left? What would they think of her?

She returned to the living room with two fresh cups.

Kathy tore open a packet of Stevia and watched the crystals disappear into her tea.

"I've no sugar," Stephanie said.

"I prefer sweetener," Kathy remarked. "I'm trying to cut down."

"Robert prefers sugar," Stephanie said, "but I deliberately don't keep it in the house. It's so bad for him."

"I know," Kathy said coldly. Every time Stephanie spoke about Robert in a personal way, she had to bite back her temper.

"How did you find me?"

"Your address was in Robert's phone. I came by here the other night; I needed to see where you lived."

"Oh, so you were the woman with the mysterious Christmas present."

"That was me."

"What were you looking for?"

"Proof. Plus, I wanted—needed—to see you and Robert together."

"And when you did . . ."

"You reminded me of how we used to look. Happy. Holding hands, kissing, content with one another, relaxed. Just . . . happy."

"I'm sorry about what's happened . . ." Stephanie began, and she was genuinely sorry.

"You didn't destroy our marriage," Kathy said bitterly. "We just drifted. If there's blame to be laid, then it can be laid at both doors."

"You never found yourself a lover?" Stephanie said with a wry smile.

Kathy laughed. "Not with two children. How can I have an affair when I have to deal with carpool and piano lessons and soccer practices? An affair needs lots of free time, opportunity, and commitment to make it work. I had precious little of any of those because I have children and a husband. And because I'm not you."

"Wait a minute—"

"Look, I've gone beyond blaming you personally; I think that if he hadn't had an affair with you, then it would have happened with someone else."

Stephanie blinked in shock and drew back a little. She recalled her own flickering fears about Illona and the way she looked at Robert. "You mean . . ."

"I mean if he was withdrawing from me and wanted comfort or companionship, then he would have taken it anywhere he could." She was unable to resist adding, "You just happened to be . . . convenient. The mistake Robert made was placing the job before his family; the mistake I made was allowing him to."

Stephanie stared at her numbly. Was what Kathy was saying true? Was there the possibility that Robert would have had a relationship with anyone, or rather, any available person?

"When I discovered that you were sending business his way, I even began to rationalize his relationship with you, saying it was purely business. Then I hated myself for thinking that he'd sleep with you just to get some work for the company."

Stephanie opened her mouth to reply, but said nothing. That thought—that bitter, foul thought—had crossed her mind on too many occasions, even before Izzie had voiced it. She licked dry lips, and her voice was husky when she spoke. "Well, that's not going to happen anymore. My boss has given me orders that R&K is not to get any more contracts from us."

Kathy sat back into the chair, absorbing the news. "Does Robert know?" she asked eventually.

"I told him last night."

"How did he take it?"

Stephanie's smile was humorless. "He wasn't pleased."

"What are the implications of that decision?"

"If he doesn't get his act together and get more work very soon, then the company might go under."

"It might be a good thing if it did," Kathy said, surprising

Stephanie with her passion. "Maybe if he could get a simple nine-to-five job, it would simplify things. He works too hard. In many ways, that's at the root of all this."

"I suggested the very same thing to him last night."

"I bet he wasn't happy about that either."

Stephanie shook her head, a ghost of a smile curling her lips. "He looked like I'd just hit him."

"Yeah, I've seen that expression," Kathy agreed. "Quite recently in fact, when I suggested I'd go back into the business with him now that the kids are older. My husband doesn't have much of a poker face."

Stephanie said nothing; she didn't want to tell this woman that only last night—probably only moments before Kathy had spotted them kissing—they had been talking about having children together.

There was a long moment of uneasy silence. Finally, Kathy spoke. "When was he going to tell me?"

"After Christmas," Stephanie said shortly. She was becoming increasingly uncomfortable with Kathy's presence in the house. She wanted her out; she wanted time to think.

"Was he going to move out?" Kathy wondered.

"He said he was going to spend New Year's Eve and New Year's Day with me."

"That's not quite the same thing as moving out." Kathy got up and stood by the window, staring out across the courtyard.

"No, it's not." Stephanie stood and folded her arms across her chest. "Kathy, I want you to know that I was the one who forced him to come to a decision about us. We've been involved for eighteen months, and serious for about six of those—or at least, I've been serious. I wasn't so sure of Robert. I was tired of the uncertainty and the insecurity. I told him to choose. I had a feeling that, left to his own devices, he'd have allowed things to drift on and on."

"He always did have a hard time making decisions." Kathy looked over her shoulder, a peculiar expression on her face. "You love him, don't you?"

"Yes. I do." Stephanie was unable to resist snapping back with, "Do you?"

Kathy turned back to the window. She could see Stephanie reflected in the glass. She had thought about this question long and hard, asked it again and again, because, in the end it came back to this one simple question: Did she love him? Even after all he'd done, even after the pain of the last few days?

"Yes."

The word hung in the air between the two women.

She turned to look at Stephanie. "Would I be here if I didn't?"

There were tears in both their eyes now, and they were staring at one another with intensity. This conversation should not have gone this way; Kathy should have shouted at Stephanie, called her names, and walked away. Stephanie should have watched the wife drive away and felt victorious. Right now, both women were experiencing the same emotion: fear.

Stephanie felt her heart begin to trip. Her mouth turned to cotton. Kathy couldn't love him . . . didn't love him . . . Robert had told her that Kathy didn't love him . . . but was that what Robert believed or what he wanted Stephanie to believe? She unfolded her arms and reached down to touch the back of the chair, feeling that if she didn't grip onto something she was going to fall.

"I still love him." Kathy swung back from the window. "Despite what he's done. He is my husband. My children's father."

Stephanie was standing frozen by the chair, staring intently at Kathy, horrified by what she was hearing. She was listening to a woman in love. In love with the same man she loved.

"He's betrayed me, betrayed eighteen years of marriage, betrayed his children who idolize him. I don't want to keep him out of spite, like Jimmy Moran's wife. If he wants to go, if he truly wants to go, if he is so desperately unhappy with me, then I love him enough to let him go. There's no point in asking Robert what he wants to do; he'll only tell me what he thinks I want to hear. . . ."

Stephanie was nodding.

"So, let me ask you. Do you want him? Do you want him so badly that you want to take him from me?"

Stephanie felt the room sway around her. Kathy wasn't supposed to love him. That's what she'd always believed, right from the very beginning, from six years ago: Kathy didn't care for Robert. Didn't love him.

But Kathy did.

And Stephanie did.

Stephanie loved him with all her heart, loved him because he was kind and gentle, made her laugh, cared for her, looked after her, was thoughtful, considerate, and had asked her to marry him.

And Stephanie had allowed herself to fall in love with him because she firmly believed that he was available. She believed that his wife no longer loved him.

Would he have made the same offer to Stephanie if he thought otherwise? Would he have had an affair with her if he thought that Kathy still had feelings for him?

She didn't want to think he would have.

It was easier—much easier—to believe that Robert had betrayed Kathy almost by accident than to accept that he'd gone out to have an affair with someone who might be able to send extra business his way.

Stephanie took a deep breath, trying to steady her nerves. How would Kathy react if she knew that Robert had asked her to marry him? *He'll only tell me what he thinks I want to hear.* Was that what had happened on Saturday? Had Robert been lying to her?

As he'd lied to Kathy?

No, he hadn't, he couldn't. This was the man she loved, the man who said he loved her. The man who wanted to marry her. That was the truth.

"Do you want him?" Kathy asked the question again. "Do you want him so bad that you want to take him from me?"

The doorbell rang before Stephanie could answer Kathy.

CHAPTER 43

The door opened just as he hit the bell for the second time. Behind the brightly wrapped Christmas presents, the helium balloon, and the bunch of flowers, Robert Walker brushed past Stephanie with a cheery "Merry Christmas, sweetheart!" and bolted up the stairs into the living room.

He stopped in surprise. There was a woman standing with her back to him, outlined against the window.

"Oh, hi. You must be Izzie . . . ," he began.

And then she turned to face him.

CHAPTER 44

There are moments etched in the memory.

Moments of passion, of pain, victory, and terror. Especially terror. When all else fades, the fear remains. When Robert Walker strode into Stephanie Burroughs's living room and found his wife waiting for him, he experienced one of those moments that he knew, instantly and instinctively, he would carry with him to his grave.

His mouth opened and closed, but he couldn't draw breath. It was as if he had been punched in the stomach, and his heart started beating so hard he was sure it was going to burst.

There was movement behind him, and Stephanie came into the room, stepping around him to stand by the kitchen.

Robert looked from Kathy to Stephanie and back again, trying to make sense of what he was seeing. A score of reasons, excuses, and stupid possibilities flashed through his head in a single moment.

Until only the truth remained.

Kathy knew.

And that brought with it an extraordinary sense of relief.

No more sneaking around, no more furtive phone calls, no more clandestine meetings. No more lies.

"Kathy . . . ," he began.

Kathy crossed the room in two quick strides, stepped up to him, and slapped him hard enough across the face to rock his head back. She'd never intended to hit Stephanie, but she'd always known she was going to strike him. That was never in doubt. Her hand stung, and she relished the blow.

Robert backed away from Kathy and turned to Stephanie for support, but the strange look on her face kept him away from her also. "You—you told her," he finally said to Stephanie.

"You see," Kathy said conversationally, not looking at him. "He never accepts responsibility. It's always someone else's fault."

Stephanie folded her arms across her chest and nodded. She'd noticed that in Robert before. Abruptly, with the two of them here in the same room, she felt like an outsider in her own home.

Robert looked from one woman to the other. "Well, she must have called you, brought you here, how else . . ."

"How else, Robert?" Kathy snapped. "Because I'm not as stupid as you seem to think I am. And you're not as clever as you believe you are."

"I think . . . I think . . ." Robert looked around desperately. "I think I should go."

"No!" both women said simultaneously.

Unsure of what to do, he put down the Christmas presents and rested the bouquet of flowers on top of them. The balloon floated unnoticed to the ceiling.

Kathy resumed her position on the sofa, and Stephanie collapsed into her usual seat. He stood for a moment, unsure what to do, then sat down on the sofa, as far away from Kathy as possible. He looked from woman to woman, noticed that their expressions and their postures were identical.

"You owe us an explanation," Kathy said.

"Both of us," Stephanie said.

CHAPTER 45

"I'm not sure what to say," Robert said miserably.

"Why don't you start with the truth, Robert?" Stephanie said.

"The truth?" He looked at her blankly and suddenly wondered how long the two women had been chatting before he had arrived, how much they knew about one another. He was hunting for a formula of words that would neither offend Stephanie nor hurt Kathy.

Stephanie leaned forward. "I've always believed that Kathy didn't love you."

He looked at her blankly.

"You told me—more than once—that she didn't love you."

Unsure where this was going, he nodded. "That's right. She doesn't."

Kathy turned ashen. "What? I've never said that! Never once." She turned from Robert to Stephanie. "I never said that to him." Then she rounded on Robert. She lunged down the couch and struck at him again, catching him on the side of the head. "You bastard! Is that what you've been saying? Is that how you've been justifying your lying affair—saying that I didn't love you!" There were tears in her eyes now, tears of rage. "I do love you!"

Robert was taken aback by the forcefulness of her response. He backed away from her. Kathy didn't love him, couldn't love him, hadn't loved him for ages. "But . . . but . . . you never said anything. . . . I just assumed . . ."

"You assumed wrong!" she snapped.

Robert drew in a deep, shuddering breath. "You don't talk to me; you ignore me. You're not interested in me, not interested in the business."

"And are you interested in Kathy?" Stephanie wondered aloud.

Kathy looked at her in surprise.

Robert looked at her blankly. Whose side was she on?

"Did you ever ask about her day? Did you ever stop to realize just who kept the house going while you were running the business?"

"Hang on a sec . . . ," he began, anger touching his voice. "I won't take that from . . ."

"From whom?" Stephanie demanded.

"From you," he finished lamely.

"I never stopped loving you," Kathy said into the silence that followed. "When I found out that you were having an affair, I hated you. But it made me reevaluate our eighteen years together, showed me some of the mistakes we've both made. It's not gone, Robert; it's still salvageable. If you want to salvage it."

Kathy still loved him.

It had been easy to justify what he was doing with the understanding that Kathy no longer cared for him and that even if she did find out, it was not going to be such a big deal. There would be a fight, sure, but then they'd separate and ultimately divorce. But it would all be fairly amicable, he had thought, because Kathy had no strong feelings for him anymore; there were times he had thought she would actually be better off and happier without him.

But she loved him.

Loved him enough to fight for him.

Stephanie watched them, saw the fear on Robert's face, the determination on Kathy's, and discovered that she wasn't listening to a couple who hated one another. In that moment, she discovered that she actually admired Kathy. It was every woman's nightmare, to face the mistress, but Kathy had found the courage to do it

She knew Kathy still loved Robert.

And Robert . . . Did he still love Kathy?

Stephanie leaned back, watching them closely. She found she was looking at a couple who still loved one another but who'd lost their way—both of them. They'd become distracted by house and home and children and job, and had forgotten what had created all of those things in the first place: their love, their relationship, their commitment.

And where did that leave her? Where did that leave Robert's promise to her?

"Do you love me, Robert?" Kathy asked finally.

Even before he answered, Stephanie knew the truth. She saw it in the way he had looked at his wife; Stephanie saw it in his face. She knew how Robert would answer, though whether that would be the absolute truth was open to question. She remembered how he'd been so desperate to keep the news of their relationship from Kathy. Once she had thought it was cowardice—and it might be that too; but now she recognized that it might also have been love. He didn't want his wife to know because he didn't want to hurt her. Was that also why he'd kept from Kathy how badly the business was doing? They were mistakes he should have shared with her. Stephanie knew that Kathy was far tougher than Robert imagined.

"Yes," he said simply, "I love you."

"And Stephanie, do you love her also?" Kathy asked, surprising them both.

There was a moment—no more than a handful of seconds—but it seemed to extend for an eternity before Robert nodded and answered. "Yes, yes, I do."

The two women looked at one another. They loved the same man. But they both knew that he had drifted from Kathy through ignorance—because he had thought she no longer loved him. He had allowed himself to enter into a relationship with Stephanie for the same reason, and she, in turn, had agreed to a relationship with him because she believed him to be emotionally separated from his wife.

"It's possible to love more than one person," Robert said slowly.

"I know that," said Kathy. "We know that," she added, glancing at Stephanie, who nodded in agreement. "But you have to make a choice now, because, Robert, you cannot have us both."

She could end it here and now, Stephanie thought suddenly. She could make him hers. If Kathy knew that Robert had proposed to her, had offered to marry her, then Kathy would get up and walk out of the room. The relationship might survive the affair, but it could not survive that ultimate betrayal. And if Kathy did walk out, what would that achieve? It would leave Stephanie with Robert. Stephanie had been afforded a glimpse of her future with Robert, and it was not what she'd imagined it was going to be.

But this was her chance to be happy.

From the moment Robert had proposed she'd been walking on air. She'd never imagined that such a simple sentence could make her feel so good. She'd spent the last few hours bubbling with excitement, planning for a future that was now—suddenly—under threat.

Kathy had come here to fight for her man.

And now it was up to Stephanie. Was she also prepared to fight for him?

The single sentence, "Robert proposed to me," would send Kathy home, devastated, and Robert would be hers. Forever. But looking at him now, his eyes wide and locked onto Kathy's face, suddenly made her wonder how he would feel if she managed to drive his wife off. She had watched him when he had told Kathy that he loved her. He meant it. Would he be able to forgive Stephanie if she drove away his wife?

But Stephanie loved him.

And sometimes you have to let go of those you love.

CHAPTER 46

"I've made a mistake," Stephanie said, breaking the long silence in the room. "A terrible mistake."

Robert and Kathy looked at her blankly.

Stephanie had the sudden urge to reach out and touch Kathy's hand. "I swear to you that I didn't know he was still in love with you. I thought he was going to leave you. I . . . I was wrong."

Stephanie stood up, and the other two automatically rose to their feet with her. She stepped forward and placed the palm of her hand flat on Robert's chest. Kathy's eyes flared, but she remained still and unmoving.

"I love you, Robert, as much as Kathy loves you. But I cannot have you. Go back to your wife. If she'll take you, that is."

Stephanie felt something break inside her as the future she'd been planning shattered and twisted away. What was left was a deep bitterness—not directed toward Robert, not toward Kathy, but toward herself. How could she have been so stupid?

Because she loved him.

Kathy looked from Stephanie to Robert. She was missing something, she knew, some nuance that she hadn't picked up. She was also sensing something that sounded almost like relief in Stephanie's voice. Then the younger woman turned and went into the bedroom, closing the door behind her, leaving Robert and Kathy alone.

Kathy turned to look at her husband. "Well?"

"Well?" His voice was shaking, and he felt hungover. "What do you want to do?" He'd run the full gamut of emotions in the last half hour. He'd gotten his wife back and lost Stephanie. On Saturday he'd been thinking about starting again; right now, he'd just been given another opportunity to go back to the beginning and start again, but with Kathy this time.

"I'll take you back, but there will be conditions," she said. "Things will change. You know that?"

He nodded. He wasn't sure what had just happened. One minute Stephanie loved him; the next she was claiming she'd made a mistake.

"And I'll change too," Kathy promised, her voice surprisingly calm and level. "We'll start again, go to therapy, try and rebuild our marriage and our relationship. But there's one question you have to ask yourself, Robert: Do you want to come back to me?"

"I never really left," he laughed shakily.

"You left me a long time ago," Kathy said sharply. "You say I withdrew from you, but you checked out of the marriage as well. Answer me."

Robert drew back from the vehemence in her voice. Where had this Kathy come from, this feisty, strong-willed, and determined woman? This was the woman he'd married a long time ago, the woman he'd thought had gone. He looked toward the closed bedroom door. And why had Stephanie rejected him? When he'd proposed to her . . . If Kathy knew he'd proposed to her . . .

And he suddenly understood then. Stephanie hadn't rejected him. He felt his throat swell and suddenly found it difficult to breath. She loved him. She loved him enough to . . .

"Robert?" Kathy said quietly.

He nodded. "Yes. Yes, I do want to come back. If you'll have me. Start again. Start afresh."

"It may not work, and we may end up going our separate ways, but I think we owe it to one another and the children to give it a try."

"Yes, yes, we do." He spread his arms. "About this . . ."

Kathy raised a hand, silencing him. "You told me you loved me. Do you mean it?"

"Yes."

"Then that's all I need to know at the moment." She pushed him toward the door. "Go home now. The children are waiting. I'll be there soon."

Robert hesitated and looked again at the closed bedroom door. "I should say good-bye . . . ," he began.

"You already have," Kathy said firmly.

Robert Walker turned and walked away.

CHAPTER 47

Kathy knocked on the closed bedroom door. "I'm going now," she called.

Stephanie opened the door. Her eyes were bright, but she was not crying. Not yet. She followed Kathy down the stairs and close to the bottom step, she shrugged and said, almost to herself, "I thought he was the one."

"So did I," Kathy whispered, looking past the open hall door to where Robert was pulling away in the car. "And he was, once."

Kathy put her hand on the knob and stopped. "Thank you," she said finally, turning around to face her husband's mistress.

"For what?"

"For not telling me about the promises he made." She leaned forward quickly and hugged Stephanie. "Take care, but—and I don't want you to take this the wrong way—I never want to see you again."

"You won't," Stephanie said with feeling.

The two women walked to the door together. Mrs. Moore, who was walking up the path, thought they were sisters, which was strange because she knew that Stephanie had no relatives in

Boston, but maybe one had come home for Christmas. She waved and both women waved back.

"What are you going to do for the holidays?" Kathy asked as she stepped out into the bitter December sunshine.

"I'm going to go home to my family," Stephanie said. "And you?"

"I'm going to do the same."

THE AFFAIR

Colette Freedman

ABOUT THIS GUIDE

The suggested questions are included
to enhance your group's reading of
Colette Freedman's *The Affair.*

Discussion Questions

1. Do you think Kathy violated Robert's trust by looking in his phone and checking his e-mails? Or do you think her actions were justified? Have you ever violated a loved one's privacy because you were suspicious?

2. Kathy notices that Robert has lost weight, tanned himself, and whitened his teeth. Was it her sudden suspicion that made her really see her husband? Do you believe couples get so used to each other that they stop noticing the details?

3. Kathy says that when she first met Robert they had sex every day. Now, they rarely have it. Do you believe couples have less sex the longer they've been together because they're bored? Tired? Uninspired?

4. Men often claim they have affairs because they don't get sex from their wives. Kathy clearly states that she still feels sexy. Do you believe it is a false impression that it is usually men who are denied sex, when in fact it is often women who are sexually frustrated?

5. Rose tells Kathy, "Men stray. It's in their nature, whether we like it or not. It goes back to the time of cavemen.... Men hunted and women nurtured. Tommy was just ... hunting." Today's media often paints adultery as a defensible misdeed. Do you believe men cheat because they are wired to do so?

6. Do you agree with Rose's decision not to confront Tommy? Do you know women like Rose who have stood by quietly as their husbands cheated? What would you do in Rose's position?

7. Do you think Maureen, as Kathy's friend, had a responsibility to tell Kathy about Robert's affair? Or do you think Maureen's

responsibility as Robert's secretary should be discretion? If you were in Maureen's position, what would you do?

8. At some point during the story, all three characters realize how similar Kathy and Stephanie look. Do you believe Robert's attraction to Stephanie is independent of Kathy, or tied up in his original feelings for her?

9. Stephanie is an extremely successful career woman. Do you think her ability to throw work Robert's way colored his relationship with her? Do you think their relationship would have lasted as long if she had stopped giving him work?

10. Do you think Stephanie and Robert could make it as a couple? Why do you believe Stephanie fell for Robert?

11. Do you think, despite his infidelity, Robert is a good father? Do you think he would want to have children with Stephanie?

12. Where do you see Robert in ten years? Who will he be with? Kathy? Stephanie? Someone else?

13. How did each of the three main characters contribute to breaking up the marriage? Do you think Kathy was complicit in Robert's affair? Who do you blame the most?

14. If you were Kathy, could you forgive Robert? In your opinion, should Kathy take Robert back? Why or why not?

15. The same story is told from three different perspectives. Do you feel that people interpret things differently primarily due to their gender or due to their fundamental need to hear what they want to hear?

16. Do you believe it is possible to love more than one person?

GREAT BOOKS, GREAT SAVINGS!

When You Visit Our Website:
www.kensingtonbooks.com
You Can Save Money Off The Retail Price
Of Any Book You Purchase!

- **All Your Favorite Kensington Authors**
- **New Releases & Timeless Classics**
- **Overnight Shipping Available**
- **eBooks Available For Many Titles**
- **All Major Credit Cards Accepted**

Visit Us Today To Start Saving!
www.kensingtonbooks.com